OPIUM

How does your story end?

Second Edition Published 2023

Cover Design/Spiffing Covers

ISBN (paperback) 978-1-7392507-2-0
ISBN (e-book) 978-1-7392507-3-7

Published by Verbatim Press

OPIUM

How does your story end?

MAISIE KITTON

For those who believed in me. x

<u>Content Warning</u>

Be aware that this novel contains graphic depictions of violence
and abuse, including death. Stay safe, and please read at
your own risk.

Contents

Key Pronunciations 11

Chapter 1: Unforeseen Contingency 13

Chapter 2: First Encounters 19

Chapter 3: Bearings 24

Chapter 4: Training 31

Chapter 5: Contest 39

Chapter 6: Flash 44

Chapter 7: Ossify 48

Chapter 8: Perpetrators 52

Chapter 9: Consequences 57

Chapter 10: Scheming 63

Chapter 11: Inconspicuous 67

Chapter 12: The Elders 73

Chapter 13: The Set-up 77

Chapter 14: Pandemonium 85

Chapter 15: Already Gone 93

Chapter 16: Fidelity 99

Chapter 17: Adaptions 109

Chapter 18: Discordance 118

Chapter 19: Atramentous 125

Chapter 20: Traitor 128

Chapter 21: Succour 132

Chapter 22: Shock Wave 138

Chapter 23: Anamnesis 143

Chapter 24: Aftershock 147

Chapter 25: Misperception 154

Chapter 26: Presage 161

Chapter 27: Misadventure 165

Chapter 28: Parade 177

Chapter 29: Interchangeable 185

Chapter 30: Exposure 191

Chapter 31: Elapsed 199

Chapter 32: Volatile 204

Chapter 33: Hunting 214

Chapter 34: Tailed 219

Chapter 35: Infiltrated 225

Chapter 36: A New Beginning 233

Chapter 37: Tripwire 240

Chapter 38: Erroneous 247

Chapter 39: Veracity 249

Chapter 40: Portent 255

Chapter 41: Groundwork 259

Chapter 42: Perspective 261

Chapter 43: Choice 266

Chapter 44: Testimony 275

Chapter 45: Acme 287

Chapter 46: Handwritten 291

Author's Note 299

Helplines – UK 301

Helplines – USA 303

Acknowledgements 305

About the Author 306

Brief Explanations 307

Key Pronunciations

People
Felan – 'Fey-len'
Blaez – 'Blaise'
Accalia – 'Ack-ay-leah'
Randi – 'Ran-dee'
Convel – 'Con-vul'

Places
Guadalupe – 'Gwad-ah-loop'
Weisworth – 'Whys-worth'

Chapter 1: Unforeseen Contingency

Somewhere on the outskirts of Guadalupe, scrawny hands shot into a dustbin. They grasped the day-old, half-eaten burger and a mouth swallowed it whole. It was the first bit of food the boy had eaten in days – he was not one to pass up the chance of a meal, no matter how meagre. He searched through the rubbish, and his scratched-up hands lifted empty packets, plastic bags... nothing edible.

He licked his lips. Maybe he shouldn't have eaten it so fast.

The first spots of rain landed on his cheeks, cold and unwelcoming, as was any type of weather change at the moment. A strong gust of wind chilled him down to the bone. His hair hung in his eyes like a thick, dark curtain, and he was swiping a trembling hand across his face to clear his vision when his fingers (none too gently) brushed against a black-and-purple bruise.

Felan stood on the voiceless motorway, looking, waiting. Nothing. Tears rolled down his cheeks as rain crashed onto his face – where could he go? He couldn't go back to the last shelter – a couple of men had kicked him out of the alcove he'd found, talking and laughing, so that was a no go.

He looked for anything, another alcove, an empty building, just somewhere he could hide until the rain passed. Especially along the Fairbank Motorway, Felan would've thought there'd be somewhere he could hole up: only drunkards and the poor lived somewhere like Fairbank, and no one used the motorway any more. The amount of empty beer bottles he'd stumbled over in the streets would have been funny if he weren't used to twice that amount in his father's flat.

Gardens were overgrown, wooden fences beaten down, and the houses themselves were crumbling from the ceiling. Numerous boarded-up doors enticed him, but he didn't dare break in. People along Fairbank were struggling enough without him taking advantage.

And anyway, who was to say the house wouldn't collapse on him the moment he walked in? He'd be screwed for sure.

A clatter ripped him from his thoughts. Turning, Felan held up an arm to shield his face from the rain and squinted into the distance. It was nothing. Perhaps it was broken fences crashing about in the wind, or maybe some more bricks had fallen down across the way, because there was nothing... There! There it was! He could barely make it out in the distance, whatever it was, and it was moving. Fast.

He bolted when he heard the familiar voices.

Rain whipped him as he ran; the footsteps never fell behind. They grew louder, not at all fazed by the rain or his frantic routes down streets he barely knew, though it seemed the people following him knew them well.

Felan ducked into the first alley he could find. It wasn't much of an alley – a narrow walkway between two houses, the floor littered with cigarette stubs. Thunder clapped. Felan was convinced the buildings either side of him shook.

A large hand clamped over his wrist and yanked him off balance. He tumbled to the floor, flat on his back, winded. He stared up. Two masked men stared back.

'She wants this? He won't last a week!' one voice said, stamping a foot on Felan's chest to keep him in place.

'It doesn't matter – she wants him anyway.'

'Who wants me?' Felan asked. They'd said that last time.

'You'll meet her soon enough, kid.'

Felan hit at the foot that held him down, punched it, slapped it, pushed against it with all his might. No give. The men laughed – cruel, rambunctious laughter – and the more Felan struggled, the louder they laughed. Despair clutched at his heart.

'Let me go!' he shouted. He didn't want any trouble. He just wanted to find somewhere to hide for the night. Was that too much to ask?

'Why don't...'

An arm choked the man from behind and dragged him away. Felan scrambled back, never one to miss the chance of an escape. But the relief of freedom was short-lived; he was trapped in the alley, backed all the way to the wall with no exit in sight. He cowered down and waited for the blow that would inevitably follow.

The blow never came.

He peeked through his hair and watched in surprise.

The arm that choked his pursuer belonged to another man, taller and stronger than the first two. They were in a fight by the looks of things. Felan didn't like fights.

'This is our territory. Back off,' the taller man said.

'We found him first!'

The taller man punched the first guy to the floor. 'Back. Off,' the defender growled, ready to strike again.

Felan watched the exchange in disbelief. This man was defending him. This man had saved him from being kidnapped. Why would he do that?

He could barely make out the conversation over the temperamental weather, but he thought he heard his saviour growling.

A flash of silver. Once, then twice. One of the men clamped a hand over his arm. A third flash, and a fourth.

'If I find you on my territory again, I won't be so lenient.'

The masked men didn't hang around, and Felan's saviour turned to face him. He slid something inside his jacket. Felan thought he knew what that something was. When the man walked over, the boy scooted back until he felt the wall behind him. The man advanced further. His eyes were pure black, though it was hard to tell from within the shadows. He had a scar on his face, red and jagged, and his mouth curled up into a knowing smirk, revealing a set of yellow, misshapen teeth.

He crouched down.

'Hello, little one,' he said. The dark eyes never left Felan's. 'I've got a place, if you want to come with me.' His voice was deep and gravelly, and his words demanded rather than invited.

Felan knew he had a choice. He could walk away if he wanted to, but this man had saved Felan from being taken away, beaten up, or worse. Maybe accepting his offer could be Felan's way of repaying him. Repayment. It was how things worked. At least, that's what his father had always told him.

Sniffing, he pulled his threadbare jacket tighter around himself. Felan didn't trust the man. The last time he'd trusted someone... For all he knew, this one could be just as dangerous as the men from before.

'What's it gonna be?'

Felan's teeth chattered.

'The rain's only going to get heavier,' the man pushed on. 'I know first-hand how cold it gets at night, especially this time of year.'

Felan bit his lip. The man was right – the clouds were getting darker by the second, and a frost was expected in a few days. What if those men came back? What if someone worse came? He tried to decode the man crouched before him. It was like staring at a blank canvas.

'You'll have a bed, clean clothes, food, water... You'll have somewhere to call home,' he enticed.

It seemed too good to be true. He would have a home?

'What's your answer?'

As Felan sat there, the rain fell that little bit heavier. The cold grew that little bit colder. He shivered more violently than he'd ever shivered before. The streets were dangerous. Even if it was only for one night, it was another night he'd be safe from those awful people on the streets that kept following him.

'Okay,' he whispered.

The scarred man stood. 'Don't fall behind.'

***

The rain didn't let up during the walk from Fairbank to a place Felan didn't know the name of, though it didn't seem to bother the man in front of him.

It bothered Felan more than he'd ever let on. He'd had enough of having wet clothes all the time and never having enough time to properly dry them. It wasn't like he could strip naked on a dodgy street and hang his clothes out to dry; someone just as desperate as him would steal them and then he'd have even less.

Felan stumbled after his saviour, half in shock, half in excitement at the prospect of clean, dry clothes. That's what the man had promised; new clothes and somewhere to stay.

The closest Felan had been to a forest was Oakley Park: it was down the road from where he'd lived before, adorned with a tiny woodland at one end, a lake at the other. Everything about it was perfect − the squirrels, the twittering birds, and the trees themselves. Bluebells and snowdrops flowered in clusters on the floor. Felan's mother had loved bluebells.

So when the man led him away from the motorway, and into a forest, Felan was mildly disappointed, for there were no flowers, and the trees themselves were bare, and the floor looked like it had been trampled on one too many times; the grass lay flat and dead. Either it was still growing or it was slowly dying. He could never tell the difference between the growing and dying.

Felan squelched through muddy puddle after muddy puddle. The man barely spared the boy a glance the whole walk.

Eventually, they left the forest, and Felan followed his saviour down a gravel path, where a large, decrepit warehouse loomed in the distance. The rain stopped. The man forged ahead.

It suddenly occurred to Felan that he didn't know the man's name. It also occurred to him that the man didn't know his. He wiped his nose on the back of his wet sleeve and quickened his pace. Despite the man's name being unknown, he'd been the only one to show Felan any form of kindness since he'd left his father's place, and subsequently, the hospital.

Felan had learned people were too busy for kindness.

They spilled into a clearing with green grass worn away in patches, shoe marks printed into the mud. Just ahead, people stood in groups, dotted all over the glade. Felan's saviour walked by all of them, entered the warehouse, and slammed the door behind him. Felan stood at the edge of the clearing, unsure if he was allowed to follow.

If the people noticed him, they didn't say anything. They wore dark clothes, they were all different heights, and some of them were girls – which, for whatever reason, he hadn't expected.

'He found him, then,' one of them said, in nothing more than a murmur.

Felan wasn't sure who had spoken. He glanced around uneasily.

Were they looking for him too?

Chapter 2: First Encounters

He shuffled on the spot and sighed at the mud squelching in his trainers. They were going to take days to dry out, and that was if the rain stayed away long enough.

Just then, Felan looked up at a shout, taking two hurried steps back. Across the clearing, two guys exchanged punches. They were in the middle of a fight by the looks of it. Felan rubbed the scar on his collarbone. He really didn't like fights. The sound of fists landing on skin played on repeat in his dreams, and it was a sound he wasn't able to escape while at school either.

Nowhere was safe any more.

He caught the eye of a girl. She couldn't be much older than him, judging from her expression, and she was just as small. Felan offered her a smile before he went back to staring at the floor. She was talking to her friends (another girl and two boys), and it was rude to interrupt another's conversation.

When he thought it was safe, he looked again.

Her hair was tied back in a loose ponytail, the strands all choppy and uneven, like she'd taken a pair of scissors to them herself. She wore dark eyeliner and...

Felan looked away. He was sure she'd smiled at him. He glanced back. Yep. She'd definitely smiled at him.

She said something to her group, pointed in Felan's direction, and walked over to him, sloshing through the mud and wet grass in black boots.

'I'm guessing you're new here,' she said.

'Something like that.'

She offered him her hand. 'Welcome to the Warehouse. I'm Blaez.'

He took it, and stared up at the old warehouse in front of him. 'Felan.'

Her hands were coarse, quite like his own. They felt comforting. Soft. Just like his mother's had been.

The Warehouse, on the other hand, was another story.

Ivy wound its way down broken gutters and crawled down the front and sides. It had one main door at the centre, a huge steel door that was twice the size of Felan. Windows lined their way along the sides, with more of them near the top of the building. The windows themselves were small squares of glass. Moss and mould grew all over, partially blending the steel structure into the forest around it.

When Felan looked back down, Blaez was staring at him intently.

'Have I got something on my face?' he joked.

She averted her gaze back up, an apology on her own face. At least, that's what Felan thought it was. It had been a while since anyone had looked at him like that, or apologised to him.

'So how long have you been out here?' she chirped. 'On the streets,' she added, when he looked confused.

'No longer than a few weeks.'

To be completely honest, Felan wasn't sure any more. The days all seemed to blur into one and after a while he'd stopped counting. There were much more important things to remember, like when the restaurant across the street of the first place he stayed threw out old food, or the warmest places to hide when the temperature dropped, and lastly when to clear off for a few hours because the wrong sort of people would come snooping.

'It shows,' she said.

Felan didn't know whether to take offence or not.

'Anyway, wait here.' Her eyes slid down to his cheek again. 'I'll be back in a bit.'

Oh, right. He still had a nasty bruise on his cheek. Blaez bounded away to her friends, hurriedly chatting. Every once in a while, she looked over her shoulder at him.

It didn't bother Felan. He was used to awkwardly hanging back while people talked.

Before long, she left her friends and joined another group,

waving her hands around, her mouth moving just as fast. Blaez's smaller size didn't affect her confidence one bit, he thought, as she skipped over to yet another group, though her expression was more subdued. She never mingled with the larger figures by the warehouse door, but when she finally came back, she led him towards them, nodded, and shoved the steel door open. It creaked and groaned. Felan was glad when it crashed shut behind them.

'The Elders,' Blaez said, as if that answered all of his questions.

'Sure.'

She beckoned him up two flights of stairs, rickety and at a slight angle.

'Nick's in charge – the one that brought you here – and what Nick says goes, to put it simply. He runs everything around here, and we all do what we're told.' They reached the top of the stairs and walked down a corridor lined with doors. 'Some of the guys refurbished the upper levels into a series of smaller bedrooms, one for each of us. Unfortunately, as you're new, yours is right at the end.'

Blaez pointed to a door at the far end of the hall.

'That's my room. Yours is the one opposite.'

'So you're kind of new too?' Felan asked. That was good. They could help each other.

'I was the newest, yes,' she said softly. She looked uncomfortable, but when she caught Felan watching her she winked. Blaez stopped outside what was to be Felan's bedroom door, pulled the handle down, and stepped inside.

Felan followed. Inside was a bed, a small closet, and tattered curtains draped over the square window. The room was kind of an L-shape, and around the corner a sheet hung from the ceiling. What looked like bathroom tiles peeked out from underneath. There wasn't much else, but he appreciated the basics, considering he hadn't even had those when he left.

'Around the corner you have a wet room. It's nothing fancy though, just something we rigged up quickly. There's a toilet in there too, right at the back. There's also a small cabinet with a few old towels folded up... Have a look,' she encouraged. 'It's yours, after all. Make yourself at home.'

Home. Finally.

He peeled the draped sheet back, saw the bowl she referred to as the toilet, the broken tiles that lined the floor, the broken showerhead attached to the wall.

'What's that connected to?' Felan asked.

Blaez peered over his shoulder. 'All the showers are rigged up to the same system which is somehow undetectable. Don't even ask me how they did it. It's quite incredible actually... The only downside is the water – it isn't always warm, and there's a limited supply. Inconspicuous, and all that jazz, but other than that, everything runs as it should,' Blaez explained.

Felan let the curtain fall back and moved to the window. The view was spectacular – he had a clear line of sight to the forest!

'We've managed to rig up the Warehouse to the city's main power system – again undetectable – so we have light and heating. There are generators downstairs in case of a power cut. We also have a main computer room; we get access to the city's security feed, and we use that room for research.'

Felan liked research. 'What kind of...'

'We don't eat together, because we don't stock up on food,' she interrupted. 'Normally, we just eat whatever we find while we're out. The funds aren't great, but Nick says they're getting better. He's planning something big.' She looked rather thoughtful, if not fearful. Felan wondered why. 'We have phones, but they won't be the ones you're used to.' Blaez removed what looked like a block from her trouser pocket.

He'd never had a phone, even before.

'This is what we call a burner phone.' She held it out for him to inspect. 'They're cheap and easily disposable. If you lose it, or throw it away, they can't be traced. They're especially useful when you're in trouble. One of the best things Nick ever invested in.'

Felan handed it back. 'What kind of trouble?'

Blaez stopped at the door and leaned on the handle. Probably debating something, he thought. His mother used to do that all the time.

'Harvey wants to see you in about twenty minutes downstairs. If I were you, I'd be there on time,' she said pointedly.

Felan glanced around his room. They couldn't have had much notice of him coming to stay, so how had they cleaned up so fast? Who had cleaned up? Did they always have rooms ready to go? How many other spare rooms did they have available?

'Were you expecting me?'

Judging by the lack of verbal response, and the hard bite to her lip, Felan thought he knew the answer.

'I'll see you later,' she said. The door closed with a click.

He sat on the bed in the corner and looked around his new room. It was so much bigger than his room in his father's flat, and in much better condition. Nick had been true to his word so far, although the dry clothes would be nice sooner rather than later. He was rather cold in his wet trousers and jumper.

Felan bounced up and down on the mattress once, just to test it. Yeah. He could make this work.

Chapter 3: Bearings

'How fast can you run?'

Harvey had short, brown hair, amber eyes, a lean build. A bit of stubble. He was nice enough, not the intimidating type, and Felan was immediately at ease upon meeting him.

They walked to the huge clearing behind the Warehouse. Well, the clearing surrounded the Warehouse, but they just called it the 'front' and the 'back'. Felan took in the green that surrounded them, so different to a front room filled with cigarette smoke and beer. No, the Warehouse was a safe haven.

'As fast as you need me to.'

'And how far can you run?'

'As far as I need to go,' he said. It was true. He went as far as he needed to go; he measured through need, not distance, and each need was different.

'Interesting,' Harvey said. He eyed Felan up and down. 'You don't look the type.'

'I've been told that before.'

'You've got a sense of humour, I see.'

'Is that bad?'

'We'll find out. But, for the time being, run around the clearing until I tell you to stop.'

He ran for an hour, doing his best to ignore the few people that had stopped what they were doing outside to watch. He sped up and slowed when he was instructed, and kept putting one foot in front of the other. And the best part? He wasn't even tired.

'Let's go back inside, Felan... I think you've proved your point!' Harvey shouted.

Success! He hadn't messed up yet.

Sweat dripped from his body. He wiped his forehead on the sleeve of his old jumper, still damp from the rain. The second he got back to his room he was testing out his new shower, because there was no way he was walking around covered in sweat for the rest of the day. Then again, he'd rather be sweating than freezing. He wondered when he'd be given the clothes he was promised.

'Did you bring any clothes with you?'

It was as if Harvey had heard his mind turn. Felan looked to the floor. 'Just myself.'

Most people would have some belongings with them, but not Felan. He was alone, with nothing but the clothes on his back.

'We'll find you some more clothes – you can't just have one set. We've got a supply in there somewhere,' he said kindly, gesturing to the Warehouse.

The arrival of a black truck saved Felan from replying. The boy watched the shadow-like vehicle with interest. His view of the driver's figure was poor, but he could quite clearly see the cold, still face, like he'd been chiselled straight from stone.

Four guys emerged from the Warehouse with Nick, and the moment the truck rolled to a stop they climbed into the back and began to unload it. Nick went up to the driver, an envelope passing between them; neither checked its contents. Nick said something before disappearing back inside the Warehouse.

'Harvey! Come and help!' a deep voice shouted.

A guy waved at the pair of them. This guy in particular had long, blonde hair, and something sparkled on his nose.

'C'mon, Felan. We'll help them unload this delivery, and then I want to show you something.'

Harvey patted him on the shoulder and headed on over; Felan hurried after him. His suspicions were correct – the guy who'd shouted to them had several piercings on his face and, on closer inspection, rings and bracelets on his fingers and wrists.

'That's George,' Harvey said, pointing to the man with all the bling, 'Ewan, Mingan, and Boris.'

Ewan was the shortest, but his bulging biceps suggested that he wasn't completely helpless. His hair reminded Felan of a horse brush.

Mingan? Wiry; perhaps he was a stay indoors kind of guy.

The most generic of the four was Boris, a man with a cut on his forehead and a cold expression, dressed appropriately in black trousers and a black shirt. Boris was someone Felan didn't want to meet in a dark alley.

'This is Felan, our new recruit.' Harvey introduced him.

All three of them scrutinised him, and Mingan was the first to move, holding out his hand. As Felan took it, scarred, spindly, blackened fingertips caught his eye.

'Electrician?' Felan guessed. His scars looked like electrical burns. Had Mingan been the one to hook up the Warehouse to the city's main power supply?

'Something like that. Good to meet you, Felan.'

'Likewise.'

'The quicker we get these boxes unloaded the better!' Boris shouted, as he climbed into the truck again.

'He's right,' Mingan said, shrugging. 'Anyway, welcome to the Wolves.'

The first box wasn't heavy, but it was awkward to manoeuvre. The rest were simple enough, and they made short work of unloading. As for Felan, he was bursting with curiosity, hoping for a glance inside one of the boxes. He wanted to know what they carried. He wanted to know how they lived, what they did, and how they survived.

Maybe Felan could help them. Nothing could be worse than living with his father or scrounging on the streets.

When they dumped the last box, Mingan said, 'We'll take them from here.' He hit the back of the truck twice with his fist. The vehicle drove off, spitting gravel and dust into the air.

'Where are the boxes going?' Felan asked.

Boris grinned. The smile looked unnatural on the man's face. 'Armoury.'

They had an armoury?

Harvey led him inside the Warehouse, through a number of corridors until he pushed open a heavy, wooden door. The room itself wasn't massive, though definitely big enough to serve its purpose, and it was by far the most dangerous room he'd ever seen. There were things he ran his fingers across that he couldn't even name.

Felan swallowed and eyed the rack of guns nervously.

***

Harvey flicked the light on. 'Here, take whatever you want.'

Felan took in the faintly lit room, scanning every corner of it. Cardboard boxes were stacked high against the back wall, and there were boxes on every shelf, all neatly labelled.

Felan turned back to Harvey. 'Are you sure?' He'd been expecting clothes, but nothing like what was in front of him.

'We have no use for them, Felan. You might as well take some. There should be some in your size in those three boxes in the corner.'

Felan wandered to the boxes in question, kneeled beside them, and carefully unpacked them; he put aside trousers (ranging from blacks to greys to browns), multiple plain black T-shirts, and jumpers (some woolly, some light); he found socks and underwear too, which looked to be brand new, and an oversized black jacket he immediately fell in love with; he toed his feet into two pairs of trainers – a perfect fit. He glanced down at his holey, broken trainers he'd stolen from a charity shop some weeks prior.

He didn't want to be the bad kid, but he never had a choice.

Felan jumped at the sound of a text tone. Harvey was already reading something on his phone.

'Have you got everything you need, Felan? Nick's looking for you.'

Felan stood, his new clothes folded neatly in his arms, shoes balanced on top of the pile. 'Yep, I'm good. Thanks for this.' He smiled gratefully at the man in front of him. He couldn't remember a time when a responsible adult had provided him with clothes or shelter. He supposed he had Nick to thank for this too; so far, he'd kept his promises. Felan liked it when people kept their promises.

'You're one of us now. Well, not officially, but you get the gist.' Harvey flicked the light off, as they left the room. 'I'll take those up to your room, Felan.' Felan tipped the clothes he'd picked out into Harvey's arms with a murmur of thanks. 'Nick's waiting for you downstairs. Oh, and I'd knock before you go in.'

Felan's knees knocked together as he took the stairs down, but when he realised other Wolves were watching him, he tried to act confident. Blaez nodded supportively at him when he found the right corridor.

The light seemed to peter out the further he walked. He stopped just outside the metal door. It looked heavy and was covered in rust. Felan knocked, unsure as to whether he should have knocked harder or more lightly.

'Enter.'

Nick's voice reminded him of the chill in the air.

Felan pushed the door and frowned when it needed a bit more force than he'd thought to get it open. It swung slowly on cracked hinges, and flakes of rusted iron stained his hands. He wrinkled his nose. He was taken aback when he plunged into near total darkness, stumbling over obstacles he couldn't see. The only light came from an oil lamp on the desk that illuminated Nick's face. The man in question tapped his cheek in an impatient manner.

It reminded Felan of his old maths teacher.

'How are you settling in?'

Felan stepped back, unsure. He was so sure he'd been called here because he'd done something wrong; according to the adults in his life, he always did everything wrong.

Felan went with a safe, 'Very well, thank you.'

'Good. It's going to get tougher for you. You're going to *hurt*. But it'll all be worth it, in the end...' Nick trailed off absent-mindedly.

Felan wondered if anyone else had received a similar talk on their arrival. He stared at the man before him, trying to understand him; Nick's eyes flashed, hard, and the blackness in them leaped closer. Felan flinched.

'You have the rest of the day to settle in, to sort out your belongings. Tomorrow, it properly starts for you, Felan. Now go,' he growled.

The oil lamp beside him flickered.

***

His clothes were waiting for him on his bed, and his two new pairs of shoes were tucked beneath it. Sure, they were out of the way, but they were visible enough that Felan remembered he had them. He filled his little closet in the corner of the room, folding up his new clothes where appropriate, or hanging them up accordingly. At the bottom of the closet there was a small single drawer, into which he emptied his socks and underwear.

The clothes he wore reeked; it wasn't until he had to physically peel them off that he realised how much he stank – he hadn't had time to have a shower before meeting Harvey. The smell forced its way up his nostrils and down the back of his throat. He tossed everything in the bin and made a mental note to himself to empty it in the morning. He didn't want that smell permeating his new space.

Felan squared his shoulders. It was time to test out that shower.

He washed the dirt and grime from his hair, scrubbed his body red and raw, not stepping out from beneath the lukewarm stream until the murky water at his feet ran clear. Reluctantly, he turned the shower off – he didn't want to use up all their water on his very first day. He didn't want to get in trouble so soon. After all, he didn't know when his invitation to the Warehouse expired, and there was always someone who needed it more than he did.

At least, that's what he always told himself. There was always someone worse off than him.

Felan spent a long time towelling himself dry. The towel itself was on the smaller side, but it was something he hadn't had before. Now, he no longer had nothing. Everything in this room was his to keep. His to use. His. All his.

Daylight began to dwindle, and he sat on the edge of his bed, dressed in a clean shirt and shorts, staring out of the window. Once the darkness came, he shut the curtains. Moonlight glided through the tiny holes – but he didn't care. There was something of a natural beauty about it, evoking in him a feeling he couldn't quite place.

After he climbed beneath the covers, curled up and faced the door, he was asleep within minutes.

Chapter 4: Training

Blaez woke Felan up early the next morning, and they walked outside together. He blinked up at the sun peeking through the clouds, smiling.

It had been a while since he could appreciate the light it provided.

'What's your favourite colour?' Blaez asked.

'I don't have one.'

'Oh, come on! Everyone has a favourite colour!'

'Alright then, what's yours?'

'Yellow,' she said, skipping across the grass. 'It's light and happy – it's what life should be.'

If only life was that simple. 'Do you really believe that?'

She threw her hands in the air, grinning. 'You gotta have some faith in the world.'

Felan wished he did. 'Purple,' he said. 'I think purple's my favourite colour.'

'Why purple?'

'I don't see enough of it.' If he was honest, he didn't have a clue. Purple was just the first colour that came to mind.

'If I see something purple, I'll make sure to give it to you.'

Felan didn't know what to say. He'd been positive Blaez would be tired of him after the day before, but she seemed more than happy to be around him. It was a novelty Felan had never really got to experience growing up. Every time he met someone new, they'd bullied him for his size, and for the different marks and colours on his skin.

Still convinced he was being an annoyance to Blaez, he followed behind her. She wasn't having any of it. She slowed to match his pace and happily introduced him to people as they passed.

'That's Convel, and that's Tate. Avoid them like the plague.'

Felan happily obliged. The men in question were big and bulky, and glared at everyone who looked their way.

She pointed to a tall girl with long, red hair pulled back by a green bandana. 'That's Accalia.' The girl in question waved as they approached.

'I've never heard that name before,' Felan said with a spark of interest. Her bandana matched the exact shade of her eyes. He wondered if it was on purpose.

'Yeah, she's unique,' Blaez said. 'And that's Randi and Caleb.'

Both were small teens, though taller than himself and Blaez. The former had shaggy, brown hair and blue eyes that pulsed with electricity. He had a slight build, and he reminded Felan of himself.

Caleb was the complete opposite; strong, but not massive, with broad shoulders and an aura of calm. His choppy, blonde hair stopped at his shoulders and it blew back ever so slightly in the breeze.

Randi reached up and fiddled with the collar of Caleb's shirt. Caleb pulled Randi's hand away, clasping their hands together.

'Are they...?' Felan trailed off, unsure whether to continue his thought. He had nothing against it if they were together, but he didn't want to assume anything. It wasn't fair to force a set sexuality on someone.

'Together? Yeah. They were found on the streets *ages* ago.' Blaez stopped walking to glare at Felan. 'Why, is that going to be a problem?' she demanded.

'Not in the slightest.'

'Good. I wouldn't want us to get off on the wrong foot.'

They walked over to the two boys just as Accalia turned up, and the five of them stood in a circle. Felan glanced around. So, these were Blaez's friends. They seemed alright.

He introduced himself with a grin. 'I'm Felan.' They exchanged pleasantries and the tension in Felan's shoulders slowly faded. Growing up, he'd learned to fear meeting new people, and Blaez's friends were no different. People hated him before he even opened his mouth, so he kept quiet. He let people say horrid things, he let people push him around, and he never did anything to stop it.

He must deserve it if the way people treated him never changed.

Which was why, when Blaez's friends accepted him, he was confused. He'd been sure they'd hate him from the off. It was what he was used to.

'We should start getting ready – they'll be out soon,' Accalia said.

'Agreed,' Caleb said, nodding.

The four of them started to stretch, so Felan did the same. His reasoning? The others had been there longer than he had, so they should know what they were doing. They knew the rules, after all, and Felan knew all about rules; rules were to be followed.

Minutes later, two men strolled out of the Warehouse. One, he saw, was Harvey and the other...

'That's Rory,' Blaez said quietly.

The man had greying, black hair and evidence of a beard surrounded his mouth. Like Nick, Rory had black holes for eyes. Felan shivered when they glanced over in his direction.

The others straightened around him, so he did too.

'And what's he like?' Felan enquired, in an equally quiet voice.

'Harvey's alright,' Randi muttered. 'He's easy-going, and he looks out for us. It's Rory you need to watch out for – he's a real piece of work. Being an Elder makes him worse.'

'Fifty laps before I even think of letting you have a break!'

Audible groans rang around the area, Felan's companions included. Harvey remained a silent observer.

'It'll be one hundred if you don't start running!'

'I see what you mean,' Felan muttered, as he joined the back of the small group. Convel and Tate ran ahead of them, and his group quickly caught up. They ran as one, in an unorganised formation, but after ten laps Convel and Tate lagged behind, and it was clear to Felan who the fittest were. Every single one of them were athletic to some degree, but some didn't run as often as others.

One thing that stood out to Felan was posture: those that couldn't run for long stooped, thinking it would help, when in reality it made it harder to carry on running because it made it more difficult to breathe.

Felan had learned that the hard way.

The smell of sweat followed them. Beads of it ran down his face, leaving a salty taste on his lips. Felan thundered past his friends and, when he finished the last lap, he stopped, still on his feet – a breather was all he needed – and could have carried on had he been asked to. He turned around; the others had all but collapsed to the floor in exhaustion, panting like dogs. The sun overhead bared its teeth on the sizzling earth, and Felan let it take hold of him completely.

'I had no idea you could run like that,' Caleb said, gasping. His chest heaved at a frantic pace.

Felan was almost sympathetic. 'Not many people do.'

Caleb moaned and raised his arm, a weak attempt to block the glare of the sun. 'I need a shower.'

Blaez flopped over beside him. 'I don't think we're finished yet.'

'You had to ruin the moment.'

'I'm just being realistic!'

'A guy can dream, Blaez! A guy can dream!'

Felan choked on his laughter, content with letting everyone bicker. Contemplating his day so far, one thing stuck out to him; people seemed to want him around. After being abandoned with his father, fear had consumed him, but outside with Blaez and the others, he felt different. He felt light. He felt happy, though he wasn't sure if that was a good or bad thing.

***

Although Blaez was close with her friends, it wasn't the same with everyone in the Wolves. Earlier, Felan had witnessed one of the Wolves trip another up, and the evil looks Rory sent to certain people. It seemed that not everyone was accepted, which meant Felan was going to try his damned hardest to fit in.

It reminded him of school.

He most certainly wouldn't be a favourite, but he'd make himself useful – so when Harvey approached him a few hours later during an impromptu self-defence class in one of the training rooms (they had training rooms!), Felan was all but willing to follow. He quickly realised it wasn't just a chat; nor was it a verbal assault, something he'd prepared himself for, and was always prepared for. No, he'd been taken aside because Harvey wanted to present him with his very own knife.

'This is yours,' Harvey said. 'Use it well.'

Felan took the curved knife in his hands and ran a finger along the blade. It wasn't a new one (the grip was worn away and chafed), but it still held a unique beauty. It was like nothing he'd ever seen before.

The sole purpose of the ground floor of the Warehouse was training rooms, though Felan had only been in one, full of old gym mats and a single punchbag. The room Harvey led him to now contained an array of moving targets, still targets, and dummies to practise on, all of which had been rigged up by Mingan with lengths of rope and circuits.

The knife tore through matter with little to no resistance. It was always a clean cut. The ferocity of the blade scared him, although he knew he would be marginally safer with some form of defence, especially if they eventually kicked him out.

His skill progressed, as time went on, under the teachings of Harvey: hand-to-hand combat, speed and agility, knives (he had yet to touch a gun, for which he secretly thanked whoever was above every night before he went to bed), and even first aid – a queasy feeling erupted in his stomach when he questioned its use.

'You never know when someone's going to get hurt, Felan. You need to know this stuff.'

That's what scared him; the not knowing, the unpredictable future which now seemed even more unknowable than before.

The knives scared him too, but not in the way they should. He wasn't scared by the fact that he was handling a deadly weapon with ease and familiarity. What terrified him was how he admired it, cold against his skin.

But he was happy, and that was all that mattered, right?

***

The deadline for his initiation grew closer, and with it came a daunting realisation. He stared at Blaez, unblinking, as he finally understood exactly what she'd said.

'You have to win this fight,' she said late one night. 'That's what all the training's for. You need to win.'

His heart dropped. 'What happens if I don't?'

Blaez cast her gaze to the floor. 'You can't stay. Nick only lets in people who are good enough,' she said. She sounded hopeful, but why? Did she want him to stay, or was she fed up of his presence already? Sometimes, he couldn't tell with this small girl.

'Why wasn't I told this before?'

It would have been nice to know that his safe haven wasn't permanent. He berated himself for thinking it would be in the first place. Nothing was ever permanent for someone like him. People, and places, came and went with no regard for his own feelings. It was the way things were, even if Felan desperately wanted something solid.

'He likes pressure, Nick. He likes to see how we fare under it – it's what it's like when we're out on a job. He likes to see how we handle it.'

He really didn't want to leave. He couldn't. He'd have nothing. Again. Nick had brought him to the Warehouse in the first place, so he must have something worthwhile to offer, otherwise what was the point? And what about Blaez – would she help him, if he got kicked out? Would her friends help him?

If he lost, where would he go? What if those men in Fairbank found him again?

Felan clenched his jaw. He wouldn't lose. He absolutely refused to lose the fight, because it would mean more than losing just that.

Every night after midnight, he crept down to the training rooms and practised until he was confident he could put up a fight. He had yet to be told who his opponent would be, but he hoped it was someone he stood a chance against. All the extra work was necessary though, no matter who it was – he had to work hard. He wanted to win.

Whenever he saw a Wolf return from a job, or a supply run, or something worthwhile for the gang, it made him practise harder. A pang of jealousy would hit him right in the pit of his stomach. He wanted to be important to the group. He wanted to fit in.

He wanted to help, no matter what.

Because they were natural fighters (something that did weird him out a little), Blaez and Accalia taught him different fighting styles and the best ways to use his knife; lightning kicks, relentless punches, and ferocious, remorseless slices. He ran around sprinting after target upon target, sparring with Accalia, and sliced through numerous dummies. He punched the final one in the mouth before decapitating it, something he'd seen his father do to the spiders that crawled out from beneath his sofa.

The spiders had never hurt anyone.

Felan stared at the knife in his hands, at the sand spilling from the dummy's neck, and back to his knife.

'I won't hurt anyone,' he muttered. He threw his knife and the blade sank into the decapitated dummy's forehead. He countered the rotation, just as Accalia had instructed.

He'd ask Blaez's friends, he decided, walking over and retrieving his knife – they couldn't have killed, could they? They all seemed so gentle, so welcoming.

Felan sank to his knees. He let the knife tumble down, and it hit the floor with an almost melodic clang. He shut his eyes and took a moment to breathe.

Closure was within reach, and he so desperately wanted it; no matter what.

He pictured his schooldays, and the unwelcome roughhousing that came hand in hand with it, roughhousing that left his uniform torn, that meant he had to walk home with one shoe in the pouring rain more than once.

His stomach churned.

Felan really did hate fighting.

Chapter 5: Contest

It was the eyes that unsettled Felan, the eyes that made him nervous – one brown and one blue; threatening, frightening, and manic.

'He won't go easy on you, Felan. He wants to make you hurt, and he's going to try his hardest to make sure you lose, so don't give in,' Blaez said.

'How can I do that? He's twice the size of me!'

'You're quicker than him – smaller too, as you pointed out. Use that to your advantage. Improvise. Every time you attack, get in and out quick. Make the first move. Don't let him antagonise you.'

'Easier said than done,' he muttered.

'Nick's testing you. He doesn't just put anyone against Convel.'

Felan shifted on his feet. He didn't want to be made a fool of in front of everyone. He thought he was past that.

Blaez sighed. 'Look, I'm only trying to help. I've got quite fond of you over these last few weeks – I don't want to see you go just yet. You're my friend.'

That, however, Felan wasn't sure about. She was nice enough, and hung out with him all the time, but she'd been giving him mixed signals for a while now, and kept secrets. He didn't know if he wanted that in a friend.

'I appreciate it,' he said.

'Felan?' a voice said. They turned to see Caleb lingering by the door. 'It's time.'

'Are you both ready?' Rory asked, more to Convel than to Felan.

'Ready,' Convel said. He tilted his head to the side with a smirk.

Felan didn't trust his voice. He nodded and shifted on the spot. One look from Convel and Felan instinctively stepped back, knife out in front of him; he wasn't going to use it, he'd decided. No way was he going to hurt someone.

They couldn't expect him to hurt someone, could they?

Members of the Wolves stood scattered around the training room, eagerly awaiting the oncoming fight. Harvey stood closest, a few feet from Blaez and her friends. For a moment, Felan thought Harvey was anxious about something. But he wrote it off quickly. Felan had grown up with anger and frustration, so he was no stranger to the faces those emotions made people pull.

The face Harvey pulled was one Felan didn't recognise.

Then it started, but there was nothing to indicate that they had begun. No signal. No buzzer. Not even a shout. All he knew was that Convel was running across the room and that was it.

Felan managed to move just in time – the blade missed by a hair's width. His mouth ran dry. *He's going to try his hardest to make sure you lose...*

Felan crouched low, and the blade swung over his head again. He jumped to the side and slashed without thinking, cutting Convel's forearm. Felan paused in horror. Thankfully the cut wasn't deep, but his fear increased tenfold at the look on the Wolf's face: pure anger. His lips formed a thin line.

Convel lunged before Felan could react. The knife caught him in the leg and Felan staggered away, swallowing the pain. He didn't cry out, but the pain festered fast, spreading shock waves throughout his entire body. He spared a glance down; blood trickled down his trousers.

Blaez had said Convel was slow – had she purposefully fed him the wrong information so he'd lose? Did she really want him gone that fast? His doubts faded at another slash. Convel missed and threw himself off balance. Felan kicked the back of his knees and, with a grunt, Convel pitched forward. Felan pounced after him. Convel spun around, slashed his blade upward, and tore through the skin on Felan's stomach. With his free hand, he punched Felan's unprotected face. A crack resounded. Felan stumbled back and, with more fervour, socked Convel right in the gut.

Blood dribbled, like a leaky tap, down the back of his throat. Felan was no stranger to the taste of it. Hell, he was no stranger to pain, but being the cause of someone else's? He backed up to rub at his watery eyes.

Convel followed.

The man clamped a hand around Felan's wrist so tight that the bones clicked and something popped. Felan dropped the knife and Convel kicked it across the floor; fear of losing reared its head like an ugly snake. He had no weapon. It was just him.

Make the first move, Blaez had said. But she'd also said that Convel was slow. Could Felan trust anything she'd ever told him?

Even if he decided he wanted to, Felan didn't get the chance to follow her advice a second time. Strong arms wrapped themselves around his waist, crushed him, and tackled him to the hard floor. Winded, Felan fought back.

Convel took a few knees to the stomach, an elbow to the eye. Felan took another punch to the nose and gained a dark bruise on the arm pinned beneath his body. A sharp pain pricked his forehead. He looked up, tears stinging in his eyes from the sucker punch. Convel's blade danced before him. Focused on his assailant, Felan punched him right in the mouth and shoved him away, pushing himself back up. He scrabbled as he tried to get to his feet. Despite how hard Felan jerked and kicked, Convel grabbed Felan's ankle, laughing, and dragged him right back down.

The knife descended and it seemed to hang in mid-air, frozen on its way to Felan. He rolled as far as he could, and his head spun when the knife skipped off the floor.

Murmurs echoed about the room. Were they not going to stop him? Convel could have killed him with that strike, or maybe even rendered him paralysed. If that was the case, did Felan even want to stay?

Improvise, she'd said.

The Warehouse was full of the only people from the last nine years who'd wanted anything to do with him. Nick had saved him.

He owed it to them, really.

Fuelled by anger and fear, Felan rolled completely into Convel and forced his knee down hard onto the man's arm. He pushed it down further, a deep satisfaction growing inside him at the shock on the man's face. He tore the knife from Convel and, with a flourish, tucked it snugly under Convel's throat.

But Convel was huge, and Felan couldn't hold all of him down.

The bigger man wound a hand into Felan's hair and pulled. Felan whimpered and grunted but held fast, his vision blurring through tears, while Convel's hands scratched red lines down his face. Felan forced the knife harder against Convel's throat; Convel spluttered beneath him. Felan pushed down harder, and harder, watched Convel's mismatched eyes shift from anger to pure, downright fear and...

Felan dropped the knife with a gasp and backed away, breathless. He'd been going to... He'd thought he was going to...

'Somewhat unorthodox,' Nick sneered from the doorway. The man gave Felan a once-over. 'My room, one hour.'

What did that mean? Was he in trouble? Had he won? Surely he'd won. He'd had Convel pinned to the ground. He was standing, and Convel was still on the floor...

'I said you could do it!' Blaez shrieked, as she slammed into him.

His anger and frustration at her flooded back. 'You told me he was slow!'

'On the uptake,' she corrected.

'You didn't say that before!'

'Oh well, you still did it! You won!'

Oh yeah. 'I won...' he mumbled. He hissed at a sudden, piercing pain in his leg. He looked down. Yep, still bleeding.

'You were incredible,' Blaez said. She kissed his cheek with a giggle.

He was being rewarded for...

'That was so cool – I've never seen anything like it!' Caleb gushed.

'Convel's rarely beaten!' Randi said. 'So that's a sight to see.'

Felan grunted. 'I was told to improvise.'

He'd nearly…

'And that you did,' Blaez said.

He swatted her shoulder and limped the short distance to the wall. He slid down with a gasp. His back was like a furnace in comparison to the wall, though the coldness did nothing to ease the pain radiating throughout his entire body.

He'd wanted to…

'That looks like it hurts,' Randi said.

'Just a little bit.'

'How much does it hurt?' Accalia asked.

'Probably as much as it hurts being stabbed.'

'I'll be back with the first aid kit.' Harvey practically ran from the room, Accalia on his heels.

Felan made a non-committal noise. 'No, I'm…'

He'd wanted to…

'Hang on, Felan. Stay still,' Blaez said. Her fingers prodded his nose, turned his head this way and that. He groaned. 'That's going to bruise… and it's broken.' She sat back on her knees.

'I know – I felt it. Twice.'

Blaez grinned. 'At least you only lost a bit of blood and not your sense of humour.'

'Hey!'

Stop pretending…

'Hmm, maybe a few brain cells too?'

'Shut up!'

Stop…

'You know what this means, Felan?' Randi said, putting a stop to another bout of bickering.

'What?' He wasn't engaged in what they were saying, too intent on keeping the waves of pain at bay, too intent on ignoring the fact he'd nearly…

'You're staying,' Randi said. 'You're not going anywhere.'

Caleb nodded. 'You're one of us now.'

Relief flooded him, as he realised the true extent of Caleb's words.

He was staying.

Chapter 6: Flash

The small embers of pride he felt later diminished almost as quickly as they came. He was going into the city with Nick, at night. This particular activity was not on Felan's list of top ten things to do.

Nick gripped Felan's upper arm and dragged him down a gloomy, lamplit street on which heavy footsteps echoed between the squalid buildings. He didn't recognise the area at all. He'd lost his sense of direction when Nick pulled him down alley number ten, or eleven; the remnants of pain from his earlier fight didn't help one bit.

They took a sharp left down another alley with shadows crawling up the walls, the ground covered in broken glass. Felan stared into the darkness, daring something to jump out of it. The street lights here had long since died, and no one had bothered to repair them.

A door seemingly sprung from nowhere, and Felan's shoes scuffed on the loose tarmac beneath his feet at the sudden stop. Knuckles crudely knocked on the boarded door in front of them. Breathless seconds went by. A hand shot out from the darkness and ushered the pair inside. Felan swallowed down his fear. There was nothing to be scared of, really. Nothing at all. He stumbled over the steps when Nick shoved him forward, hitting the floor. Felan gasped in pain, as the movement jolted the cut on his leg.

'Get up,' Nick hissed.

The smell hit him first, a sour odour buried within the walls and the carpet. The weak lights flickered on, showing dark stains ingrained in the floor, ghosts of now defiled intricate designs. Torn curtains lay strewn on the floor, and small dust particles floated in the air whenever a breeze blew through the cracked window in the far corner. An assortment of instruments was piled up high along one wall, the tips of them secreting liquids of varying shades. Fluffy mould gnawed away at the wallpaper.

This room could have been his father's flat, though there was a distinct lack of alcohol.

'Found another one, have you?' a voice asked.

Felan jumped. He turned to see a man emerging from one of the back rooms he'd previously overlooked, cloth in hand; his *only* hand!

'They come when I need them,' Nick said.

Felan frowned, and looked from the new man to Nick, confused. Why had he been brought here?

'The same as usual?'

'Yes, Larry. Same as usual.' Nick turned to Felan; the boy shrank back. 'Sit in that chair. I'll collect you when he's finished.'

'Why? What's happening?'

A triumphant smirk gazed back, and Felan wished he'd never said anything.

'Be patient.' Nick stormed into the darkness.

The first of the abandonment shakes settled in, and Felan found he couldn't stop the trembling of his hands.

Someone cleared their throat.

'Oh, sorry. I'm Felan,' he said, offering a hand.

Larry said nothing about the shakes when he took his hand. He wondered if Larry knew what they were.

'Larry,' the man said.

Tattoos crawled up Larry's neck in a variety of colours. They covered his arm, some obviously experiments, and others clearly invested with time and care. Larry's arm was his palette, though Felan was keen to know how the man managed to tattoo himself with one arm. He was short in stature and a little on the dumpy side. A coarse and rough exterior met an aura of kindness; Felan felt sure he would come to no harm with him.

The boy sat down in the chair when Larry gestured for him to do so. 'What's going on?'

'You're getting a tattoo.' Larry spoke slowly, with an obvious slur to his words. There was no alcohol on his breath.

Felan nodded. Nick had saved his life, and if this was the price to pay, then so be it. And anyway, after seeing Larry, he wasn't completely against the idea. He wanted to have designs on his skin too. He wanted to belong, and *same as usual* sounded like they all received the same tattoo. To belong somewhere...

That was all he'd ever wanted.

'Sorry,' Larry said, 'but I need you to take your shirt off.'

He complied. Larry made no comment on the countless white lines on his back and chest, and he made no comment on the fresh bruises that covered his body. Felan shivered when Larry dabbed alcohol over his right shoulder; goosebumps appeared along his arms, and, when Larry turned away to fetch something, Felan recoiled spectacularly as a needle swung into view. Larry didn't say a word. Red-faced, Felan scrambled back onto the seat.

'This is going to hurt.'

Larry flicked the tool on. Felan bit his lip. He tasted blood the second the needle made contact with his skin, over and over again, but it didn't hurt like he'd thought it would.

Curious, Felan stared at his shoulder. Tiny droplets of blood rose to the surface, and every few seconds Larry paused to wipe it away on a cloth. It made the pain worse though, the constant stopping and starting. It always did.

***

The size of the tattoo shocked him – he hadn't known what to expect, but he'd thought it would be bigger for the amount it hurt. A symbol, no bigger than an orange, sat snug on his shoulder. It resembled an animal head, but...

'A wolf,' Larry answered, as he covered the design with something that resembled plastic, or was that cling film? 'Everybody's is the same.' Larry unplugged the machine and dragged it over to the corner. He was surprisingly strong for a man with one arm.

Felan took that as his cue to put his shirt back on, careful of the wrapping. When was Nick coming to get him? Although he didn't mind Larry, he couldn't wait to get back to his room, where it was warm. He couldn't wait to get back to – well, he guessed they were his friends now. He couldn't wait to get back and just *rest*. His leg throbbed harder and harder, and the bruises had darkened all over his body while he received the tattoo.

If Larry had seen the change in colour, he didn't say anything. Felan thought he wasn't the first one to stumble through Larry's door, Nick in tow.

The boy froze at a loud crash outside. Larry spared him a single glance before he went back to cleaning the equipment. Felan settled. If Larry wasn't concerned, then why should he be?

Felan fell off the chair (again!) when the door to Larry's place crashed open. Nick waltzed in, a shadow made of coal, downright fury in his eyes; they zeroed in on Felan, who sat on the floor in shock. Nick looked just like his father when he...

'Out now!' he growled. He slurred his words and his breath reeked of alcohol.

Felan trembled. His father's breath had smelled that way more than once, and when that happened...

'Now!'

When he still didn't move, Nick struck Felan across the cheek. Felan didn't make a sound. Nick grabbed his wrist and hauled him out of the building.

He was plunged into darkness, and into the biting wind.

Chapter 7: Ossify

He was pretty much a walking icicle by the time he got back to the Warehouse.

Nick barged past, knocking Felan into the wall in the process, and disappeared down the corridor. A door slammed shut and the action reverberated throughout the whole building. Felan rubbed his shoulder uncomfortably. Had he done something wrong? He remembered the trip out, trying to figure out why Nick had turned on him like he did – and violently flinched at the echo of a slap. He must've done something wrong. Nick wouldn't have hit him for no reason.

Felan hid in his room, ashamed of the red mark on his cheek. The bruises from the fight hid it well – it didn't even look amiss on his body. He touched it with his fingertips and, with a sinking feeling, remembered how long it took for bruises to fade. This was something he couldn't wash away with a shower, or even rest away with a good night's sleep. No. This was something that would stay, semi-permanent, in full view of everyone else. What would the others think? Would they know?

A knock at the door startled him.

'Felan?'

'In here,' he called.

Harvey peered in. 'Come with me.'

He had little to no misgivings with Harvey; it was Nick and Rory who made his skin crawl. At least with his father, he knew where the line was, to an extent, but with all these new people? He still had to decode them. So far, Harvey was safe.

Harvey led him downstairs into a sort of basement. Felan grinned excitedly. A room full of switched on monitors and computers, and a friendly face!

'Get over here, Felan!' Randi waved. 'I need some help.'

Felan looked questioningly to Harvey.

'I need you to help him with encryptions.'

'How did you know I can do it?'

Harvey winked. 'I'll be back in a while to see how you're getting on.'

Man, he hadn't touched a computer in so long...

'If you hop on that computer, you can help. It'll be quicker with two of us...' Randi suddenly stopped. 'You do know what you're doing, right?'

Felan cracked his fingers. 'Absolutely.'

'Good.'

Of course he knew what an encryption was. He'd spent enough time trying to decode them in the library, the only place where he had access to a computer. It had given him something to do and an excuse to avoid his father on a daily basis. Not that he could ever avoid his father for long.

Encryption used mathematical equations to hide information so that it couldn't be deciphered. It was used to convert documents and files and messages – and just about everything – into gibberish and meant the wrong sort of people couldn't access it.

His fingers flew across the keyboard for a few minutes. He paused with a frown. The cryptography security needed to be sufficient, otherwise they would be open to a brute-force attack or something much worse. He didn't want that. He had to prove that he was trustworthy. He had to prove his worth.

'I'm thinking we make the encryption longer,' Felan said.

Randi didn't take his fingers off the keyboard. 'It'll take longer.'

'It'll make everything safer.'

'Noted.'

They worked in a harmonious silence, their fingers tapping on the keys. Monitors flickered on and off. It was actually sort of fun. The door sometimes opened too, but neither of them turned, too engrossed in the task at hand. To have someone checking up on him was an odd feeling; his father had never done that growing up. This was different, a change of circumstance, and he liked it, so much so that he didn't want to mess it up. He'd been thrown a lifeline, a second chance, and he wasn't one to waste such things when they came about so rarely.

'I didn't think you'd know as much as you do.'

Felan snorted. 'I surprise people like that.'

'Yeah, I see what Blaez meant.'

'About what?'

'You.'

'What about me? What did she say?'

Randi laughed. 'Never you mind.'

'Hey...'

The door to the sort-of-basement opened. 'Are you nearly done? Because I need a word with Felan,' Harvey interrupted.

'Funnily enough, we've literally just finished up,' Randi said. He spun in his chair and smiled.

'Good,' Harvey said. 'You're free for the rest of the day, Randi.'

Randi's face lit up. 'Cool! I'll see you guys later!'

Harvey patted him on the shoulder as he tore from the room. Then, he gave Felan his full attention. 'Come on, I've got something to tell you.'

Curious, Felan followed Harvey to a room he'd never seen before. 'Where are we?' he asked, peering into the dark space.

'It's one of the boardrooms.' Harvey flicked on the light. 'It's where we have meetings and such.' Inside, there was a rounded table at the centre, surrounded by a number of plastic chairs. It could hold about six or seven people, nine or ten at a push, but a job that needed that many people? It was unheard of and completely preposterous.

'So why are we here?' Felan asked.

Harvey gave him a sideways glance. 'I'll tell you when we get inside.'

Felan sat down on one of the plastic chairs – it was surprisingly comfortable. The door closed heavily behind them. This couldn't be good. He'd done it now, surely. He must've done something wrong, because why else would he be called in to have a private conversation?

He looked at Harvey through his hair and swallowed. 'Am I in trouble?' Despite the trust Felan had in the man, he was still wary; of everything. Good things had been taken away from him so frequently in his life that Felan never assumed anything, or anyone, would stay.

'Head up, Felan.' Harvey said it so softly Felan was sure he'd misheard, but he did what he was told. He didn't recognise the look the man gave him. 'Not in the slightest.'

Felan's mouth opened in surprise. He wasn't in any trouble?

'In fact, we need you to help with something.'

'Okay?'

'We need some supplies, and we – as in, you and I – are going to get them.'

'What?'

'In two days, we're leaving to go into the city to get some supplies. There's a small shop that we're going to hit.'

'What do you mean, *hit*?'

Harvey gave him an exasperated look. 'You know full well what we are and what we do.'

Did he though? And more importantly, did he want to be a part of *that*? He wanted to stay, but he also didn't want to hurt anyone.

'Are you in?'

They'd taken him in without question, without wanting anything in return. So, the least he could do was help. That's all they wanted, right? They wanted someone to help – he could do that. He could help them. Maybe that would secure the Warehouse as his new home.

'Yes.'

'Good,' Harvey said. 'I'll come and find you tomorrow so we can run through the plan.'

'Okay – what do you want me to do now?'

'Take the rest of the day off, Felan. You've worked hard today.'

At the unexpected compliment, he blushed. He didn't know what to say. It had been a while since he'd been praised.

He'd almost forgotten what it felt like.

Chapter 8: Perpetrators

*The five-year-old stumbled down the bank, running by the pond.
His mother chased him, laughing, with the child squealing as she
got closer.*

'Mummy, come catch me!'

*He ran around the pond, only stopping when he tripped up on
a jutting tree root, sending him sprawling onto the grass. Felan
cried out in surprise. He looked up from where he had face-
planted, and the smile on his mother's face made everything okay.*

***

Felan couldn't have asked for better company for his first ever
job; his partner was silent, but wary and focused.

Well, it was less a job and more robbing a shop on the corner
of the street for money and alcohol.

For Nick.

At the crack of dawn, they gathered all the necessary
equipment before sprinting from the Warehouse and heading
into the city centre; their shadows morphed as they ran, and the
silhouettes never formed a solid shape.

They stopped just down the street from the shop. Above them,
pastel colours in the sky gave way to neutral blue.

'Are you ready, Felan?'

The boy blanched when Harvey pulled a pistol from his jacket,
holding it with ease in his gloved hand.

Was he really going to use that?

Not trusting his voice, Felan fumbled through his many layers
of clothing and drew his dagger. The metal shimmered in the
morning light. They could already hear the sound of sirens wailing
far, far in the distance, maybe the result of another offender.

'Felan?' Harvey pressed.

'Yeah,' he said, his mouth dry. He hid his knife from view once again. 'I'm ready.'

As one, they barrelled through the automatic doors. Harvey pointed his gun at the shopkeeper, and Felan hurried over to the alcohol cabinet to begin filling his backpack. He included as much of the strong stuff as he could; he knew it put Nick out of it much quicker, and an out of it Nick was a manageable one.

Harvey rifled through the till, broke open another glass cabinet for other random valuables. Felan's hand shook so hard he almost dropped his bag containing over fifteen bottles – Nick might have just murdered him.

A bullet rang out. A thump followed. There was no way Harvey had just...

'Felan! C'mon, let's go!' Harvey yelled over the scream of the sirens.

He looked at Harvey with wide eyes.

'Felan. We need to go!'

He didn't argue, following Harvey from the shop. His feet slapped on the cracked concrete, steady and constant, and he recoiled at a screeching of brakes behind him, followed by the bangs of car doors being kicked open. He glanced over his shoulder. A multitude of guns were aimed right at them.

Was this what normally happened?

Bullets streaked past them, shattering windows as they whistled through the gaps between their heads and their feet. Felan ducked to the left when he felt a sudden breeze beside his ear.

Felan eyed the fork at the end of the street and nodded once to Harvey when they got close. They tore down their different paths and Felan's feet pounded down the narrowing alleyway, putting as much distance as he could between him and his pursuers. He ran faster than he'd ever run in his life, he was sure of it.

If he got caught, it would be the end of his second chance.

He stumbled to a halt some twenty minutes later, muscles aching. Felan slumped against the wall and let his eyes slide shut as he caught his breath. The bag slipped from his back. He held it gingerly in his hands; all of that, for *this?*

But the world was never kind enough to give him a break.

Hands grabbed him around his neck and forced him to the floor. He landed with a heavy thump, momentarily winded. The bag fell through his fingers, but he didn't hear any of the bottles smash. Felan tried to scramble to his feet, but the hands squeezed his neck tighter. He thrashed his body on the floor, flailed his legs out to try to get a good kick on his attacker, but he couldn't do anything.

His father's hands around his neck squeezed tighter. His vision blurred. Felan couldn't breathe. He was too small to fight him off.

Felan brought his hands up to join those around his throat, fingers scratching and fighting. Looking up, he met the crazed blue eyes of what appeared to be a homeless man. Ragged hair – sloppily cut at the shoulders – framed his face. His eyes had a deep-blue tinge that swirled like a hurricane about to strike its next victim. And they were fixed intently on him.

A rusty knife appeared and started its descent towards Felan's throat, inching closer and closer. Releasing his grip on Felan's neck, the man shoved an arm there instead, forcing the boy flat on the floor. Felan stopped scratching at the arm on his throat and pushed a hand towards the knife, attempting to force it in the opposite direction. His hand slipped, and so did his reality. The knife descended further. With a grunt he gripped it with both hands, content with pushing it away from him for now. As long as it didn't impale him, he didn't care where it ended up. His heart pounded. The gap between the tip of the knife and his exposed neck shrank centimetre by centimetre, so he made a last, feeble attempt at pushing the bigger man off him. He didn't want that rusty knife anywhere near him, thank you very much.

The tip of the knife pressed into his throat, and Felan thought he was dead. Just like that. It was all over.

No.

Not when he'd just found a place to call home.

It wouldn't be taken away from him.

Not this time.

Closing his eyes in strain, Felan pushed upwards suddenly and the man toppled sideways, for the moment, off balance.

That was all Felan needed, his weeks of training with Accalia and Blaez coming right back to him.

Felan managed to arch his back enough that he could push himself up with one arm, losing the grip on the knife and jabbing at the man's ribs. The man's head flew back. Felan followed through by digging his elbow into his attacker's abdomen, the sudden and unexpected ferocity knocking the man back. It gave Felan enough space to twist his arm into his back pocket to extract the knife he hid there. Unsheathing it, he pushed the man off him completely. The boy stumbled to his feet, gasped heavily as he placed a hand on the wall to keep himself standing. He made eye contact with the man, and Felan hesitated.

'Go to your room now!'

Felan frowned in confusion. 'But Daddy... I wanna watch toons. Mummy said I could.'

A sharp, stinging sensation hit his cheek. He backed up and stared into his father's anger-filled eyes, whimpering as the man held his wrist too tight.

'Don't speak about her again!'

Felan struggled in his grip. Another slap caused Felan to wrench himself away and bound to his bedroom, tears streaming down his cheeks.

He would never forget the look of pure hatred in his father's eyes.

The homeless man ran at him, and Felan slashed his knife. A huge gash opened on the man's chest, and blood stained his dirty clothes. The man snarled at him, but backed away, astonished. Fearful.

The smug look was wiped clean off his face.

Taking two large steps forward, Felan screamed as loud as he could and drove the knife towards the man's unprotected chest. He could have sworn he heard bones snap as it sank deeper and deeper, and then blood poured from the wound as he pulled it back.

The homeless man grunted and sank to his knees.

Felan looked to his feet, saw the blood flow thicken and watched in fascination as it slowly twisted its way towards him like a snake. His ears rang. His heart throbbed. His whole body ached. He stayed focused on the blood that sloshed about his feet, until it began to seep rather alarmingly into his new shoes.

He vomited twice. He blinked hard. 'No...' he whispered. 'No. That wasn't me.'

Looking around frantically, he found his bag on the floor, kicked to the side. Felan stumbled over with feverish abandon. He checked the contents before he set off again.

No bottles had broken.

Chapter 9: Consequences

Shadows followed Felan back towards the Warehouse.

Once the coast was clear, he ducked into a public bathroom and scrubbed his hands. The cold water ran red and stained the sink. He scrubbed and scrubbed, aware of how the door rocked on its hinges, but nothing, *nothing*, could swipe that image from his head. The door swung and crashed with a bang. Felan scarpered.

As was normal for a Saturday, Farley Street was bustling with people, lined up and down with stalls. His mum had taken him here once or twice as a kid, but it had been years since he'd ventured so far from his father's flat.

The sounds of chatter around him turned into a dull buzz at the back of his mind, and when his stomach growled, he eyed the fruit stand ahead with hungry eyes. A punnet of grapes caught his attention, balanced precariously on the edge. With his head down, he tried to not look guilty. He swiped the punnet straight off the table and carried on. Not a single person batted an eyelid; no shouts followed him; no footsteps chased him... nothing. Not daring to believe it, he peeked up a little. An elderly woman smiled warmly. Felan pulled the punnet of grapes closer to his chest.

Did she not see him steal them? If she had, why was he being rewarded for such behaviour?

Forgoing getting on the underground, like he'd planned with Harvey beforehand, Felan sprinted as far as his body would take him.

It took him far.

Far enough away from the city for him to not feel so trapped. Something about the constant flood of people and shadows of buildings had trapped him in its flow; he'd been kicking and fighting but could never quite breach the surface of the water. He stopped running at the sound of a scream. A group of kids played in the park.

He smiled.

Benches littered the circumference of the park, and in between stood wooden planters filled to the brim with flowers of all kinds. He'd always liked poppies the best. He took a seat furthest from the kids and ate the grapes slowly, making sure to lick his lips. The happy squeals of the kids pulled his gaze over to them more than once.

He remembered playing in a park with his mother, the sun hot on his cheeks, the grass as green as emeralds.

The grass at his feet now stood feeble and dry.

Sparrows and robins hopped atop a barbed wire fence that ran around the circumference of a tiny woodland – so tiny in fact that Felan didn't think he could even class it as one. A cluster of trees, maybe? Dirt footpaths criss-crossed the park like a cardiovascular system, leading in every direction and no direction at all, though no matter which way he looked, the city buildings loomed overhead.

Popping the last grape into his mouth, he tossed the container into a dustbin. He wasn't full in the slightest, but at least he'd eaten something – and any food was more substantial than just water from his shower. He stayed on the bench, thinking for far too long, and the darkness came, faster than he remembered. What felt like a cold hand clamped over his mouth and sucked the air from his lungs.

He was late.

He looked up. The sky was no longer blue, instead grey and dark. Felan held the bag to his chest and ran full sprint. His muscles groaned and contorted in anger and discomfort; the feeling was mutual, and never really faded.

A sudden flash of movement, and he whipped his head to the right. His hand instinctively reached for his knife. He felt stupid when he realised it was just his shadow. Nothing to worry about. It ran beside him, a blur of darkness that never fully formed. A nocturnal, distorted shape that provided little comfort.

Far, far in front of him, the Warehouse rose behind a hill. He'd taken a different route back, deciding it would be good to know what lay in each direction. Distorted light filtered through the many windows. He wished the ground would swallow him up; he was *really* late.

A draught greeted him when he pushed the door open.

'It took you this long to get back, did it?'

Felan jumped at the abrasiveness in Harvey's voice. Normally, he associated Harvey with a gentler tone.

'I had to take a detour...'

'So did I, but I wasn't delayed for half a day, Felan!' The man stared at Felan, who wanted nothing more than to cower down. 'Upstairs. Now,' Harvey hissed. He pointed a steady finger to the ceiling.

Felan shuddered. He walked upstairs, aware of the eyes that gouged into the back of his skull and of Harvey's thundering footsteps right behind him. How embarrassing! His first job, and he'd already royally screwed himself.

Once he'd made it to the relative safety of his room, he stood by the window, a large distance between him and Harvey, who shut the door a little too calmly. He shook his head, rested his palm on the closed door.

'You have no idea how angry Nick is.'

Felan retreated. 'I...'

'What's that on your shirt?' Harvey asked.

'What?'

Felan looked down. Blood stained the lower left of the fabric. With a trembling hand he touched it. Still wet. It clung to his skin like moist powder.

'It's nothing,' he said quickly. 'I'm fine.'

'You're bleeding...'

'It's not mine, alright!' Felan yelled.

It was hard to tell what Harvey was thinking when Felan couldn't read faces well.

'It's not mine,' Felan repeated, sitting on the edge of his bed.

'What happened?'

Felan glanced up at the change of tone. The sound of the gunshot echoed in his head. He flinched. He jumped to his feet a second later.

'What happened? You're asking me what happened? *Me?*' he spat, incredulous.

'Yes, you! You're the one that decided to not come back! Despite having a phone on you, may I add.'

'And you're the one that pulled the trigger!' Felan roared.

Truth was, he'd completely forgotten about the phone because he was far too busy fighting to stay alive. Harvey bared his teeth. Felan sat back down and dipped his head in shame. He kept messing everything up.

'It's my job,' Harvey said, his voice tight. 'It's what I do. It's what we *all do*.'

'You could have given him a chance to run.'

Now it was Harvey's turn to sit down. He sat on the bed next to Felan, and the boy stared. Lines on his forehead, shadows beneath his eyes – how had he not seen it before?

'Nick has eyes everywhere,' Harvey said.

His father was the same; he'd seemed to know where Felan was, even when he was trying to hide. It appeared to him that Harvey couldn't just do what he wanted to do, and neither could Felan. It was kill or be killed. But he hadn't had a choice against the homeless man; Harvey had when it came to the shopkeeper – nothing could justify taking the life of an innocent man.

'Then defy him.'

'I can't.'

'Why not?'

The man leaned in close. 'Why can't *you*, Felan?'

For the first time, Felan saw the danger in his expression. Saw the tiredness, the fear, and the flecks of doubt. Just add that, Felan thought, onto the list of things he hadn't noticed earlier.

'That's what I thought,' Harvey growled. His face flashed with a cold fury that didn't look right on him; he slammed the door shut when he marched from the room.

The bag hit the floor with a clink, the bottles nudging one another. His thoughts went to the shopkeeper, the blood on the floor by his head. To the homeless man, how blood had poured from his chest, the eye of the tornado quietening down to a bleak wind. He scratched his hands with a whimper. He'd done that. He'd been the cause of everything.

He didn't remember standing up, but he jumped back in fright when his bedroom door opened. Nick barged in and grabbed the bag with an evil smirk. 'That's one case of affairs sorted. Now, why was this not delivered directly to me the second you walked in?'

He had no answer to give, and nothing to justify himself with. A simple *I forgot* would not suffice. Maybe with homework that response would have worked, but this? There was no defying Nick.

Felan stared at the floor. He thought he could still see the blood on his hands, feel it dripping, warm and wet, down his fingers.

Nick raised his hand and brought it down hard; it hurt, though Felan didn't react. He nodded once it was over and didn't lift his gaze. He thought back to how he had been saved – now he truly understood the consequences. The man's next words brought back memories of heavy rain and a second chance. 'I won't be so lenient in the future.'

His cheek stung, but who was he to complain? He'd failed at his task, and he had to be punished. He'd caused harm to another person, and he had to be punished. He had to be punished. It was only right.

If Harvey's footsteps were thundering, then Nick's were roaring earthquakes that rendered the entire Warehouse silent. For a brief moment, Felan feared his door might be torn off the hinges. The memory of blood on his hands made him tremble.

Blaez. She was in the room across from his. She'd know what to do. He hadn't seen her downstairs when he arrived, so maybe she was in her room? God, he hoped she was there.

He knocked on her door quietly. His hands shook.

He heard movement on the other side. 'Just a second!'

In a moment of pure defeat, he wrapped his arms around himself, though it failed to give him any comfort. It had been a long time since Felan last had a hug from somebody, so long ago he didn't really remember what it felt like.

'Felan?'

He kept his gaze on the floor, on its cracked surface, on the mud and shoe prints that wore it away. He didn't want to look her in the eye. If he did, what would she see? Would she still see Felan, the boy? Or would she see a murderer? Someone who had taken the life of another out of fear for his own safety? A coward?

Her dainty fingers brushed against his cheek. Felan flinched away at the jolt of pain.

'Oh Felan, what's he done to you?' she whispered.

He finally looked up. Her black eyeliner remained a daily constant, but today it had no effect. Today, all he knew was the definition of being completely and utterly helpless.

Today, all he'd learned was that nothing he did was right.

'What happened?'

He tried to speak, but he couldn't make the words come out. Felan shook his head and covered his mouth with the back of his hand. Blaez blurred in front of him.

She took him in her arms and drew him close. His body shook, no matter how much he begged it to stop. He shouldn't be like this. He deserved what had happened. He deserved punishment.

Why did it suddenly feel like the whole world had ended?

Chapter 10: Scheming

No one asked about the bruise on Felan's cheek.

The three of them sat around the table, in the centre of the boardroom, waiting for the briefing. He glanced at both Blaez and Randi, at their impassive faces, the way neither of them were surprised to be there. Felan fiddled with the hem of his shirt. They might not be surprised, but he sure as hell was. He'd thought that, after his dismal performance with Harvey, he wouldn't be invited out again. The thought saddened him somewhat; he liked being helpful.

The door opened and Felan tensed in his seat.

No Nick. No Rory. Harvey was Harvey, and despite their spat Felan still liked the guy. He saw it in the way Harvey greeted them all with smiles, like a father would. Tala, on the other hand, was still a mystery to him. She was calm and fierce at the same time, with reddish-brown hair tied back in a plait, long enough to reach her waist. She was mute too – that was a talking point. She couldn't intimidate with her words, but she had a stare that left those who disobeyed stammering at her feet. Felan, luckily, hadn't faced that particular look yet. She was also kind, a quality a lot of the Wolves lacked.

'Sorry we're late,' Harvey began with a smile. Tala signed something with her hands; Felan understood the gist of her movements.

'Now, what you're going to do isn't overly dangerous, but don't think for a second that it's safe.'

Felan suppressed a laugh. He'd been a fool to believe stealing alcohol from a corner shop was safe. 'Safe' didn't exist. Not even in the Warehouse were they safe. It was just how it was. Felan hadn't felt safe since his mother died; what else was new? He was used to not feeling safe. There was always someone, somewhere, out to get him.

'What do you want us to do?' Blaez asked.

'Yeah. You don't have to sugar-coat it. We know the risks. We're not stupid,' Randi said.

Felan knew what would happen if he so much as opened his mouth. His father had ingrained it in him, at a young age, not to speak out of turn. The consequences hurt.

'There's been reports of a disturbance in the towns to the west. We need you to check it out.'

Felan leaned back in his chair with a frown. Wasn't that the police's job? Then again, Felan thought, they'd never really done that job up to now.

'Why does it have to be us? We're the least qualified,' Randi said.

'That's exactly why we're sending you three,' Harvey said. Tala nodded.

Felan's frown deepened. 'How does that help us?'

'How else are you supposed to learn?'

The question sounded so simple, so innocent, but it was so ridiculous that Felan laughed.

'I don't know – maybe send someone qualified with us? Show us how it's done?'

Harvey sat back in his seat. 'I'm afraid that's not possible.'

'Why not?' asked Randi.

'Nick's orders.'

Ah – that made sense. Felan wasn't being sent out for good behaviour. He *had* done something wrong.

But this was good. This would give him a chance to right that wrong and get back in Nick's good books. It would be a good thing – he could prove himself useful after all.

'What are we looking for exactly?' he said.

'Listen, you're there for one purpose – watch and observe, get as much information as you can,' Harvey said.

'But I don't get why we're getting involved, I mean, the Wolves as a whole. It doesn't affect us,' Felan said. He looked from Harvey to Tala suspiciously. 'What's going on?'

'Nothing that you three need to concern yourselves with,' Harvey said.

'By sending us out, you've already concerned us!'

Tala rose to her feet and angrily waved her hands about, making gestures, tearing her hands apart. It was the loudest he'd ever seen her.

Blaez was the one to break the angry silence that followed Tala's outburst. 'What do we do if more trouble breaks out while we're there?'

The Elders looked each other in the eye. Tala cracked her hands. 'Stop it before it gets out of hand,' Harvey said.

'You want us to show ourselves?' Felan asked. A flash of annoyance sparked in Tala's eyes.

'Let me remind you of the objective,' Harvey said, leaning forward. 'Get as much information as possible.'

They nodded. Felan clenched his fists under the table.

'You leave at first light.'

***

Felan stayed up, until the early hours of the morning, on the computers, searching.

Take them down. Take them out. Avoid murder if possible.

Felan's fingers twitched on the keyboard. Murder was out of the question. He watched the cameras situated at the perimeter of the town; narrow walkways and secluded areas stood out as possible hiding places. He followed the walkways, the paths, the empty streets, observed the empty houses, working to find a path that could get them in and out in one piece.

Felan lulled himself into a peaceful state of melancholy: the constant clicks of the mouse, the constant tap of the keys. One of the screens blinked out of focus, and it broke the spell momentarily. A rhythmic noise from the floor above roused him. At first, he thought nothing of it. It was probably someone tossing in their sleep, or a rodent scratching about somewhere – yet he quietened, eager to hear the commotion, if there was any, and his fingers stilled completely.

Felan closed his eyes. There it was again! The same rhythmic noise from before! But what was moving around so early in the morning? A loud crash resounded far above him, and something scurried away. His eyes snapped open. Yep. Definitely footsteps. He crept from the computer room and up the stairs, taking care to stay in the shadows so whoever or whatever it was didn't see him coming.

The footsteps grew louder and louder – until they stopped. Felan covered his mouth with his hands. He could *hear* the person's breath. They were just around the corner!

The footsteps faltered. Paused for a beat. Started back up again.

He slowly followed, making sure to stay within earshot.

The front door squeaked and Felan jumped.

How were they now way ahead of him?

He ran to the door, not understanding how the footsteps had got so far away from him in such a short space of time. They should have been right around the corner, not two floors below where he had been minutes, maybe even seconds, previously. He made to sprint down – but if he did, the person would be long gone by the time he got there, vanished in the night. He reached the stairwell as the door swung shut. He cursed, and something flashed in the window. He climbed up to it and perched on the ledge, just in time to see a figure disappear into the forest.

Felan leaned back against the wall, still staring out. Somewhere a raven cawed. Then it fell silent.

Even in pure darkness, he knew that person anywhere. He shook his head. He must have orders from Nick. Nick must have told him to do something, because, otherwise...

What the hell was Harvey doing creeping around the Warehouse?

Chapter 11: Inconspicuous

They were out of the front door by the time the larks began to sing.

Instead of a restless chatter on the way there, it was more of a restless quiet.

Felan hadn't divulged to the others about what he'd seen the night before, hence his solemn silence. He wanted to make sure his suspicions were correct before he made any assumptions – after all, Nick could have sent him. There could be a perfectly reasonable explanation. It might not be as big of a deal as Felan was making it out to be.

But he hated it when people kept secrets.

'I know you said you're okay, but are you sure everything's alright?' Blaez asked.

'Dandy,' he muttered.

She didn't ask again.

Felan made a signal with his hands when they reached the first landmark – an ancient willow tree a few miles from the town – and the three of them fanned outward. The sound of their footfalls dissipated as they slunk about in the shadows, creeping through the shrubbery. The closer they crept, the lighter the sky became. Felan winced at every snap of every twig.

Soon, the town was in Felan's line of sight. He stopped at the next landmark – a pair of unmarked headstones – and whistled. The others stopped too. The town seemed normal enough. A bit quiet, but then again it was early. The locals shouldn't be up for a while yet, giving them plenty of time to get into position. After a few more watchful minutes, Felan signalled to push forward. They converged, and crept their way down the overgrown path Felan had discovered the night before, the crumbling walls either side of him laced with ivy and woodlice.

He held his hand up, signalling for them to stop again, and peered around the corner. The street was deserted.

'Okay, coast is clear. Let's make it to the back now, and then we can wait for something to happen,' he whispered.

Blaez and Randi nodded in agreement. They scuttled like beetles and burrowed into the bushes that strangled the circumference of the town. They spread along it and lay in wait.

The silence unnerved him, and he had a prickling feeling that they were going to get caught – he just knew it. He slid his hand into his pocket, relaxing as soon as his skin kissed the cool metal of the knife. He did the same with the other hand; the pistol burned a hole in his pocket. The night before, Harvey had met them in one of the training rooms, and Felan had used a gun for the first time. He much preferred his knife.

On his belt, his burner phone hung, ready and waiting for use.

Felan cursed under his breath. What was the bloody point? Then lo and behold, townspeople *finally* started milling about just like any other day. He stayed hidden, listening to snatches of conversations, sure the others were listening too.

'That poor thing! But what can I say? We all warned her – we all warned her what trouble that boy is. You just can't tell kids these days.'

'How much? For one packet? That's ridiculous!'

'Mum, come and play!' A little girl with blonde hair ran over to a broken fountain at the centre of the square.

Felan's arm slipped a little, as his head fogged up. He corrected himself, annoyed, but that annoyance drained from him as quick as it had entered.

'Seen anything today?'

'No, sir. Not one goddamn thing,' replied a much younger voice.

Footsteps faded away, and Felan crept as close to the edge as he dared. What the hell were they looking for? Who were they looking for? There was no way they knew he was there. Unless they were all waiting for the same thing – yeah, that was it. They were all waiting for the same thing. He relaxed back down.

Sticks and rocks dug into his elbows and, when he shifted to get comfortable, one of the branches poked him rather aggressively in the eye.

A sudden shout from across the square jolted Felan back into action. Wiping water from his eye, he crawled his way towards the others. The shouts grew louder.

'Watch it,' Randi hissed when Felan bumped into him.

'Sorry,' he mumbled. Blaez appeared on his other side.

'You're late! Where the blazes have you been? Where are the supplies?' an older man shouted at a young boy, no older than Felan himself.

'I couldn't get them! Maddison refused.'

They weren't a boy – they were a girl, her hair hidden beneath a hat.

'What does Maddison expect us to do? We've already given her as much as we can. We can't give her any more! We don't have the money! I told her that last time her men came gallivanting around here!'

The whole town seemed to pause. Every head in the vicinity turned to face the older man and the girl.

'I can go to someone else,' the girl finally said. 'I can get it cheaper…'

'No. We need to stick together now. It was a mistake, letting you go alone.'

'What if they come back again?' the girl asked, frightened.

The man put a hand on her shoulder. 'Then we'll just have to tell them. *Again.*'

Townspeople nodded along with him, still focused on the conversation. Perhaps that was why it was so easy for the men to emerge from the back alley, behind everyone.

Screams. Shouts. Yells. Wails. The sounds of guns and pistols. Laughter. Felan couldn't pinpoint the exact moment it started, but when he blinked, the town was in chaos. Men fighting men. Mothers and fathers protecting their families. Men hitting women. Men hitting children. Bodies hitting the floor.

'We need to get out of here!' Randi shouted.

'What? And just leave them here?'

'Felan,' Blaez said. 'You know the objective. We got what we came for, and now we need to leave. Preferably now.'

He tore his gaze from his friends to the town square. 'They can't defend themselves. They're hurting little kids!'

'Detaining them. For now,' Randi replied quickly.

'Why detain them? Why not let them be?'

'I don't know. We need to report this back to Harvey and Tala,' Randi said. 'Felan, come on!'

Felan was torn. He knew he could go out and help, but it wouldn't achieve anything. He'd just get caught, along with the rest of them, and that wouldn't help anybody, like nobody had helped him until...

'I've seen them before!' Felan realised.

'What? Seen who?'

'The men that started the attack. I've seen them before!'

'Where?'

'Before you found me – they were chasing me for days – two of them kept following me. They caught me too, and nearly dragged me off to someone. Then Nick showed up,' he said. Felan watched the scene with keen eyes; the men were focused on the children, in the same way they'd focused on him.

'Dragged you off to who?' Blaez asked.

'I don't know – they never said her name.'

'Her? Then surely it must be Maddison, if these are the same men,' Blaez said.

They watched the chaos unfold further. The men forced the adults to their knees, and the men dragged the children, two or three at a time, back the way they'd come. The youngest child looked to be no older than five. In the distance, Felan heard doors slamming and engines revving. Cars to transport the kids, he realised.

How had he not noticed?

Felan saw the little girl with blonde hair get thrown over a man's shoulder and carried off, screaming her head off, little arms and legs flailing all over the place.

'Stop, please! We've already told you – we don't have any more money. You ask too much!' the older man pleaded. He sported a bloody nose, and two of the men held him on his knees.

'New rules!' one of the men shouted. 'If you don't pay on time, we take the kids.'

'No!' A woman bolted after the men, and he realised with dread that it was the little girl's mother. 'Give my daughter back!'

A single gunshot and the woman lay dead. With a snarl, Felan pulled out his knife and made to throw himself into the fray; Blaez and Randi held him back.

The man shot a second bullet into the sky. 'If you do what you're told, you'll get the kids back. You've been warned.' He turned and walked away. A few of the men stayed behind.

'Get back to your business,' one of them said. 'The quicker this is dealt with, the better.'

One by one, the townspeople stood. The older man and a few of the wives rushed over to the fallen mother. Husbands and fathers helped the women up, let them cry, and glared over at the few men that dared to stay.

'When will we get our children back?' someone said from the crowd. A tiny baby wailed and the mother shushed it.

'When they've paid off your debts. Now, are you hiding any more kids?'

'Of course not! You've taken them all!'

'You better hope that's true, because if you've lied, and you're harbouring any others...' He let the threat hang empty. Felan hated bullies.

'Felan... Felan!'

He blinked. Crouched in front of him were Blaez and Randi.

'We need to go – how are we getting out of here?'

'There's an exit to the left. Follow the shrubbery around, and we can squeeze through without being seen,' he said to Randi. He didn't put his knife away while they crawled towards their exit.

Randi went first, followed closely by Blaez. Felan had got halfway through when the terrified scream of a girl caught his attention. He zeroed in on the scream, saw with a sense of dread the girl he'd thought was a boy get cornered by two men, the same two men that had cornered him, he realised. They forced her to the floor. She'd tried to hide. The girl had tried to...

'Felan!' His friends shouted.

The girl looked up and made direct eye contact with him. Felan couldn't look away. He knew those eyes, pleading for help, pleading to be saved, pleading for anyone to do something. She screamed as a foot held her down, as her hands were tied behind her back, and as she was dragged away.

'Felan, we need to go!'

Feeling oddly out of sorts, he let his friends pull him through the narrow gap between the two buildings and ran after them. They didn't look back.

Would that have happened to him, had Nick never showed up that night? Would they have dragged him away, kicking and screaming? Because, while Felan had Nick to swoop in and save the day, that girl had no one. Not a single person spoke up to defend her. Not one person made any move to help her.

Not even Felan.

He was a coward, and he always would be.

Chapter 12: The Elders

'You're back early.'

After they exploded into the clearing, Harvey didn't even give them time to catch their breaths. He ran straight over to them. Felan stumbled to a stop, hands on his knees, still holding the knife. Harvey looked them up and down.

'What happened?'

Not one of them answered his question.

'What happened out there? Are you alright?'

This was the man who had taken them under his wing. This was the man who looked out for them. But this was also the man who kept secrets and sneaked around in the dark.

'We're fine,' Felan answered.

'The town got attacked. They had everyone detained,' Randi explained.

'They took the children,' Blaez finished.

Felan thought he saw a flicker of doubt, of fear, engulf Harvey. 'They can't have.'

It vanished when the front door slammed open. Rory stormed out. 'Get inside, you three. Now!'

***

The Elders stood within Nick's quarters.

Nick, as menacing as ever, stood by his desk; Ralph stood with his arms crossed, face calm like a daisy blowing in a breeze, not a care in the world. The grey streaks in his hair offered a guess at his age, or his experience. Perhaps even both. Stephen and Tala stood either side in mid conversation, and their hands flitted back and forth like they were playing a game of 'High Low Chicka Low'. His mother had taught him that one when he was little. Stephen was young for his position, but more than capable. Harvey and Rory stepped into place, and the horseshoe of six Elders was complete.

'What did you see?' Harvey asked.

Felan gathered his thoughts.

'The town was... quiet. Nothing was amiss, except that, I guess, prices were a bit steep, and they were struggling. Normal things for a small town. A young girl came back, said something about someone named Maddison refusing them something, and asking for more,' Felan said. Blaez and Randi nodded in agreement.

The Elders shared glances with each other.

'It was chaos. Men dressed in black flooded into the square. They... they detained everyone, forced people on their knees, took the older children, and...' Felan shook his head. Coward.

'And we got out of there,' Randi finished for him.

'What did these men look like?'

'Like Felan said... dressed in black. Jackets. Boots. Guns,' Blaez listed off without hesitation.

Tala signed something frantic with her hands.

'No,' Felan said eventually, 'no one saw us.'

Right there, midway through the meeting, he saw the girl. She flickered in his vision, pinned to the floor. A bloody coward.

'We got out before they could,' Blaez said.

Not quite, Felan thought.

The air in the room went cold and thready, as if guzzled away by some machine starved of warmth.

'How many of them were there?' Ralph asked.

Then endless questions, the drilling, the interrogation. It reminded Felan of school, when the teacher organised a class debate. Felan remembered sitting at the back of the room, head down, content to stay out of the way. Here, however, Felan was expected to talk, so he said as much as he dared.

After all, people who talked too much were punished.

Ralph waved his hand a good while later. 'Okay, that's all. You can go now.'

'What? Is that it?'

Everyone in the room looked to Felan.

'And what exactly are you expecting?' Rory said, glaring.

'I don't know, some answers, maybe? We could've died! We could've got caught, and we don't get to know anything!'

'It's not in your brief to know anything. You're new. You get the information. We deal with it. That's how it is,' Nick said.

'But I've seen those men before!'

'And that immediately entitles you to know information you're not supposed to have?' Rory said sarcastically.

'The night you saved me,' he said to Nick, 'from those two men. They'd been following me for days, saying they were going to take me to someone, a woman – it was Maddison, wasn't it? Maddison sent those men after me, just like she sent those men to the town, and now you expect me to just let it all go? To pretend that there isn't a crazy woman out there taking children?'

'Enough!' Stephen growled. 'You've said enough!'

'And you've said nothing!' Felan shouted.

Dead silence. Blaez and Randi looked fearful, stuck in place behind him. He hadn't realised he'd moved forward at all. Fingers drummed slowly on the desk, and Felan lifted his head, meeting Nick's hollow stare.

'As I said already,' Nick drawled, 'it is not in your brief to know anything.'

'And how is that fair?'

Felan recoiled in horror the second the words moved past his lips. He knew better than to speak out of turn. He knew not to antagonise people. He'd learned that lesson long ago, in the light of the television, past midnight, when he couldn't sleep.

He should've known better.

Nick rose to his feet and glided through the darkness, leering down at Felan. He trembled. He'd been there before.

'Whoever said anything about it being fair? You signed up for this. You don't tell us what to do.'

Felan kept his lips sealed. So much for getting back in the man's good books.

Nick's mouth quirked upwards in a smirk. 'You're learning, I see, little one,' he chuckled. 'If we hadn't found you, you would have been taken. You would have died, weeks ago, but thanks to me, you have a home – and now you have to earn it. If you step out of line again...'

Five long seconds passed. A strong hand crashed down on his face and forced him all the way to the floor. Felan gasped in pain, but stayed exactly where he was. In the dirt. Where he belonged.

'I give the orders, and you – *all* – obey.'

Felan didn't know what hurt more. The sting on his cheek, or the fact that Harvey made no move to intervene.

Chapter 13: The Set-up

Felan and Blaez lay side by side on his bed after another morning of rigorous training – which had lasted until Nick had a bloody, stupid, BAD idea.

'Rob a bank – is he off his nut?' Felan whispered.

'As crazy as it sounds, he knows what's best for us. He must have a plan, at least,' Blaez said, shrugging. She didn't seem at all fazed.

Felan was. 'Are you not the tiniest bit... apprehensive about this idea of his?'

'Why should I be? He has the ideas, and we carry them out. That's how it works.' She looked to him. 'Are you saying you are?'

Felan scowled. 'You're acting like a sheep.'

'Humour me.'

'Well, yeah. I mean, something could go wrong...'

Blaez laughed in his face. 'Felan, our job has "wrong" written in the title! It's what we do. Surely, you at least trust him by now?'

'And you do?'

'What, and you don't?'

He played with a loose thread on his shirt. 'There's a big difference between tolerate and trust.'

'He saved your life...'

'Exactly the reason I tolerate him. But that doesn't mean I trust him. Not after what he did.'

He felt visibly sick every time he saw the red mark on her face. He didn't care about the marks on his own body. What he did care about was being unable to stop it happening to someone else, especially someone he cared about.

Blaez cast her eyes down. If Felan didn't know any better, he'd say she was resigned to this sort of treatment. Then again, so was he. 'I guess I don't fully trust him either, but I trust that he knows what he's doing.'

Felan always wondered how someone so small could contain so much power and energy and intellect. Her hair stayed the same, choppy in length, and her eyeliner never lost its punch; he was sure she slept with it on. She was always so strong.

'We'll just have to...'

Footsteps paced up and down the hallway outside. He held his finger to his lips. Blaez rolled her eyes. He slipped off his bed silently and stood behind his door, waiting for someone to show themselves. He could see the shadow underneath it, could hear the breath of whoever was stood outside his room, listening in, eavesdropping. The footsteps walked back the way they'd come, and Felan swung the door open, staring wildly around him.

He should be looking right at the culprit.

'Who was it?' Blaez whispered.

'No one. Nothing. There's no one there,' he said. But he knew who had been.

'What do you mean there's no one there?' Blaez joined him at the door. They both peered down the hallway, watching it fade to black. Nothing.

'Let's go back inside,' he said.

'Okay.' They retreated into the safety of his room and collapsed onto his bed. 'We're gonna have to be careful,' Blaez said astutely. 'Anyone could have heard us.'

Let them hear. Let *him* hear, he thought with malice.

But Nick had taken him in. Nick had given him a home. He was supposed to be thankful to Nick, for giving him a second chance. How would it make Felan look, if everyone caught him saying awful things about Nick? Only bullies spoke ill of others behind their backs.

He'd kick him out for sure.

'People are always listening,' she carried on. 'Especially Nick. He knows everything that goes on in Guadalupe. It's what makes him so...'

'Intimidating?' Felan supplied helpfully.

'Yeah.'

'He saved me though.'

'Yeah.'

'He saved you too.'

'Yeah.' She paused. 'I guess he did.'

Felan nudged her knee with his. 'What does that mean?'

She nudged him back. 'It means we're lucky to even be here at all.'

Judging by the absent look on her face, Felan knew she didn't mean a word she said. And Felan quite agreed. 'Did you ever have a pet growing up? I mean, *before*.'

Her face darkened. 'No.'

So it *was* too good to be true. He didn't know what he'd done, but he'd upset her, the one person willing to spend any shred of time with him. It always happened sooner or later anyway.

He was good at upsetting people by just existing.

Felan shifted on his bed, angling himself away from her. 'I'm sorry – you probably want to spend some time with your friends.'

He waited for the hurried scramble out his door, for the slap, for, well, anything. What he wasn't expecting, however, was a friendly pat on his hand. 'It's okay, Felan. I want to spend time with you. Besides, they know where I am.' She still had that vacant look about her, but a smile was a smile.

Felan felt his cheeks heat up. It wasn't every day someone told him they wanted to spend time with him.

'I feel like I'm taking you away from them.'

'They understand,' she said, 'and they have friends of their own.'

He turned so he was lying on his side, facing her. 'Do they?' So far, he'd assumed that Blaez's friends were strictly that. Blaez's friends. He hadn't seen them with any of the others, so he'd assumed.

Assuming. That's all everyone ever did.

'Well, Randi and Caleb always like some alone time,' she said with a wink. Felan flushed a deeper shade of red. 'And Accalia gets on with pretty much everybody. Trust me, they're not going to be short of company.'

'As long as you're sure.'

'If I didn't want to spend time with you, Felan, I wouldn't be here,' she said. 'Oh, that reminds me.' She reached into her trouser pocket. 'Close your eyes, and hold out your hand.'

He raised an eyebrow. 'Really? Are you really making me do this?'

'Come on!' she giggled. 'Do as I say!'

Felan did as he was told. Something small dropped into his open palm.

'Okay, you can open them now.'

She was wearing the biggest smile he'd ever seen. He looked down. 'You remembered,' he said softly.

'I found it in one of the storerooms – I saw it and I thought of you.' She clapped her hands excitedly. 'What do you think?'

In his hand sat a small, purple brooch in the shape of a grape. It was plastic, and worn, and looked like it had been trampled on a few times.

It was also the first gift Felan had been given in years. It also meant Blaez listened to what he said, and remembered things.

Felan liked grapes. He looked up to Blaez's expectant face. 'It's great.'

He guessed he didn't sound or look all that elated, because her face fell. 'Do you not like it?'

'I love it.'

She looked away. 'If you don't, it's fine. It's only a stupid thing anyway.'

'No, really. I love it.'

She glanced back, unsure. Felan disliked how unsure and uncomfortable he made people. It wasn't on purpose, but he guessed he just had that look about him. Not for the first time, he wished he was invisible.

'Why are you so scared to show people how you feel?'

'What?'

'Your words have no correlation to the expression on your face. Honestly, it's kinda creepy. Sometimes it's like you're not really here at all.'

Felan never had been good at talking, and he also didn't fancy getting into his whole daddy issue sob story, so he said, 'I didn't have friends, before I met you. I don't know how I'm supposed to act. I don't know what I'm doing, and sometimes... if I expressed how I felt, things would get taken away. I didn't want the same thing to happen to you.'

'You're stuck with me now,' she said with a wink, slipping her hand into his. 'And you're doing fine. I just want you to express yourself more. Of course, it's fine if you're not comfortable doing it,' she added hastily. 'All I know is forlorn Felan, or expressionless Felan. I haven't met excited Felan, or happy Felan... I want to meet him. I'm sure he's a nice guy.'

Felan pinned the brooch to his shirt. 'This is the nicest thing anyone's ever done for me.'

She gave him a winning smile. 'You're welcome. Now come on – let's go explore the forest!'

It took them a total of thirty seconds to race each other down the corridor, to trip down the stairs, to fly out of the Warehouse door towards the forest in the setting sun. They leaped over fallen tree branches and followed the paths, though they made sure not to venture too far from the Warehouse.

Felan got to the finish line first (a small fairy ring they'd discovered days before) and threw his hands in the air in victory.

Blaez slammed into him three seconds later. 'It's not fair – you're faster than me.'

'You could try harder.'

'If I try harder I'll die.'

'Yeah, please don't do that.'

They sat, with their backs against a tree, with a great view of the fairy ring. He'd never been so intrigued by a circle of mushrooms before. 'Fairy rings are caused by fairies or elves dancing in a circle,' he said. He had done a project on them in school once. The other kids had laughed at him. They had called him a fairy, he remembered. They had called him lots of unpleasant things.

'Do you really believe in that stuff?'

'Why not? As you say, you've got to believe in something. Anyway, I don't, like, *believe* believe in them, it's just sometimes fun to think about.'

'As in, fun to imagine a world where everything is better?'

He cast a sidelong glance at her. 'Something like that.'

She made a *carry on* gesture with her hand. 'I'm intrigued. Do tell me more about fairies and elves.'

'Are you being sarcastic?'

'I don't know yet.' She grinned. 'Just tell me!'

'Fine!' Felan laughed. 'If humans entered the ring to dance with them, they would be punished. The human would be forced to dance, and they wouldn't be able to stop until they went mad, or they died of exhaustion.'

'That's... uplifting.'

'Not all the stories are negative, though. Sure, sometimes fairy rings symbolise bad luck, but they are also said to be good luck charms.'

'How can something be both?'

'Apparently, fairy rings improve fertility and fortune, so people grow crops and let their livestock graze nearby. Other legends say that a fairy ring in your back garden would bring good luck to the house as long as it remained whole.'

'So what happens if we break it?'

'Probably nothing,' he said. 'It is superstition after all, but... I'd rather not tempt fate. Not here.'

Blaez drew her knees to her chest. 'Let's focus on the good luck portion. If we don't step inside it, nothing bad will happen.'

'I like that idea.' Felan picked out the dirt under his fingernails.

'This is good,' she said.

'How can a fairy ring mean everything's okay?'

He'd read about them as a kid, but he'd never seen one before, no matter how many hours his mother helped him search through woodland for that stupid project. Not until the Warehouse.

He couldn't tell if it was something out of a dream or a nightmare.

'Something good will come from this,' she insisted. 'Otherwise we might as well not bother trying at all.'

Felan thought he was a very trying person. He tried to stay out of people's way. He tried to stay quiet while other people were talking. He tried to pretend he didn't exist to other people as much as possible; but it was impossible to act invisible with Blaez, when Blaez was the first person to truly see him.

His mother had always told him to try hard at life, but what did he want in life any more? Friends, he thought. A family. Somewhere to call home. He had that at the Warehouse.

So why did he suddenly want something… more?

A soft pitter-patter broke Felan from his thoughts. He looked up. 'It's raining.'

'It's only light rain. We can stay here for a while longer,' Blaez said, yawning. She rested her head atop his shoulder and shut her eyes.

Felan froze, not moving a muscle. He clawed at the dirt beside him and tried not to freak out. No one had ever fallen asleep on him before. He'd fallen asleep on his mother countless times, and with her, and there had been that one time after…

He clenched his fist so hard he snapped a twig. Blaez shuffled closer.

For so long, he'd dreamed of having a friend, of having someone to confide in, someone to share his dreams with… and his nightmares.

Could he relax with Blaez? Could he have a moment of clarity with her? Could he have *this*? He wanted it, oh he wanted it so badly, but what if it made her go away? What if something else got taken away because he decided to indulge? After everything he'd been through, could he really let his guard down? What if something bad happened?

He stared straight ahead. If this was his second chance at life, he was going to embrace it. Slowly, he lowered his head, millimetre by millimetre, until it lay atop Blaez's own. The areas of his skin that touched hers tingled, and heat bloomed and spread all the way to his fingers and his toes, racing up and down his limbs like clockwork.

Her hand found his in the dirt and squeezed. Felan squeezed back. They didn't let go.

'Thank you for being my friend,' he said.

'No,' she said. 'Thank you for being mine.'

Felan had finally shut his eyes, content, when the sky rumbled. He glared upwards, lifting his head. Typical. Just when he finally allowed himself to relax, the rain bloody *poured*.

Blaez snapped her head up, as a rather alarming amount of water soaked them both. 'I'm calling it,' she said. 'Let's go!'

They slipped and slid along the muddy path, giggling like little kids, as they raced each other back inside, their clothes sodden from the downpour. They stopped at the end of their hallway, in front of their respective rooms, the floor damp where they stood. Mascara ran down Blaez's face, but the light in her eyes undid him. He dashed over and hugged her tight, smiling when she hugged him in return.

This was what he'd been missing for nine years.

Chapter 14: Pandemonium

As the sun peeked through his curtains, Felan woke with a bitter taste in his mouth.

He stumbled to the wet room and gulped down water from the showerhead. He coughed and spluttered, and sank to the floor with his knees pulled to his chest. Cold water trickled over him. The boy paid no mind. He sat there, clothes drenched, and let his head droop down.

Thirty minutes later, he made his way to the armoury. Caleb and Randi were armed and ready, standing chatting in the hallway. They said hello as Felan walked by. He pulled a pistol from the rack (he wasn't going to use it) and slid it into the new holster on his belt; his knife already hung sheathed. Blaez was in the corner of the room, packing... Was that a sniper rifle?

Felan nearly passed out from shock. Blaez? She was the sniper? But she was so gentle, and kind, and...

There was no way the small girl could be one. She was so... so... She'd killed before? She'd killed people? She'd killed people!

Then again, Felan reminded himself bitterly, so had he.

He watched her remove and reattach the scope, and fiddle with it until she was satisfied, then she disassembled it and packed it away into a case that fitted inside her rucksack.

Oh yeah. A rucksack would be helpful.

He peered inside the closest one; a first aid kit and a burner phone rested in the small pockets in the lining. He zipped it up and waited.

Starting out slow and sluggish, the energy within the Wolves began to creep up. Felan felt it himself, on top of the crippling fear that sat heavy in his chest. His fingers played with the hilt of his knife absent-mindedly. Sure, he'd stolen before, but those were insignificant, tiny things that didn't make much of a difference. Someone's life savings? That definitely made a difference.

A shadow next to him made him jump.

'Blaez? Oh my God,' he wheezed out.

She laughed. 'You're out of it, Felan.'

'Well, yeah. I'm bored waiting for everyone.'

'Or, is it because you're ner-vous,' she sang.

'Are you?'

Talking like this with Blaez, he almost forgot that she was a killer, but with every word, he imagined her pulling the trigger, her cold eyes, a blank expression on her face. His mental image didn't look like Blaez at all.

Her face dropped. 'We all are... we just, we try not to show it.' She frowned. 'Are you feeling okay?'

'Fine,' he said. It was all very well focusing on the fact that Blaez had killed before, but he'd killed too. How did that make him any better than her, or any of the others?

'Time to go!' Harvey called.

Some of the guys let out whoops of excitement. Felan swallowed dust. When Nick had first announced who was leading the raid, Felan wished he could shut himself in his room and hope people forgot he existed.

He didn't want someone who crept around to lead the raid – what if he got them all killed? What if Harvey left them all behind and made away with the takings himself?

Felan watched Harvey lead them out of the armoury and zeroed in on the black glove on his hand. He'd been wearing it more and more often – but why?

And then they ran, merging into the pack, as they sprinted into the forest. He kept pace easily and found himself near the front. They all ran in close formation until they reached the underground, where they split off into smaller groups. They rode the train into the city centre, and Blaez, Convel, Felan, and Tate couldn't have been happier to stick together.

Felan turned his back on them and gave Blaez his undivided attention, despite his misgivings around the girl.

'You're the first one to split off,' he said, grabbing a handle when the train jolted. The other passengers mumbled and groaned.

'Yeah, what about it?' she asked.

'Well, you know, be careful.'

'I know how to take care of myself.'

'I know, but… just, be careful.'

Because, what would he do if she got hurt?

Her face softened somewhat. 'I will. This is our stop, guys. Let's go!' Blaez called over Felan's shoulder. He turned, but Convel and Tate had already fled for the doors. 'They're eager,' she offered.

'I wonder why,' he said sarcastically. He followed them anyway, off the train, and climbed back up to the surface. They all stayed in their smaller groups and made their way down the street – they'd be less noticeable like that. All the way down Jubilee Way, families with little kids ran around, eating ice cream and queuing up at hot dog vendors. Cars honked all the way down, and people dressed in posh suits waved at each other from across the street.

All too soon, the multistorey car park solidified into view. He turned to wish his friend luck, but she was already a shadow darting through the bystanders, already long gone. She would be fine, he knew. She was a sniper, and snipers were trained to kill. *Blaez* was trained to kill.

Part of him hoped he'd wake up and it would all be a bad dream.

The first unit consisted of Boris, Chad, George, and Lewis, who split off as Nick commanded. They funnelled themselves down the narrow alleyway and turned a corner.

Accalia and Caleb peeled off in different directions. Unlike the others, they stayed on Jubilee Way. Accalia lingered behind a rusty car next to the kerb, pretending to check her phone, and Caleb ducked behind a skip beside a block of flats some builders were renovating. He took his phone out and did the same as Accalia.

The old scrapyard came up quickly on their left, and Felan followed Convel and Tate inside. The others were already there. Hopefully, by the time the signal came through, all memory of them would have faded from the minds of the bystanders.

The old scrapyard on Jubilee Way was just that: an old scrapyard that no one used. People were too materialistic to throw things away. Felan knew the feeling. Behind him sat piles upon piles of broken tyres and wheel spokes and torn furniture. There were also rusty signs falling from collapsed posts, so Felan guessed at some point there had been an order to the chaos, to tell people where to dump their unwanted items. A ratty teddy bear stuck out from beneath a table leg. It was missing one eye and its ear was ripped open, the once white stuffing all dark and dirty.

Felan wondered if he was dark and dirty on the inside too.

He craned his neck to get a proper look at Blaez's hideout across the way, but he couldn't see any sign of her, only the highest stories of the car park. The hustle and bustle of Jubilee Way around the corner reminded him of what they were about to do. The screams of delight from the kids were about to be screams of another nature.

He glanced around the group of Wolves. He was only friendly with Randi, and the boy in question was nowhere near him. Felan thought perhaps Randi had done that on purpose.

Harvey pocketed his burner phone. 'That's the signal.'

Convel and Tate left the scrapyard first, making a beeline for the Jubilee Bank doors that were made entirely from glass. They broke the glass and barged through, pistols in hand. Felan followed the rest of the Wolves inside and flinched at the first gunshot, the second, the third. The white marble of the interior echoed with screams and blaring alarms. Andy and Mingan chased a number of hysterical workers up the staircase. Ewan and Lee bounded after them.

Crowd control, Felan remembered.

'Felan! Come on – we need to get this system crashing!'

Harvey and Randi sat at the front desk, fingers flying over the keyboards. *Oh yeah.* He rushed over, slipping on shards of glass, and took Randi's seat in front of a monitor. As he worked, he caught glimpses of Randi running in circles, reaching for power outlets and cables and cutting wire after wire. The alarms mounted on the walls flashed yellow, and orange, and red, and flickered like flames. They stopped screaming after a while. Randi had destroyed those too.

In all honesty, Felan thought Jubilee Bank needed better security. Twenty fingers furiously tapped, motivated by the noise from upstairs. The quicker they crashed the system, the quicker they got out of there – he didn't want to be there any longer than they had to be.

'Done!' Felan shouted, getting out of his seat. Randi took over, already working on the next phase of the plan.

Harvey stepped away. 'See you on the other side, Randi.' He glanced at Felan. 'Top floor.'

Felan didn't exactly have much of a choice. He followed Harvey, and they sprinted up the stairs, using the banister to launch themselves further. Their shoes crushed glass as they rounded a corner and bounded along a corridor, and then reached another flight of stairs.

The Wolves left damage in their wake; the remains of expensive-looking chandeliers showered the floor. The occasional smear of blood made his stomach roll. At the signal to stop, Felan nearly collapsed. Harvey steadied him.

'Are you alright?'

Fearing he would vomit if he opened his mouth, Felan settled for a nod.

'Good. You go left, I'll go right. Once you've got as much as you can, head straight to the roof. Believe me, we haven't got long until the cops arrive – be on your guard,' Harvey warned, patting his shoulder. 'See you soon.' The man ran back the way they'd come.

Was every raid they undertook always this chaotic?

The first few boxes Felan came across were already open, the contents strewn carelessly over the corridor floor, expensive jewellery and hard cash. He slung his rucksack from his shoulders and started to stuff it with wads of money, more cash than he'd ever seen in his life. Felan cleared up the floor as best he could and finally found an unopened box. Driving his knife into the cracks of the tiny door, he levered it open.

He froze.

A picture.

People he recognised.

He remembered them, from his mother's side – God knows how long it had been since he'd seen them... And they had seen him and done nothing. They'd seen the state of the flat and the bruises on his face. They'd cut their trip to Guadalupe short, and Felan had never heard from them again.

That was the first time Felan understood what betrayal meant.

He surged forward and sank his fist into the frame. His knuckles tore through the face of the father and ripped a jagged line through the neck of the mother; the infant in her arms was unaffected by his bout of rage.

Felan proceeded to ransack the box completely and left nothing behind. Why? Because they'd left him behind.

He looted a few more boxes until he filled his rucksack. With one last look at the broken picture, he turned on his heel and ran, heading up to the roof. He spilled out of the fire escape, closely followed by Harvey. He hadn't noticed the man was so close behind him. He wondered if Blaez was watching them.

The six of them peered over the ledge.

Far below, Convel, Tate, and Randi bolted down the street. Caleb appeared and pulled Randi down by the sleeve, while the other two stopped either side of Accalia. Waited. Sirens screamed from all directions. Twelve cop cars zoomed around the corner, their blue lights lighting up Jubilee Way. Pedestrians on the streets scattered, getting as far away from the commotion as possible. Felan heard children crying all the way from his position on the roof of Jubilee Bank.

He hated it when little kids cried.

The Wolves around him dived for cover. His friends down below stayed out of sight.

'Felan,' Harvey shouted. 'Get down!'

He didn't. He watched the cars swerve and speed down the street. 'What's the point? They know we're here anyway.'

'But they don't know our current location! Get. The hell. Down!'

He did just that when a bullet streaked through the air.

He sank behind the ledge, terror in his veins, as more and more bullets whistled past. He risked a peek.

The bullets, he deduced, weren't aimed at them.

One of the cop cars veered hard to the left, and a tyre spun off and hit the windscreen of another; both cars crashed with a squeal of brakes. The cops from inside dived out.

Felan watched the shadow on the multistorey car park with a mixture of dread and awe. He hadn't known she was that good a shot! She fired again. Windows exploded. More tyres popped and burst.

It seemed that Blaez wasn't fazed by the erratic movement of the cars.

Then, Blaez stopped shooting. He guessed that maybe the cops were too close for her to get a steady shot – but that was good. She hadn't hit a person yet, at least not directly.

The first two cop cars parked in front of Jubilee Bank. People emerged from the cars, guns in hand, just as Boris, Chad, George, and Lewis erupted into the street from the alleyway. They ran with shouts, and stormed through the first wave of cops. They slashed with their knives and shot the cops down before running away towards Accalia and the others.

Bodies. They'd left bodies.

How many of those cops had families? Friends? People that would miss them?

The rest of the cars arrived, and more cops, guns in hand, leaped out. They advanced with small steps, wary, as momentarily the sounds of bullets faded out. Had they not seen the guys earlier, killing their colleagues? One brave cop made it to the front steps of Jubilee Bank and peered inside.

The gunshots started up again as soon as they left the safety of their cars' shadows. Gesturing to each other, the cops hurried inside and Felan imagined they took cover. They looked so small down there, like ants, or a swarm of flies.

More of them dropped to the floor and didn't move again.

Felan peered further. A hand on his wrist yanked him back down.

'What the hell is wrong with you?' Harvey growled. 'If they'd seen you, you'd be a corpse with a hole in the head, lying on the floor, right there.' He pointed to the floor at their feet.

Felan's heart pounded in his chest. This wasn't Harvey, not the Harvey he knew anyway. Felan stood again, backing away from the ledge. Harvey followed, and the others watched, reaching for their weapons.

'Am I not allowed to look after myself now?' It was what he'd grown up doing. It was what he'd been doing for months, even after joining the Wolves. In fact, Harvey was one of the ones who'd been pushing for it.

'You're putting us all in danger!'

'What about them down there? They're risking their lives, and we're trapped up here!'

Harvey shoved the boy to the floor.

Felan flushed bright red, out of anger more than embarrassment – and fear – and climbed to his feet.

'Now, we go.' Harvey and the others climbed over the ledge. Felan blanched. That was the plan? *Climb down?* Felan glanced over the ledge after them – Lee was already two floors down.

He could stay. He could stay on the roof, wait it out, plead his innocence. He could get caught, and he could tell the cops everything about the Wolves, and what they did.

Could he do that though, to his friends? To his new-found family? The only people in this city who wanted him? Needed him? And after everything they'd done for him, could he bring himself to betray them like the world had betrayed him? Like his biological family had betrayed him?

After securing the rucksack on his shoulders, Felan scrambled up and stood atop the ledge.

It was a long way down.

Chapter 15: Already Gone

Fleeing in the shadow of Jubilee Bank, Felan felt invincible.

His rucksack slapped hard against his back, the contents jingling about, and the extra weight made it harder to run. As they were running down the street, other Wolves merged with his group, and for a moment, Felan thought they were safe.

Then the cops sent a storm of bullets after them.

Accalia and Caleb shot randomly at the cops and stumbled while reloading. While some cops dropped to the floor, screaming, some fired back.

Felan swallowed bile as he ran. He couldn't afford to get distracted. He had to get out of there. They *all* had to get out of there.

It almost didn't register in Felan's brain when Randi stumbled ahead of him. He clamped a hand down on his shoulder, running significantly slower than before. A red patch blossomed from beneath his hand, and Felan rushed to his aid.

He couldn't believe it when the others ran past.

Were they serious? They couldn't leave Randi by himself... he'd get caught. He'd die.

Felan didn't want Randi to die.

Accalia pulled the trigger once more, a sharp zip that ended with a smash. A shop window shattered somewhere behind them, and pedestrians screamed and cowered down.

Blaez joined the fray shortly after: three booming bullets streaked through the air, one after another, and three cop cars exploded as if they were on a fuse, sending shock waves rippling beneath their feet. It was like running atop one of those waterbeds he'd read about once, and everyone managed to stay on their feet.

Everyone except Randi.

Felan reached him just as the boy crumpled. Wrapping an arm around his waist, Felan dragged him off down a side street just off Jubilee Way, away from everything. He sat his friend against a wall. His head lolled onto his chest.

'Go, Felan,' he managed to say. 'Just go.' His body went limp.

'Randi?' Felan shook him. 'Randi?'

Nothing. Just haggard breathing and more blood than Felan knew what to do with. A shadow fell over them – Felan leaped to his feet, knife at the ready. If it was the last thing he did, Felan was going to protect Randi. He knew what it was like to be left behind, to have no one on his side. He'd just thought his new-found family would be different.

Caleb held his hands up, white in the face. Felan lowered his guard.

'He's still alive,' Felan said, taking stock of the tears rolling down the younger boy's cheeks.

Caleb collapsed to his knees beside Randi, stroking his hair. 'Thank God,' he cried. 'Thank God.'

'Take my bag and go, Caleb,' Felan said. He chucked the rucksack at the boy's feet. 'I've got him.'

Caleb's face crumpled. 'I want to stay.'

'Run, Caleb.'

'I'm not going without him.' He narrowed his eyes at Felan, and didn't take his hands off his boyfriend.

Then, Felan understood, because despite being friendly with the pair of them, neither of them knew him all that well, and Felan didn't really know them either.

So how could he expect Caleb to be okay with leaving Randi behind with a stranger?

'I'm on your side,' Felan said. 'I'm on your side, and I'm going to bring him home. But I can't do that if you're here. The others are still close – you can catch up, and get back safely.' He reached over and squeezed Caleb's arm. 'I'll bring him home.'

Caleb stared back. A cop car zoomed by, heading in the direction of Jubilee Bank. Randi hadn't moved. Pedestrians screamed down the street, and the sounds of sirens made Felan's head spin.

'I trust you,' Caleb said, tears dripping down his cheeks. 'Please don't let him die.'

'I promise,' Felan said. 'Now go, Caleb. I've got him.'

Caleb kissed Randi on the forehead, and ruffled his hair once more. Another cop car went screaming by.

'Go!'

Caleb grabbed the rucksack and ran.

Once he was out of sight, Felan let the panic overtake him. What was he meant to do now? He was by himself, and he had made a promise he probably shouldn't have made. Sounds blurred around him, and he stared at Randi's unconscious body. A deep voice broke through the haze.

'Leave him, Felan. He's already gone!' Felan looked up. Harvey stood at the mouth of the side street. 'Come on, let's go!' the older man shouted, angry and irritated.

Felan couldn't care less. He was not going to abandon Randi when the boy had been nothing but welcoming since his arrival.

No one deserved to be left behind.

'He's still alive! We can't just leave him!'

Harvey shook his head a few times, glaring, jaw tense. And he ran.

Felan had known it would happen, but it still stung. It stung to know that no one ever stuck by to help... Randi was barely fifteen! Gathering his thoughts, Felan surveyed the situation.

There were flashing lights he hadn't noticed before, and even more sirens. Three ambulances braked outside Jubilee Bank and paramedics spilled out.

Just how many cops had they killed today? How many had Blaez killed, had Accalia killed, had Caleb killed? How many cops now lay lifeless because of his friends?

Randi groaned.

Felan clenched his jaw.

But the cops had shot back.

They'd hurt his friend.

He pulled down Randi's shirt to reveal the wound, and a fresh wave of blood ran down his arm. Felan poked it gently and peered closer; he couldn't see the bullet at all. He pulled Randi forward. There was no exit wound either, and of course he'd foolishly given Caleb his bag, far too worried about not delivering goods to Nick than remembering the first aid kit stashed inside.

'Idiot,' Felan cursed himself. He tore a strip of his own shirt and wrapped it around the wound as far as it would go before he tied it off, suddenly glad Harvey had insisted on basic first aid training.

Blood spotted through the few layers of fabric, but it was the best Felan could do in the situation.

He snaked an arm around Randi's waist, pulled Randi's arm around his shoulder, and held it there. The boy groaned again.

'Randi, I'm gonna get you home, but I need your help,' Felan puffed, taking the first step. He nearly sent both of them tumbling to the floor. Carrying someone else proved much harder than he'd originally thought, especially considering how small a person Felan was, and he tripped a few times before he found a rhythm that worked. To start with, Randi helped. He moved his feet and it lessened the burden, but before long Felan was back to dragging him, Randi's strength long gone.

Stumbling down the street in plain sight, covered in blood, was a mistake, but there was no other option. He didn't know any of the shortcuts yet and didn't want to risk getting lost; Randi's life was in jeopardy.

For some reason, they didn't get chased. Felan didn't question it.

Luck was on his side for once – and if good luck was carrying a dying friend down the street, he didn't even want to hazard a guess at what bad luck would look like.

When Felan recognised them, he took the familiar back alleys and secluded walkways, but he steered clear when he didn't, and when he could go no further, he lugged Randi into an abandoned house, praying they weren't being followed. His shirt resembled a crop top, having had so much torn off it. He hated to part with new belongings, but his friend's life was worth more than a stupid shirt. Anyway, Felan was sure the Wolves had plenty spare in that warehouse of theirs.

Laying Randi down beneath the stairs, Felan sat vigilant, in sight of the doorway. The house had been the first place he'd stayed after he ran away, after leaving that little boy behind; surely, he was no better than Harvey. People left other people behind all the time. He saw it every day.

The difference was, a small part of him said, he'd had no choice when it came to that little boy. Harvey had a choice when it came to Randi, and by extension, him.

The floorboards groaned, and a chill slithered in through the broken windows. Felan had been there when the windows broke – a guy had thrown something at Felan, but he'd missed. Felan had been showered with glass before scarpering, running as far away as he could. The guy had caught up to him weeks later, with a few of his friends, and followed him, taunting him with promises and sickening threats. Nick had saved him.

The abandoned house had been the first place Felan felt safe in since his mother died, and it had been ripped from him the moment he had let his guard down.

If there was one thing he had learned about the streets, it was this: to never let his guard down.

Twenty minutes later, when he was positive they hadn't been followed, Felan made a move, and by the time they'd stumbled across the city, it was dark. Dread settled in his chest, dropping down, coiling in the pit of his stomach, when the Warehouse came into view. Stars twinkled, mocking him from millions of miles away. They shone down and lit up the dirt track in the distance.

Randi's weight grew heavier. All he heard was the sound of dirt underfoot. The howling wind bit into his arms, and his face, and the bitter cold settled deep into his bones.

Felan lost all feeling in his hands. Randi almost slipped from his grasp and Felan forced his body to hold on, walking in a zigzag in order to stay on his feet. Well, it was more of a stumble, as he couldn't see, couldn't breathe, couldn't think.

Felan's stomach growled. He couldn't remember the last time he'd eaten… it must have been days ago. He swallowed away the hunger pains, although the cold air did little to appease him. His throat was like sandpaper.

The terrain grew rougher. The dirt changed to sizeable rocks, loose and unstable, and snagged his feet when he lacked the energy to lift them off the floor. He fell to his knees at one point, crying out in the effort it took to get back up; the wind roared louder. He thought he heard shouting. He blinked a few times. An exhausted grunt fell from his lips.

He tried. He tried to help Randi. He didn't try hard enough. Felan slumped to the floor, catching Randi as a last act of his consciousness.

He remembered hearing a huge bang. The lights to the Warehouse seemed to glow brighter than ever and blew out his pupils. His felt his eyes roll, haggard breath on his arm. Something sharp dug into his cheek. The touch of a warm, calloused hand on the back of his neck.

It all dissipated to black.

Chapter 16: Fidelity

He was alone when he woke up.

Felan shivered and pulled the covers closer.

Hang on – covers?

He blinked the sleep from his eyes and looked around. He was in his room, his door closed, the curtains drawn shut. What the hell? He'd been outside. Cold. Exhausted. Carrying Randi. Randi! Where was he? Was he alright? Was he alive?

Felan sat up and groaned; every single part of his body hurt – aches and pains shot down his legs, across his chest, and he had a pounding headache to top it all off.

'Brilliant,' he muttered. His throat hurt. He rubbed his head and lay back down. Despite the exhaustion still buried in his bones, weighing him down, he couldn't sleep. There was no solace in the solitude of his room.

'Felan?' a voice asked.

He was surprised by the figure peeking through the doorway.

'Are you awake?'

'Unfortunately.'

Walking in, Harvey offered him a smile, but it didn't reach his eyes. He was uncomfortable, Felan thought, but this was good. This was the Harvey he knew, not the monster that had invaded him at Jubilee Bank. The man dragged a chair to the side of Felan's bed and sat down. He tried another smile. It was a little more successful. 'How do you feel?'

'How do you think I feel?'

Harvey moved. Felan stiffened – then he saw the bottle of water in his hands, held out towards him. A gift, no, a peace offering. He thought back to Harvey's actions at the top of the bank, his suspicious behaviour, and every single thing that had him doubting the man in front of him.

The pain in his head worsened, and he took the bottle. The water soothed his throat and numbed his headache enough for a sigh to escape his lips.

'Better?'

Felan forced himself to sit. 'Not really.'

'I'd be worried if you were.'

'And are you?'

'Am I what?'

'Worried.'

Harvey ran a hand through his hair. Felan eyed the movement warily. The man's hair was greasy, and the lines on his forehead had deepened since Felan last saw him.

'I'm surprised you're up – you put your body under a lot of strain,' Harvey said. A frown scrunched his eyebrows together.

Felan shrugged. He'd received worse from his father over the years. He'd recover in no time, he thought, playing with his hands, focusing on the cracks and the scrapes on them. He remembered the adrenaline of running. He remembered the blood that had stained them too.

'How... how is he? Randi, I mean.'

Harvey crossed him arms. 'Alive.' Then, 'You saved his life.'

'That was kind of the point,' Felan said, resisting the urge to roll his eyes. 'So how long have I been out?'

'A week!' Harvey roared. He stood up so abruptly that the chair toppled over with a crash, and Felan flinched back. Harvey advanced on the boy, who fell from his bed, scrabbling back until he hit the wall. He slipped and fell numerous times as the familiar fear gripped him.

'What the hell were you thinking? Were you trying to get yourself killed?' In Harvey's rage, spittle coated his lips and flew in all directions.

Felan blinked.

His father grabbed him by the shoulders and shook him, hard enough to hurt, hard enough to leave marks. Then he was on the floor, a shooting pain in his wrist.

'She's gone, Felan!' his father yelled. 'She's gone, and it's all your fault!'

He shrank under the intense stare Harvey stunned him with.

'Did you forget our number one rule? Did you forget everything we ever taught you? We were ready to leave Randi behind – he knew the risks when we took him in, and he agreed!'

'Okay – maybe Randi knew the risks, maybe you all knew them, but I didn't! I had no idea what the hell I was getting myself into!'

Maybe he shouldn't have said that out loud.

The sound of Harvey's voice echoed around the room, and Felan started to shake. The volume increased, as if someone had their finger pressed down on a TV remote, the plus volume button forced down hard.

Felan didn't move an inch, despite the shivers and the shakes that took control of his body, nor did he open his mouth to defend himself. He took the word barrage and let it wash over him. No soap. No lather. Just coarse and rough waters; exactly what he was used to.

The thunder boomed, letting loose huge crashes that ricocheted around his skull. Felan cradled his head in his hands. His body started unconsciously at every sudden flash of lightning, every growl of thunder. Those blue flashes sent jolts of electricity rippling across his window.

He missed his mum. Only two weeks without her. Only two weeks of this, and he was tired. Far too used to it. Far too used to it already.

And then Harvey stopped and looked at him. At least, that's what it looked like to Felan. Harvey reached a hand out to him and dropped it just as fast. He stood back and turned the chair upright. He sat with an audible '*oomph*'.

'I shouldn't have said all that,' he said.

Felan nodded, but his expression betrayed him; Harvey's face fell. But Felan didn't get a chance to feel bad for it, because a wave of exhaustion hit him. He yawned, staggered to his feet and collapsed back onto his bed. A serene blankness washed over him, and something warm covered his hand, patting it gently. Felan wanted to tug away, but he was so tired...

The warmth left, never came back, and he fell asleep the way he'd woken up.

Alone.

***

'What the hell happened to you?'

Despite his misgivings about her morality, he couldn't hide the anger, and the surprise, and the shock he felt at seeing such a painful bruise on her cheek.

Blaez smiled. 'Who do you think?'

Felan ground his teeth together in anger. Why would Nick hit her like that? He understood why he was hit himself – he needed to be punished after all – but what could Blaez have possibly done to receive something as painful as that? He wanted to reach over and touch it. He wanted the ability to touch it and make it disappear.

'Why did he do it?'

She didn't stop smiling. 'I missed.'

'Missed what?'

'My shot. Well, it was more than one shot, but it's the same difference.'

Felan rubbed his forehead. 'Come again?'

'He gave me this *lovely* present because I missed every shot the other day,' she said.

Oh. She was talking about the raid. 'But you didn't miss – you hit your mark. Every time,' he said. She hurt people. She killed people. She was a killer.

He stared down at the floor.

'I guess you're right, Felan,' she said. 'I hit what I wanted to hit.'

Suddenly the floor wasn't so interesting. 'What are you talking about? Blaez, you've done nothing but confuse me since I've woken up. Please can you stop talking in riddles – I've got a bloody headache and trying to understand what you're saying is making it worse.'

'You're no fun.'

Pain darted across his skull. 'Blaez – please.'

Blaez crossed her arms and leaned back in the chair. The bruise looked so wrong on her face – so did labelling her as a killer.

'I'm an expert sniper, Felan. And you don't need me to tell you what that means,' she said. He shook his head numbly. Of course she was a killer – how could she not be? 'But that's not the whole deal. I *am* an expert sniper, an expert sniper and proud of it. I can hit whatever I want from up close, far away... distance doesn't matter. I can hit *anything*. It takes me seconds to adjust. It's instinctive to me.'

'Brag about it.'

'I do. All day,' she grinned.

Felan felt sick to his stomach. She was proud of that? Being a killer?

'They get angry, Nick and the others, every time I miss, but to me it's a huge relief.'

'Huh?'

'I'm not a killer,' she said. 'I don't aim to kill – although admittedly I have shot someone in the leg once. It gave Caleb time to run away. No. I aim to miss... I always miss, because my aim isn't on the cops, or the people Nick wants me to hit. My aim is on the windows, to shatter the glass, to distract people. My aim is on the floor at their feet, the air around their heads, to scare them away. I aim to cause chaos, not to kill.'

For someone with such steady hands, it was strange that now they trembled like a lost kitten.

'An expert sniper that refuses to kill,' Felan whispered. And he'd thought she was a killer? How could he have thought that? They were *friends*. Friends didn't think that.

What was wrong with him?

All of his misgivings about the girl dropped into an abyss and Felan gladly let them fall. She hadn't killed anyone.

But he had.

What did that make him?

'You sound relieved,' she said. There was a small smudge to her eyeliner – he suspected she'd rubbed it while talking, while he wasn't paying enough attention. Her lips remained a thin, white line. She pulled her knees to her chest, rocking slightly; she was small enough to be able to curl up on the chair and not fall off.

'I am,' he said. The guilt was astronomical. If Blaez hadn't been in the room, he'd probably have drowned himself in the shower for an hour or three, punched a wall, screamed into a pillow... anything to lessen the shame he felt at labelling Blaez a killer.

'That's why you were acting weird,' she said suddenly.

'Yeah.'

Hurt flashed in her eyes. 'Me? Felan, you thought I'd...' Even she couldn't say what he'd been thinking.

He hung his head in shame. 'I know. I'm really sorry. I just assumed...'

'That because I'm in a gang, I'm exactly like Nick?'

'Well, yeah.' She thumped him hard in the shoulder. 'Hey!'

'That's for assuming,' she said, smiling playfully.

Felan didn't smile back. He couldn't.

'And you? Have you, you know, killed someone?'

He thought about lying, but the answer was written clearly on his face.

'My first job with Harvey,' he whispered. He kept his gaze on the floor as he told the story. 'It was self-defence. Blaez, I swear it was self-defence.'

A hand on his arm. He looked up. 'I believe you.'

And it was like Atlas took back the burden of the world again. Atlas would bear it now. Not him. Not Felan. 'Is there anyone else here like you?' he asked.

She poked him. 'Like us, you mean?'

Felan wiped at his eyes. 'Fine. Like us.'

Blaez curled up tighter into a ball. 'Randi and Caleb. They lived in a care home together – it's where they met – but it couldn't handle that many children, too much poverty, and you can probably guess what happened after that.'

'They ran away?'

'They were thirteen – thought that the younger kids would be better off if they had two less mouths to feed, two less bodies to clothe, and so on.'

'That sucks,' he said.

'Agreed. Anyway, Accalia's like us too.'

'Really? But both Accalia and Caleb shot at the cops the other day!'

Blaez winked. 'They took a page from my book.'

'Oh.'

'Yeah, *oh*,' she laughed. 'Anyway, Accalia – her parents went to fight in the war and they never came home.'

Felan knew about the war she was talking about. It made city life worse because all the money went into funding the army, rather than maintaining the safety of the citizens.

'She lived with her grandpa for a while, but he passed away not long after. She was too young to live by herself, but she was too old for an orphanage, so she wandered around until Nick found her.'

'Sure. Anyone else?'

Blaez shook her head. 'For a while, Harvey was.'

'But he's not any more,' Felan said. The man had shot a clerk in the head at point-blank range.

'I don't know what happened to him. He's not who he used to be, Felan.'

'I know.'

'You didn't know him before – he looked after us. I guess he still does, but he's barely here any more.'

Felan didn't tell her he'd found Harvey sneaking around. 'You think he's up to something?'

'No. I think he knows exactly what he's doing.' Her face dropped, and her chin hit her knees. 'Listen, Felan... I wanted to tell you about the sniping. About me. I really did, but I wasn't sure how you'd react. You're new to all this... whereas I've had years to come to terms with it. I know what it feels like to have the floor ripped from beneath you, and to get thrust in a situation you don't know if you're comfortable with. I didn't want that for you,' she said. She waved her hands around in a helpless gesture. 'I didn't want *this* for you.'

Felan offered her a smile. 'It's okay, really. It was just a bit of a shock. I am sorry for thinking you were like everyone else.' He glanced down. 'There was a moment then, during the raid, when I thought about handing myself in to the cops, and telling them everything.'

Blaez cocked her head to the side. 'Why didn't you?'

'Because you're the only people that seem to give a damn about me at the moment. I didn't want that to get taken away because I was scared.'

'You know, Felan, you're allowed to be scared.'

'I've had enough of being scared.' Felan brought his knees up to his chest. Echoes of his father lingered in the corners of his mind.

Blaez clenched her fists into balls, and Felan thought she was about to start shouting at him. Or hit him. It was an action he'd learned to look out for with his father, when the man had him trapped in a corner. *Before.* He deserved the hits, and the shouts, and he supposed he probably always would.

Felan picked at a scab on his arm; he didn't remember where he'd got the injury from. 'It's not what I thought it was going to be,' he said.

Blaez leaned over, grabbing his arm. She had tears in her eyes. 'I wish I could have warned you. I wanted to warn you so bad – but Nick already had you from the start.'

Felan looked down. 'This is how it starts, isn't it?'

'It's going to keep happening, Felan.'

He thought about all those empty rooms upstairs, the rooms they were currently renovating, the rooms he now understood were to be filled with more people, more kids.

Just like him and Blaez.

'It's not going to get better,' she said.

Reaching a hand out, Felan cupped her cheek. She leaned into his touch. 'It's going to be okay. Have some faith, yeah? That's what you always tell me.'

'In the little things,' she said. He removed his hand from her cheek and bopped her nose with a finger. She scowled. 'This has to have happened to us for a reason. The universe wouldn't put us through this just to make our lives worse. There has to be a reason we're here.'

Felan shrugged. 'Maybe there's no reason for it. Maybe that's the way life is.'

She shook her head, smiling. 'I never thanked you for saving Randi's life.'

'It was nothing.'

'It was against the rules.'

'Sod the rules.'

'I quite agree.'

'Don't let Nick hear you say that – you might get another bruise.'

Blaez pulled a face. 'Oh ha ha, Felan.'

He grinned, and it felt amazing to be able to. For a moment, the pain left him, the memories left him, until it was just him and Blaez in his room, laughing.

He didn't remember falling asleep.

***

Not even the prospect of being shot scared him as much as Nick did.

He guessed word had got back to Nick that Felan was mobile again, because within five minutes of drills in the training room, Accalia poked her head in. 'Nick wants to see you,' she said.

It was never good when Nick summoned him. How could it be? He'd done the wrong thing, and he had to be punished. He forced himself to walk down the dark corridor to meet him, his knees growing weak. He still wasn't feeling one hundred per cent, but when was he ever?

He pushed open the door when invited to and froze. Nick sat at his desk, waiting, a finger tapping a steady rhythm on the surface. Felan nearly let his knees buckle.

'So,' Nick growled, 'I heard about your little adventure. Explain.' Nick stood and his black eyes shone menacingly.

'I – I couldn't leave him there. He was still alive. I couldn't just let him die.'

'Oh, you could have. You could have easily just run with the rest of them.' The man's shadow slowly advanced in the dark, and Felan followed its movement on the walls. Fear gripped him, and he couldn't move. 'So why didn't you?'

A chuckle in the dark. Breath on the back of his neck. Still, Felan didn't move.

'Pathetic,' Nick said, just above a whisper. He pressed a sharp nail against Felan's neck and slowly dragged it across the skin.

The boy let out a gasp. The nail dug in deeper.

'If you want to survive, you need to learn to not care.'

Felan curled his hands into fists to stop them from shaking. This was the man that hit Blaez for missing her shots. This was the man that didn't care about the lives of his Wolves. Before long, his hands weren't shaking from fear.

'Always put yourself first, otherwise you won't make it out there.'

He tried to ignore the nail that dug in deeper and deeper. The nail that all but cut his airway off. One finger. One placement. One quick death, if Nick chose.

'You need to learn what it means to obey me, Felan,' Nick said.

A small trickle of blood ran down his neck.

'And I hope this gives you an indication of what'll happen to you if this happens again.'

Felan stayed frozen on the spot long after Nick left. He pressed a hand to his neck, winced, and brought it up to eye level. Barely there, in the cover of darkness, but it was there.

The sheen of blood.

Blood on his hands.

That was a fact he couldn't deny.

Chapter 17: Adaptions

One pointed look from Harvey, and another scathing look from Nick, and Felan volunteered himself for the next supply run.

What he didn't expect was three of his friends to volunteer to go with him, so that's how he found himself sat in one of the boardrooms with Accalia, Blaez, and Caleb.

Why had his friends volunteered to go with him? Why would they put themselves forward for something like that in the first place? He didn't have a choice. They did.

What the hell were they playing at?

Caleb should be staying behind with Randi. Randi was still recovering, though he was moving around a bit better; he had been written off job detail, and while Felan was relieved the boy had been given time to recover, part of him was jealous. Jealous that he didn't have to go back out onto the streets, where anything could happen.

'Let's head out,' Accalia said, standing up. They'd planned all they could, and now it was time to set the plan into motion.

Even if none of them liked it.

'I'll meet you guys outside,' Felan said, a little breathless. 'I've left something upstairs.'

Accalia and Caleb nodded and carried on. Blaez stopped in her tracks.

'Is everything alright?' The black eyeliner made her eyes pop.

'Yeah. Give me a few minutes,' he said, and promptly jogged away. He nodded to a few Wolves he passed along the way (they didn't even acknowledge him) and bounded up the stairs two at a time. Once he'd shut himself in his room, he dipped his head down, tried to slow the anticipation in his heart, and thought about what they had to do.

Rob a pharmacy – in broad daylight. Get away without getting caught.

A piece of cake, really, in comparison to what had gone down on Jubilee Way, but that didn't make the new job any less terrifying.

What if someone else got hurt?

Felan tightened his belt and dusted off his shirt and trousers, as he walked back downstairs to the armoury. He reluctantly picked up his pistol and slid it into the holster on his belt, covering it with his shirt; it wasn't visible to the eye unless he lifted the clothing, and neither was his knife – he carried that everywhere. He removed a rucksack from the shelf and slung it over his shoulders.

His friends were waiting for him outside, Accalia with her green bandana and her rifle, Caleb with two pistols and a knife sheathed into his belt. He tucked a tiny blade up his sleeve with a wink. Blaez enclosed her sniper rifle in her ski sack, fully assembled and ready to fire, and two knives hung on her hips.

None of them were killers, he reminded himself. His friends hadn't killed anyone. They were just that, his friends; he needed to remember that.

'Is everyone good to go?' Accalia asked. The girl wasn't used to giving orders, or being in charge for that matter, but she couldn't have refused. It should be an honour to lead a job. Blaez had told Felan that Accalia had a future with the Wolves, whatever that meant.

Felan wasn't sure if Accalia was pleased about that.

'Not quite. Felan, can you take my bag?' Blaez asked.

'You'll have no first aid kit,' he said.

'It's in my ski sack. Stop worrying so much,' she said, stuffing her rucksack in his. 'Okay, now I'm ready!' A breeze blew by, creating a sail out of her choppy, black hair.

Accalia sprinted into the forest, and the rest followed closely. Felan hung at the back, keeping an eye out.

He wasn't quite sure for what.

***

Being the poorer part of the city, the Fringe teemed with people. Here things were cheaper; no one had the money to afford luxuries from the city centre.

Felan nursed a cup of tea. The street was on the nicer side, despite the dirt cheap products. A balcony above him spewed flowers, most likely weeds, but it added colour to such a dismal place. His father's flat had been in the Fringe, though on the other side of the city.

He'd lost sight of Blaez some ten minutes ago, as she scouted the area. She returned grim-faced.

'How's it looking?' Caleb asked.

She sat down heavily. Accalia wordlessly slid her untouched tea across the table. Blaez gulped it down in seconds.

'Packed,' she said, wiping her lips. 'All elderly.'

Felan thought back to the older woman who'd watched him steal grapes and smiled. She would not have the same reaction if he'd threatened her with a gun. She would not have the same reaction if she saw what he was capable of.

Felan had never associated the word *dangerous* with himself before.

'The plan stays the same. Our best bet now is to have two of us keeping watch, while the other fills up the bags. Blaez, you'll stay on the roof up there.' Accalia pointed to a balcony some floors up. 'It's just across the street. I know you're used to long distance, but if something happens, we're going to need backup immediately. Don't take any chances for yourself. We need this to run smoothly, with no casualties,' Accalia said. 'Caleb and myself will cover you, Felan. We have our burner phones, so if anything goes wrong, we can all contact each other; namely Blaez.' She turned to her. 'You see anything wrong, anything at all, you alert us, and we'll get out of there. We'll rendezvous as soon as we can. We're not taking any chances today.'

Felan stared through the pharmacy window at the elderly people inside, the way their bodies bent low and awkward, how they moved slowly. 'Agreed,' he said.

Caleb rested a hand on one of his pistols and flicked the safety off. Felan gulped down the last of his tea and set the mug down. He never had liked tea, but there wasn't a lot of choice when he had no money.

'Everyone set?' Accalia asked. Felan tilted his head down in affirmation. 'Good luck,' she said.

Blaez left the table first and did a complete U-turn. She climbed the metal stairs beside the little cafe and disappeared.

Accalia stood with her fists clenched. 'Let's go, boys.'

They walked across the street. The bell above the door tinkled as they entered. Accalia pulled out her rifle, and Caleb held his pistols in the air.

All hell broke loose.

'If you could please all back away into the corner.' Accalia sounded much more confident than she looked. 'Please, we don't mean any harm.'

The crowd of elderly people awkwardly shuffled away into the corner Accalia indicated, grumbling and sniffling, the shop worker standing protectively in front of them, anger clear as day on his face.

Felan wished things could be different. He caught the bags thrown at him and headed for the shelves – the quicker this was over with the better. He emptied shelf after shelf of he didn't know what. Christ, he'd never seen any of this stuff before.

'Please, stay quiet,' Accalia instructed.

Caleb joined her, his pistols in the air by his head. 'We don't want to hurt anyone. We'll be out of your hair before you know it.'

The shopkeeper looked like he wanted to say something but, apparently, thought better of it.

Felan zipped the first two bags tight and tossed them back. Accalia and Caleb slung them onto their backs. Felan shoved everything he could find into the second two bags: packets and bottles, painkillers, bandages, antiseptic cream...

Three phones buzzed in unison. Felan stopped ransacking and pulled his out.

Get out!

He cursed, stumbling to his feet. Sirens wailed far away.

'We need to go!' he yelled, and slung a rucksack over each shoulder.

The three of them bolted down the street. Felan looked behind, up at the balcony. A shadow waved him away. The sirens grew louder. Blaez fired. A multitude of screams followed.

He ran faster when the other two pulled ahead of him. He looked as he ran, at the shops, the street signs, anything to get a grasp of where exactly he was, and where they were going. They turned a corner, chased by sirens, and the sight of the abandoned railway caused dread to settle inside him.

One way in, and one way out.

But he followed them down and along the tracks, because he trusted his friends with his life; it was kind of hard not to. He heard Blaez fire again, and again, yet it did little to ease his fear. She was still trapped on that roof, with no way down, and she'd made it very clear she wouldn't kill. She'd made it very clear what her morals were, and Felan had never been more terrified.

He didn't notice that the others had stopped until he crashed hard into them.

'Jeez, a bit of warning maybe?' Felan groaned. He picked himself up off the tracks. His friends didn't move. 'Why have we stopped?' he asked.

Accalia clamped a hand over his wrist. 'I think there's people down here with us,' she whispered.

Felan listened. Footsteps. 'Is it not people walking above us on the streets?' he asked, although he knew that wasn't the case. He looked up anyway, saw some light filtering through the drains above them, saw liquid dripping down from the surface.

'No. No... Listen.'

The footsteps gradually grew louder, faster, frantic. The three of them all looked around for something to hide behind – for anywhere to hide – but there was nothing except darkness. Accalia pointed her rifle into it. Caleb and Felan pressed their backs to her, held their pistols steady out in front of them, in the direction of the pursuing cops.

'No chances,' Accalia said, firm.

His hands shook around the pistol – he'd avoided having to use it so far. He didn't want to use it. Please, he really didn't want...

Something shifted to his left, a loud grating sound, and his pistol automatically turned to point, like it had a life of its own. The noise echoed like crazy. He stared hard into the darkness. He could see something moving... something shifting...

'What is it?' Caleb whispered.

'I don't know.'

'Remember, no chances,' Accalia hissed.

A figure emerged from the darkness, and Felan's finger moved to the trigger.

'No... no don't shoot!'

He recognised the voice in the shadows, the lean figure, those glowing amber eyes. The shadow stepped closer.

Felan held up his pistol. 'What the hell are you doing here?' he growled.

Accalia and Caleb were silent beside him, half paying attention to them, half focusing on the oncoming footsteps from both sides.

'Saving you, what does it look like?' He looked dishevelled, like he'd just run non-stop for hours.

'We can fend for ourselves.' How the hell had he found them? Where had he even come from? There was no way he wasn't following them.

Harvey ignored him. 'Come on – they'll be here in seconds!'

'Who'll be here?' Felan asked warily.

'Not now!'

They followed Harvey into a drainage pipe, hidden behind what looked to be an old manhole cover. Felan's feet sank into something warm, something wet; he tried his best to keep his mouth shut.

He peered through a crack in the cover. It was still dark, and there was no movement outside just yet, but the footsteps prevailed, growing louder and louder. There was a flash of light, and a group of men appeared right outside the manhole cover.

Felan looked to Harvey.

The man held a gloved finger to his lips.

'They're not here. They must have gone another way...'

He opened his eyes – he knew that voice! Torchlight flooded the old railway track, illuminating the group further. The huge men were armed to the teeth with knives and pistols, all dressed in black. Felan muffled a gasp behind his hand. They were the same men that had tried to take him – the same men that had taken all those children from the town, the town that was so far away from the Fringe.

What were they doing this far across the city?

Before he could ponder further, cops thundered around the corner and attacked. The police dragged away three of the men (Maddison's men, Felan realised), all three unconscious; one remained unmoving on the floor. Forgotten.

Felan managed to speak, but it was difficult with his mouth so dry. 'How did you know they'd be here?'

'Be quiet!'

Felan huffed. Harvey might have helped them, but it didn't change the fact that Harvey was definitely creeping around, especially in those dark clothes of his. It didn't change the fact that he didn't trust him as much any more.

'Actually, how did you know we were even here?' Felan asked again. 'I haven't seen you since last week – where've you been? Why show up now?'

'Shut up!' Harvey hissed for a second time.

'They're not cops, Harvey,' he said.

Harvey said nothing. The man didn't take his gaze off the crack in the manhole cover.

Felan rolled his eyes. 'Whatever. You guys carry on. I'm gonna go and find Blaez – she needs to know there's people lurking around everywhere,' he said.

He reached to open the cover to venture into the abandoned underground, but a hand grabbed his wrist and pulled him back. The wetness crawled up his trouser legs inch by inch.

'No. You're coming with us,' Harvey said, voice hard and serious. 'You're coming back with us. No arguments.'

'I'm not leaving her behind.' Felan tore his wrist free and glared at the man in the dark.

'And what about Nick? What do you think he'll do if you come back late again?'

This wasn't the Harvey he knew.

'Screw Nick!' Felan yelled. 'I'm not letting my friend die when there's something I can do about it!'

He reached for the manhole cover again. Harvey shoved him hard into the wall. In a second of pure terror, it was his father that leered over him, not Harvey. It was his father breathing angrily down his neck, not Harvey. It was his father. It was always his father.

Felan hated how much the physical contact affected him every time.

'I don't want to hear you say that again,' Harvey warned angrily.

'And what do you *want* to hear me say, huh?'

'Enough.'

'No! I couldn't care *less* about what you think, or what Nick thinks. He's not here right now. He doesn't make the decisions if he's not here. Accalia's in charge. The decision is on her.'

'The decision is on me! While you're in my company, I'm in charge!'

'And you're not even supposed to be here! Stay out of it!'

Harvey leaned in closer. Felan backed up. 'I'm an Elder, and you're scared, Felan. I can smell fear on you. You *reek* of it,' he whispered.

'Maybe,' Felan said. 'But maybe I wouldn't be so scared if you told me why Maddison's men were still looking for other children to kidnap. Or maybe even, *how they knew we'd be here!*'

Harvey growled right in his face.

'That's what I thought,' Felan said, shakily. He couldn't find the strength to step away; couldn't find the strength to look away. Who did Harvey think he was?

'Stop it!' Caleb cried.

Felan snapped his head round and flushed. He'd forgotten they had company.

'Harvey's right, Felan,' Accalia said quietly. 'The safest thing for Blaez is if you come back with us.'

'How can you say that? She's your friend!'

'That's exactly my point. If she sees you, she'll be distracted. You'll distract each other. She's safer making her way back alone. She's more inconspicuous that way.'

Accalia was right, of course, but just because she was right, it didn't mean he had to like it. Nothing about this was right: leaving Blaez to fend for herself; Harvey showing up *exactly* where they were; Harvey hiding them from Maddison's men. None of it made sense. He hated not being in control. The last time he'd lost control, someone had lost their life.

'And besides, she can take care of herself. She knows what to do in these kinds of situations.'

Blaez did have a solid head on her shoulders, and she was a quick thinker, but she was up there alone, with her rifle, a sniper that refused to kill.

A shadow on the balcony.

Alone.

Harvey shoved aside the manhole cover. He checked the coast was clear before he waved them forward, and Felan stepped over the forgotten body. Harvey replaced the cover and their hiding place vanished from sight.

'We still have lots of ground to cover,' Accalia said.

Felan tossed the heaviest rucksack at Harvey, who caught it and wordlessly pulled it on. The four of them ran in the darkness, following the track to the entrance on the other side of the Fringe.

He couldn't stop looking back at the body on the floor. Were they really going to leave it there? To rot? For the rats and rodents? He thought back to the small town – they'd probably buried the mother, the mother Maddison's men had killed. The odd gunshot could be heard, rattling the ceiling above them, and he wondered if that was Blaez, making good on her promise, hitting things to make a distraction, to give them time to get away, and hopefully to give herself time to get away too.

Or maybe it was something else entirely.

Chapter 18: Discordance

'Isn't there somewhere you should be?'

Felan looked from Harvey to Nick nervously. If looks could kill. Only Harvey could maintain that eye contact with Nick; Felan thought Harvey was... challenging him? It was what all the bullies had used to do at school when they fought over who would beat him up that day.

Nick smirked when Harvey eventually stalked from the room, but when his gaze settled on Felan, he glared. 'It took you long enough to get back – where's the sniper?'

'There was a change of plan. We went on without her,' Caleb said before Felan could come up with another excuse.

'Come and find me when she returns. We'll talk then.' Nick left the room with an air of irritation. He reeked of alcohol. Accalia, Caleb, and Felan shared a glance.

'What do we do now?' Felan asked.

'Refill the medical supplies, I guess,' Accalia said. She walked over to where Harvey had thrown his bag, picked it up, and tossed it to Caleb like nothing had happened – as if they hadn't left Blaez behind.

'Where do you think she is?' he asked, fiddling with his shirt sleeve.

'On her way back,' Caleb said, his hand on the door. His face held something akin to pity, although there was an indifferent presence to his body, like he didn't care any more, like he'd been through this scenario before.

He had, Felan realised, with Randi.

Images flashed through Felan's mind, clip after clip of Blaez and where she might be, with no end in sight. The small shadow he'd left on the balcony. Completely fine. Injured. Dead.

Felan clenched his fists. No, she wasn't dead. He'd know if she was.

'How can you be sure? We left her there, alone. Anything could have happened to her.' He scuffed his shoes on the floor. Sweat and fear. He reeked of it.

'She knows what she's doing, Felan. You have to trust her,' Accalia said. Her green bandana seemed duller than normal, not fixed into place as it usually was.

Felan followed them out of the room. He felt the absence of the shadow beside him as something physically cold, something like an ice cube in the palm of his hand.

The armoury wasn't deserted. Four Wolves crowded in one corner, staring at their phones. Felan looked closer. They weren't the usual burner phones – they were proper ones, the expensive kind that all the kids in Felan's year at school carried around.

'Nick says it'll pick up soon,' Kit said eagerly. 'He's had this planned for months!'

'It took him long enough,' George said.

'It couldn't have come at a better time either – we really need the money,' Lewis interjected.

Felan didn't think he'd ever spoken to any of them, seeing as he mostly stayed out of their way.

Chad suddenly let out a whoop of excitement. 'I'm off, boys – I've got a hit!' He picked up a brown satchel (since when had they had satchels?) and ran from the room. The others let out similar noises of excitement and replicated Chad's actions.

'What was that about?' Accalia murmured.

'No idea,' Felan said.

She shrugged. 'I'm sure Nick will fill us in later on.'

Felan busied himself with unpacking supplies. 'I wouldn't be so sure of that.'

***

Felan huffed and punched the desk.

'*Occupy your mind with something else,*' Accalia had suggested hours before, but no matter how much he tried, his thoughts always wandered back to Blaez. It overcame his senses and sent his head spinning, his vision swimming, and his balance shaking.

Blaez running through the dark, her clothes torn, blood dripping down her face...
Blaez limping through the forest, cries of pain echoing around her. Eyeliner smudged...
Blaez collapsed on the floor, a pool of blood beneath her. Body twitching. Eyes rolling shut...
Blaez underwater, gulping down mouthful after burning mouthful. Eyes wide. Body convulsing. Hair like a halo, splayed around her face. And then she floated, slept beneath the surface, a ribbon of blood leaking away...

Felan pounded his fist on the keyboard with a growl. He jumped when a voice spoke.

'They were wild animals. Feral. No controlling them.'

His face fell at the sight on the screen. One of the elderly ladies he'd seen in the pharmacy was being interviewed by a reporter. She looked frightened. Tears cascaded down her cheeks, and Felan raised a hand to touch the screen. Her whole body shivered, and an elderly man's arm (maybe her husband's) wrapped around her waist to console her. Felan retracted his hand and slumped in his chair.

'My wife's been waiting weeks for those antibiotics – God knows how long she'll have to wait now that those hooligans have stolen them!' The elderly man's bottom lip wobbled.

Felan swallowed down bile.

'The victims of the robbery are still being treated for shock. Luckily, this time, no one was seriously harmed. The robbers were teenagers, we were told by countless witnesses, and armed. Now, it is very likely that this group of teens are part of the ongoing threat to our city.' Graphs flickered on the screen, a plethora of colour Felan took no notice of. 'It has been reported that gang activity over the last year has risen by twenty per cent – with crime amongst our children up by twenty-five per cent. It's a worryingly high number. In the last six months alone, there have been over fifty reported cases of child abduction, of our children going missing – do not let your child become another statistic.'

Felan stiffened. It was all very well reporting these facts, but what had the city done to prevent it? What was the city going to do to bring those missing kids home? The tiny bit of hope in him drained away, and at the sight of the headline, flashing red on the banner at the bottom of the screen, he glared at the man talking.

Adolescents shoot up elderly.

Felan switched the monitor off and left the room. The old lady... she'd been waiting for antibiotics, antibiotics he'd just stolen. Had he condemned her to more months of suffering?

He stormed all the way to his bedroom, stripped off, and ran a cold shower, as fast and as hard as it would go. Felan stood beneath the water, no longer feeling the cold. His body shivered; his blood scorched his veins. Water plastered his hair flat and it stuck to the back of his neck. Twisting, he glared hard at the tattoo embedded forever in his skin.

Water splashed over that too, and numbed the burn of submission.

Felan stood naked and vulnerable beneath the tiny jet of cold water, the palms of his hands pressed onto the tiles. He dipped his head down. Water trickled into the corners of his mouth, ran in his eyes and bathed him in an icy tomb. He gasped for breath.

He just needed to feel nothing for a while.

***

Blaez returned just after dawn.

He waved from the roof, on the off-chance she would see him, and much to his joy she raised a weary hand in greeting.

He didn't blame her – she must be exhausted. As his friend neared, Felan climbed down the face of the Warehouse, eager to welcome her home.

She stumbled on the gravel in front of him, her head bowed down, and he pulled her into his arms, feeling himself relax for the first time since they'd left her behind.

Felan ruffled her hair gently, her body trembling against his. It still smelled of Blaez. He closed his eyes and rested his head atop hers. She was safe. She was *home*. Her arms wrapped around his waist and she leaned onto him.

'I'm glad you're okay,' he whispered.

Blaez squeezed him once more and pulled away to look at him. 'I need to see Nick.'

'Now might not be a great time for that,' he said. He shivered at the memory of the stench that had followed Nick out of the room the day before. He knew Nick wanted to see them all the second Blaez got home, but they'd wait until he wasn't quite so drunk.

Felan didn't like drunkards.

She nodded. Doubt flickered on her face when she looked to the Warehouse; its shadow held them captive.

'Ralph then. Can we talk to Ralph?' she asked.

'Yeah, but not right now.'

'Why not?'

'Because you're going to go and get cleaned up first. Then we'll go and see him.' He gave her shoulder a playful swat.

Her eyes closed, and he reached to grab her. She yawned again. 'Thanks.'

'You good?'

'Amazing.' Blaez squared her shoulders and walked to the door. She turned back before she went inside. 'Thank you,' she said. 'For waiting.'

He blinked, taken aback by the display of vulnerability. 'You're welcome.'

***

Blaez knocked on the door, swift and sharp, and she pushed it open after confirmation from the other side.

Felan had never been inside Ralph's office before, so he'd always imagined it to be like Nick's. Instead, the curtains were open, and daylight lit up the room. The window was open too, and the sounds of the leaves rustling in the trees eased Felan's nerves somewhat.

He hadn't been sure what to expect.

Definitely not this.

Ralph sat, slouched, behind his desk, and looked up with an expectant expression on his face.

'Are you free for a chat?' Blaez asked.

Ralph puffed out a mouthful of smoke. Felan saw the cigarette held between two fingers. 'I thought Nick wanted to see you.' His green eyes were bright and piercing, and he seemed very much at ease.

'We're on our way there now,' Blaez said. Felan gave her a look. He thought they'd agreed to wait?

'Very well,' he said, taking a drag of the cigarette. 'What is it?'

'I found something on my way back,' Blaez said.

Ralph leaned back in his chair, cigarette smouldering. 'Well?' he asked, eyebrows raised.

Blaez reached into her pocket and removed a pistol, a midnight-black pistol, and set it on the desk. A dark symbol stared back at them, barely noticeable, engraved right where the palm of someone's hand would lie.

Ralph tensed in his seat. 'Where did you find this?' He traced the symbol again and again, as if trying to make it disappear. But it was like a tattoo. Permanent. No disappearing.

'On my way back here – I was still in the city. I saw the pistol and thought nothing of it, thinking we could make use of it here, but then I saw the symbol. I thought my eyes were playing tricks on me.'

Felan was definitely missing something.

'What does that symbol mean?' he asked, and moved to stand beside Blaez.

Ralph stared out of the window, chewing the end of his cigarette absent-mindedly.

'The Protrudes,' she stated.

He didn't know what on Earth that meant, but from the reaction of the Elder before him, he concluded it wasn't something to be taken lightly.

'It means the Protrudes are on the move again.'

Chapter 19: Atramentous

'What's a Protrude?'

'They're a rival gang,' Blaez explained. 'Long history; nothing good.'

Well that was just brilliant. 'So what do we do about it?'

'For now, nothing.' The grey streaks in Ralph's hair had never looked darker.

Felan found a spot on Ralph's desk and willed himself to stay calm. 'I thought we kept each other safe,' he said. The words sounded childish, even to him. Hadn't his fellow gang members left Randi to die? Hadn't they abandoned Randi when he needed them most?

'We keep each other alive…'

Felan scoffed.

'*When the situation permits it!*'

'Right. I forgot you get to choose.'

Cigarette ash fell onto the man's fingers.

Blaez shifted nervously on her feet. 'Are there no precautions for us to take?'

Ralph barely glanced up. 'We act like we don't know anything. It was only a matter of time before something like this happened. We're lucky to have lasted as long as we have.'

Felan couldn't believe how calm the man was over the whole situation. 'So what do we do in the meantime? How long is it going to take until they stop?'

Ralph let out a guffaw. 'There's no stopping this, Felan. That would be like trying to stop time. Surely you understand the concept?'

Felan held back a snarl. Of course he understood the concept of time – hadn't he wished his childhood to speed up? Hadn't he prayed every goddamn night that he would get to leave his father? Hadn't he prayed for his bruises to fade? And if they didn't, hadn't he prayed for someone to notice what was going on?

'I'm not a child.'

Ralph laughed.

Felan ignored the jibe. 'We have Maddison's men kidnapping children, we have a rival gang after us...' He trailed off at the look that flitted across Ralph's face. 'You're joking – you're joking!' he exclaimed.

Ralph took one final drag. 'And he finally figures it out.' He chucked the cigarette out of the open window.

This time, Felan turned his unbridled anger on Blaez. 'You knew? You knew about this and didn't tell me?'

Hurt flickered across her face. 'Actually, I didn't.' She gave him a cold stare. 'I knew about the Protrudes, and I knew about Maddison, but I had no idea. No idea at all.'

He was too angry to feel guilty. He turned back to Ralph. 'What else have you kept from us?'

'Nothing of your concern.'

'But it is! Do you understand that, or has the smoking destroyed a few brain cells too?

Ralph's eyes flashed. '*Hold. Your. Tongue!*'

'It's all very well sending us back out there, pretending to know nothing, but Maddison's men, the... Protrudes, whatever they're called, are going to come right back for us! We're the target! And you're sending us right back out there where she can easily take us!'

Ralph pushed his chair back. 'Welcome to gang warfare, Felan,' he said. The Elder opened his desk drawer. He pulled out another cigarette and lit it. 'Now go and see Nick – I daresay he's been anticipating your arrival for some time now.'

'We haven't finished...'

'GET OUT!' Ralph sprung up from his chair and knocked a stack of papers to the floor.

Blaez grabbed Felan's hand and they bolted.

***

He curled his hand around his new phone, rereading the text again to make sure he was headed in the right direction.

Despite being newer than a burner phone, it still resembled a brick in his hand, black, black, all black – it had a tiny blue screen that lit his face a little – though it could be used more than once. Felan would've preferred a burner phone, now that he knew what the new ones were for.

He pulled his jacket tighter around his body, willing it to ward off the cold – why was it always so cold at night? Why couldn't it be warm, just once?

If he could, Felan would have dumped the satchel in the closest dustbin and run. He wanted nothing to do with it – he knew what it did to people. The shame of what he was about to do, the guilt, shortened his stride; did he want to do this?

A car honked its horn somewhere in the distance. No. No, he didn't. The thought of being found by Maddison's men stayed at the forefront of his mind. If it came to it, could he... could he do *it*? Could he pull the trigger?

He rounded the corner; a stocky figure leaned against a wall, his face covered by a hat and scarf. Felan quickly walked over, shoving his phone in the satchel that hung from his shoulder. His heart hammered in his chest, so fast he thought it might jump out of his throat and take off down the street. He thought of the mess it would make if it did.

'You're late, boy,' a gruff voice said. 'Have you got it?'

Felan reached into his satchel and pulled out a small ziplock bag.

'Perfect.' The man held out a roll of cash.

They exchanged hands. A single tear rolled down Felan's cheek, unnoticed. The man walked away. Felan covered his mouth with his hand to silence his breath; it was okay. He didn't know the man, and the man didn't know him – just quick and simple and okay. He dried his tears. Nothing to worry about. Just get to the drop-off, take the money, leave. It was as simple as that.

Felan jumped when the phone dinged. He pulled it out and read the message – another drop-off a few blocks away. With a sniffle, he tucked the roll of cash away into the satchel and set off.

He had a long night ahead of him.

Chapter 20: Traitor

A shout roused Felan from his restless slumber – he'd just got back from drop-offs a few hours before, and it had taken most of that time to fall asleep. He left his room just as Blaez left hers.

'Any idea what's going on?' he asked.

'Nope.'

They quietened as they merged with the other Wolves, all looking equally confused, if not annoyed, that they'd been woken in the early hours of the morning. Slowly, dread filed into the room, pooling in Felan's stomach, one piece at a time. Blaez's hand curled around his. He slipped his fingers between hers and didn't let go. Caleb caught his gaze over the sea of people, looking as baffled as Felan.

Once everyone was in, the door crashed open again. Harvey tumbled through, covered in blood and dirt, a rope tied around his wrists.

Stunned silence followed. Seeing the state the man was in, Felan went to meet him, all quarrels aside, to help him, to free him, to do *something*. But Blaez held him back and shook her head.

Nick stormed in, his expression on fire. He kicked Harvey in the side of the knee, and the man hit the floor with a groan. Everyone mumbled amongst themselves, their voices growing louder, confused. Nick stamped and kicked, and once satisfied, he let Harvey be. Harvey coughed and wheezed, his blood smearing across the floor.

What had Harvey done to make Nick hate him so much?

Felan glanced around the room. Was no one going to help?

The dread settled completely at the accusing stares, the evil looks, the glares that were aimed at the man on the floor.

Harvey tried to rise, grunting with the effort, his face screwed up in pain. Felan caught his gaze for a moment, just a moment, before Nick stepped between them. Felan shrank down under his calculating glare, squeezing Blaez's hand like his life depended on it.

Confusion crashed down on the room.

'The Protrudes are back,' Nick said.

Blaez's hand in his steadied him. Harvey didn't have his glove on...

'They're spreading their wings on our territory. On Guadalupe.'

More angry shouts. Why didn't Harvey have his glove on...?

'Maddison wants control of the city.'

So it was true. Angry shouts rose in volume, and Felan resisted the desperate urge to cover his ears. Nick let the noise grow and grow, held up a calloused hand, and the noise shattered to the floor like broken glass.

'For a while now, she's seemed to have a new goal in mind.'

Felan didn't take his eyes off Harvey. In pain, hurt, open wound, no black glove...

'I know now what she wants,' Nick growled. Spit flew from his mouth as quick as the anger sparked in his body, and one look to Harvey and it burned into an inferno. 'She has contacts in the forces. She wants to take us out, one by one.'

A sudden, familiar stench hit Felan like a bullet to the chest, and he fought to stay upright. It was a stench that lingered in the hallways of his home; a stench that made his father's breath reek of anger and madness.

Alcohol.

Part of him hoped Nick had made a mistake, that the alcohol had influenced his judgement too much. The smell hacked into Felan's bloodstream, and he was taken away by an intense riptide that left him struggling to keep his head above the water.

'Our friend here has been helping her,' Nick finished, with an angry gesture to the man on the floor.

Felan resurfaced and began to tread water, desperate to understand. He needed to. Why would Harvey do something like that? It didn't make sense – Harvey wouldn't do that. He cared about them.

One look at Harvey, the remorse and the pain, and Felan knew. It all made sense. It was Harvey. Harvey was the reason the Protrudes knew exactly where to find them. Harvey was the reason the cops had got a head start on them. It was all Harvey. He'd betrayed them all; he betrayed Felan, and that betrayal hurt more than anything else.

He'd known the man had changed, and now he knew why – Harvey hadn't thought twice about giving them away. He'd thought Harvey wanted to protect them.

It seemed that all Harvey had ever wanted was to protect himself.

Felan dipped his head down. He couldn't look the man who'd betrayed them in the eye. Instead, he focused solely on Nick. Felan might dislike the man, but at least he wasn't a traitor.

Nick's hand disappeared behind his back and returned with a knife; it shimmered something beautiful. Nick grabbed Harvey's hair and pulled him to his knees – he pressed the knife to his throat.

Blaez held onto Felan's arm, her body shaking. Felan couldn't look away. He'd never seen Harvey so tired, so broken, so helpless than in that moment. Dead. The thought clamped a vice around his heart.

'Why?' Nick snarled. He shook Harvey's shoulders and the knife broke skin; a tiny indent on the side of his neck. The blood splatter down his face indicated a broken nose.

Felan stopped breathing.

No. No, he wouldn't. Nick wouldn't do it. He'd give him another chance. Yeah. He'd give him another chance to prove himself. Nick did that for Felan when he failed, so he had to do it for Harvey as well.

Harvey might have betrayed them, but it was Harvey who'd helped them escape capture. Why had he helped them escape when he was the one to give them away in the first place? Was it guilt at betraying them? What had motivated the man to save them?

Harvey opened his mouth to speak, and Nick slit his throat. Blood spilled through the gash and swallowed his voice. Harvey fell to the floor, choking and twitching and writhing like an escaped demon. No one moved. Nick watched on with a knife, a bloody knife, in his hand.

'Traitor!' Nick shouted. The others joined the chorus.

Tears welled up. Despair and horror showed like fireworks on Caleb's and Randi's faces, huddled together in shock. Felan saw only anger in everyone else.

The first tear fell, and his lungs contracted painfully. A stone-like weight settled in his chest; he swallowed the sick feeling back down, again, and again. His body seized up, but somehow, he moved, working his way through the Wolves that gathered closer, towards the body on the floor. He smelled the blood. He walked over it. Everything blurred. He stumbled closer. There, in the centre of Harvey's palm, stood the symbol, stark against his pale skin: an arrowhead.

Felan's memory failed him. He remembered screaming. He remembered being dragged from the room. He remembered arms that pinned his flailing limbs.

He stared into Harvey's lifeless eyes, and something deep inside him shattered.

Chapter 21: Succour

Time was a brutal being. It took things, and it gave things away just as fast. It made things fade.

Time was one of Felan's greatest foes.

He barely slept, he didn't eat, and his drop-offs remained unanswered, while he instead opted to stay on the Warehouse roof all day. He only climbed down when the darkness came. Visions of blood and emptiness haunted him as if on a constant loop with no pause button, with no option to eject the disk.

A few times he'd looked at himself in the mirror.

He didn't recognise the boy that stared back, the underneath of his eyes black and red; it wouldn't have surprised him if he'd been crying blood and tar the whole time.

Felan didn't like looking at his own eyes any more. Blaez's he could handle, as long as he didn't think about how they'd look if she died, but his own were too far gone down that particular path, and no matter how hard he blinked them away, the dead eyes he'd witnessed kept coming back to haunt him: Harvey's, the raging hurricane in those of the homeless man, the clerk – his eyes had been closed, but Felan had seen them open moments before.

Felan sat up in his bed, bones cracking, head foggy, sight hazy, wondering how, in a whole Warehouse full of people, he'd managed to wind up alone.

He clambered to his feet, wrenched the tiny window open, squeezed himself out, and climbed all the way to the top. He sat himself against the railing, wrapping his arms around the metal bars. The forest ahead was starting to wake.

Trees spiralled and twisted upwards at odd angles. A single vine of ivy wound its way up the bark of an older tree, seemed to strangle the hoary oak, just as the sun reached its peak. He watched in vague fascination. A broken honey texture flickered on the ground, and the scent of the early morning hit him.

A flock of birds flew over his head, twittering and singing. It was as if they threw their souls into every note they belted out, put their everything into the music, lest it be their last song. A young doe approached the clearing cautiously, scanned the area. He stared at her, observed her movements, and marvelled in her bravery. He wished he was brave. He shifted his foot. She dashed back into the forest, nothing more than a shadow slipping between layers of darkness.

He stayed like that all day. The cold air burrowed deep into his skin and settled into his bones. Where the sun slowly fell from the sky, the moon swooped back up and settled into its grave. Constant clouds shattered the shadows and Felan rubbed his tattoo, stuck in an endless cycle of submission.

'I thought I might find you up here.'

The forest looked different at night. A fine layer of fog dusted the tops of the trees like snow.

'Accalia's been promoted,' Blaez said.

Felan thought of Harvey and swallowed. He thought of Harvey, and how he'd never find out why he did what he did. He'd never find out the truth.

'Nick's making plans to deal with the Protrudes – all the Elders are.'

'I assume they're not plans for a diplomatic conversation, are they?' Felan coughed, his voice hoarse from lack of use. He gripped the bars tighter. 'Why are you here, Blaez?'

She sat down next to him. 'Because I'm worried about you. It's like you've been a ghost since…'

Felan clenched his eyes shut. 'That's not gonna make me come inside.'

'Note taken, but I just wanted you to know. Harvey, he… he meant a lot to all of us too,' she said. 'We're all feeling it.'

He lay on his back and stared up at the inky blackness above him. Two days prior, Convel and Tate had returned and announced that they'd dumped Harvey's body somewhere it would never be found. Felan thought it must have been in the forest, because there was nowhere else to dump it within walking distance. He thought about the day he might accidentally stumble upon it, rotting and swarming with flies.

The thought made his stomach churn uncomfortably. Goosebumps rose along his arms.

'How could he do that to us?' Felan asked.

Blaez's skin brushed against his. 'I've asked myself the same thing, but I can never come up with an answer.'

'It was him – he was the reason our job went so wrong so fast. The Protrudes have contacts in the cops, and Harvey has contacts with us; it's no wonder they knew where we'd be.'

'I know,' she said softly. 'You said he saved you from being caught?'

Felan nodded. 'Not before he set us up, and because of Nick, I'll never understand why.'

Blaez curled up like a cat into his side. 'Emotions suck,' she said.

'Everyone feels things differently.'

'The principles are the same though, right?'

'The principles don't matter,' he mumbled. He waved his hand in the air. 'You know, as a child, I used to watch the stars every night. I used to sit on my windowsill and stare at them for hours. I didn't understand how they stayed so bright, especially when the world was so dark. I didn't get how they stayed constant. I never understood how the stars were always there, when people came and went all around me. It didn't make any sense to me,' he said. 'I learned later stars do die. In fact, they explode. Something called nuclear fusion.'

Blaez rested her head on his chest.

'Stars burn to emit light, and when they run out of one substance, they just burn the next. It carries on, and on, until they run out of things to burn. Only then will they collapse in on themselves. They collapse into... well, I like to think they collapse into shells of their former selves when they die.'

She propped herself upon one elbow. 'And then what?'

He shrugged. 'Nothing. They live like that forever. But it makes me think.' He paused. 'People die when they run out of fuel. They have no reserves. When their time's up, time's up. It's undetermined, yet it's like that for a star too – they just get to live for so much longer than we do.'

'Do you think that, when we die, we'll become stars? I like the idea of watching over the world at night. I like the idea of guiding someone home.'

Felan wrapped one arm around her. He'd missed her company, far more than he'd thought possible. 'We've done things, Blaez. I've done things, but I like to think someone knows who we really are, after everything that's happened. I like to think someone can see through this, and see that we're not bad people.' He thought for a moment. 'Do you regret it?'

'Regret what?'

'Choosing this life?'

'It wasn't a choice, Felan,' she said. 'I had no other life to choose. And I know it was the same for you.'

He yawned, and for the first time in a week, he felt he could sleep peacefully. But – there was one last thing. He was curious, and in this strangely intimate moment, he felt bold enough, and felt the nerve to ask his friend, 'How did you get here?'

She froze, and he regretted saying anything at all. She sat up and crossed her legs, some distance between them – distance he'd created. Felan hoped beyond hell he hadn't messed up.

'It's a long story,' she said finally.

Felan relaxed, crossing his own legs. 'I mean, I have time,' he offered. He heard her mind turning. Heck, he even *felt* her mind turning.

'Parents.'

One word. Just one word, and a wave of horror floored him. The terror he'd felt as a child flared in his veins and he trembled. 'Blaez…' He trailed off. His voice cracked.

'You don't have to stay anything, Felan. I'm over it,' she muttered.

He made to take her hand, but thought better of it when he saw how white her knuckles were. 'I know from experience, Blaez,' he said carefully. 'These kinds of things – they don't go away.'

She looked like she'd been burned. 'You think I don't know that?' Angry tears fell, and she swatted them away. 'Every time I'm alone – how can I not remember? How can I not remember the years they had me locked up?'

He ran a hand through his hair. Felan wanted so badly to wipe away her tears, and hold her, but he stayed away. He knew she'd lash out. Then he saw something he thought he'd never see; Blaez crying. Not silent tears. Not the few and far between sniffles. Sobs. Sobs that shook the entirety of her body.

'God, Blaez, I'm sorry,' he said. 'I'm so sorry.' He stumbled over his apologies, rambled and backtracked, cursed, and apologised again. He was thankful for the cover of darkness; the darkness, somehow, made everything safe. It made everything okay, even when it wasn't.

'No!' she gasped out. 'You did nothing wrong. It's…'

'Don't you dare say it's all you.'

'It is…'

'It's other people,' Felan said. 'This wasn't you.'

Blaez shuddered. 'What about you, Felan?' she asked with a sniffle. 'I only guessed at first, but… what happened to you?' She wiped her nose on her sleeve.

Felan clenched his jaw. He'd expected it from the second he opened his mouth, but somehow, he still wasn't prepared. He didn't want to answer, because really, he didn't know what had happened to him. What happened was vivid in random snippets, but blurry in others, and it became hard to distinguish fantasy from reality.

'He put me in the hospital,' Felan said.

Empty bottles smashed onto the wall above his head.

A fist to his temple. A fist to his nose. Knees on the floor. A foot to the side of the head, his ribs, his stomach. Glass everywhere.

He stumbled through the sliding doors of the emergency room and promptly collapsed in a shivering heap, covered in blood.

He woke up in a hospital bed, and the covers swamped his body. Fragile limbs. Bandages on his arms, something on his cheek. Delirious. He had to get out.

He left in the night, although not much worry came from it. After all, it was just another missing child. What was another one?

A gentle hand on his shoulder made him blink. He pushed away the memories and looked right at Blaez. He tried to say something, *anything*. He choked. He'd never given it much thought. To be honest, he'd never had a chance to think about it – staying alive unsurprisingly took up a lot of a person's headspace. No. He'd just left it where it was, slowly rotting, until the smell of decay hit him hard. He choked again, and nothing could stop the tears flooding his cheeks.

'I've got you,' Blaez said, wrapping her arms around him.

'Why did this happen to us?'

'I don't know,' she said. 'I really don't know.'

Chapter 22: Shock Wave

Felan made his way down to the training rooms. If he was going to mope about, he might as well let off some steam while he did it. Accalia had suggested it to him in passing the other night, and he thought he'd take her advice.

Caleb ran up to him the moment he walked through the door. 'Have you seen Randi at all today?'

'No, why? What's happened?'

'No one's seen him since last night. He never showed for training this morning.'

Felan clapped his shoulders in what he hoped was a supportive manner. 'If I see him, I'll let him know you're looking for him.'

Days passed. There was still no sign of Randi, and Caleb was beside himself with worry. Felan had caught him out searching for Randi more than once over the last few days. Not that Felan would ever tell on him.

Felan itched all over. There were only so many times he could punch the same punchbag before he split his knuckles, and even then he kept punching. Blaez, upon seeing the blood smeared over the bag, dragged him away to wrap his hands.

His sleep never improved. The guilt, the worry, the horror – it all festered in the dark. The dark used to be safe. The dark made him invisible. The dark used to protect him.

What a fool he was to think things would ever get better.

He set off on drop-offs early, deciding on taking the woodland route to the city for a change. It was a way he didn't take often enough, considering his love of nature. He spied deer tracks in the dirt, wishing he could follow them like he used to with his mother. They never found anything at the end because the tracks kept going, but once Felan swore he saw a white deer in the distance.

He jogged for a while, liking the feel of air heavy in his lungs, surprised that the leaves on the trees were a mottled brown in places. To Felan, time didn't work the usual way any more. One day it was blistering heat and the next freezing icicles.

Today, the heat scorched everything, he thought, as he wiped the sweat from his forehead, after two hours of traipsing the city streets. He still had five drop-offs to get to – not a bad day's work really. He'd made nearly six hundred in the Flax! He didn't dare touch the money to buy himself some water – Nick would find out, and he'd never get a cut again. No. He didn't want to risk that. Better to suffer now and get rewarded later on.

The Flax was also known as the inner ring of Guadalupe and was where the richer people of the city lived. Prices were high and so were sales. People strolled along, stopped for conversation, smiled at each other, helped each other. Here, there was a calm atmosphere, and that wasn't something Felan encountered often in the city.

At the sound of coins hitting the floor, he turned, trained his eyes on the small pile that rolled to a stop. He looked around. He couldn't even tell who'd dropped them in the first place. He bit his lip. No one seemed to care. He spun the other way. Nothing.

He couldn't imagine having so much money he wouldn't notice if he dropped some.

His stomach rumbled and he checked his phone – he had thirty minutes until the next drop-off. The nearest fast-food place was across the street, he saw, as he scooped the coins into his hands, already walking. He counted them slowly as he stood in line, not bothered about having to wait; he was more bothered about the satchel full of money, and drugs, and weapons.

'The cheapest burger you have, and a bottle of water,' he said when he reached the counter. His mouth watered at the smell. The girl behind the counter nodded and reached behind her for the food, pre-cooked, and slid a bottle of water over to him. He tipped the coins into her open palm, blinking hurriedly when he realised he'd been staring at her bright green nails.

The girl laughed. 'Thank you,' she said.

'Yeah, thanks.'

Felan sat by the window and slung the satchel at his feet, unwrapping the food. He couldn't remember the last time he'd eaten warm food. He couldn't even remember the last time he'd eaten. The second his teeth sunk into the bun he was in heaven. He'd forgotten what a meal like this tasted like, and he could feel it gliding down his throat, piling up inside him. It was better than any blanket.

Here, he could pretend to be normal. He was just another normal teenager eating fast food in a restaurant with air conditioning to escape the heat. He had no problems in life. He had a real family, and somewhere safe to live.

He took another huge bite, and caught the eye of a small girl with her mother. She watched him from across the room, so he smiled. Her face lit up in wonder, and she waved back, her small hand flapping about excitedly. The mother reached over to still her daughter's hand, looking around to see what had caught her attention. She smiled at Felan, and he felt the sudden urge to run. He put the bottle in his satchel and tried to leave as calmly as possible. He pushed open the doors.

Shouts and sirens pierced his ears. Immediately, he searched for cover – how had they found him so quick? He'd done nothing wrong! He held the satchel close to his front; he couldn't be found with all of this on him. That would be the end of everything.

The cars zoomed right past him and around the corner. Curiosity got the better of him. He walked in the direction of the commotion, through crowds of people running into him. A smashed window brought him to a halt. The grocery store across the street teemed with movement, two cop cars parked on either side, five cops total. He frowned. No Wolves were due out that day. Who...

Six people dressed in black leaped out of the window and sprinted to the left, guns in hand. The cops took cover and fired, but the men were already away. Three cops jumped into a car and set off in pursuit. They turned the corner in a matter of seconds.

Maddison. The Protrudes. *They were here.* Was it a coincidence that they'd happened to rob somewhere nearby? Every time he saw them, each event occurred nearer and nearer to the centre of Guadalupe. He slid his hand into the satchel and brushed his finger over his knife. He'd be fine.

He hoped.

Something in the shop moved. A head reared up from behind the counter, visible through the window, and the red hair sent Felan reeling backwards. Another Protrude leaped out of the window and ran right, unarmed from what Felan could see. The last two cops said something into walkie-talkies, climbed into the car, and zoomed off. Felan closed his eyes, a mental map of the city forming behind them, and he took off running.

He zigzagged through people, down side streets, down alleyways. He saw glimpses of red hair through the gaps between buildings – the cop car was never far behind. Dammit. He needed to get there before it was too late; screw the drop-offs. He wanted answers.

Skidding down another alley, he grabbed his pistol and flicked off the safety. Sirens echoed all around him. Someone with red hair sprinted past the mouth of the alley. Felan rolled to a stop and fired one well-aimed bullet. Brakes squealed, and the car careered out of control.

Satisfied, Felan took off again, crossed the street, mindful of the few cars and stumbling over the kerb, and sprinted even faster. He recognised the street the redhead ran towards; he knew what was at the end of it.

Somehow, the guy hadn't even noticed he was being followed. Felan tackled him down an alley. A fist split his lip. 'Stay quiet,' Felan growled, holding a hand to his mouth. He picked himself up off the floor and checked that nothing had spilled from his satchel. Blood trickled down his chin.

'What the...?'

'I said, be quiet,' Felan said. He shoved the man to get him to move. 'Now go. Down the alley, and take a right.'

The man didn't move. It didn't look like he would, but sirens were always a good incentive.

'Through there,' Felan said, before the man even asked.

He nodded and shoved the peeling door open. Felan slammed it closed behind him. Inside, an empty room greeted them. Wooden floorboards squeaked beneath his feet, and Felan managed to avoid the holes in the ground. He saw the shards of glass next. Following the trail, he found that someone had boarded up the broken windows with loose bits of flooring. Hence the holes. The stairs had taken a beating and were blatantly unsafe to climb; Felan hadn't dared the first time he was here, and he wasn't about to try gymnastics any time soon.

Far above, daylight beamed down through sections of ceiling that had collapsed into piles of debris. The whole place smelled of damp.

Felan crossed the room and slid down the wall opposite. He kept his eyes on the redhead the entire time, though the man hadn't approached. Yet. His lip throbbed, and in between taking sips of water, Felan held the bottle to it, grateful for the coldness.

'What the hell was that, kid?'

And oh God, even just the sound of his voice made Felan shake.

Chapter 23: Anamnesis

The young boy opened his eyes to see a crack of bright light through his mismatched curtains. It was supposed to be overcast today, so they were going to spend the day inside watching toons.

But Felan wanted to go outside. He was all ready to jump on his mother to wake her, but he guessed it was still too early in the morning. He yawned, threw his covers off, and padded over to the curtains to open them. He jumped up onto the windowsill and sat down with his back against the wall to watch the sunrise.

He was a curious child and so asked a lot of questions. He had always been fascinated by science and nature, always wanting to know how things worked, and, despite being on the receiving end of the bullies, he'd been told he was advanced for his age.

He heard a soft knock on his door. He smiled when he saw his mother's face peeking from behind the door frame. In the light, his mother's hair shone golden.

'Hey, little one,' she whispered as she stepped further into the room, arms opening wide for Felan. He leaped from his perch and flung himself at his mother.

'Mummy!' he shouted. He wrapped his arms around her neck, smiling as she laughed and pulled him close, kissing him on the forehead.

'Happy birthday, Felan,' she said, setting him on his feet. 'Are you going to watch cartoons with me all day?'

'Mummy! Have you seen outside? It's all pretty colours!' He pouted. 'I wanna go outside! We can watch toons later?' he pleaded.

She stroked his cheek gently. Felan liked it when she did that. 'Little one... you know we don't have much money.'

'I know, but I don't wanna stay inside all day! Please Mummy... it'll be fun! We'll get ice cream at the park and see the ducks!' He bounced on the spot in poorly contained excitement.

'Okay, Felan, let's get changed first, yeah? Then we'll head out.'

'Yes! I'll wait here, Mummy!' He shoved his feet into his favourite (and only) pair of black shoes, excited for the day that lay ahead.

***

The water rippled in the slight breeze. The layers of blue got deeper and darker, much to Felan's fascination. Mother and son sat hand in hand as they ate their ice cream on the old bench in Oakley Park. The sun above them had singed the grass at their feet, some invisible force wearing away the patches since the last time Felan had been there.

His mother chuckled as he managed to get ice cream on the end of his nose, but loudly protested as he smeared melted ice cream over her face. She tickled him the second he'd finished eating, his laughter coming out in raspy gasps and squeals.

Usually when it was sunny, everyone was out in the field kicking a ball around or playing Frisbee. Felan preferred to sit by the pond and watch the ducks, asking his mother an endless stream of nonsense questions.

As they left Oakley Park, his mother held his hand and ruffled his hair.

'Did you have fun today?'

'It was awesome, Mummy!' He bounced in his steps, but a frown appeared on his face. 'I just wish Daddy wasn't working. He would've had fun with us.'

'He's trying to get more money, so he can buy you that toy you've wanted for ages.'

Felan nodded. 'It's been the best day today, Mummy... I love you,' he said sincerely. He didn't think she heard it enough any more. She always looked sad when she thought he wasn't looking.

'I love you too, little... Felan!'

His mother threw him onto a patch of grass with no warning. Felan scraped his elbows as he tried to catch himself. He sat up, *confused. Was this a new game? If it was, he didn't like it very much. He looked over to where he'd last seen his mother. All he saw was a faint trail of exhaust fumes. He stood up on weak legs, rubbing his elbows, confused by the screams.*

His mother had been right beside him.

Then he saw the body in the road. It had long, blonde hair, and Felan would know that hair anywhere.

'Mummy?'

She didn't get up.

'Mummy?' He walked over. 'Mummy, wake up.'

A pair of arms caught him around his waist and pulled him back.

'Stay here, kid. You don't want to see that,' a deep voice said.

'Why won't she wake up?' he asked the man.

The man wore shorts, and a beige shirt, and had cropped, red hair. He looked kind, just like his mother. 'She's not going to wake up,' he said. 'She's going to sleep for a long time.'

'No. She said we'd watch toons later.' He thrashed in the man's grip. 'Wake up, Mummy!'

He sank to his knees, though the man's strong grip kept him in place. He heard sirens in the distance, and he turned his head to watch the arrival of the flashing blue lights, and people dressed in yellow. As they reached his mother, the strong arms spun Felan around so he could no longer see.

'Mummy... No... Mummy!' he cried, as he tried to fight the arms. A soft hand touched his tear-stained cheek, and he stopped resisting enough to stare up at the man in front of him.

'My name's Tristan. What's yours?' he asked.

'F-Felan. And I'm not supposed to talk to strangers.'

'That's very smart, Felan. Hey, do you want to ride in the back of the car?'

When Felan nodded, Tristan waved at the people dressed in yellow and they exchanged some words. The boy stood up, wiped his face, and grasped Tristan's hand tightly. The man offered him a smile, but it was like his mother's – it didn't reach his eyes. They walked over to one of the cars and climbed into the back seat.

Within seconds, Felan drowsed, his face buried in Tristan's chest. His mother let him fall asleep on her all the time.

'I'm so sorry, Felan,' he whispered.

Felan whimpered and held on tight. Tristan was nice, like his mother.

The car sped off, and Felan dreamed of Oakley Park.

Chapter 24: Aftershock

The memory faded away like smoke.

'You helped me once. It's only fair I returned the favour,' Felan said.

'I've never seen you before, kid – are you okay?'

That's right, Felan thought bitterly. The adults always forgot. He looked the man right in the eye. 'There was a young boy that day, about to run over to his dead mother – but you steered him away. You didn't let him see.' He took another gulp of water.

The man stepped closer.

'You rode with him in the car. You sat with him for hours in the waiting room. You comforted him when he cried. You stayed with him until he fell asleep.' Felan chucked his water bottle down. 'Then you left him alone.' He rose to his feet. 'And for that he'll never forgive you.' He pinned the man against the wall with a knife to the throat. He growled.

The man's eyes flashed in recognition. 'Felan?'

'You left while I was asleep, Tristan. I woke up and no one was there. Do you know what that's like?' he shouted into the man's face. His hands trembled. He gripped the knife tighter.

'Put the knife down,' Tristan said. 'Put it down, and we can talk.'

Felan threw the knife and it stuck to the door. 'Go on – say something!' he roared. 'You owe me that much at least!'

Tristan rubbed his throat. 'I was running late – I couldn't stay long.'

Excuses. They always made excuses. It's why Felan had never trusted an adult again, after his mother. Harvey had come close, and then he betrayed them all. If there was one thing Felan had learned, it was that adults always made excuses, and children were always to blame.

'That's not enough,' Felan said, glaring.

'What was I supposed to do?' Tristan said, exasperated. 'Your father was on his way. You were in safe hands.' He moved to pat Felan's shoulder.

Felan backed away. 'Don't come any closer.'

'Okay, fine, but you were in safe hands...'

'Safe hands! Are you insane?' he yelled.

'What do you mean?'

'How was I, a *child*, in safe hands with that *monster*?'

Tristan grabbed Felan's wrist against his will. 'What did he do?'

Felan tried to shake his hand off but nothing would relent the grip on his wrist. His chest tightened. The tattoo burned and simmered on his skin.

Weak.

His father's hand on his wrist was like pressing a smouldering cattle prod to his skin. It burned, and it burned, and it always left marks.

'Felan – what did he do?'

His head smashed so hard into the table, he saw nothing but white for minutes.

He couldn't defend himself.

He let his dad punish him.

He let his dad hit him.

He let his dad kick him.

The whole time he stayed silent.

A crack in his arm and he screamed.

Another kick for making noise.

A self-inflicted bite on his hand to stop the screams and the cries. Pain in his hand, as he broke the skin.

Blood ran down his knuckles, and his teeth sunk ever deeper.

'Felan – Felan! It's alright!' a voice shouted, above the thick black smoke.

Tristan could have prevented everything if he'd just stayed a few hours longer. Tristan could have been his hero.

'What did you mean before?' Felan asked quietly, realising that in his anger he'd forgotten to ask.

'Before what?'

'When you said you were late and couldn't stay – what did you mean?'

He knew, but he wanted the man to admit it. He wanted the man to admit to what he'd done, how he'd left an innocent child alone while he returned to Maddison and robbed somewhere. Maybe he even killed someone.

Tristan hung his head. 'I can't say.'

Felan crossed his arms. 'It wouldn't have anything to do with the Protrudes now, would it?'

Tristan stared in shock. 'How do you...?'

'I'm not an idiot.'

Reluctantly, Tristan held his left hand in the strip of light; he uncurled it to reveal a black arrowhead tattoo. Despite having known it was there, Felan still froze. It still sent fear right to his bones. Tristan was one of the men that...

'It's not what it looks like,' Tristan began. 'Please understand that...'

'You're working for a psychopath that kidnaps children? Yeah, I understand,' he spat.

'I can't deny that, but it's not what it looks like.'

'I can see perfectly well, thank you!' A beat. 'Were you there, in the town?'

Surprise appeared on Tristan's face. 'No, actually I wasn't. I was meeting a friend,' he said softly.

Felan had to leave. He couldn't be seen with a Protrude. Nick would find out, especially if Felan failed to complete his drop-offs. Nick knew everything. Nick would know.

Panic rose in him.

Tristan stepped closer again, and Felan eyed him dangerously. He stuffed his water bottle inside the satchel and slung it over his shoulder. 'Whatever, I need to go. I've got places to be,' he said.

'No... stay. Just a bit longer,' Tristan said.

Felan stopped in his tracks. What did the man want from him? Had he lied before? Did he want to kidnap him and take him back to his boss? 'If Nick finds out I helped you, I'm dead,' he said. 'So, so dead.' There. A bit of fear never hurt anyone. That should make him back off.

'Nick?'

Felan wrenched his knife from the door and pointed it at Tristan. 'You can't mention me. Forget you saw me. Pretend I don't exist.'

'Nick?' Tristan's entire face dropped. 'Tell me you didn't... tell me you didn't join them.'

Felan licked his dry lips. 'What choice did I have? I was alone, starving, cold,' he listed off. 'They saved me from men, YOUR MEN, and offered me somewhere to stay. I couldn't turn that down.'

Tristan's eyes went straight to the satchel. 'What's in the bag, Felan?'

He pulled the satchel to his chest protectively. 'Nothing. None of your business.'

The man sighed in disappointment. The disappointment always hurt more than a slap did. 'You know, you don't have to do the drop-offs.'

Felan cursed. It seemed Tristan knew anyway. What was the point in pretending any more? What was the point in keeping secrets? 'I don't have a choice.'

Felan didn't like secrets. Secrets got people hurt. Secrets tore people apart.

'You do. Trust me, you have a choice,' Tristan insisted. 'Come with me, and I can help. I know people who can help. You can get out of this life, Felan.'

'I'm not a child any more. I don't need your help.' His hand shook as he spoke. Was there really a way out? He glared. No. Tristan was toying with him. That's all anyone ever did. Adults always lied to him.

He raised his knife to Tristan's eye level. The weapon's reflection danced in the water in Tristan's eyes. A blade had never looked so beautiful.

'It's not safe…'

Felan pushed past him, cutting him off.

He hesitated at the door.

'Get the hell off our territory, Tristan,' he said shakily. 'You can go back to, to, Maddison, and you can tell her to kindly leave.'

'Please…'

'It's not your territory. It's ours.' Felan shoved the door open and took one step out. 'We'll fight for it, if we have to.' He slammed the door shut behind him and turned away.

What monster had infiltrated his body? He wouldn't fight! He didn't want to fight. Why had he said that?

He ran, fighting the urge to stop, fighting the urge to go back to Tristan and ask him for help. He had drop-offs to get to, and he had to get back to the Warehouse.

Felan wiped his eyes as he ran, angry at the tears falling down his cheeks. He should never have helped Tristan in the first place, should have just left him to his fate, as the man had done to him; but he knew he never could have lived with himself if he hadn't helped him.

Felan liked helping people.

After rushing the last drop-offs, Felan ran some more. He needed to distract himself from the memories that kept coming back.

He remembered being told he'd be moved somewhere safe, into a house with other kids like him.

'Boys, you mean?' he asked.

'No,' the nurse laughed gently, 'other kids that have been in the same situation as you. They'll have marks on their skin too.' She pointed to the bruises on his body.

Felan stared at the colours and patterns that stained his skin, and poked them with his fingers. 'Oh.'

'Is that okay, Felan?'

He nodded.

'Okay, I'll be back soon. Get some rest.'

She didn't come back.

He was used to adults breaking their promises, so he expected it. Some of the lights switched off outside his room, and Felan got up. He changed into some clothes the nurse had laid out for him a few days prior, and climbed out of the window.

***

A day after he ran away, he came across a boy of similar age. He was sickly thin and covered with rags. He'd run straight to Oakley Park and found him hidden inside a bush.

'What's your name?' Felan asked, taking off his jumper and laying it over the boy.

'I don't remember,' the boy whispered, voice so hoarse Felan nearly didn't hear.

'We don't need names anyway. We have each other. That's more important.'

The boy smiled, and his lips bled.

'I'll be back soon,' Felan promised.

He came back with an empty plastic bottle and some scrap food wrapped in a napkin. He scrambled down to the pond and filled the bottle with water; not the best idea, but it was something at least.

He crawled into the bush. The boy was still awake. Felan showed the bottle. 'I've brought you something.'

Hungry eyes widened, and the boy opened his mouth eagerly. As gently as he could, Felan poured drop after drop on the boy's tongue. He let him swallow it, let it wet his mouth, before he poured more in.

'I've got some food too.' He unwrapped the scraps and fed the boy small pieces, not really knowing what he was doing. 'It's not the best food, but it'll be good to eat something.'

'Thank you,' the boy whispered.

Felan fell asleep, and he woke up shivering. He looked over to the boy, who lay still. He crawled over and shook him.

Cold as ice. Blue lips. Almost frozen.

Felan cried for the boy as he put his jumper back on. It had done all it could for the boy, as had Felan.
Then he ran, water bottle in hand.
He ran as far as he could go.
Felan saw the newspaper the next day: 'Young boy found dead in Oakley Park.'

Felan shoved his way through crowds of people, blinded by tears.
He'd never felt more trapped.

Chapter 25: Misperception

Felan wandered mindlessly about the city, aware of just *what* he was carrying, stashed away, in his satchel.

He thought moving would calm him down enough to think properly – but it only made his thoughts move faster and faster, and he didn't know where he was and how long he'd walked for, or where Tristan was or where Randi was, and his hands wouldn't stop shaking, and his body wouldn't stop trembling, and he couldn't think straight because he couldn't *stop moving...*

His phone wouldn't stop buzzing. No. No, he couldn't do more drop-offs. For a start, he didn't know where he was, and he just wanted to get back to the Warehouse. He just wanted to hide for a while and wait for the world to settle.

He wanted everything to be okay again.

Thankfully, it was Nick with a general summons for everyone to get back to the Warehouse. Felan had never been happier to do as Nick said. He took note of the street signs around him. He didn't recognise any of them, and if he didn't get back pronto, Nick would be angry – but how could he do so if he didn't know the way back?

Digging around in his satchel, Felan found some spare change, potentially enough for a ticket. He followed the signs to the closest underground entrance, peered over the heads of people on the street as he went.

He froze.

People walked into him, grumbled something about stupid kids. He mumbled an apology to people that didn't listen and walked slowly, making sure to hide behind others so he didn't get caught, but not so much that he couldn't see ahead.

As Felan crossed the street, Randi turned and stared.

Shock laced his friend's face, and Felan thought he could smell the fear from metres away.

Randi bolted.

Felan took off after him, squeezed through crowds and didn't apologise. For a minute, he thought he'd lost him, but shouts and angry yells from ahead kept Felan on track. He got to the corner of the street in time to see Randi disappear down an alley.

It didn't make sense. The direction Randi was headed... it was out of Guadalupe, even further out than the Fringe, all the way on the east side. Was that where he'd been this whole time? Was that why no one had seen him? He'd done a few drop-offs in the Fringe, but never further.

'Randi! Randi, stop!'

Felan's feet pounded on the concrete. Blood thrummed in his ears like an arrow in flight. Randi skidded on loose pebbles.

He found himself growing angry. Why was Randi running from him? They were friends, weren't they? At least, they had been, before. Felan had saved his life, and this was what he got in return? Silence? Rejection?

And people wondered why he found it so hard to trust.

He put on a burst of speed when Randi turned another corner. The sun was at its peak, the shadows at their largest, and next to each boy, a twin shadow ran alongside them, deformed and in a race of their own.

'Get out of here, Felan!' Randi yelled.

After a while, Felan started to recognise the alleys and passages they ran through, and he realised they'd been running back and forth down the same labyrinth network.

Randi was toying with him.

'Wait!'

'You're ruining everything! Stay away!'

Randi zigzagged, wormed his way down backstreets Felan had never seen. They definitely weren't in Guadalupe any more. Felan skidded around a corner. Good, a dead end. That meant Randi couldn't go anywhere.

Felan watched as Randi climbed the wall at the end of the alley, with a speed that suggested, perhaps, he'd climbed it before.

'What are you doing?' Felan tried to scramble up after him. He couldn't find a hold. He couldn't find a goddamn hold.

Randi looked down at him, smiled a smile so small that it might not have even been real. 'You won't understand, but I'm sorry – it'll be okay soon.'

'What are you talking about? Just come back!'

'Sorry, Felan,' Randi said. He tipped over the other side.

'Randi! Randi, wait!'

Felan's shadow snapped at his heels as he climbed the wall, and when he peered over the top, he couldn't believe his eyes.

Situated in the flat expanse on the other side was a large warehouse – about five times as big as the one he lived in – and he watched Randi sprint towards it.

He pulled himself up to get a better view.

All he saw was green and grey, typical of any settlement outside of the city, and outside of the Fringe. Groups of people dressed in black hung around an empty hangar, the sounds of conversation travelling across the ground. A man with red hair stepped outside the warehouse.

Felan's concentration faltered. He slipped and fell, landing hard on his ankle. He gasped in pain and tried to stand. He collapsed heavily into the wall.

Tristan was already back. His ankle throbbed. Tristan must have left right after him. He swallowed down a cry of pain. He'd found Randi. Felan tried to take a step, but his ankle couldn't hold his weight. Randi was on the other side of that wall. Felan kept a hand on it and tried to walk again. Randi and Tristan knew each other. Felan fell to the floor. Randi was a Protrude. Felan picked himself up. Randi was a Protrude. Felan limped and didn't fall. Randi had deserted them all. He grabbed the satchel.

Randi had left them.

Randi had found somewhere else.

Randi had left them all behind.

Blinded by tears, Felan limped his way back to the city. Another person he trusted, gone. Another person he trusted, leaving him behind.

It couldn't be. No. He was spying, getting information for Nick. He must be. It was the only explanation that made sense. Randi wouldn't desert his boyfriend for no reason.

But the Protrudes kidnapped children, so why would Nick send him there? Why would Nick send him directly into danger? Felan wiped his eyes. Isn't that what Nick did anyway, with the drop-offs, with the raids, with the jobs? Isn't that what was expected of them anyway?

How was this any different?

***

He ignored the glares that greeted him when he limped into the room. To be honest, he didn't really see them. All he could see was Randi, running, away from them, and away from him.

Blaez crossed her arms when he took his place beside her. 'Where've you been?'

'Later,' he muttered. Felan pretended Caleb wasn't in the room. He pretended he knew nothing about his boyfriend's whereabouts; he didn't want to get the kid's hopes up for nothing.

Nick stepped out of the shadows. 'And at last, the straggler has returned.'

Felan wondered if anyone could hear his heart beating.

'There's a raid coming up, bigger than anything we've ever done before. Make sure you're ready.' Nick aimed that last part at Felan, he was sure of it.

Bugger.

'The Protrudes are encroaching further on our territory,' he said. Felan thought back to Tristan, and how the Protrudes had been in the Flax earlier that day. 'We're going to fight back, and we're going to fight back hard.'

Nick said other things, though Felan tuned them out. When people began to leave the training room, Felan limped over to

Nick and withdrew the money he'd made on his drop-offs; Nick took it with a greedy smile and left the room.

Felan sighed in relief. If his punishment was no cut of the money, that was fine by him. He didn't want it anyway.

'Talk to me, Felan,' Blaez said.

'Let's go to the roof.'

They collapsed there some minutes later.

'What happened to your face?' Blaez asked.

Oh yeah – he'd completely forgotten Tristan had sucker-punched him earlier. 'Ran into someone.'

'Hmm. And your ankle?'

'Fell off a wall.'

She rolled her eyes. 'Only you would be that stupid.'

'That's not nice.'

'I *was* being nice.'

Felan poked her. 'Hey.'

'You were so late today, Felan. I've never seen Nick that angry.'

Felan glanced her way. He'd never seen her so quiet and reserved before. She might deny it, but something had definitely happened the other night. He wasn't stupid.

He just hoped that one day she realised he was there for her in the same way she was always there for him.

He sighed. 'I did my drop-offs, like he asked.'

'And that took all this time?'

He knew she didn't mean to sound condescending. Sometimes it happened, by accident. People put the wrong emphasis on the wrong words and it all went south, so Felan brushed it aside as he always did. He ignored the pang her words made in his chest. 'The Protrudes were in the Flax,' Felan said, and told her everything he'd seen.

'But that's our territory!' she exclaimed.

'I know. That's what I thought,' he said, then, 'I know one of them, Blaez. I tracked him down. Someone from my childhood.' The memory of it came hurtling back.

Her hand brushed his. 'Felan...'

'He found out what I was doing, what was in the satchel, who

I was with.' His hands started to tremble. 'He offered me help. He offered to get me out.'

'Oh, Felan...' She took his hand and held it in both of hers. The gesture was somewhat comforting.

'I can't stop thinking – what if I accepted his help? What if I let him get me out? But I knew I couldn't – I have friends here, people who care about me, people that've given me my life back, given me a home. I can't desert them. I can't desert you, not after everything you've done for me.'

But, he thought, *is this the life I want?*

'It might've been a ruse,' Blaez said, slowly. 'Lure you back to where they're living and kidnap you that way.'

'Exactly,' Felan said in a hushed voice. He'd told her what he said to Tristan. 'And now Nick's said *that*... what if Tristan was actually being sincere about wanting to help?'

Blaez shuffled over, and he dropped his head onto her shoulder. 'Be careful, Felan. I understand you know him, but if he's with the Protrudes... that can't be anything good.'

'I know.'

'It'll sort itself out. You'll see,' she said, wrapping an arm around him.

'What if I come face to face with him again and I have to hurt him?'

He hadn't meant to say it out loud. He hadn't meant to sound so scared. He hadn't meant anything, and yet...

'We'll think of something.'

'I don't know who to trust any more, Blaez. I don't know what I want.'

Everyone in his life he'd got close to had either left him behind or betrayed him. What the hell was he going to do on the day Blaez and the others left too? He was so close to tears, and it was pathetic. He was old enough to not cry over everything. He was old enough to be brave. He was old enough, he was old enough, he wasn't old enough...

'You can trust me,' Blaez said. 'We're in this together; just promise me you won't do anything stupid.'

'Since when have I done anything stupid?'

'Felan, please.' Perhaps it wasn't the time for jokes. 'Promise me.'

'I promise,' he murmured.

'Pinky promise?' She let go of his hand and extended her little finger to him.

He interlinked his pinky with hers and relished in the feeling. 'Pinky promise.' He hadn't made one of those since his mother died. 'Is now a bad time to mention that I found Randi?'

Like he'd anticipated, she'd detangled herself in seconds and stared at him with an unreadable expression.

'What? Where is he? Why isn't he with you?'

Felan explained everything. 'He's a Protrude, or at least he's pretending to be one.'

She jumped to her feet. 'We have to tell Caleb!'

'Blaez... no.'

'Why not? He's been worried sick!'

He limped after her and groaned out, 'He's doing something for Nick.'

She turned suspicious eyes on him, and he wondered if he should have kept it a secret after all. 'And how do you know that?' She put her hands on her hips, waiting.

Felan sank gratefully to the floor. 'I don't, but what other reason does he have for being there?' He hissed at a particularly painful twinge.

'Why can't we tell this to Caleb?'

As much as it pained him to lie, he knew it had to be done; for both of their sakes. 'He's with the Protrudes – think, Blaez. He'll want to go and find him – that could blow Randi's cover, and it'll put them both in danger. The last thing I want right now is for anything to happen to either of them.'

'Me neither.'

'It'll be okay – they'll be okay,' he reassured. He swallowed a painful lump in his throat.

'I hate lying,' she said.

Felan stared out over the dark forest. 'I know. I hate it too.'

Chapter 26: Presage

'This is most... surprising,' Nick drawled. Sat behind his desk, he smiled knowingly.

Felan stopped in the middle of the room. Maybe it wasn't the best idea after all, but he needed to know if Randi was there on *his* orders, and if he was safe. Or at least, as safe as he could be living with child abductors.

'I was just wondering if you've heard anything from Randi – if you've found any leads on where he is.'

'He updates me twice a week.'

Randi would get in contact with Nick, but not with his own boyfriend? Not his friends?

'You know where he is then.'

'This might come as a shock to you, but no. I don't know where he is,' Nick said, amused.

'You're lying.'

'A bold accusation,' Nick said. 'You're not as clever as I thought you were.' He leaned back in his chair. 'Randi's running an errand for me, like I asked him to.'

Felan felt the doubt in his chest lessen. He'd been right. Randi hadn't deserted them.

'I chose him because he's the most reliable, and he'll get it done efficiently. We all make sacrifices here, especially when it's for the greater good.' He finished with a growl that trailed off in a rumble, and the hairs on the back of Felan's neck stood in salute.

'That's sick!' he shouted.

It wasn't until he shouted that he saw the empty vodka bottles on the desk. Felan backed away, numb, his fingers tingling – he knew what was coming. Nick strode forward like a thunderstorm. A fist sunk into his chest. The boy cowered. He wouldn't give him the satisfaction of hearing his cries of pain; he would never give *anyone* that satisfaction again.

Nick pinned him to the wall before he could catch his breath. One steel hand crushed his windpipe, and the other slammed relentlessly next to his head. With each slam, Felan flinched. With each slam, bile rose in his throat.

'Sick! You call that sick!' Nick roared.

Spittle landed on Felan's cheek. The hand around his neck squeezed tighter. Nick's hand slammed into the wall harder and harder. Felan's ears rang louder with each slam. He forced himself to stay quiet, and he bit his lip, hard. Blood dribbled down his chin, warm and wet, and he couldn't wipe it away. For a scary moment, Felan thought Nick was going to kill him.

Then he let go.

Felan's body submitted and he fell limp to the floor, unable to hold himself up.

He coughed and spluttered, retched, and forced himself to stay silent. He blinked, blinked away the yellow spots that danced in his eyes, blinked, and when Nick advanced, he crawled back on his hands, scrabbled at the floor to get away – yes, he could see the very sharp knife in the man's hand. Nick twirled the knife and tested it on his own skin. He whipped something at Felan, who ducked and cowered away. It hit the wall with a bang and clattered noisily to the floor.

'You call someone making a sacrifice for others sick?'

Felan wanted to run. He shouldn't have come. He shouldn't have bothered. He should have just obeyed, and kept quiet, and done what was expected of him, like he'd been taught to do. He wanted to run away.

He couldn't.

The man crouched in front of Felan, the tip of the knife pressed at the base of his own ring finger. Blood welled there, and Felan couldn't look away.

'I've told you already – always put yourself first, or you won't make it.' Nick looked Felan right in the eye. He plunged the knife into the knuckle of his ring finger and twisted the knife deeper; a sickening pop followed.

Felan watched in horror.

'This is sick, Felan,' he said, motioning to his hand.

The boy watched red travel over Nick's skin like external veins. With perverted precision, he sliced his way right through the bone. The finger fell to the floor.

His fascination was shameful.

'I think you need to learn the difference,' Nick said. He stalked over to his desk and took huge gulps from one of the bottles.

Felan retched and refused to vomit. Nick crouched down before him again.

'Why don't you just behave, Felan? Then I wouldn't have to do things like this to make you understand.'

The boy shied away. His breath stank. Nick held his arm tight.

'If you just behaved, I wouldn't have had to cut my finger off.'

Felan nodded.

'Why don't you just behave? Why don't you just do as you're told? It would make your life so much easier. Things wouldn't hurt if you behaved.'

Felan nodded. That's what his dad had always said. It was true. If he behaved, he didn't get hurt. Nick was telling the truth.

'Is this how you repay me?' Nick asked, softly, a tone Felan had never heard from his mouth before. 'I give you a home, I give you your life back, and all you do is disobey. Do you understand how much that hurts me?'

Felan blinked away the tears.

'I thought you could help me, Felan, but you need to stop disobeying me. You need to stop questioning me. You're not in charge, remember? This,' Nick pointed to his finger on the floor, 'was your punishment for disobeying me. Take this as your punishment, and learn from it, before it's too late.'

Felan let a traitorous tear slide down his cheek.

'You don't want to hurt me any more, do you? No, you want to help me, don't you? You want to stay here, where you're protected,' Nick encouraged.

He did. He did want to stay. He didn't want to hurt anyone ever again. He wanted to help people. He wanted to be *safe*. 'Yes,' Felan whispered.

'That's good to hear, Felan. Really good. Can you help me now?'

'What do you want me to do?'

'I've got some drop-offs – can you do them for me?'

Felan stumbled to his feet. 'I'll leave immediately.'

'That's excellent news.'

He stumbled down the dark corridor, rubbing his aching neck. He thought of Tristan. Harvey. Blaez. Himself. Everyone else that stayed at the Warehouse. Even the Protrudes. All of the other people in the world who'd done awful things. Maybe they were good people, underneath. Maybe they were good people without a choice. And Felan... he didn't have a choice. He wanted to stay. People cared about him. People wanted him. Why didn't he just obey? Like Nick said, things would be easier. He wouldn't hurt as much.

Felan ran through the forest, a satchel slung over his shoulder.

Things would get better.

They had to.

Chapter 27: Misadventure

An incessant tapping roused him from his sleep.

Felan sat bolt upright, immediately wide awake. The sound faded out for a second, and he cocked his head. There it was again! The same incessant tapping from a few seconds ago! He opened his eyes, letting them adjust to the darkness of his room. As quiet as a grain of sand shifting on the shore, he slipped out from beneath his covers and padded over to the window. He peeled back the curtain, and there it was.

A raven sat on the ledge outside his window. Tapping. Tapping. Tapping. Felan frowned. Of all places, why here? Why had this night shadow chosen the Warehouse as its roost for the night? He tried to shoo it away, tapped on the glass in return, but the tapping turned desperate. The sound sped up, and Felan found himself watching and staring with a morbid sense of dread. It reminded him of those insane piano pieces, where the keys followed each other in quick succession, faster and louder and more desperate than the last...

It stopped.

When the raven finally took flight, Felan felt as though something in him had shifted, that something had changed. He shivered and stood by the window for a long time. He traced the fading bruises around his neck with his index finger, and when he did go back to sleep, he was haunted by the sound of incessant, desperate tapping.

***

Blaez led the trio into a run. Felan kept a close eye on Convel from behind – he was still convinced he'd tried to kill him during his initiation. They ran through the forest but took a new path to the underground. Felan eagerly looked about at the change of scenery.

Disappointment ensued; all he saw was an isolated cluster of slums beside a small farm. There were cows in the field, and a lady was digging. Convel either didn't notice her or didn't care, because they swiftly moved on.

They walked onto a street at the south-west edge of Guadalupe and scurried down to the underground. As expected, it was mostly deserted, with just a few people on the platform, their faces bent to their phones. Felan watched Convel eye them with interest – once a thief, always a thief. They shared a glance, and Felan glared. They couldn't get distracted. *They had to help Nick.* After their last encounter, Felan had begun to believe the words, but the tightness in his chest didn't loosen. He told himself it was the nervousness of the job.

The train screeched to a halt, and they climbed into a carriage. A woman sat, headphones on, at the other end.

'The second we get off, I'm heading out on my own,' Blaez said. 'I'll be a few streets away, on the clock tower. I'll be watching you, as well as watching for cops – I'll help out as much as I can and keep them off your backs.' She only looked to Convel. 'And no killing bystanders.'

'Nick doesn't care what we do,' Convel scoffed. 'As long as he gets what he wants, he doesn't care.'

'We need to be careful, Convel. The moment you take out your weapons, all hell will break loose. The cops will arrive, and we need to be long gone.' She looked cautiously over her shoulder. The woman was still engrossed on her phone. 'Get in and get what we came for, and leave as quick as we can. When you get inside, split up and head for empty corridors. Fill your bags quietly, and get the hell out of there,' she recited.

Felan nodded. They'd gone over the plan hundreds of times already. Convel pretended to yawn.

'What about the guards?' Felan suddenly thought aloud.

'Avoid them, if you can. But if it means you get out quietly, dispose of them; I'd prefer it if you incapacitate them. But just get out.'

Their car came to a stop, and Felan looked up in surprise. That was quick. They hurried out as the doors slid open, and Blaez took off.

'Go careful, Blaez,' he muttered.

Convel laughed.

'Got something to say?' Felan asked, dangerously.

'Nothing,' he said, grinning.

Felan stalked up the stairs to the street. Convel overtook him. Felan kept a cautious eye on him.

One couldn't be too careful these days.

***

Vermillion was an area of the Flax closest to the centre of Guadalupe, containing Vermillion Bank and various high-end clothing stores. Honestly, Felan quite liked a vintage shop, but there was no need for so many expensive ones like these.

Felan looked to the clock tower where Blaez would be and saw the small shadow on the roof, blended almost perfectly into the tiles. At least she was safely out of the way. He observed Vermillion Bank: smaller than the one they'd stormed before, but still tall and with no latched windows. He was already annoyed that he'd let Blaez go alone. Last time she'd been too close to the commotion to get away.

Convel strode into the building.

'Thanks for the warning,' Felan said.

He leaned against the wall across the road and counted down the minutes; they went by too fast for his liking, adrenaline pumping through his body.

And then Felan walked into the bank slowly, not as confident as Convel, and headed right. He climbed up flight after flight of stairs. The corridors were never deserted, either families or security guards hanging around every floor, and it occurred to Felan that Nick hadn't checked out the place beforehand. His plan had been to complete the job on a lower level, fill his bag, and leave quietly.

He was going to have to change that plan a little.

His throat ran dry as he climbed higher. It reminded him of the bruises he'd hidden beneath a scarf – he couldn't let Nick down. Finally, he found an empty floor near the top, two cameras mounted high up on the walls on either side.

'Act normal,' he mumbled. He slipped out his knife. He paused, waited for alarms to sound, for the rush of movement. Nothing. Felan slid his knife into the crack of the closest door and tried to wrench it open. He wondered how Convel was getting on, then realised he didn't actually care.

The door wouldn't budge. He retracted the knife and examined it; a few scratches along the edges. No nicks. He jammed it in again. Nothing. He even tried running the knife down from the top of the door to the bottom, and back up again. Still nothing. Felan scowled at Nick's lack of preparation and jabbed his knife in the gaps over and over again in silent anger.

Was he setting them up for failure?

For the longest time it didn't look like it was going to work, and Felan began to think he would leave the building in handcuffs – but then the tip of the blade snagged on something. He grasped the hilt with two hands and twisted the knife to the side as far as he dared. The snag began to loosen.

Yes!

He shoved all his weight onto the knife, and the door opened with an audible pop. Sheathing the knife, he slid his fingers into the gap and pulled; it opened enough for him to slip through.

He dropped his rucksack to the floor and began to fill it, cramming in as much as possible, opening drawers and cupboards and anything he could find.

The door squeaked. Felan spun around, staring into the face of an equally stunned guard. Before the guard could shout, the hilt of Felan's knife hit him squarely on the forehead and he stumbled back. It was a skill he and Blaez had perfected, on the quiet, in place of outright murder. Felan punched the man in the temple and he crumpled to the floor. He dragged the unconscious body further into the room, lest anyone see him. The walkie-talkie on the man's uniform crackled.

'What was that? Is everything alright up there, Hayden?'

Felan froze. Dammit. He unhooked the device and fumbled with it – he was pretty sure he had to hold down the little button.

'It was nothing – kids playing in the corridors,' Felan said evenly.

'There are no kids with you. Hayden, where are you? I don't see you on the cameras,' the voice said.

Felan thought quickly. 'I'm in room 75B,' he said, remembering the fancy lettering on the door.

'Come out where we can see you.'

Felan cursed. He dropped the walkie to the floor and scrambled for his knife. He shoved a few last-minute items into his rucksack before zipping it shut.

'Hayden, come in.'

The boy shrugged on his rucksack.

'We're sending the guys up.'

Felan bolted from the room.

Alarms blared.

Footsteps crashed up the stairs, and Felan cursed again. He had no choice now but to climb. He ran down the corridor and up the stairs, round and round, ran along another corridor and up some more stairs. A guard ran at him, clearly on his way back down. Felan took a hit to the shoulder, and the arm, before he managed to strike the guard in the face. Felan shook him off and sprinted away.

Get out. Get out. You have to get out. Just keep going.

Shouts from below made him run faster, and he ran until he could go no higher; and no way was he going back down to say hello to the guards. Besides, it wouldn't take them long to restrain him because Felan wouldn't put up a fight. He didn't want to hurt anyone else.

He saw the windows and weighed his options. There was a slim chance.

Felan was accustomed to slim chances.

He took the burner phone from his bag and thumbed a quick message to Blaez: *Window. Top floor.* He tossed the phone to the ground, broke the glass container on the wall, and swung the hammer he found inside at the window with all his might.

The impact shook the window frame, and jolted up his arms, a tingling sensation taking over. Rolling his shoulders to try to alleviate the tingle, he swung again. Nothing. Footsteps thundered towards him.

Why wasn't it working?

He swung again. The glass shattered into what resembled a spider's web, and splinters shot out in all directions. Felan barely remembered to shield his face as the window exploded altogether. Fragments of glass hit him in the face; it stung more than he'd thought it would.

Glass remained lodged in the panel, but the hole was big enough for him to climb through. The shouts grew louder, louder than the alarm, and he launched himself out of the window. His trousers ripped. His skin tore. A few weightless seconds and then Felan balanced himself on the tiny ledge.

Footsteps and voices entered the corridor, and there was no time to make sure he had a good enough grip as he started his descent. He let himself slide down when necessary, tried not to yell when he missed his footing. Police sirens wailed. He couldn't tell if they were headed in his direction.

A guard peered out of the broken window, at that moment Felan slipped again, grazing his hands. He looked up and stared into the barrel of a gun. Felan ducked, a bullet skipping off the brick just above his head.

He swung further to the right to avoid the second bullet, which narrowly missed his arm. Felan hurried down, heart in his throat, body spread across the face of the building like a spider – he had to get out of their line of sight. He slipped down and struggled to find another grip. Glass smashed above him, showering him with tiny pieces.

A guard climbed out to the ledge and fired down at Felan. The bullet ricocheted. Felan's hand gave way just as he found grip with the other and pulled himself to 'safety'.

He dropped down to another ledge, then another.

A bullet zipped through the air. Blaez! She'd pulled through! She could keep them distracted while he made his escape. At least, that's what he assumed the new plan was.

Another bullet zipped over and hit the glass of the window he'd smashed; shards rained down and he hid his face in his shoulder, spitting dust from his mouth.

Blaez let loose another bullet.

A guard tumbled from the ledge with a shout. They screamed all the way down, and they hit the floor with a sickening thud.

Felan stared at the shadow on the clock tower in shock. No, no she hadn't...

A bullet landed frighteningly close to Felan's head, and he slipped; he skinned his hand and tore through his trousers some more until he caught himself. If he hadn't been holding the wall so tight, he might have seen the horrible tremble that possessed him. The boy looked down. A skip stood below him, a body crumpled beside it, unmoving. He swallowed down bile.

It was too far to fall. He could risk it at two floors, maybe three at a push. He used the pipes, and the windows, and the cracks in the walls as aids. Bullets barely missed him.

Blaez didn't fire again.

Felan let go of the wall, as the cops barrelled down the street below. He landed in the skip with a heavy thump; it wasn't exactly a soft landing, but it was better than the pavement. He patted himself over quickly, checking for injuries. A bit of a jolt, falling three floors, but he was alive. He spilled onto the pavement and walked around the body. He pulled the pistol from its holster.

He wasn't going to use it.

He wasn't.

He flung himself out of cover and saw Convel crouched behind a parked car on the other side of the road, impatient, as if he'd been waiting for a while. Felan couldn't care less.

Convel signalled and sprinted left, while Felan sprinted right. They weaved through the lines of traffic and people, and ignored the honking horns. Convel came up beside him and they ran side by side – he couldn't tell who was enjoying it more, but they were getting away.

Nick's plan was working; the cops didn't know who to go after when they had six raids taking place simultaneously in the Flax.

Lost in the thrill of escape, the freedom of running, Felan ran headlong into a chest. He looked up. Tristan. And friends.

No Randi in sight.

Blaez shot at their feet, Convel and Felan tumbling one way, and the five Protrudes another. Blaez fired again, and the Protrudes backed away.

Mouth open in what Felan knew to be shock, Tristan stared at him, and more so at the pistol in Felan's hand. The disappointment in the man's gaze was gut-wrenching. Felan wanted to hide the pistol, hide his shame, from Tristan; but why did he want to hide?

Tristan had this coming.

Tristan left him alone.

Felan's hand clenched around his weapon – he wasn't going to use it. It was for show, more than anything. To scare Tristan and his friends off so no one would get hurt.

Convel fired his pistol. 'Get off our territory!' he snarled, angry. He fired again. Felan stared at the bodies on the floor. Tristan still hadn't moved, hadn't flinched. Convel adjusted his aim.

'No!' Felan shouted, throwing himself between them. 'Don't shoot him.' He stared down the barrel, hot and gasping, and *oh God!* What was stopping Convel from just shooting him *and* Tristan?

Convel shrugged. 'Fine. He's all yours.' He wiped sweat and blood from his forehead.

'What?' he recoiled. The pistol burned his skin.

'Shoot him.'

Terror filled his body. Like a spider spinning a web, one glistening, sticky string at a time, the terror formed an intricate riddle he couldn't quite figure out. Why would Convel assume he wanted to kill Tristan himself? He didn't want to kill anyone!

'Why don't you just do as you're told? It would make your life so much easier. Things wouldn't hurt if you behaved.'

'You don't have to.'

'I don't need your help.' Felan remembered their last conversation very well. He pointed his gun at Tristan with a glare – to intimidate him, not to use it, he told himself.

'I know you, Felan. You won't shoot me,' he said.

'Oh – you know each other, do you?' Convel said in pleasure. 'Just wait until Nick finds out!'

So much for team spirit.

'Why are you here?' He wished his hands would stop shaking.

'Put the pistol down,' Tristan said. He took a step closer.

Felan fired at the floor. 'Don't come closer.' He blinked away the tears. He wasn't weak. Not any more. Who did Tristan think he was?

'Fine. I'll stay here.'

He felt breath on his neck and froze. 'You know, this is why your father did what he did to you,' Convel said.

His father didn't need justification for what he did.

'You always wanted your father to love you – this is why he didn't.'

'You don't know anything!' Felan snarled. He turned on Convel, completely forgetting Tristan was even there.

'Your mother died to be free of you. You're a burden.'

'Shut up!'

The tears came unbidden. He willed them away. He didn't want Convel, of all people, to see him like that. He didn't want Convel to know how easy it was to get to him. But it was too late.

Convel smiled horribly. 'I told them the first day Nick brought you back that he should have left you. You were weak.'

'I earned my spot here,' he said, voice shaking. His hand wavered.

'You got lucky. You're worthless.'

'I got the stuff today,' he argued.

'You're not helping now – you're *useless.*'

Felan saw red, so much red, and he exploded in rage. He remembered shouting. He remembered seeing nothing. He remembered the way his father...

Tristan cried out in pain. The red faded – the end of Felan's pistol was smoking. His eyes followed it. No... no, no, he hadn't. He couldn't have. 'I didn't... no, I didn't,' he whispered. Blood gushed past Tristan's fingers, and the man groaned. 'I'm sorry,' Felan whimpered. Convel ran off, laughing.

'Felan,' the man gasped. He collapsed to the floor. 'Felan, run.'

Felan hadn't realised how close the cops were. 'Tristan...'

'GO!'

Like the coward he was, he scampered after Convel, though he failed to notice the cop car until it slammed to a stop in front of him. Felan hit the bonnet, shocked, and could already feel bruises forming on his legs from the impact. He stared into the faces of the cops behind the windscreen. Was this it?

A bullet blasted through the windscreen, then another. The cops lay still in their seats, jaws slack, eyes open. Felan turned in time to see Convel duck behind a parked car, the end of his pistol smoking.

A bullet scuffed the floor at Felan's feet. 'Put your hands up!' a cop shouted from somewhere.

In a surge of panic, the pistol tumbled from his hands and he held them high. He couldn't do this. This wasn't him. He didn't hurt people.

'Turn around and get on your knees!'

He did so slowly, and made eye contact with a cop, a cop who had a gun aimed at Felan's chest. He looked at the boy with such disdain, the same disdain Nick aimed at him, and it supported Felan's belief that he'd deserve this treatment wherever he went. It didn't matter if this had been a second chance. It didn't matter if it wasn't going as well as he'd hoped.

He would be forever met with disdain and misery, and nothing was going to change that.

The cop snarled, held his finger to the trigger. 'On your knees!' Another bullet sounded, and the cop fell to the ground. Felan jerked back as blood hit his face.

'What are you doing? Get up!' Convel grabbed him by the arm and shoved him forward.

Felan stumbled and struggled to catch himself.

Convel spun around and shot again. He spun in a circle and fired three more times. Three more silences. 'Run!' The mismatched eyes of his fellow Wolf burned with a hunger Felan hoped he would never possess.

Felan bit back a scream as a bullet sunk deep into his forearm. He had never felt pain like it.

Blood flowed out of him in rivulets; though he didn't have time to stem the bleed. He fell, skinned his knees, and scrambled away.

Why had Convel helped him?

The unmistakable sound of Blaez's bullets somehow composed him – perhaps it was the knowledge that his friend was watching out for him, following his progress. Blaez's shadow crawled around the clock tower and vanished moments later.

He thought he might be crying, but he couldn't tell over the constant screaming of sirens fading in and out. The screams of bullets echoed in his mind; Convel's face, his words, echoed in his mind; they ensured he ran faster and harder and didn't dare stop.

Blaez waited at the railway entrance. Convel was nowhere to be found.

'Felan, I...' She tried to speak, but her words failed her.

'Where's Convel?' he asked. He held his bloody arm awkwardly to his chest. Pain laced the limb, hitting him in waves of increasing intensity.

'Already gone down there,' she said. 'Felan...'

'Let's go.'

'I didn't mean...'

'I said let's go.'

A guard had fallen to his death. He'd shot someone. Convel had *murdered*. He walked down into the underground and overtook a woman dressed in very formal clothes. She took one look at Felan and gasped in repulsion. He bared his teeth at her and growled. She hurried off, her heels clicking as she did so.

Felan had never been so disgusted with himself.

'Ah, so he finally shows.' Convel stood by a bench, face stuck somewhere between humour and anger.

'No thanks to you,' Felan seethed. How could Convel stand there, okay with what he'd done?

'I saved you! You should be thanking me!'

That might be true, but he'd rather be caught than get another man killed.

'I didn't ask you to.'

They walked into the carriage and kept as far from everyone else as possible. Blaez moved to shield Felan from view; after a nudge from Blaez, Convel did the same – and he clamped his hand down hard on Felan's arm. The bullet ground against bone.

'Ow, let go! What the hell are you doing?' Felan hissed.

'You're covered in blood. I'm trying to help you,' he whispered angrily.

'I don't need your help.' He gagged into his shoulder – the smell of blood worked its way up his nose and down the back of his throat. Then he remembered the splashes of blood all over his face. He rubbed at his cheek, stomach churning at the red that came off on his sleeve.

'Look at him – he hasn't got the stomach,' Convel said.

No. No, he absolutely did not have the stomach, and he wasn't ashamed to admit it.

A soft hand rested on his shoulder. 'We'll sort you out once we get back,' Blaez promised.

Felan tried to get the images out of his head, but they were burned into his mind, along with the rest of them, along with the silences.

Chapter 28: Parade

Convel had gone on ahead of them, refusing to acknowledge their presence, and when Felan and Blaez returned to the clearing in front of the Warehouse, Convel was already in a conversation with Tate, their hands gesturing wildly.

Felan took solace in the fact that Nick wasn't back. That was good. That gave him time to think of what the hell he was going to do when Convel inevitably told him about Tristan.

He stumbled and hit the floor, blood sticking to his skin like dried paint, all crinkly and slowly peeling away in crunchy, crispy flakes. Another wave of pain hit him.

Blaez sank to her knees beside him and rifled through her bag. 'I need to get the bullet out,' she said.

'It's fine. I can't feel it anyway…'

'Exactly why I need to get it out.'

A pair of tweezers came into view, and he clamped his mouth shut. Accalia appeared, seemingly out of nowhere, bracing his arm, a bandage at the ready. Blaez leaned in close. He squirmed.

'Hold still,' she said. 'And don't tense your arm. Try and relax.'

'I'm trying.'

He groaned as she dug around. He'd thought getting shot was bad, but its removal was even more painful; he imagined fire, walking along burning coals, and being smothered by smouldering lava. He'd been burned before, more than once, and the bullet was worse. Somehow, having something inside his skin hurt more than something burning him from the outside.

In the end, it was all the same.

In the end, they both left ugly scars on him that he couldn't scrub off.

'Have you got it yet?' he asked.

'Nearly.'

She tugged the tweezers out. Blaez dropped the bullet into his open palm.

'That's it? All that, for this little thing?' he scoffed. He rolled it around with his fingers; it was literally the size of his fingernail. 'That's pathetic.'

'Yeah, and look at the damage that pathetic bullet did to you,' Accalia said pointedly. Felan couldn't even see the skin of his forearm because there was so much blood.

Blaez glared. 'And you said you were fine.'

Felan's eyes wandered while he let the girls finish their work. A few people milled about outside, and a pile of rucksacks sat by the front door. *Loot*, Felan thought.

Most of the groups had returned, though Caleb had been due back hours ago. Felan wasn't overly concerned. He and Blaez had been late back too, and they were okay, for the most part.

As usual, Nick was nowhere to be found.

Accalia wiped blood on her trousers. 'Okay, I think we're good.'

Blaez wrapped his forearm, over and over again, and tied it off with a neat bow. She nodded in satisfaction. 'That should hold.'

'Thank you.'

'Just try not to get shot again.'

***

Caleb stumbled into the clearing, red in the face. He had no bag, his jacket was missing, and, most startlingly, he was alone.

'You were supposed to be back hours ago,' Rory accused.

Caleb nodded, panting.

Accalia walked up to him and put her hands on his shoulders to steady him.

'Thanks,' he gasped.

'Where's Ralph? Where's Mingan?' Accalia asked.

'We got cornered. I saw an opening and I took it.'

Tala made a series of gestures with her hands.

'They were together last I saw them,' Caleb answered. 'We got separated.'

Another series of gestures.

'Not injured,' he said.

Tala walked over to another group and motioned with her hands, already in another conversation. Rory stared hard at Felan and smirked as he walked by. Felan cursed – Convel must have told him, the sneaking rat.

'We're glad you're back safely,' Accalia said, smiling reassuringly at Caleb.

'Who's left to come back?'

'Everyone's back, except the rest of your group, and Nick.'

'Anyone injured?'

'Felan got shot, cuts and bruises, but nothing life-threatening.'

No, he thought. He wasn't a threat to his own life, but he was a threat to others. He hurt people, even when he didn't mean to. It was always by accident, always when he lost control – but then was it really accidental when he let himself lose it?

He'd nearly killed Convel in their first fight (though Felan had come out of it worse), he'd actually killed a homeless man, and he'd shot Tristan.

How many more people were going to get hurt because of him?

'Ouch,' Caleb said.

He wasn't going to lose control any more; he wasn't going to hurt anyone ever again. Felan clambered to his feet. He stumbled, his head spinning, and it took four hands to keep him upright. Since when had Blaez had three heads?

'Are you sure you should be standing?' Caleb asked.

'Yeah. I'm good. Nothing to worry about.'

'Felan,' Caleb said. 'You don't look so good.'

He wasn't. He really wasn't. He'd hurt someone who was only trying to help.

How did the others cope with killing? How were the others okay with taking a life? How were they okay with doling death out like a gift? He supposed it was a gift, to some. A long time ago, it might have been a gift to him too. Perhaps it still was.

He didn't fight when Caleb sat him back down.

'Wasn't yours supposed to be a quick in and out?' Caleb asked, incredulous.

'He got found out and had to improvise,' Blaez said. She told the story to their friends while he sat there, dazed. 'They had a run-in with some Protrudes.'

'Their appearances are becoming more frequent,' Accalia said.

'And they're getting closer,' Caleb added.

'Yeah – we don't even have a plan to stop them,' Blaez said.

Felan made a wounded noise at the back of his throat. They didn't have a plan to stop *him*. If anyone needed to be stopped, it was Felan. 'Convel should have left me there.'

Blaez cupped his cheek, looking into his eyes. 'For whatever reason, he didn't.'

'I wish I knew why,' Felan said.

'I agree – it wasn't like Convel. He has a habit of running away when things get rough.' Blaez glared angrily across the clearing at the man in question.

'I know the feeling,' Felan murmured. He ran away too, every time he made a poor choice or lost control. He'd done it with his father, he'd done it with Tristan, and he'd done it to himself. He wanted to run. He needed to run.

Felan could never outrun himself.

'Are you feeling alright?' Blaez asked, quietly, so the others couldn't hear.

Had Nick not arrived at that precise moment, Felan thought he might have said something.

The man emerged from the forest, as menacing as ever, and waited just beyond the treeline. Someone walked out behind him. The person was dressed head to toe in black clothes, their hands were bound with rope, and they had their head down.

Caleb burst forward in a sprint. Felan predicted the action and leaped to his feet, grabbed him by the waist and pulled him back. God, why did everything *hurt*?

'No, let me go!' Caleb shouted. 'Let me go!'

Felan grimaced through Caleb's flailing, the bullet wound burning something crazy. Blood soaked through the bandage and, within seconds, the white fabric was the same deep shade of red as his arm.

Nick held a hand up. 'If you don't restrain him, you're all in for it.'

The person dressed in black hurried between them and fell to their knees. 'Don't hurt him,' they begged. 'You promised you wouldn't hurt him. You said if I went, you wouldn't hurt him. I went, and now you're threatening to hurt him.'

Mutters started to build up, whispers, the windfalls of rumours that wouldn't die down for weeks. Nick stepped closer, gesturing to the person on their knees.

'This is what happens when young people think they know better than their Elders.' Nick grabbed the person by the throat, turned them around, and slid an ugly knife beneath their jaw.

Randi's jaw.

Caleb whimpered, and Felan remained the barrier that separated them.

Randi couldn't keep his eyes off Caleb, an intense longing that hurt Felan's wounded soul.

'After what happened with Harvey, I thought this wouldn't happen again!' Nick pulled Randi's head back, forcing his face up to the sky. 'Our young friend here has been supplying the Protrudes with information.'

Randi paled.

Caleb fell limp in Felan's arms.

'No,' Blaez whispered.

'And like last time, he must pay for his disloyalty,' Nick snarled.

Murmurs of agreement rippled around the clearing. Felan looked from one Wolf to another; they all shared a wildness, a wildness he for one did not possess. A wildness he *hoped* he didn't possess. A wildness he hoped he...

'No! He wouldn't do this – I know he wouldn't! Please, no!' Caleb begged.

Nick had to be lying. Nick had said he sent Randi to the Protrudes... but what if Randi went behind Nick's back? What if he took that opportunity to betray them? What if Randi wanted them all dead?

Felan glanced around the clearing, at the people he considered friends.

Who could Felan trust, really?

Who else was lying?

Felan must have loosened his grip for a second because, before he knew it, Caleb sprinted away, and managed to slip past Accalia and Blaez, the pair of them in shock. Felan ran after him and tackled him to the floor some distance away. 'Stay down,' Felan hissed. Caleb continued to fight. 'Stop it!'

Felan pleaded in his mind for Caleb to stop. Nick was planning something, and they were all in the middle of it.

'Keep. Him. Restrained!' Nick roared.

Other voices joined the roar. Birds perched atop the trees took flight. Felan didn't blame them.

If he could, he'd run too.

'Caleb, stop. Please stop.'

At the sound of Randi's choked up voice, Caleb stopped completely, all the fight draining away from him. Felan climbed off him, but kept his hands in place just in case. Caleb looked at Randi with the most heartbroken eyes Felan had ever seen. Randi couldn't even wipe away his own tears, so the boy looked up, focusing on something high in the sky. Felan looked up fleetingly too, wondered what Randi found so captivating, so intriguing, so calming. He saw nothing but black clouds.

'No, no, no I'm dreaming,' Caleb muttered. 'He wouldn't do this. No, no, no...'

The knife pierced Randi's chest, and the pieces inside Felan shattered to dust.

The colour drained from the boy's face like water from a bath. Randi choked. Caleb screamed. Over and over again. Inhumane screams. Randi coughed once, then twice.

The guilt ate Felan, chewed him up, and spat him back out. If he'd managed to convince Randi to come back...

Randi's gaze managed to find Caleb, heard the screams, *saw them*.

Felan pulled Caleb closer – Caleb grabbed him hard, hard enough to leave bruises, and Felan didn't have the heart to pry him off. He deserved it, didn't he?

Nick withdrew his hand. Randi fell face down to the floor, twitching, choking.

Everyone left the clearing, until it was just the five of them, Felan's first friends.

Caleb collapsed to his knees beside Randi and turned him onto his side. 'We can save him!' he said, glancing hopefully to Accalia. 'We all have first aid kits – we can still save him!' He started to laugh, and Felan forced himself to look away. He blinked away the tears as he stared at the floor. 'Guys?' Caleb said.

No answer.

'Cal,' Randi whispered.

Caleb didn't look down. He kept his hopeful gaze on Accalia. 'Accalia?' he said. When she did nothing, he looked to Blaez. When *she* did nothing, he looked to Felan. 'Why is no one doing anything?' he cried.

'It's over, Caleb,' Accalia said, finally.

Felan crawled to his feet. Randi wheezed and writhed in Caleb's lap.

'Cal,' Randi said again. 'Cal, please...'

He turned on his side and heaved. Crimson coated his lips when he turned back.

'I'm sorry, Caleb,' Randi choked. He lifted a trembling hand to Caleb's cheek and rubbed his thumb along his jaw. Caleb let out a sob, covering the hand with his own. He kissed his boyfriend's forehead.

'It's okay,' he whispered. 'You're okay. You're okay.'

'I couldn't...'

'You're gonna be okay, Randi.'

To his credit, Randi tried to smile; it turned very quickly into a groan and a grimace. 'I tried...' He broke off in another cough.

Randi's hand fell from Caleb's face and hung limp at his side. 'I tried,' he repeated. His chest heaved in agony.

Caleb held Randi's face with both hands and rubbed away the tears that leaked out of the corners of his eyes. 'I know,' Caleb said. 'You tried so hard.'

Randi's eyelids fluttered shut. 'I love you,' he mumbled. His chest continued to heave.

Caleb continued to dry Randi's tears, and pressed a bittersweet kiss to his bloodstained lips. 'I love you too. You're gonna be okay,' he soothed. 'Just go to sleep. Just go to sleep.'

Blaez cuddled into Felan's side, her cheeks wet from crying. He pulled her closer. He *needed* her closer. He needed to know she was alive and breathing, anything to take his mind off...

She hid her face in his shoulder when Randi's eyes shut for the last time. Felan refused to let his tears fall. He didn't deserve the tears. He didn't deserve to feel sorrow.

No.

He deserved the guilt that sent his head spinning.

Chapter 29: Interchangeable

'He shouldn't be allowed out on these sorts of jobs any more. He's useless, and he nearly got us all killed. He should just stick to drop-offs and leave it at that,' Convel accused. 'And Blaez missed – again!'

Rory glared in their general direction. 'Is that so?'

Felan wiped sweat from his hands, staring in disbelief. Accalia and Caleb had only just walked away with Randi's body a minute ago. They were doing this now? So soon after...

'Listen – all that matters is that we got what we went for, and we all got back.' Blaez tried to placate him, her eyes red from crying.

Felan didn't like it when Blaez cried.

'Silence!'

She didn't try again. Felan didn't even bother. No one listened to him anyway.

'Blaez. Come here,' Rory instructed.

She went without complaint.

'You need to work on your aim,' he said. The way he spoke, like he was talking to a little kid, condescending, and about something as trivial as *this*?

Blaez, with her short stature and choppy hair, looked tiny in comparison. 'It got jammed! I swear it jammed when I pulled the trigger!' she exclaimed.

Felan didn't react – lie or not, Blaez sounded honest and truthful. He remembered her pulling the trigger, a guard falling to his death, her stopping; had it been an accident? Had she missed like always, but the guard tripped? Blaez wouldn't have killed him on purpose.

So far, it seemed Blaez was the only person he could trust. If he couldn't trust Blaez, then what was the point?

Rory backhanded her so hard she stumbled and hit the floor. Felan growled, angry at himself for not stepping between them and taking the hit instead, but he knew if he went over, she'd get worse.

'Someone might think you didn't want to help us any more, Blaez.'

His friend recovered quicker than he'd ever seen her do – or anyone, for that matter. 'No, yes... of course I do! It's the least I can do – you took me in and gave me a home. Of course I want this!'

Rory gave her one last, deploring look. 'Remember that next time.'

Felan seethed, but then Blaez did something that shocked him. When Rory finally turned away from her, Convel grinning widely, she looked to Felan and winked. She winked. She bloody winked at him from the floor.

Somehow, he found the strength to smile back. Maybe there was hope for them out there, somewhere. It was dashed away when Rory cast a withering glance in his direction.

'As for you, Felan,' Rory spat, red-faced. 'Go and see Nick. I daresay you're overdue for a punishment.'

Felan walked with his head held high.

Blaez would be okay, he didn't need to check on her. She could look after herself better than he could ever attempt to. Besides, if he went over to help her up, she'd scowl and slap his hands away.

He entered the Warehouse, and the sounds of the others training down the corridors reminded him of what he should be doing to better himself, of how well he should be doing. He'd been at the Warehouse for months, yet he was on his way to Nick's for another telling-off. Christ, he wasn't a child – he could make his own decisions.

Apparently, his decision-making wasn't up to scratch.

What would his mother say if she could see him now, if she could see exactly what he was capable of, if she could see exactly what he'd become?

His friend had died because Felan hadn't tried hard enough.

That single thought turned his face into stone as he knocked. For the first time ever, Nick held the door open for him.

'Did you enjoy the show?'

Felan tried to think of a time where something hadn't hurt. He came up empty. No matter what he did, he ended up hurt, or hurting someone else.

Nick stalked towards him, knife in hand – still covered in blood. Randi's blood. He flicked the knife in Felan's direction and droplets of cold blood hit him on the face. His stomach twisted horribly. Randi's blood.

'You've lied to us, Felan,' Nick said. 'You've lied to me. I thought we agreed that you would help me, but instead you've disobeyed me. Again. Befriending a Protrude, nearly getting your group killed because of your inaction earlier today, nearly getting caught – need I continue?'

The boy stared at the floor. It was pointless trying to fight.

'And Randi, well... you ruined that one for us.'

It still *hurt*. The way everyone acted like nothing happened, like one of their own didn't just get *murdered* moments before, how everyone was *okay* about it.

'I think you'll find that one was you,' Felan said quietly. 'You sent him out there.'

A pause. 'Yes. I sent him out there to retrieve information about the Protrudes. Numbers, figures, names... anything. He failed.'

'And how did that justify you killing him? He was a child!' He bravely met Nick's gaze – and recoiled almost instantly.

'A damned disobedient one at that,' Nick spat. 'He refused me. He knew exactly where they were – he was with them for months! I killed him for his disobedience. And now, what am I going to do with you, hmm?'

He circled Felan with silent footsteps. A sudden slash on his arm made him gasp. 'You get involved, far too involved, in matters that don't concern you.' The knife slashed his cheek. 'You got far too involved about Randi.' A slash to his waist. 'Far too involved in Harvey.' A slash to his palm.

Felan didn't utter a single sound.

'Before I saved you, Harvey was willing to do anything for me. I'd instruct, and he'd do it – no questions asked. Ever since you, he stopped. He stopped obeying me, for you,' Nick said. He was hidden in the shadows and Felan couldn't find him. 'He messed up. He gave away too much information to Maddison. He was a double agent – he worked for both of us, and in the end, he was loyal to *her*.'

Felan's mind whirled – Harvey was a double agent? Harvey had stopped, for him? He bit his lip hard at a particularly slow and long slash to his thigh.

'He was loyal to you, and because of you, I lost any means of gathering information. Again.'

The knife hit the floor, startling the boy, as he'd been expecting another slash. Instead, Nick punched him in the face. He stumbled, and another punch to the chest sent him reeling. Coughing, Felan caught himself, forcing himself to stand on weak legs.

Would it always be like this?

Nick clamped his hand down hard on Felan's injured forearm, dug his fingers in so deep the ruby-red bandages came loose.

Felan blocked out the pain. He couldn't stop thinking about Harvey. He'd worked for both gangs?

Why would Harvey choose Maddison over him?

'They're both dead, Felan, and it's all your fault,' Nick whispered.

'She's gone, Felan. She's gone, and it's all your fault.'

The knife poked at his throat, and he waited for the final cut. It wasn't anything less than he deserved.

Quiet laughter trickled into his ear. 'I'm not going to kill you. It seems punishment has no effect on you.'

Felan said nothing.

'It's not your fault, I suppose, given the way you were raised – but I would like to be respected.' Nick held the knife in front of Felan's nose; his and Randi's blood shimmered on the blade. 'By taking out the threats, I'm trying to keep you safe. Do you understand that?'

Felan couldn't stop staring at the blood that flickered in front of him.

'You're a danger to yourself, Felan, and worse, to the people around you.'

Felan shuddered. He thought that about himself already, but it hurt more coming from someone else.

'A different method, yes. That'll keep you in line. Arm out, Felan.'

He raised his arm. It shook tremendously.

'There's no need to be afraid – I'm going to help you,' Nick said, and before Felan realised it, Nick was rebandaging his arm for him, gently and softly, with clean bandages. Where had they come from? 'See. I'm helping you – so why is it so hard to help me?'

Felan's father had never helped him like this. His father never bandaged the wounds he inflicted. He'd left Felan, a child, to heal his own wounds, to look after himself, to lick himself clean like an animal. Felan remembered locking himself in the bathroom at ten years old, holding a towel to his arm and begging it to stop bleeding.

He'd been late for school that day, and no one cared about the reason why.

Nick's ministrations didn't hurt one bit, and he thought that maybe this was the way it should have been.

'We're going to make an agreement here.'

'Okay.'

'If you slip up again, do *anything* wrong, Blaez gets the punishment.'

Panic seized him with icy hands. 'No! No, you can't hurt her – please don't hurt her!' He latched onto Nick; his small hands clamped down on Nick's arms to get him to listen, to pay attention, to *understand*. He couldn't live with himself if something happened to Blaez – not when he could have done something to prevent it. 'Please,' Felan begged. 'Please. I'll do anything.'

He couldn't watch another friend die because of him. He couldn't.

Nick cupped his cheek with one burly hand. 'Fine. I won't hurt her – but you have to help me, Felan,' Nick said. 'All you need to do is help. That's all I'm asking of you. Doesn't that seem so simple?'

It did and it didn't. A blow to his temple sent Felan reeling.

***

When he came to, Felan thought he was back at his father's flat. His father knocked him out all the time, and Felan found himself waking up covered in blood in random spots around the flat most days.

It wasn't until he saw the empty bottles in the dark that he remembered where he was.

He couldn't tell the time of day, as Nick's room let in little light, and the man himself was nowhere to be seen. Sitting up, his head throbbed. He made to stand, both hands on the wall to support himself. Unsteady knees gave out beneath him, and he hit the floor with a cry of pain.

He remembered the punishment. He ran his finger over the bandage that covered his forearm; smooth, caring, and gentle.

A promise.

An *agreement.*

Felan hauled himself to his knees and slumped against the wall, gasping through tears. He didn't know why he was so surprised at his treatment – violence was all he knew when it came to the people meant to care for him.

He didn't deserve to cry; that was for everyone else. He'd got his mother killed. He'd got Harvey killed. He'd got Randi killed. He'd shot Tristan. Now he was getting Blaez...

'Stop crying,' he muttered to himself. He didn't have the right. Too many people. Too many people hurt because of him.

It was his fault.

It was always his fault.

Chapter 30: Exposure

'Oh.'

Someone had blatantly trampled through it, the fungi mutilated and crushed into the dirt, and their fairy ring was no more.

Felan wasn't surprised. Nothing good in his life lasted forever. Nothing was safe when he was in the vicinity.

He fell to his knees, tears stinging his eyes, and brushed the broken circle with his fingers. Felan dared the evil spirits to cast even more misery on his life. He dared the creatures to take something else. He dared them to curse him.

Blaez found him later, shivering in the dirt. She helped him inside, rubbing a hand up and down his arm.

'It's broken,' he whispered.

'I know.'

It scared Felan how easily the others moved on.

It scared him more that it was expected of him too.

***

He tried to avoid Caleb, but the endless meetings, the endless paired work, made that impossible. Nick told him he had to overcome the guilt. Nick told him he had to ignore it and carry on.

What better way to do that than to look guilt in the eye?

'We're together on drop-offs today,' Blaez said, interrupting his train of thought.

'Wait, really?'

'Yeah! But I'll meet you outside. I've forgotten something in my room,' she said.

'Okay!' he shouted after her.

He was surprised. After what happened last time, it was rare for Nick to let them out together. Not that he was complaining

– drops-offs with Blaez were always fun, and it meant he could keep an eye on her too.

'Right – armoury. Satchel,' he said to himself. He walked through the door and froze. Caleb sat in the far corner, huddled against a stack of boxes, twiddling a knife between his fingers.

Felan tried to get his stuff quietly – it was best to just pretend he hadn't seen him – but as he turned to leave, he walked smack bang into the table, sending a whole tray of bullets flying. He cursed and scrambled around on his hands and knees to pick them all up.

Caleb barely reacted. 'Oh, it's you,' Caleb said.

'Who did you think it was?' Felan asked, flustered.

Caleb looked up. 'I've just escaped from Accalia,' he said.

'Ah.' The girl hadn't left Caleb alone since... well. Felan shook his head and wandered over, awkwardly standing next to him. He rubbed the back of his neck, still red in the face.

'You can sit down,' Caleb muttered.

Felan set the satchel down beside him and crossed his legs. 'What are you doing down here?'

'Keeping out of everyone's way.'

'Why?'

Caleb scoffed. 'Why do you think, Felan?'

'Oh.'

'Yeah, oh.'

No matter how hard he tried to ignore the guilt, it wouldn't go away. It stayed, stuck to him like superglue, an anchor to a barely seaworthy boat. Someone he knew had *died*. He stared at the knife in his friend's hands – they were shaking so much, and Felan couldn't think of a single thing to say to make it better.

'Why does everyone I love keep secrets from me?'

Felan asked a very similar question of himself every day: *why does everyone I love leave me behind?* He swallowed, wishing beyond anything that he could provide a solution, hating himself for not being able to ease his friend's turmoil. 'I can't answer that.'

'Harvey lied to us. Randi lied to us. Lied to me. *Me.*' Caleb threw the knife so hard it stuck fast into the wall opposite. 'I thought we knew each other – we've been together since we were twelve, and we told each other everything. Why would he do something like that?'

'Maybe he thought he was doing the right thing,' Felan said. Caleb stayed quiet. His whole body shook. 'Hey, Caleb,' Felan said, resting a hand on his friend's arm. 'He loved you.'

Caleb gave him a look devoid of any emotion and shook him off. 'I don't know any more.'

'He did. He really did care about you,' Felan insisted. The look on Randi's face that day...

Caleb sniffed. His eyes sparkled with unshed tears. 'Yeah? Then why did he betray me?'

Felan's heart broke all over again. 'I have no answer for you,' he whispered. This was why. This was why he tried to avoid Caleb.

What kind of friend did that make him?

***

He sprinted after Blaez into the forest, racing her along the paths and through the dying bushes. They did this sometimes in their free time. They'd fill a water bottle, pick a direction, and run.

Those days were Felan's favourites.

They raced for miles, satchels slapping against their sides. Blaez tripped on a root, and Felan zipped by, taking the lead while she caught her balance. She was more chivalrous than him, because when he tripped and actually hit the floor, she stopped to help him to his feet.

'Are you okay?' she asked, giggling.

'Yeah, fine,' he said, dusting himself off.

'You dork.'

'Thanks, Blaez.' They took the rest of the journey at a walk. 'How many drop-offs have we got to do?'

'Thirty.'

'Damn.'

'Most of them are close by, so it's not so bad – and really, it's fifteen each.'

'Good point,' he said. 'Ouch!' He turned to Blaez, pointing at the tree beside him. 'Did you see that? The tree attacked me!'

'How does one walk directly into a tree?'

'With great skill and amazing sight.'

'Yeah, you're amazing alright.'

'What's that supposed to mean?'

She grinned at him. 'Never you mind.'

'So, I was wondering – I know we have all those drop-offs, but do we have time to go somewhere today?'

Blaez swiped a branch out of her face and held it out of the way for Felan. He muttered his thanks. 'How do you mean?'

'There's something I sort of need to show you.'

'We've got two drop-offs for tonight at five thirty – we have to be back in the city by then,' she said. She reached into her satchel for her phone. 'There, I've sent them to you.'

'I can make that work,' Felan said. 'If we can get the others done quick, we can go straight there.'

This was the test, he thought. This was the test to see if he could trust Blaez as much as he hoped he could. He was sure he could.

But still.

They reached a fork in the path. Felan was sad to part ways so soon. It felt like he hadn't seen Blaez for ages.

'Agreed.' She bumped his fist with hers. 'See you in a few hours.'

'Go careful,' he said.

She flashed him a smile. 'Always.'

***

'This is a dead end, Felan – where are we?'

Being there brought back memories from last time. He pointed to the top of the wall. 'I fell from there,' he said.

'What the hell were you doing up there – and all the way out here?' she asked, staring at him suspiciously. 'Felan, we're not even in Guadalupe any more. This is further beyond the Fringe than I've ever been!'

He'd been expecting the anger. 'I chased someone here,' he said. The wall looked exactly the same, but much had changed in him since he'd last looked upon it. So much had *gone*.

'Who?'

'Go see for yourself.'

She looked at him in incredulity. 'You seriously want me to climb up that?'

'Blaez.'

She muttered something unintelligible, probably something sarcastic about how she hated him, as she pulled herself up the wall. He followed close behind, fully expecting a punch to the head when she saw what was on the other side. Although they were friends, he had no idea how she'd react. He had no idea what she'd say. He had no idea how he was going to keep her safe, not if he kept secrets from her.

Blaez dropped low when she saw what was on the other side.

'Felan, what is this?'

'This, Blaez, is the Protrudes' base.'

He stared for a moment at the vast number of people that ambled around the clearing before he realised exactly what he was seeing.

Guard duty.

The Protrudes were on guard duty.

He wondered just how many of them had been stolen from their homes.

'How on Earth…? How long have you known?'

Felan looked at his hands. 'I never told you the full story – it was Randi. The person I followed. I found him in the city, but he ran from me. He led me here. He kept telling me to leave, but I kept chasing him.'

'Felan…'

'I knew where he was, but I said nothing. Not even to you. And what you did know, I made you keep it quiet,' he said. 'Now look what's happened. I knew, and I said nothing. Did nothing.' He saw Caleb's face, heartbreak, and tears, and anger, and he clamped his jaw shut.

'I thought for sure Nick had made a mistake,' Blaez whispered.

Felan screwed his hands so tightly that he thought he might've broken a finger or two. 'Nick told me he sent Randi here to gather information. Nick lied to everyone.'

She grabbed his shoulder a bit too hard. 'What are you talking about?'

'Randi was here on Nick's orders, and so was Harvey.'

She was going to hit him. He knew it. She was going to hit him and send him tumbling back down. 'It's my fault they're dead,' he said. 'It's all my fault.'

'Felan...'

He didn't understand what she was waiting for.

'No,' he begged his friend. 'Don't even try to say it's okay. He's dead because of me. They're both dead because of me. It's all my fault.'

Why wouldn't she just hit him already? Hadn't he done enough to warrant a punishment?

Blaez's hands were soft, softer than he remembered them being, and her thumbs stroked his cheeks. He kept his eyes firmly shut. His dad had done that before sometimes, acted all worried and promised to help, though when Felan did reach a hand out, his dad would slap him away with a laugh; it made the rejection burn more than it usually did.

Blaez wasn't doing any of that.

She was so close he could *see* the tears in her eyes, how they shimmered and sparkled like stars in the night sky. She wasn't punishing him; she was comforting him.

'It wasn't your fault, Felan,' she said. 'Either of them.'

He shook his head. 'I've ruined everything.'

She continued to stroke his cheeks with her thumbs, like his mother used to do when he cried. The gesture was safe, Felan knew. Blaez was *safe*. He lifted his gaze.

A single tear traced the lines of Blaez's face, and he watched it drip, drip, drip onto the fabric of her jumper. 'No, no. This wasn't you. They just... maybe they just made all the wrong choices.' He followed its trail with his finger. 'And we didn't?'

And for a moment, just one moment, Felan imagined a different world, a world full of colour, and life, and no darkness. He saw himself running through a field of grass, hand in hand with her, where the tinkling sound of her laughter echoed. He saw himself growing up somewhere else, somewhere away from the broken grandeur of the city, somewhere quiet, somewhere safe; somewhere his mum could have lived, where he could have lived, and maybe Blaez would have been there too.

They would be free. Free... what a feeling that must be. What a feeling it must be to feel the open air, like a bird, flying with no limits, uncaged. Not locked away with the key lost in the rubbish.

'I like to think we didn't,' she finally said. 'I can't help but think Randi found something here – something that was worth his betrayal.'

Tristan. They had to have bumped into each other, being so close in proximity. He wondered if Tristan had offered Randi help too.

Blaez brushed his cheek once more before letting go, settling herself beside him. 'When I was young, I always liked the idea of saving lives. That idea never came to be. Instead, I ended up here,' she said. 'I've been taught to defend myself and the people I love – I guess it's similar, but it's not the same. I still end up hurting people, and accidentally...' She broke off, and Felan watched the guard from the bank hit the floor, over and over again. It had been an accident. Nothing more.

From the wall, the Protrudes looked like bugs. They didn't look threatening in any way. 'Do you think we'll win?'

'No,' she said. 'But neither will they.'

Feeling brave, Felan stood up and took her hand. 'And what about us?'

She squeezed. 'We'll be alright. Keep our heads down, obey the orders. We'll be okay.'

Felan stroked his thumb over her knuckles. 'You know what I admire about you, Blaez?' he said. 'I admire your faith in everything.'

'You'll get nowhere without faith. It's what keeps me going. Now come on – we need to get back. We don't want to be late for the drop-offs.'

Chapter 31: Elapsed

Felan thought maybe it was Nick's idea of a sick joke, that the man purposefully chose his drop-off routes so he'd catch a glimpse of Oakley Church in the distance, atop a neat row of houses he used to walk by as a kid. The kids who lived there used to play football in the street, and they drew pictures on the pavement with broken pieces of chalk they found in the bins.

At seven years old, Felan walked by hand in hand with his mother.

At sixteen years old, Felan walked by with a satchel full of drugs.

And the church itself hadn't changed at all. The stone path to the door was clear, though a variety of weeds including dandelions grew in clumps along the edges, and the door itself stood white and bold. Weather-worn bricks festered with lichen and yellow mould from the base all the way to the slated roof. The slates themselves stood fast and didn't seem to be in any danger of collapsing. As he peered through the window on the door, neither did the nave or the chancel. Up and to the left, the bell turret shot into the sky like it always had. Felan had always thought blue was a strange colour for a bell turret, but each to their own.

Headstones littered the church grounds, and Felan averted his gaze more than once from the loving words of family members, knowing they weren't for him to read. Some of the graves had fresh flowers laid on top. Others sat barren and overgrown.

The stone path forked at the door. It continued on round to the right, but on the left, the stone path gave way to gravel and wound around the other side. Felan's shoes crunched on the gravel – making noise at a church always felt sacrilegious. Christ, these people were resting. They didn't need stupid kids coming and ruining what was supposed to be eternal peace.

Felan stopped in his tracks at the sight before him. He growled. A rage pounded away at his ribcage, begging to be let loose.

How dare they?

How dare they forget?

Felan stumbled over and collapsed to his knees.

How was he supposed to visit any more if he couldn't reach her grave? He stretched out a hand to touch the brambles that had grown since his last visit, but retracted it.

His hands shook as he texted Blaez the address, and they didn't still in the hour it took for her to arrive.

She approached from the side entrance, cautious and wary. He waved at her from across the way, and she picked her way through the gaps in the graves and the headstones.

'I got here as fast as I could,' she said, coming to a stop beside him. 'What are we doing here?'

Even an hour in silence hadn't diminished the rage he felt at seeing the state of his mother's grave. How could they let it get so... uncared for? Why did no one look after it?

If Felan only had his mother growing up, then who did his mother have to lean on?

Blaez kneeled beside him. She bumped his shoulder. 'What's going on?'

'My mother's buried here, in an unmarked grave.' He pointed to the bramble bush. 'She's under there, Blaez. She's somewhere in there.'

He'd only managed to visit a handful of times, but he'd always been able to recognise the grassy mound. With the bramble bush in place, he couldn't get within ten metres, let alone see it.

'Was she beautiful?'

'She was amazing in every way.' Felan traced a finger along one of the stems, wondering how the bush had grown so big so fast. 'But she was also sad, and lonely. She thought I didn't notice.'

He'd always noticed the faraway look in her eyes when she thought he wasn't looking, the frown on her face, and the sadness in her gaze. He'd give anything to have those images erased from his memory. Her smile was fading from his mind, and so was her laugh, her touch, and her words.

Felan didn't want to be alive on the day he forgot about her completely.

'At least you guys had each other,' Blaez said.

Not even his mother's siblings ever stopped by to mark her grave. They hadn't paid a penny towards the measly funeral service. No. They'd let strangers bury her, and they left her alone and forgotten, and hadn't stepped foot in Guadalupe again.

'I didn't want this for her, Blaez. She was supposed to be remembered.'

'She'll be remembered by you, always. And if you like, she can be remembered by me too.'

'Will you remember me?' he whispered softly.

Blaez froze. 'What are you talking about?'

'A few months ago, I checked the records in the library.' He ran a hand through his hair. 'I'm registered as dead, because they didn't find me, and there are so many other kids registered as missing or dead, and no one's doing a damn thing about it.'

The cops and the nurses and everyone else meant to save him had given up on him. If they'd done that to him, what had they done to the others?

'Maybe, if we ever get the chance, we can change that.' Blaez took his hand. 'My parents never looked for me and forgot about me within days. I doubt they'd even recognise me if they saw me in the street,' she said bitterly. 'I'm not on that list. I'll never be on that list.'

'You're...'

Felan cut himself off. He'd been about to say, *you're lucky*, but how was her family forgetting her lucky? Felan was only on that list because he'd run from the hospital. He suspected that if he'd run from his father's place, the cops would have been none the wiser.

'We're all going to be forgotten, in the end,' he said. 'No matter how we live our lives, the good or the bad, the history we leave behind... eventually it will all be forgotten and trodden into the dirt, and it'll be like we never existed.'

'Then we make sure they remember us. We start something that will live on forever. We start something that will enact change.'

'They forgot Mum, and they've already forgotten me. I don't want to end up in an unmarked hole in the ground because I can't afford my own headstone. I don't want that for myself, and it shouldn't be like that in the first place. No one deserves to be forgotten like that, like they were nothing.' Felan's mouth ran dry. 'My mum was everything to me, and this is what happened to her.'

'It wasn't your fault.'

He looked down in disgust, gesturing to himself. 'She loved me, Blaez, and look how I've used that love.' He killed people, he stole, and he sold drugs. He turned that love into violence.

Blaez threw her arms around his neck and buried her face in his shoulder. He cringed but hugged her back.

'Felan, you listen to me, okay?'

He nodded.

'You are one of the most loving people I've ever met. You do everything you can to protect the people you care about, and you don't stop. Ever. And no one has ever cared about me like you do. You wait for me to come home safely, and I love you for that.'

He should be ashamed of seeking comfort when he didn't deserve it. Not after what he'd done. 'It's not enough, Blaez. It's never been enough.'

'You are enough, Felan. You will always be enough. Do you understand that?'

Felan thought it best not to answer. He didn't like lying, so why lie to Blaez?

Like she could hear his thoughts, she pulled away and kissed his cheek. She sighed. 'I'm not forgetting you, Felan. I can promise you that.'

He really didn't deserve a friend like Blaez, and she deserved way better than him. His mother deserved a better son, and he deserved every blow his father gave him.

'My mum is buried beneath a city that thrives on corruption. She's buried beneath a city that drained away from her every good thing she had. And now...' Tears sprung to his eyes, unbidden, and dripped down his cheeks. He should be embarrassed about wetting Blaez's jumper. 'And now it's doing it to me too.'

It was a strange feeling, to feel everything at once. Felan could list off twenty different emotions, but not a single one corresponded to him. He felt far too calm for the situation at hand, and far too... distant. He hadn't been expecting to visit his mother's grave. He'd promised himself he would never show up empty-handed again, and, well... there went that promise.

He knew that, deep down, everything he did stemmed from anger: at his father, at his mother, at the cops, at the nurses, at the bullies from school, at the teachers, and the city itself.

At Felan.

But the anger was hidden beneath layers of thick skin, layers he'd spent years building up so nothing could break through.

Then Blaez came along, bless her heart. Her heart that had been broken too many times for such a kind person. He wished he could be more like Blaez.

An alert sounded on one of their phones, and Blaez was the first to pull away. 'I'm sorry, Felan, but we need to go.'

Felan stared at the bramble bush, the damned bramble bush that separated him from his mother. He wished that one day he could hack it to pieces.

'We can come back another time,' she said softly. 'Please, Felan.'

They left Oakley Church hand in hand, Felan stoic and cold, Blaez with remnants of mascara running down her face. The gate closed behind them, and Felan had a feeling, a feeling that churned in his gut, that he wouldn't be coming back to Oakley Church ever again.

Chapter 32: Volatile

'What do we do, Felan? We're late for the last drop-off.'

After their 'detour', as Blaez had so kindly put it earlier, they'd barely made the last few drop-offs on time; they were late. Really late. So late, in fact, that darkness was falling before they were finished. Felan had been late to drop-offs before. It wasn't a particularly enjoyable experience, especially when the customer was hidden at the end of a dark alley threatening to knock his teeth out if he took too long to retrieve the goods.

But he had a plan for the last one. 'Just go with it.'

'What do you mean, *go with it*? Go with what?'

He put a hand on her shoulder to stop her from walking, pulled her into an alley, and pointed to a rather large man waiting on the corner of the street. 'You see that man? That's Bruce. He's a rough customer. You stay here, out of sight. Don't make a sound.'

'I'll come...'

'No.'

Throwing her hands in the air, Blaez backed up and leaned against the wall, out of sight. Felan continued onwards and crept out onto the street. He swallowed before he spoke, and hoped he didn't sound too scared. 'You're late!' He came to a stop in front of Bruce, far too close for Felan's liking, but he tried not to show it.

Bruce cracked his knuckles. 'No, I'm not – we agreed five thirty.'

'And I amended it to five,' Felan said quickly.

'I didn't get no text!'

'That's not my problem.' His heart thudded beneath his ribcage. 'Now either you pay double, for keeping me waiting, or you walk away empty-handed.'

A rogue hand shot out and pinned Felan to the wall – his feet couldn't touch the ground. 'Who do you think you are, kid?' Bruce's fist was ready to fly.

Felan ignored the way the hand clenched around his windpipe. 'The only thing standing in the way of you and your next high,' he spat.

'Why you little...' Bruce punched him hard, so hard Felan's head slammed into the wall, again and again. Black tinted his vision for a few seconds and, still dazed, Felan smiled toothily at Bruce. He felt blood drip down his chin.

'How much do you want it, huh? Because, if you don't decide in five seconds, I'm leaving. I don't have time to hang around.' Felan spat blood in Bruce's face and slipped a hand into his satchel.

After seeing the state of his mother's grave, Felan wasn't in the mood to hold back.

Bruce laughed with furious eyes. 'And how do you plan on getting away? You're just a good-for-nothing street rat.'

Felan pressed the tip of his knife to the man's gut. 'I am more than a street rat.'

'Are you trying to scare me?'

His head slammed into the wall again. The hand around his neck squeezed tighter. Felan jabbed the knife a little deeper, aware that the layers around his heart were tearing at the seams, ready to collapse all around him.

'Fine,' Bruce griped. Warm spittle sprayed everywhere and Felan fought the urge to gag. 'Take your filthy money.'

Bruce rounded the corner, a hurry in his step. Blaez appeared from the shadows a moment later. Felan tilted dangerously as a bout of dizziness hit him, and the street danced sickeningly while he climbed to his feet.

'He hit you.'

He blinked away the lingering vertigo. 'It worked, didn't it?'

She eyed the wad of cash in his hand, the knife in the other. 'I see that.' If she saw the blood that stained the blade, she didn't react.

'We didn't miss a drop-off,' he said.

He wouldn't admit it, but opening up to Blaez had rattled him more than he'd thought it would. She was the first person he'd ever disclosed his past to, and it was terrifying to be seen as vulnerable. He wanted nothing more than to get back to the Warehouse and lie on his bed in the dark.

Alone.

Recharge.

Start again in the morning.

'Bruce's punch didn't miss, that's for sure,' she said. She pulled a clean cloth from her satchel and wiped his face free of spittle and blood. 'That's already bruising.'

Shying away, he sheathed his knife and tossed the cash in his satchel. 'Come on,' he said.

Red stained the cloth in her hand. She gave him an odd look. 'Are we heading back?'

'Yeah.'

'Fine, but at least let me sort your face out first – it's still bleeding!'

'I've had worse.'

'Why are you being so stubborn?'

'Blaez, it's nothing,' he reassured her, 'now let's go.'

Before they could leave the alley, Blaez shot a hand out to grab him. 'Wait!' She tossed the cloth in a dustbin, took a few hesitant steps forward, and peered over his shoulder at the street. 'Let's go back to the Warehouse another way.'

'This way's quicker,' he said.

'Felan... this is the Slum.'

He'd heard about this street long before he joined the Wolves. He'd heard stories from his mother, and in more detail from the man who raised him. He had nightmares for weeks, thanks to the way the stories were told. The Slum teemed with drunkards and druggies, and was notorious for its drug dens, and for drop-offs. For whatever reason, he hadn't had the pleasure of visiting yet. Until now. But whatever. If it was the quickest way back to the Warehouse, he'd be damned if he took a longer route.

'So?'

She crossed her arms. 'I don't like this way.'

'Why not?'

Her body fizzled with electricity. 'Does there have to be a reason?' she snapped.

'If you've got something to say, say it.'

She glared at him, and he felt he should know the reason why. He felt he should know why she didn't want to go that particular way. But a part of him didn't give a crap. He just wanted to get back to the relative safety the Warehouse provided.

He just wanted to be left alone to wallow in his own pity.

'Whatever, Felan. Let's go. I wouldn't want to hurt your ego, your pride, whatever! Let's go.'

She stormed her way into the fray, chin in the air, tense. The shouts increased tenfold. There were more than a few people milling about in the street – one might think it was the early hours of the morning, given how many people were stumbling, and staggering, and hollering. Many of them were smoking. What, Felan didn't want to know.

He wondered what they'd think of two kids passing through the Slum; he thought the sight of parachuting rainbow unicorns might surprise them less.

Blaez stuttered to a stop. She looked so... so... visible? Was that the right word? She looked so visible when she didn't want to be, like she would rather be anywhere else in the world.

'It's okay,' he said. 'Just grin and bear it.' He grabbed her wrist, momentarily surprised by her taut muscles, and tugged her along. She didn't struggle. 'See, not so hard.' He turned his head, grinning back at her.

She glared. 'I can't believe you.'

'You really are something else, Blaez.'

'I could say the same thing about you.'

She slowed, as they approached another group of people. They were more boisterous than the last, the men all over the girls, despite the occasional protest. Smoke spiralled into the darkening sky. The lights outside the clubs pulsed and flickered.

Blaez stumbled. 'Felan, stop.'

'Nope. The quicker we walk the quicker we'll get back.'

She squirmed in his grip. 'Let go.'

'It's fine – it's only for a moment.'

'I swear to God, you let me go right now!'

'Look, we're nearly there!' he called, pointing across the way. It was true. Past one more group of people and they were Warehouse bound.

Blaez tried to prise Felan's hand off. 'You're hurting me!'

Why couldn't she see that he wanted to get back to the Warehouse? What was her problem?

Just then, her palm landed across his cheek, a perfect slap, with enough force to send his head to the side. He released her, and she swept his legs out from beneath him. He lay flat on the floor, winded, and the ground dug uncomfortably into his back. She held him down with one black boot on his sternum.

He was shocked to see tears spilling down her cheeks.

'I don't believe you!' she shouted. 'I know you're hurting, but that's no reason to treat me like this!'

'Treating you like what? I'm trying to get back to the Warehouse!'

'Who was I raised by, Felan?' she yelled. She forced her boot down harder. Her lips wobbled; eyes angry. 'You should've realised. And just because you're... you're upset, about opening up to me, it doesn't mean you get to treat me like dirt! You don't get to push my feelings aside because you don't understand your own. You don't get to ignore my needs because you're trying to shut everything out!'

Felan deserved every ounce of pain that came his way, and if he could, he would have taken the pain he'd inflicted on Blaez and forced it upon himself tenfold.

'Blaez... I'm so sorry. I – I wasn't thinking...'

'You never do!'

Her face drained of colour, and she crumpled before him. She hunched over, dug her boot deeper, and Felan let her. He let her bow her head, let her tears fall. He really thought she was going to break down.

'I'm sorry,' he said.

The words didn't feel like enough. He didn't think there was anything he could say to make up for his behaviour, for betraying her like he had.

He felt he'd be atoning for his mistakes for the rest of his life.

Somehow, she didn't break down. Felan thought she must have a stronger leash on her emotions than he did on his own, because she got a hold of herself, took a deep breath, and stared at Felan with the most vulnerable face he'd ever seen. A bead of sweat dripped down her nose.

'They shouted; at me, most of the time. They threw things at me while I was…' She shook her head. 'Being here… I don't like it. I told you I didn't like it, and yet you dragged me along anyway. You hurt me anyway.'

He'd carved those lines into her forehead with his own hands.

Felan didn't deserve to cry. It was his fault Blaez was upset. He had no right to tears, but he had every right to the guilt that ate away at his insides.

'I'm so, so sorry.'

'Whatever.' He thought she was going to hit him again. Instead, she helped Felan to his feet and dusted off his clothes. 'I don't need your apologies, or your pity. I just need you to think, Felan. Think about the people around you. For your sake, and for theirs.'

'I swear it.'

'Good.'

'We'll go back the way we came – head to the Warehouse another way. The route's clear,' Felan observed.

'No point. We're here now. Might as well finish it.'

'Blaez…'

'Enough.' She held her hand out. 'Just walk with me.'

***

Felan snapped his head around when he heard the shout.

He saw the big guy first, the girl second, a girl that couldn't have been much older than Felan. The guy reached for her with beefy arms and unsteady feet.

She tried to dodge his advance. 'Leave me alone!'

The guy tugged on her cardigan. Tearing ensued.

'I bought that yesterday, arsehole!' she shouted. 'I'm not interested!'

He slammed a hand on her arm. She shoved it off and sent the guy it belonged to staggering away. He came right back. 'Woah there, chill out,' the guy slurred. 'I'm not gonna hurt you.'

Felan felt the hatred bubble inside him. His mother had kept some details of those stories from him. Maybe she'd thought she was protecting him, by hiding the harsh reality of the world.

Sometimes, Felan wished she'd been honest with him about the world from the start.

'Blaez,' Felan ground out.

She looked just as angry as he felt. Scrap that, she looked downright murderous; her eyebrows pinched together, a hawklike look in her eye. 'I know.'

They walked over hand in hand.

'Don't touch me,' the girl said.

The guy didn't leave. 'Come and have some fun.' He staggered around some more and caught himself on her shoulder. She shoved him off with a huff.

'No thanks,' she said.

Any sober man would have noted the tone of her voice and backed off.

'Someone as pretty as you shouldn't be out here all alone.'

'I'm with friends,' she said, glaring.

'I don't see any friends, girl,' the guy guffawed. 'Let me buy you a drink – it'll loosen you up a bit.' He fiddled with something in his pocket.

Felan growled, low, at the back of his throat.

'No.'

'You'll have more fun with me.'

'I don't I think I will.'

The guy coughed in her face. Felan wasn't sure who was more disgusted. 'Come and dance,' he slurred.

'No.'

Felan was close enough to hear the guy's next sentence: 'I'll show you a good time.'

'I seriously doubt that.'

The guy grabbed her wrist. 'Come on, love. We'll have fun!'

The girl punched the drunkard in the face. He flailed around and tore the cardigan clean from her body, revealing more skin. He pulled her to him, fingers clenched over her bare arms, his lips much too close to her ear. 'I like the feisty ones.'

'Let me go!' she screeched.

'Be still!' He shoved her so hard she crashed into a dustbin before slamming into the floor.

He blinked.

Felan didn't remember moving.

He blinked.

He was next to the guy.

He blinked.

The guy was on the floor, amidst a mess of broken glass and rubbish.

He blinked.

'What part of *no* did you not understand?' Felan roared. He kicked glass shards at the drunkard on the floor. No one batted an eyelid.

Felan crouched down beside the girl, who looked at him warily. 'I apologise. I had no intention of hurting you... only that scumbag behind me.'

The girl nodded. She rubbed her hands over her bare arms. The vest she wore barely covered anything.

'I don't like bullies,' he carried on. 'You looked like you could use some help.'

Blaez handed the girl her torn cardigan back. 'I'm sorry we didn't intervene earlier – this might not be so torn up if we had,' she said.

'You've done plenty,' the girl said softly. 'Thank you.'

A buzz from Felan's satchel caught his attention. He cursed, pulling out his phone. It couldn't be another drop-off because they had nothing left to sell, so who...?

Just a meeting, it seemed, as he scanned the text from Accalia, though it was a meeting they'd most definitely be late for.

They were hours away from the Warehouse, and soon it would be completely dark.

And his face ached, although in the grand scheme of things it wasn't that big a deal. The place where had Bruce hit him wasn't bleeding any more, though he traced over the area and found two cuts on his cheek. That arsehole was probably wearing a ring or something. His skin was tender, and bruising, but that was nothing new. Always a new bruise, always a new injury.

His skin had always been, and always would be, marred.

He also didn't want to get on Blaez's bad side again.

Felan shoved his phone back into his satchel after thumbing out a reply to Accalia. 'Blaez...'

'The frown looks cute on you,' the girl said to Blaez.

Felan flickered his gaze between Blaez and the girl with a small smile. She slipped something inside Blaez's hand, gave it a squeeze, and let go. Blaez blushed horribly. He almost wanted to poke fun.

'Thank you both – for everything. Catch you later!'

The girl disappeared inside a club, wrapped, Felan couldn't help but notice, in Blaez's favourite jacket. He nudged Blaez's shoulder. 'Come on. They're expecting us back.' She looked at the club anxiously. 'We've done all we can for her.'

They made no effort to run. He gulped in the cold air and drank in the darkness. Blaez was quiet beside him. He watched her, the little lingering smile on her face, a smile he'd never seen before. She uncurled her hand and revealed a slip of paper. Blaez read the numbers with the softest eyes he'd ever seen her wear.

'Are you going to see her again?'

The smile fell and she ripped the paper to shreds. 'No.' A gust of wind carried them away. 'It's not fair on her,' she said.

Felan slung an arm around her shoulders. Somehow, they were fine. One minute they were at each other's throats, and the next, they thought the world of each other. He sighed. What were friends for, hey? She leaned into his side as they walked, but clearly thought better of it, because not even a second later she pushed him away, tense.

'We should never have made that detour,' he said. Blaez didn't agree, but she didn't disagree either.

'I'm sorry,' he said. 'I just thought you deserved to know the truth. About everything. And by coming back the way we did... I put us both in jeopardy.'

They both had drunkards for parents. Felan should have known better.

'I'm sorry,' he said.

Blaez held a finger to his lips. He shut up right away. She turned her head and stood on her tiptoes. Felan shivered involuntarily at the feeling of her warm breath on his neck.

'Felan... I think there's someone following us.'

Chapter 33: Hunting

'Got them,' Felan said.

The them in question? A Protrude who, from what Felan could guess, had been following them for a while. They wore black clothes, and if he and Blaez hadn't been aware of the Protrude's movements, they would have missed them loitering in the shadows.

'What're they doing?' Blaez asked, pretending to fix the collar of Felan's shirt.

Felan shrugged, squinting through the darkness. 'On their phone, I think. Should we get closer?'

As the words left Felan's mouth, the Protrude looked up, saw Felan watching, and fled down the street.

'Damn – they saw me watching.'

Blaez grabbed his hand and ran. 'Quick! Let's see where they lead us!'

They unapologetically pushed past the drunken people on the streets and forced themselves through the clouds of swirling smoke barely visible in the dark. He recognised the street they ran down, and he knew what was at the end of it. Blaez, he noticed, realised too.

Just how much longer were the Protrudes going to follow them?

'We can't let them get over the wall!' Felan said.

Without warning, Blaez zipped left, down another alley, and the dark swallowed her whole.

The Protrude stopped running. Felan slowed to a walk and advanced, knife in hand. He wasn't taking any chances.

'You're cornered,' Felan called out. The touch of his knife comforted him. He hated alleys, and the dark, yet his life seemed to revolve around them. 'You've got nowhere to go.'

'You shouldn't have followed me here,' the Protrude said. Felan stiffened. He recognised that voice. He associated that voice with the dark. 'You're on our territory now.' The man turned. 'You made a big mistake coming here.'

Felan got a good look at his face. His chest stuttered. 'You?' The man grinned. 'Miss me?'

'Why were you following us?' Felan demanded.

He hoped Blaez knew what she was doing. Where was she?

'You might as well come with me,' the man said, removing a rather large knife from his belt.

Glancing around, Felan stepped back, slowly. He'd been in this exact scenario once before, a while back, and he wasn't at all keen to repeat it. 'No thanks.'

'Where's your little girlfriend? Did she get scared and run off?' he cooed.

Felan kept his focus on the knife in the man's hand. 'She's not my girlfriend.'

'You're not brave, kid.' The man smirked. 'I know deep down you're pissing yourself.'

He cringed. 'I wouldn't go that far.' He let the man get closer. Accalia's voice rang through his head, loud and clear. *Get them close, then surprise them.*

The man pointed his knife at Felan's face. 'Ran into some trouble, did you?'

'What does Maddison want with us?' Felan countered.

The man leered closer. 'You'll find out soon enough, I'm sure.' He reached out to grab Felan, who ducked and backed away some more. The man followed.

'Come on, stop playing.'

Felan stopped.

'I see you're learning. Good.'

He flicked his gaze into the darkness. He smirked back. 'Not in the slightest.'

There was a loud *thunk*, and the man collapsed to the ground. Blaez materialised from a passageway, a brick in hand. She tossed said brick away and nudged the Protrude with her boot.

'Where were you?' Felan panted, hands on his knees.

'Improvising.' She glared at the unconscious body. 'He'll hurt when he wakes up.'

'Good,' Felan said. 'He deserves it.'

'Even better, we've got a perfect cover story!'

'How so?'

'God, Felan, you really are slow sometimes,' she said, laughing. 'We can say we chased him and he led us to the Protrudes' base. We won't get in trouble for *withholding crucial information from the Elders*,' she air quoted, pulling a weird face.

'That's brilliant!'

She kicked some dust at the Protrude, her face twisting in disgust. 'Let's get going – we're late as it is.'

***

Blaez advocated for killing the Protrude on the spot. 'He's scum, Felan.'

Felan wanted the Protrude to feel the same fear he'd felt that night, at the prospect of being dragged off somewhere entirely new and potentially dangerous. Also, Felan thought, it might get Nick off his back for a while, even if it did mean condemning the Protrude to an unpleasant meeting. After hearing his thoughts, Blaez quickly agreed. They gagged and bound the man with bandages from their satchels, and when he awoke, he struggled.

When Blaez told the man what she wanted to do to him, the man gave in and started walking.

'Good – you're learning,' Felan said. 'How does it feel to be on the receiving end?'

The silence was answer enough and lingered all the way across the city to the Warehouse clearing.

'I'll get the door,' Blaez offered. She ran ahead a few steps and yanked it open.

Rory stood on the other side, ready to swing. Fury sparked on his face. 'And what time do you call this?'

'We've got something to show Nick.'

'You don't get to give orders, boy!' Rory shouted. Then he noticed the man. 'Get in before I change my mind!'

Felan led the Protrude into the Warehouse and into a darkened training room, where he promptly shoved the man forward. Blaez flicked the light on. 'What do we do with him now?' Felan met the Protrude's defiant glare. 'Nick can deal with him.' Triumph soared in his chest when the Protrude looked towards the door, horrified.

As if summoned, Nick stumbled through the door and fixed his gaze on Felan.

'You both missed a *very* important meeting,' he spat.

Felan seriously doubted that.

Blaez nudged just that little bit closer to him. 'We know where the Protrudes are,' she said.

Nick sneered. 'A likely story.'

Felan pulled Blaez aside. It left Nick with a clear view of the man on the floor, the man who looked just as frightened as Felan had that night. The night Nick saved his life.

Strong hands grabbed Felan by the collar. 'Explain.' Felan held his breath. He reeked of alcohol.

'He followed us,' Blaez said. 'We chased him, and he led us right to their place.'

Nick studied Felan for the longest time with those black eyes of his before letting him go. Felan reached up to sort his collar out. He wasn't weak. He wasn't.

'Where are today's takings?'

On autopilot, Felan dropped money into Nick's outstretched hands. Drug money. Felan looked away.

'How's our little agreement working out?'

'Fine,' Felan said quietly. Nick patted his shoulder and pressed some cash into his hand. His touch burned.

'Keep it up.'

Nick then took the cash from Blaez's hands, and Felan did his best to hide the trembles that wracked his body. He despised his fear of Nick, and more importantly, the anger at himself.

Nick circled the Protrude again, and again, silently watching him, a constant, menacing cycle. Felan thought he might've seen a stain on the Protrude's trousers. Each step made the Protrude flinch.

Felan blinked.

He couldn't watch this. He couldn't do this. He made to leave the room, but before he did, he looked back to Nick. 'The Fringe. On the east side,' he said, trying to remember how to breathe. 'That's where you'll find the rest of them.'

He wasn't dismissed, but he didn't think Nick would care. He'd done as he asked. He hadn't done a single thing wrong.

'What was he talking about? What agreement?' Blaez demanded, having caught up to him on the stairs.

Felan swallowed. He had to keep her safe. She surged ahead and blocked the stairs, hands on the banisters.

'What did you agree to? Answer me!'

'Can you do me a favour and leave me the hell alone?' he shouted.

Felan shoved her out of the way and stormed up the stairs. His bedroom door slammed shut. Why did she always have to pry?

His thoughts shifted to the Protrude downstairs. The man deserved it; he deserved to be at the mercy of Nick, for what he'd done. He'd tried to kidnap Felan. He'd helped detain a whole village and take their children. He'd tried to kidnap Felan again.

God knows how many other children and people he'd manipulated and stolen away. He deserved everything that came to him. If that man and his friend hadn't chased Felan that first time...

Felan never saw that man again, and Felan felt no better for it.

Chapter 34: Tailed

Ralph and Mingan showed up two days later, covered in dirt and grime – exhausted, but alive – and everyone crowded inside the largest boardroom, listening in.

'We were in the shop for a second, and the sirens went off – the cops were already outside. It was like they knew we were coming, and that's what we don't get,' Ralph said.

Mingan stepped forward. 'We didn't even get a chance to do anything – we had to run, but we got separated. Caleb just happened to be in the right place at the right time, so he got away, like we'd told him.' Caleb was nowhere to be seen. 'But we were stuck. We were followed for so long. We could barely move without being seen. The place was crawling with cops.'

'Then yesterday, everything went silent. They were right behind us the whole way, so we had to take detours – we looped around the whole city twice! But they were always on our tails. Then nothing,' Ralph said.

'It's like they…'

'Everyone out,' Nick said dangerously, his gaze focused on Felan. 'This doesn't concern anyone but the Elders.'

Felan bristled at being interrupted. 'Hang on…'

'Let's go,' Blaez hissed, dragging him from the room. She dragged him all the way up to his bedroom, not speaking the entire way.

Not until they reached the safety of a closed door.

'You can let go now,' he said. She relaxed her hand on his wrist, and he shook her off, scowling.

'You can't keep doing that,' she said.

'Doing what? Voicing my thoughts?'

Felan kicked his shoes off under his bed and thumped a fist into the wall. Why was everyone telling him what he could and couldn't do? Why was everyone speaking to him like he knew nothing?

'No, annoying Nick like that. It's not going to help you in any way,' she said. 'You need to be careful.'

Felan thumped his fist into the wall again. 'He can't do anything to me.'

'He will, Felan. He will,' she pleaded.

He dragged his eyes to meet hers – angry, and wild, and feral. Despite the make-up, she wasn't a normal girl; far from it, in fact. She was vulnerable, and she had issues.

Just like him.

'No, he won't.' Felan sighed. 'Nick threatened me with you. He said if I didn't obey, he'd hurt you instead, because his punishments don't work on me.'

He watched the gears turning in her brain. 'And *that's* why you've been so overprotective.'

'Yeah. Yeah, I guess it is,' he mumbled.

'I don't need you to do that. That's my burden to bear, Felan. Not yours.'

'You're not understanding. If I slip up...'

'Then you slip up. I can take it.'

'You shouldn't have to!'

'And neither should you, Felan. Do you understand that? Do you understand that if you carry on like this, not looking after yourself, you'll end up hurt, injured, maybe even dead? You can't keep throwing your life away like it means nothing to you – you have to start looking after yourself.'

'What about you?'

'I can't believe we're having this conversation.' Blaez laughed to herself. 'I can take care of myself, and I don't need you, or anyone else, to look after me.'

Felan fiddled with the bandage on his forearm. More often than not, it stayed white, but there was the odd day where red bled through. Wounds were an inconvenience – they took far too long to heal, and they hurt long after they stopped bleeding.

He thought about how he'd run from everything, to try to leave it behind. He thought of how it stayed with him, because it was a part of him. He remembered grieving his mother in the dark. He remembered mourning the loss of what a father should be. He remembered crying over the little boy in the park he couldn't save. Harvey. Randi. And the nameless ones – they were the worst.

'Aren't you afraid you'll go mad?' He feared he already had.

'Yes, and no. But it'll work out. You'll see.' Blaez patted his leg once and left the room.

'Helpful as always,' he muttered to himself. With a yawn, he took off his jacket and shirt, tossed them onto the floor, and curled up under the covers, tried to fall asleep...

He couldn't.

Something wasn't right about Ralph and Mingan's return. There was no way the cops would just let them go like that without some ulterior motive; he was convinced that the cops had known exactly what they were doing when they let Mingan and Ralph go. And that's what he thought they must have done.

Let them go.

Felan threw his shirt back on, slipped on some shoes, and silently walked to the computers in the sort-of-basement. He opened up the security feed of the city. He switched from camera to camera, keeping an eye out for anything strange.

Nothing. There was no cop activity, which was very unusual. Cops always patrolled the city at night... well, not *always*. He'd seen cops on duty eating fast food inside their cars more than once, and he had even found some of them sleeping.

So much for the safety of the citizens.

Felan checked every camera four times over, and the unease grew. He saw no one, no drunkards lurking, no workers on their breaks, no druggies, no beggars, no nothing. It was like watching a ghost town.

His stomach twisted.

He brought up another page with a few strokes on the keyboard. His heart skipped a beat. He frantically clicked and typed, and reopened the feed, this time without the interference.

Not a single siren. Not a single flash of light. Just a train of shadows. He zoomed through the cameras until he reached the front of the train and gasped – a steady stream of cop cars, all headed for the same destination.

He grabbed the torch on the desk beside him and sprinted up the stairs two at a time. 'The cops are coming!' he shouted, the beam of light waving around frantically. 'We have to leave!' He skidded down another hallway. 'Wake up! The cops are coming!'

Door after door slammed open, and angry faces greeted him.

'What are you yelling about?' Ewan ground out, looking like he'd just been wrestling with a clawless bear, wincing as Felan aimed the torch in his face.

'The cops are coming!' he shouted again. That woke everyone up. 'Get up, and get out!'

If he'd done as Nick said and left it alone…

'How do you know this?' Accalia said, already dressed and alert, despite the rude awakening.

'I watched the security cameras. They don't have their sirens on, or their lights. Hoping to take us by surprise, I think,' Felan said quickly. 'They knew we'd be watching the cameras – they set a trap!'

'That's enough shouting, I think,' a voice said. Felan jumped. Nick was right behind him, as menacing as ever.

Felan swallowed his fear. They had to listen to him – they were all in danger! 'Nick, please,' Felan said. 'The cops are coming! We can't stay here!'

A resounding slap echoed down the hallway. 'Silence!'

He stared at the floor, quietly seething, torch clenched tightly in his hand.

At least it wasn't Blaez.

It could've so easily been Blaez.

'We're leaving,' Nick stated. 'Split up. Carry as much as you can – leave as little trace as possible. Don't be followed.'

'Where will we be going?' Accalia asked.

'Head south-east. There's a backup base ready and waiting.'
He evaporated back into the shadows.

Felan wished he had that ability.

In a blind panic, everyone rushed around, back and forth, armed themselves, packed up as much as they could carry. At most, they had ten minutes. The lights stayed off, since to turn them on would surely alert the cops, but torches flicked on and off. Someone shook him. His cheek burned. 'Felan! Get your stuff!' It was Blaez, swaddled in clothes and bags, make-up unspoiled; somehow. She had magic hands. 'Snap out of it!'

He was in and out of his room in less than a minute, stuffing his few belongings into one bag – his new pistol being one of those things. He clipped his purple brooch to his shirt.

He'd hoped that, after leaving his first home behind, that would be it.

No such luck.

His knife hung at his hip. Just knowing it was there quietened the restless beast inside him.

His room. The first place he'd *really* called home.

'Come on!'

He tore down the stairs after Blaez and into the armoury, where the others had completely ransacked the place. Boxes upturned, crates on their sides, dirt on the floor, empty racks, nothing left bar a few of the older pistols. He picked through the remains – a few bullets, a few boxes, a few ziplock bags for drop-offs; he couldn't leave those behind.

Somehow, it would be his fault if something important wasn't taken with them.

'Where are Caleb and Accalia?' he asked, suddenly realising their lack of friends.

'They already left with Tala and Stephen,' she said. 'Caleb had a bad night.'

He looked to the side entrance, where everyone was leaving in trios or pairs, hurrying on their way, leaving Blaez and Felan alone in the armoury. Nothing remained.

'Got everything you need?' he asked. He stepped out of the back door and into the darkness, Blaez right next to him.

'Yeah,' Blaez said. 'Lucky you were watching the cameras.'

They froze. The night life stilled all around them.

'The computers,' Felan said. 'Blaez, what's on them?'

'Everything,' she whispered. 'They have everything on them.'

Felan turned back to the Warehouse and stared at the looming shadow in horror.

Chapter 35: Infiltrated

'What do you mean by everything?'

'Files. Data. Information.'

'Why wasn't I told about this earlier?' He'd worked on those computers before – why didn't he know what was on them?

'I wasn't even supposed to know. It was Randi who... anyway. It doesn't matter,' Blaez said.

'Of course it matters!'

'What matters is that there's a file for each of us!'

Felan cursed. He hated to think what his file said. 'Containing?'

'Randi didn't get the chance to say.'

Felan clenched his fists. If the cops got hold of them, they'd never be able to get away from this life. They'd never be able to start again. He didn't care about the others so much, but Blaez, and Caleb, and Accalia... he could still help them.

He hurried back to the Warehouse.

Blaez blocked his path. 'What are you doing?'

He pushed past her. 'Hard drives.'

'There's no time – they're nearly here!'

'Humour me.' It would be close, but there was time. He could get in, and hopefully he could get out.

'Felan, we have to go!' She tugged hard on his arm; he tugged back harder and knocked her off balance.

If he could just erase all the data from the hard drives. If he could somehow help...

'It's over, Felan. We need to get as far away as we can. They won't be able to track us if we leave now,' she pleaded.

He thought she might be crying, but in the dark he couldn't see. 'And this is the problem, Blaez. I'm not allowed to protect you, but you're allowed to protect me? That's not fair,' he said.

'Now you have to make a choice. If you want to go, go. But I'm staying right here.'

'I'm not letting you go back in there by yourself,' she said.

'Come on then! It's not like we have all the time in the world.'

That comment earned him a solid punch to the shoulder.

Using the shadows, Felan slunk back inside and crept into the sort-of-basement, Blaez right beside him. Perhaps he should have wished she'd left, but right now, he felt relief that he wasn't alone in the empty warehouse.

The computer he'd recently vacated blinked in the darkness – Felan jumped right on it and opened up page after page, flitted through different screens, very aware of Blaez standing right behind him.

'What's your plan?'

'Delete everything.' Simple. Easy. He liked those sorts of plans. In and out. He hoped.

'Nick *will* murder you for erasing them. He's spent years on those.'

'I think he'd appreciate the fact that I didn't let the cops get everything. And anyway, if he cared that much, he'd have stayed and got them himself.'

Or he had them backed up elsewhere, which Felan liked to think was likely. Either way, it didn't change the fact that there were still files on the computers ready to divulge all their secrets.

She snorted once and quickly quietened down. 'Whatever – you carry on here, I'll watch for the cops.' She walked to the door without a second thought.

'Blaez,' he called over his shoulder.

'Yeah?'

'When they come, please don't leave me here.'

The dark hid his face, but it couldn't hide the tremor in his voice. His voice betrayed the fear he felt deep inside, like a maggot burrowing deeper and deeper: a constant itch, and a constant nagging pain.

He hadn't felt fear like this in so long, and it scared him.

'I promise,' she said.

Deleting the data wouldn't be enough – a simple file recovery program would restore the information with a few simple commands, and the cops would get it all back in seconds, and Felan might as well have done nothing.

He pulled open the special software and furiously typed away. Despite Blaez keeping an eye out, he sat on the edge of his seat. The dark always made him uncomfortable.

As of late, he'd begun to despise it.

Blaez's quiet footsteps stopped behind him. 'They're in the forest on foot, but there are a few cars on the track.'

'Good – I'm nearly done here.'

'How much longer?'

'Five minutes?'

She let out a low whistle. 'That'll be close.'

'Yeah. Which prompts my next question; where can we hide? Because something tells me that hiding under these desks won't suffice.'

Blaez didn't bat an eyelid. 'There's a storage cupboard on the fourth floor – it has a secret compartment.'

'It'll have to do.'

'Indeed – I'll be right back,' she said.

He silently cheered when the progress bar appeared on the screen. Now it was just a waiting game.

And the bar couldn't have moved any slower if it tried. He'd told Blaez five minutes – but it wasn't looking good. It had been frozen on sixty per cent for a while.

'Don't freeze,' he muttered. 'Please don't freeze. Don't freeze.'

'Felan,' she whisper yelled. 'If we don't head upstairs now, we won't get a chance to.'

'It's not finished,' he said. 'Blaez, there's still forty per cent to go!'

It wasn't frozen. He refused to believe that the software had failed. It couldn't have. He'd only updated it a few days ago. It should be breezing through.

'It's frozen, Felan,' she said. 'We tried, and we failed. Now please, let's go.' She reached for the plugs.

'No!' He pushed her arm away. 'Don't you dare.' The bar suddenly jumped ahead. 'There's still twenty per cent left – if they get in, they can easily disable the program. I can't leave until it's finished.'

'I promised I wouldn't leave you here.'

'Fourteen per cent...' he announced.

'Felan!' It sounded like she was gritting her teeth. 'Let's go!'

'Twelve per cent...'

'They're right outside,' she said, shaking his shoulder. '*We. Have. To. Move.*'

'Ten seconds, Blaez,' he said. 'Please.'

'*We don't have ten seconds!*'

'Done!'

Felan leaped from the chair and bolted up the stairs with Blaez.

When they reached the front entrance, he peered around the corner. Apart from the voices he could hear outside, the coast was clear. He stepped out into the hallway, and when nothing happened, he beckoned Blaez to follow. They tiptoed with minimal noise. Felan cringed when the first stair creaked under his foot.

Silence.

Felan looked over to the front entrance.

Blue flashes lit up the corridor.

He cursed. 'Go... go!'

They crept up the flights of stairs. Sweat clung to him, his skin clammy and uncomfortably warm, his legs weak.

Halfway up the third flight, the door opened far below them. It was quiet; had they actually been asleep, they would never have heard it. With a flick of the wrist, Felan beckoned Blaez to go ahead. She rolled her eyes, but didn't complain. Well, at least not verbally. He looked down. Shadows filed in below.

'They're in,' he whispered.

She grabbed his sweaty hand and pulled him forward. He happily obliged. His bag hit the corner with a thud, but they didn't slow down. They had no time.

'Just up here,' she said. She pointed out the storage cupboard when they neared it. Funny, he'd never noticed the damn thing before. She found the handle and they hurried inside. Blaez began to climb over the mountains of boxes, and Felan followed suit a second later. He hoped the cops couldn't hear them.

Blaez started to tap on the back wall.

'What are you doing?' he hissed. 'They'll hear you!'

'No, they won't. Hold the light up.'

He flicked on his torch so she could see. She grabbed hold of something, and pulled – part of the wall swung forward. Felan shone the torch inside. There was just enough space for the two of them.

'Now we hide,' she said.

Felan climbed in first, their bags abandoned behind rows of boxes – he hoped the cops didn't snoop through their stuff. That was the last thing he needed. Blaez shuffled up close to him and yanked the section of wall back. Felan switched the torch off.

He pressed his ear against the wall, listening. He could hear footsteps, faint, but they were getting closer, louder. 'They're here,' he whispered.

Some sort of signal went off, a shrill alarm, and shouts, and crashes, and bangs, and gunshots followed. Felan jumped horribly. Blaez shrieked amidst the chaos and hid her face in his chest. He wrapped his arm around her, as much as he could in the cramped space, and shut his eyes. He hated how loud it was. It went on for what felt like hours – in reality, it was probably a minute or so.

The noise died, and the cops shouted to each other across the building.

'Clear!' a deep voice said.

'Nothing here, sir!' another cop yelled. Definitely female.

'Negative!'

Felan didn't move. Had his heart not been running a marathon, he might've fallen asleep. He had a new definition of exhausted now. All thanks to the cops. They'd tried to catch them in their sleep – talk about cheating.

He pulled Blaez closer when a box tumbled to the floor inside the room; nowhere near the compartment they were in, but *someone was there!*

'Looks like they knew we were coming,' the first voice said. Felan stifled a chuckle – there was always one to state the obvious.

'He warned you! He told you not to run in – now look what's happened! They've dispersed, and now we have to start all over again!' The second voice didn't sound too happy to Felan.

'We needed to take action!' the first voice exclaimed. 'The longer we waited, the further they branched out!'

Felan imagined him with a thick moustache, thick beard, a balding head. Oh yeah, and slightly on the chubbier side – he sounded completely winded by the four flights of stairs. How he'd become a cop was beyond Felan.

'And if we'd waited, we'd still know where they were!'

Felan liked this guy – he seemed cool, collected. Like he knew what he was doing, like he had a plan. Not at all like his superior.

'Mr Bailey – may I remind you that you're on probation. I can easily have you thrown back inside if I please.'

'You put me on probation because you didn't want a perfectly good officer sat behind bars.'

Was the system seriously so corrupted that the superior ignored the basic guidelines of the law?

'You agree with him, don't you, Mr Bailey?'

'I do.'

'But do you understand that he's spent too long in the field to understand *our* part in this?'

'It's *because* he's spent so long in the field that he understands what needs to be done!'

'My job is to terminate the threats…'

'*Our job* is to protect the city!'

'…in this city and restore her.'

'And what a marvellous job you've done, sir! You've completely destroyed any chance we had of stopping them for good…'

'They'll slip up, Mr Bailey,' he said loudly. 'All criminals do. It won't be long before we catch wind of them again – they can't keep running forever. Think of it like hitting an ant's nest. It breaks, but the queen lives. And they'll lead you straight back to her.'

More boxes tumbled to the floor.

'But we don't know where they are!' Mr Bailey shouted. 'Don't you get that this is what they do? They'll never stop running! Not if we don't catch them – and you've ruined that for us now!'

'No! I didn't ruin this – he did! He's so blinded by his desire to...'

The voices petered out. Dammit. He hadn't learned what was going on, only that some of the cops hadn't wanted to attack them. Did that mean that they had someone on their side? Someone that wanted to help? Someone that wanted to... What did they want?

Blaez sat up as much as she could. 'Did you hear that?' she asked.

He struggled to find his voice. 'Yeah.' He shifted to find a more comfortable spot, but it only made the cramps worse.

'We're screwed... *Randi went to the cops*?'

'Or maybe they tracked Mingan and Ralph here?' he suggested.

'I thought that before, but now I don't think so. Randi was alive when we planned that job – with everyone hitting different points. He must've known about it – Nick could have told him, so he'd have some room to negotiate, to give the Protrudes information, and that's why they ended up going after our group. It makes sense!'

She was sort of right, but it also didn't make *any* sense. Felan couldn't believe it. Either Randi had sold them out twice, or the cops had amazing luck.

'But why would Randi put us in danger like that? We were friends,' Felan thought aloud.

If Randi had sold them out, then it was Randi's fault that Felan got shot, and that he'd accidentally shot Tristan. If Randi hadn't sold them out, the Protrudes would never have known where they were, *the cops* wouldn't have known where the Warehouse was. Now, because of Randi, they had to flee like cowards.

Because of Randi, everything was in ruins.

'I really don't know,' she mumbled miserably.

Felan ran a hand through his hair. It was sweaty and gross, and the tiny compartment was already packing a smell. They couldn't leave either.

The cops would hang around for a few hours at least, picking through every room, checking, and double-checking, and triple-checking...

And so they waited.

That was all they could do.

Chapter 36: A New Beginning

What had Randi been *thinking*, going to the cops like that? And even ratting them out to the Protrudes in the first place? What was it he'd said? *'You won't understand, but I'm sorry – It'll be okay soon.'* What didn't he understand? What was Randi planning?

Whatever it was, it clearly hadn't worked – and now Felan would never understand because the secrets had died with him. Perhaps that was for the best. Maybe it would be better if he never knew; that way he couldn't be disappointed.

It was why Felan hated secrets so much. They just made everything worse.

His life was crime and bloodshed. That's what he'd managed to do with his life, with his mother's sacrifice. Felan had managed to kill people, hurt people, betray people, lie, cheat, steal, beg, *give in*. It was something he could never get away from, no matter how hard he tried.

They ran while the coast was clear, in a direction Felan had never run before. The trees gave way to bushes, and the bushes themselves were wild, wilder than the bramble bush that covered his mother's grave, and untamed. They saw remnants of human footprints in the ground, and they knew they were heading in the right direction.

'I think we're clear,' Blaez said.

'We'll walk for a while,' he said. 'We've been running for hours.'

'That was close. I can't believe it actually worked!'

He gave her a look. 'I thought you said you always had faith?'

'I do,' she chirped. 'But every time I'm still shocked.'

'That makes absolutely no sense.'

'It does to me!'

Felan shook his head in disbelief. What a weirdo. They left the forest behind and walked on, edging around four villages in succession. People milled about, but they kept their distance, not wanting any contact. If the cops came sniffing, townsfolk would pass on how they'd seen two kids traipsing by.

It was safer to steer clear of people and pretend they didn't exist. Felan was excellent at pretending he didn't exist.

'It sounded like they wanted to do more than arrest us,' she said.

'I got that too – when the guy started going on about exterminating threats and whatnot.' The cops saw them as rodents, he thought, not humans. Not kids.

Blaez nodded. 'Do you think we would have got a trial?'

'A trial for what?'

'If we got arrested, do you think we'd get a trial?'

Felan shrugged. He'd thought about it before, not that he'd admit it. 'I don't know. I'd like to think we would get one, but you heard them. They want us gone. Chances are, we won't get one – we'll go to prison, no matter the regulations.' Bloody corrupted system.

Felan faced Blaez and walked backwards. He clapped his hands together. 'Right, I do have a question for you, Blaez – you're smarter than me, so you'll probably know the answer.' He stumbled over a fallen root but quickly righted himself. 'That didn't happen!'

'Duh,' she said, smirking.

'The cops... why now?' Felan asked. He glanced over his shoulder every now and then, much to Blaez's amusement. 'They've known for weeks where we are. Why wait until now to attack?'

'Easy,' she said. 'Planning. Movements like the one last night? They take ages to plan, and by the sounds of it, not all of the cops were happy with it, especially Mr Bailey,' Blaez said.

'Mr Bailey seems like a nice guy.'

'Yeah.'

'And he's on probation? How does that even work?'

'Not a clue. All I learned was the cops are just as corrupt as everything else.'

Blaez laughed when Felan tripped again. Hmm. Walking backwards wasn't doing it for him. He made the executive decision to walk normally.

'Yeah, and that the guy in charge isn't too happy with us,' Felan said.

'That too.'

The fact that a small group of people could get under the cops' skin so easily – he wasn't proud of it, but he wasn't ashamed of it either. Satisfied would be a better word. Felan was satisfied he'd annoyed people that had never helped him in the past.

There was no greater joy.

Well, there probably was, but he was yet to discover what that greater joy was.

Felan pulled out his phone when it buzzed. Accalia had sent him a string of numbers.

Blaez's phone buzzed too.

'All jokes aside, these are coordinates right?' he asked.

'We'll see where they lead us,' Blaez said.

'Let's run again – we'll get there faster.'

'Race you?'

Felan barked out a laugh. 'You're so going to lose.'

***

A rugged field greeted them.

'I don't understand.' Blaez frowned. 'I'm looking at the coordinates Accalia sent – there's nothing here.'

'It'll be here somewhere,' he said. 'Let's keep looking.'

They walked off in different directions, searching. They were definitely late to the new base (they were always late these days). The journey should have taken them one day at most, not three; to be fair, he'd saved all their identities from being exposed, so that had to count for something, though he had a feeling Nick wouldn't be so understanding. He was due a punishment anyway, especially after the slap a few nights ago.

That was nothing more than a warning for what was to come – and for Blaez too.

She was in danger. Again.

He slashed his knife through the grass in front of him, kicked sticks out of the way, and carried on searching. No matter what he did, he always seemed to put everyone in danger. He waded further in, slashing as he went. He hadn't realised grass could grow so tall.

'Come on, where are you?' he muttered to himself. He thought, by now, he'd have seen signs of traffic passing through; footprints, litter, anything.

'Have you found anything?' Blaez shouted from across the field.

He turned around and got a mouthful of grass. 'No,' he yelled, spitting it out. 'There's nothing here!'

He listened for her voice and cut his way to her. Felan laughed when he saw bits of grass stuck in her hair. He picked them out one by one, stifling his laughter the whole time.

'Maybe we got the coordinates wrong?' he suggested.

'No. I don't get things wrong. We should be right on top of it!'

Felan stared at the floor. 'It's because we are!' he exclaimed.

'How do you mean?'

'We're standing on it,' he said.

He crouched low and sifted through the grass. Blaez followed suit beside him, and they felt their way through inch after inch of grass. Knife in hand, he cut through roots and stalks until he reached soil. Felan slashed his knife, over and over and over. Finally his knife clanged against something solid. 'Over here, Blaez!'

A metal ring saw the sun, perhaps for the first time in years. It was rusted, and dirty, and teeming with woodlice.

Felan yanked on it hard. Nothing. Blaez appeared beside him and took the ring in her hands.

'Three, two, one...'

The sounds of chains clanking rang below them. A metal door tore out of the ground, ripped up grass and dirt that had spread and grown over it, and revealed darkness down below.

'Torch?' he asked.

Blaez searched the bags, and handed his one over.

'Thanks.'

He switched the torch on and shone it into the dark – an empty room by the looks of things. Felan hopped down first and shone the torch beam all around: a door on the far side, an old desk directly across from it. Groaning pipes ran all around the room.

Blaez landed beside him, and the door above them slammed shut; gears and chains clanked and groaned.

'Okay?'

'Yep.'

Not even his jumper protected Felan from the cold of the room. He made his way over to the desk in the corner, rubbing his arms. The few sheets of paper crumbled under his touch and collapsed into piles of dust and cobwebs.

'This is old,' he said.

Blaez drew lines in the dust. 'I wonder where we are?'

'I don't know.'

'Whoever was here before is long gone,' Blaez said, shining the light of her torch around the room.

'We need to find the others – we're late. Again.' He pulled open the door, and light blinded him.

The others must already be here, he thought.

'Felan, look,' Blaez said.

The door creaked on its hinges and slotted perfectly back into place; with no handle, the door matched the generic pattern of the wall of the corridor.

'A perfect hiding spot.' He traced the patterns with his fingers, over the non-existent gap between wall and door. Amazing.

A hand on his shoulder brought him back to reality.

'We need to go,' Blaez urged.

They followed the corridor, which spilled into a large hall. Tables and chairs filled it – a room bigger than any of the ones at the Warehouse. More corridors twisted away on each end of the hall. Felan couldn't wait to explore.

Blaez nudged him.

Two of the larger tables had been shoved together, and at them sat the others, waiting, two empty chairs beside Caleb – who sat there with a blank face, a blank existence. Felan sat next to him with a smile. Caleb stared straight ahead. Felan looked around the table. He received nothing but sneers in return.

'Read the coordinates upside down, did you?' Rory grinned wickedly.

'We got held up,' Felan said coolly. He crossed his arms.

'By what?'

'The cops.'

'But you left with everyone else, did you not?' Nick's voice came from behind him.

Felan tensed. He hoped the others didn't notice. He hadn't realised Nick was in the room.

'I remembered the hard drives.'

'Is that so?'

Blaez picked up the story for him and explained what had happened, and what they'd overheard. She took Caleb's hand. 'I'm so sorry. It looks like Randi went to the cops.'

His face betrayed no emotion. 'Don't touch me.'

She let go fairly quickly. 'I'm sorry,' she said again, then looked up and down the table. 'That's what happened, and that's what we overheard.'

'What do we do now?' Andy asked. His stubble had grown out and he looked slightly wild.

Nick slowly walked to the head of the table and took a seat. 'We fight back.'

Convel grinned. 'How soon can we start?'

Nick held a hand out to silence him. Felan seethed. Had that been Felan speaking, he'd have got a thrashing.

'We've let the Protrudes get away with too much. They've invaded our territory, taken what's ours, and are pushing us too far. It's time to take back what's ours and fight!' Nick roared.

The hall erupted in a torrent of shouts and cheers. Felan looked up and down the table: these people were devoted, submissive, *blind*. A roar from beside him broke his heart – Caleb.

Anger burned in every inch of the boy. He snarled and shouted with everyone else, and for the first time, Caleb looked like he belonged with the group.

Felan felt eyes on him. Convel. The man bared his teeth and looked Felan up and down in disgust. Feeling out his knife, Felan bared his teeth back. The knife helped him stay in control.

'What do we do about the cops?' That was Ewan.

'Whatever you like – just don't get caught.' With that, Nick swept from the room. A shadow streaked along one wall, then vanished.

Felan looked to Blaez, to Accalia, back to Blaez.

This was it.

This was the part where everything changed.

Chapter 37: Tripwire

It didn't take long to make the underground base usable again. Once the dust was cleared, the rooms aired and tidied, and the many rodent infestations fixed, the base resembled one of those old-timey mansions; except it was underground. The corridors were more like tunnels, some of which they had yet to explore, and some were so dirty Felan didn't think they'd even been used the first time.

After the base had been running on backup power for days, Mingan finally sorted out a permanent electricity supply, and Kit figured out the water supply hours later. Felan was left to boot up the computers by himself, which was fine by him. He was the only one left that was well versed in computers, and he liked alone time. Once they were up and running, he helped Accalia set up security cameras around the new base and made sure the feed was clear, and smooth, and everything ran as it was supposed to.

Just to be on the safe side.

He didn't want to lose his home again.

While he worked, Felan looked at the news. It was usually the same old boring things: another car crash, or another betting shop closing, or it was a report on underage drinking, or another report detailing how civilians were being hurt in the streets, or more and more reports of missing children.

Felan thumped the desk. It was all very well telling everyone, but when was anyone actually going to do something about it?

And before long, the drop-offs resumed too. It took longer to get into the city, but that was okay with Felan. Any time outside was a gift, because it was suffocating, living underground without windows. He couldn't even hear the rain. No more staring out into the forest.

Just webs of tunnels, and corridors, and darkness.

***

An almighty explosion shook the ground beneath his feet.

'Jesus,' Felan muttered. 'That was a big one.'

Convel and Tate had a thing for bombs, he'd found out. They made their own with whatever supplies they had. The bigger the bomb, the more intimidated the Protrudes would be, apparently.

It had worked for a week, he remembered. Convel had set a bomb in an old factory, relatively close to the Protrudes' base, and boom! They had free reign of the city, but after a week, the Protrudes hit back. They hit an old workshop near the Warehouse, and that was Guadalupe. Explosions went off at random times, and never in the same place.

That's when the news reports had started to get interesting.

'These explosions are no longer the result of what we've been calling "Lone Wolf Terrorist Attacks". Experts say these bombs are intended to intimidate rival gangs – what we're experiencing is a turf war. It's also known as a very destructive variation of gang warfare.'

So yeah. Felan liked to keep the news on, since it meant he could keep up on what the Wolves were doing.

Ever since Nick banned him from taking part in anything other than street work, it was hard to keep up with everyone. There was only so much Accalia could tell him, and no one else talked to him. Blaez was banned too; she was as clueless as he was. They caught snippets of conversation through the walls, or in the corridors, but nothing big.

So, the news it was.

Felan picked up the crisp packet he'd stashed in the computer room and tore it open, devouring the contents. It wasn't the healthiest option, but it was food. It was all he could find at such short notice, and it was all he'd get until he went out on drop-offs again.

He couldn't wait to get back outside in the open air. He really didn't like living underground. He crumpled the crisp packet and tossed it into the nearest bin.

Where would Blaez be now?

Her location was all over the place as of late. Some days she was on drop-offs and he wouldn't see her at all. Some days she didn't leave the base, on cleaning duty or sorting through the cupboards and taking inventory. Some days she went outside for some fresh air. Some days she kept watch in the city and reported any activity – but that was usually while doing drop-offs.

And some days she stayed holed up in her room, face buried in whatever book she'd found that day.

Licking his fingers (ready-salted crisps were underrated), he headed down the two flights of stairs to her room. Felan knocked on the closed door.

'Come in,' Blaez called.

He grinned and pushed the door open. Blaez lay atop her covers, book open in her hands. He thought it might have been a children's book, but she stashed it away beneath her pillow before he could read the title. Her cheeks reddened.

'I see someone's had an easy day today,' he cheeked.

'Hey! I've been taking inventory all morning – where've you been?'

'Computers.'

'Ooh,' she said sarcastically, 'because that's so hard.'

He wiggled his fingers, making them crack. 'It physically ruins me.'

'I can see,' she said. She crossed her legs. 'What can I do for you, Felan?'

He made sure the door was firmly shut. 'Tell me about bombs.'

'About... bombs?' she enquired slowly, her face stuck mid shift between amusement and puzzlement.

'Yeah.'

'Well, no bomb is the same. You can add slightly more of one thing, and slightly less of another – but all are volatile. Add people like Convel and Tate into the mix? They don't care what goes in as long as it makes a bang.'

'Okay, and that's why you don't use bombs? That's why you use your sniper rifle – because it's... predictable?'

'Partly,' she said. 'Bombs hurt people. Bombs are unpredictable. You can't control them. But a gun? Or even a knife, actually – I can control it, at least until I pull the trigger, or I decide to swing. And being long range like I am? It means I don't have to partake in the violence if I don't want to. Sometimes it's bad enough watching through the scope.'

Felan understood that. At least now they could both take a step back from it. He still couldn't believe it. It was the perfect present, not that he let on at all. Though he didn't love being on the streets, either. He knew what to expect, who to expect, and that was tedious. Customers had started to recognise him, and he knew they recognised Blaez too.

It was getting dangerous.

'At least now we don't have to...'

The door burst open and revealed a distressed Accalia. 'I've been looking everywhere for you two!'

Felan hoped to hell she hadn't overheard their conversation. 'Why?'

'Have you heard about Caleb?'

Felan and Blaez exchanged a worried look. 'No? What happened?'

Accalia sighed. She stepped in and shut the door. 'He came back covered in blood. From what I gathered, his drop-off got violent and wanted a fight. You know Caleb, especially as of late. He was more than happy to give him one,' she scolded. 'He refused any treatment and went off to have a shower. Says he's fine.'

'Rubbish,' Blaez said. 'He hasn't been alright since...'

All three of them looked down.

'We can't help him if he doesn't want the help,' Felan said finally. 'It's all very well being around, watching him, being near, ready to step in, but if he doesn't want the help, what's the point?'

Accalia nodded. 'Right – I just wanted to keep you guys in the loop, but I need to get back to work now.' She paused at the door. 'I suggest you guys do the same.' She left the room as quickly as she'd entered.

Blaez leaned her head on Felan's shoulder. 'What are we gonna do, Felan?'

He wished he had an answer.

***

Felan wiped away the blood dripping down his cheek.

Bruce definitely hadn't forgiven him for their last encounter. The last of the bruises and cuts had just healed; now he had more to showcase to the world. There were *always* more bruises to showcase to the world.

'Fan-bloody-tastic,' he muttered. With a few more profanities, he wiped himself clean – it wouldn't do to wander the streets of Guadalupe covered in blood, not that anyone would really care.

Feeling peckish, Felan counted the money in his pocket. He had a few coins – it wouldn't buy much, if anything, but the crisps seemed ages ago. The coins jingled in his hand while he walked over to the little bakery and ducked inside. A middle-aged man greeted him.

'This is all I have,' Felan said. He tipped the money onto the counter. Maybe this was a bad idea – smelling the freshly baked food was awful. What if the man took the money and asked him to leave?

'You can have one of the rolls,' the man said. 'And I'll throw in a bottle of water.'

Felan almost broke down in tears. 'Thank you. Thank you so much – oh, don't worry about a bag,' he said.

The baker put the plastic bag back with a laugh. 'Saving the environment, are you?'

'No,' Felan said, taking the roll and the bottle of water. 'I'm going to eat it now.'

'Ah,' the baker said. 'Have a good day.'

'And you – thanks again.'

He bit into the roll. It was still warm, and food always tasted better when it was warm. He took another bite. Fresh food was a luxury he could never afford.

The baker seemed nice enough, and he'd given Felan a drink. Maybe the world wasn't quite so against him after all. If he ever got more money, he'd go back to that bakery and buy more goods, and pay the baker back. He hated owing...

An explosion rattled the street.

Felan knocked into a middle-aged couple as the ground shook, and they steadied each other with frantic apologies. Windows shattered and blew glass all over him. He shielded himself best he could and felt sharp scratches on his skin.

A plume of smoke rose from the next street.

It had to be the Protrudes, because the Wolves didn't set up bombs in the street. It wasn't their way. And anyway, the bomb the others had scheduled wasn't until later, and it was to be near the Protrudes' base.

Then the screams and shouts flooded in.

Felan stared at the sky in horror. The Protrudes had set off a bomb in the middle of a busy street in the Flax. Families. Children. Everyone. He ran, fuelled by a desperation to soothe the crying children, to help, to atone for his mistakes and wrongdoings. Sirens screeched around him. He gawked at the scene: blood, a few bodies, crying children, burning debris.

Why did he allow it to happen? Why did he continue to stay with people that made the world a worse place?

Because that's what they did, right? They hurt people, heck, *he* hurt people. Blood on his hands, nightmares in his head – when Nick took him in, violence hadn't been what Felan had had in mind.

Quite the opposite, in fact. Felan didn't want to hurt people, and he rather hoped they wouldn't hurt him.

The Protrudes, however... They would pay. They'd pay for Randi, they'd pay for Harvey, and they'd pay for every single home they invaded, for every child they took and coerced.

They'd pay for the lot.

He finished his drop-offs in record time and rushed back to the base. He liked the walk back because it wasn't just a forest any more. There were fields to walk through, small rivers to cross, villages and towns to avoid – though none of them were major settlements. A maximum of thirty houses in each town, but he liked to keep his distance. He didn't know if they were friendly or not.

Felan fumbled for the handle buried within the grass and pulled it open. Dirt rained down into the hole, and daylight flooded in. He jumped inside. The door swung shut behind him.

He turned at the sound of a whimper. He flicked the light on – the room lit up. He found the source of the noise and his heart sank.

Huddled in a corner was Blaez, knees pulled to her chest, rocking back and forth. He dropped to the floor beside her, a thousand thoughts rushing through his mind. Finally, he settled on one:

'Did he hurt you?'

'No. No.' She snivelled into her knees.

He rubbed her shoulder, his heart pounding, and pounding, and pounding. 'What happened?' Her body shook. 'Blaez, talk to me,' he said softly. He'd never seen her cry like this before. What could have possibly happened to make Blaez so upset?

She lifted her head. Blotchy, swollen eyes. Eyeliner, and snot, and tears ran down her face. 'There's been an accident,' she whimpered, and her whole body shuddered.

Chapter 38: Erroneous

Blaez wouldn't react like this unless someone...

'Who?' he managed to ask.

She shrank herself tighter into a ball. 'Caleb was helping Convel and Tate set up the bombs. They went off ahead of schedule.'

So that meant... no. No. It couldn't have been them in the street. They didn't set up bombs in the street. They didn't hurt civilians. That was the rule. And why was Caleb even with them? 'Is he okay?'

Blaez held back a sob. 'Convel and Tate were unharmed, minus a few scratches.'

Anger. That's what he felt. Pure anger. He didn't give a crap about them. 'Where's Caleb?'

Blaez shook her head.

'Blaez. Where's Caleb?'

She started to sob. 'They said there was no way he'd have been able to make it out. When it went off, he was right beside it – the charge didn't work or something. It malfunctioned and exploded, and... and...'

And he'd been just around the corner in the bakery. He'd been *just* around the corner from them. He could have done something to stop him. He could've helped. He could've stopped it from happening in the first place. He could've done *something*!

'He's dead, Felan,' Blaez cried. 'How many more of us are gonna die?'

He squeezed into the gap next to her and hugged her. He didn't dare move as she clung to him, and he forced himself not to cry. He forced the anger down, down, down. He willed his emotions away so that he could comfort Blaez.

'It was an accident.' That was all he could think of to say. Did he believe it? Nope.

How many more of them had to be sacrificed?

'They'll be together now,' Felan said, thinking of his friends, friends lost to violence he partook in. 'They're together, and they can work it out.' They'd be happier up there, away from the violence. They could relax and actually live. Something they never got the chance to do the first time around.

'Right. You need to go and sort out tomorrow's drop-offs,' Blaez said without emotion.

'I'm not leaving you here by yourself in this state.'

'I just want some time alone,' she said. 'Please, Felan.'

He sighed. 'Fine – I'll sort yours out too.'

'Thank you.'

He squeezed her shoulder once more and clambered to his feet. God he was exhausted.

'Wait!' she called as he walked out of the door.

'What is it?'

Blaez trembled in her spot on the floor and curled up even more.

'Felan – there's something you should know...'

***

Felan burst into the infirmary. Sat by one of the beds furthest from the door was Tala, exactly where Blaez had said she'd be. Felan walked over. On one of the beds, smothered by sheets, lay a little boy. Bloody bandage over one eye. Stitched-up cut on his forehead. Pale. Felan stopped at the foot of the bed.

He struggled to understand Tala's hand movements, but when he finally got it, he clutched the bed frame to stop himself from collapsing.

Felan, this is Edward. His parents were killed in the explosion.

Chapter 39: Veracity

'What are you doing here?'

'Felan...'

'You need to leave.'

'Not until you hear what I have to stay.'

'You're ruining everything! If I don't bring back the exact money for the exact number of drop-offs...'

'How much do I owe you?'

He stared at the redhead like he'd grown a third eye. 'What?'

'How much do I owe you?' Tristan repeated.

Felan checked the contents of the bag. 'Thirty.'

Without hesitation Tristan dropped the cash into Felan's hand and took the ziplock bag.

Great. That was brilliant. The only person who showed any inkling of wanting to help, and they were an addict.

Tristan must've seen the look on Felan's face. 'I don't use, Felan,' he said, as he slipped the bag inside his jacket. It looked fancy, and was that leather?

'Why am I here? Because either you're trying to kidnap me, or you want to get high. Which is it?' He rested his hand on the hilt of his knife, ready. He glanced around the corners to make sure no one was sneaking up on him. They'd get a good shot at it from behind the skips.

'Relax, Felan. I'm not doing either,' Tristan said. 'Look, I needed an excuse to talk to you. This was the only way I could think of.'

'Then I'll make sure to refer you to someone else if I see your number again.'

Tristan blocked his exit. 'Talk to me, Felan.'

The boy ignored the man in front of him. He peered down the alleys, across the street, everywhere someone could be lurking.

Nick could be watching. Anyone could be watching, waiting to see what he'd do. He couldn't talk out in the open. It wasn't safe.

'Not here,' he said. 'I'm not talking here.'

***

Felan decided he shouldn't be allowed in fancy places – he stuck out like a man wearing a full body cast at a swimming pool. Everybody inside the coffee shop was dressed up in suits, like they were on their breaks at their really important jobs. They stared at Felan in distaste. Even Tristan didn't look that bad – he had a suit jacket and jeans. Felan had a ratty satchel, holey shoes, and tattered jeans and jumper.

No matter that the coffee shop wasn't busy; it was obvious he didn't belong.

The waitress arrived and placed their drinks on the table. Tristan thanked her. Warily, Felan brought his drink closer to him and gave it a sniff. Warm and sweet, just as he remembered. It had been a while since he'd had hot chocolate.

'It's not been poisoned or anything,' Tristan said.

Felan took a sip and glared. 'Bite me.' Now that he mentioned it, Tristan could have slipped something...

Stop it. He'd watched the waitress bring the drinks over, and he'd had his eye on it since. Tristan wasn't out to get him.

'How are you, Felan?'

'What kind of a question is that?'

'I thought I'd start off easy.'

He pushed his hot chocolate away from him and tried not to think of Caleb. His friend. Dead. *Killed.* 'I don't want to answer.'

'That's okay,' Tristan said, taking a sip of his coffee.

'I'm sorry,' Felan said. He didn't look up from his drink. 'For what happened last time I saw you.'

'Forget it.'

'*I shot you!*' Felan hissed. 'I can't just forget that!' He glanced around again. Thankfully, Tristan had decided to sit them at a booth in the back, away from most of the other customers.

'The man you were with was goading you. It wasn't your fault.'

'How can you say that?'

'Quite easily,' the man said. He leaned back in his chair and stretched, grinning. 'I'm right as rain.'

'Did the cops get you?'

He hesitated. 'A buddy managed to get me out of there.'

'What buddy? Convel...'

'Killed the rest of them?' Tristan said. 'That he did. But did you think we were going into that without backup?'

Felan sipped his drink. It warmed his insides, a nice change from tap water – or whatever water he could find. It tasted sweet and rich on his tongue, like velvet. The last time he'd had hot chocolate was when his mum was still alive. At least, the days she could afford it.

'How many drop-offs do you do a day?'

Felan lowered his head in shame. 'Between twenty to thirty,' he mumbled.

'Do they all get so violent?'

Felan brushed a finger over his cheek where he knew Bruce's parting gift still sat. 'A few.' He couldn't relax. He kept waiting for someone to jump out and attack him. His body was tense, coiled up like a spring ready to fly.

'Okay.'

Felan blanched. 'What? That's it? That's what you cornered me for?'

Tristan unbuttoned his jacket. 'Unless you have more to tell me?'

It was tempting, he had to admit. To tell him all about Caleb, about Randi, Blaez, Accalia, even Harvey and Nick. Everyone else. Little Edward, who still lay unconscious in the infirmary. Little Edward who'd have no idea where he was when he woke up. Little Edward who'd be forced to...

'I have to go.'

Nick would be watching. He knew it. Nick was always watching. That's how he always knew everything that went on.

Felan abandoned his drink and fled the coffee shop, hands shaking, bottom lip trembling, compelling himself to put one foot in front of the other.

'There is a way out, Felan,' Tristan shouted after him. 'You just have to ask.'

***

He found Blaez in the infirmary. Edward was regaining colour, and that was good, but the bandage over his eye was still bloody. In some ways Felan wanted him to remain in the bed forever; that way he'd never have to do the things that Felan did. He noticed, for the first time, just how small the boy's hands were. He couldn't imagine a knife in those innocent hands.

'He's so tiny,' Felan whispered.

'He shouldn't be here.'

'Neither should we.'

Blaez tucked a strand of Edward's hair behind his ear. 'You're right. We shouldn't.'

Felan, his mind made up, tapped Blaez on the shoulder. 'Can we talk?'

'Talk?'

He looked around, over his shoulder, made sure no one lingered in the hallway, behind the door, behind the beds. He nodded once, but kept his head down.

'Oh Felan,' she mumbled. 'Come with me.' Blaez lead him up to the top floor, into a room full of dust – a room they had yet to venture into and sort through. He meandered around the table, the two stacks of boxes, and the broken cabinet.

'I saw Tristan again.'

'Right,' Blaez said. 'Okay.'

He remembered the conversation in vivid detail and relayed it to her. 'He said he could help me.'

She paced around the room. Felan felt dizzy just watching her. 'Do you believe him?'

He could still taste the hot chocolate if he closed his eyes. 'Part of me does, and the other half is screaming at me that it's a bad idea...'

Blaez stopped pacing. She walked over and brushed his cheek. Oh yeah. He kept forgetting that Bruce had roughed him up a bit. Some would say he was used to that kind of treatment.

'Are you saying...?'

Tears dashed down his cheeks before he could stop them. 'I want to get out of here, Blaez. I don't want to hurt anyone any more – I don't want to live like this! I want out.' He took Blaez's face in his hands. 'And I want you to come with me.'

But already she was pulling away. 'What about Accalia? What about Edward?'

His hands fell uselessly to his sides. 'That's the thing...' He trailed off.

'No.'

'Blaez, please...'

'I'm not letting any more of my friends die. Not while I can help it,' she said fiercely. 'I might want out, but they come first.'

He closed the gap between them, and for every step back she took, he took another. He had one last idea, and he had to try.

'Blaez... do you remember the conversation we had, where you explained to me that you wanted friends who put themselves first, no matter the cost?'

'Don't...'

'And that's what I've done. I've put myself first, and I want out.' His heart jittered when she stopped moving away from him. 'What would Accalia want you to do? Would she want you to stay here, or would she want you to get out the first chance you get?' He reached out and grasped her hand tight. She didn't pull away. 'Blaez... Accalia's safe. She's an Elder now, and you know she won't let anything happen to Edward. You know she'll get him to safety if she has to.'

Unshed tears sparkled in her eyes. 'How can you be so sure?'

He picked up her other hand. 'I'm not, but do you not trust Accalia to do what's right?'

'Of course I do.'

He stepped in even closer. Her breath on his face tickled. She smelled of furniture polish. 'Do you trust me?'

'Do you trust Tristan?'

He nodded. 'More than Nick. Tristan seems genuine.'

'We all thought that about Nick too,' she whispered.

'Tristan came back. Even after I...' He cut himself off. Not one of his finest moments, even if the man was okay. Felan still had nightmares about it.

Blaez's nose tickled his. 'Even after you shot him?' The playfulness came back.

Felan winced. 'Yeah.' He prayed he'd said the right things. It was true though, all of it. If Blaez wanted friends that put themselves first, then she had to do the same.

Blaez bumped her forehead against his. His heart skipped a beat.

'I trust you,' she murmured.

'So you'll come with me?'

'I'll come with you.'

'Are you sure?'

'Nope. So let's do it.'

Chapter 40: Portent

'Three.'

Nick's face was a thunderstorm; crackling with lightning, booming thunder, flickering darkness.

When Felan messed up, or made mistakes, or didn't obey orders, Nick was angry – but that was no comparison to the storm, to the *rage*, Felan now witnessed. It wasn't much different to the rage that boiled inside him every time he saw the empty seat at the table.

'Three of our own have been killed – all because the Protrudes couldn't stay away.'

Killed? They'd been *murdered* – two of them by Nick himself! Call it treason. Call it disloyalty. Whatever. That didn't change the fact that Nick had slit Harvey's throat and driven a knife through Randi's chest. Killed. Nick made it sound like it had been an accident, like all of it was an accident.

That wasn't the Protrudes. That was Nick. It had all been Nick.

A chorus of shouts replied. Nick circled the tables.

'We're not afraid,' the man said. 'We're not afraid to do what needs to be done.'

Felan didn't know about the others, but he was terrified. Never had his father induced such fear in him as a child, and yet Nick, in a matter of months, had revoked every bad memory of Felan's father and implanted his own.

'I need two of you to set up cameras around the perimeter of the Protrudes' base.'

'Me,' Blaez volunteered.

'And me,' Accalia said. 'We can do it.'

Felan remembered his rushed instructions to Blaez as they filed into the hall: *Whatever Nick says, just go with it.* They could figure out their plan of action after.

'Someone to watch the cameras once they're up.'

Just go with it. Felan raised a hand.

'Watch their rotation. Watch their deliveries. Watch what they do. Watch *them.*'

He swallowed the anxiety. 'Got it.'

The last time Nick had been relatively civil with him...

'I need some of you on weapons duty – see what we have, what we can salvage, organise everything. And I need the rest of you to do everything else. Drop-offs. Supply runs – nothing major. I don't need you lot to get arrested before we can make a move.'

Felan glanced up and down the table. Tala was absent, but he knew exactly where she'd be.

Nick pointed to some of Felan's least favourite people. 'Convel and Tate are already working on another batch of bombs – deadlier than the last.' Felan's eyes flickered to the empty seat. 'A few of you will set them up all around the perimeter, out of sight, all within range of each other – do this when the patrol is at its weakest; you'll confer with Felan. Once they're primed, we'll wait. We'll go silent for a few days. No one leaves. Let the Protrudes think they've got the upper hand. Get them to let their guard down. Make them comfortable,' Nick derided. 'Then, when I give the signal, we head over to their base. Once we're all in position, Convel will detonate. They'll panic. They'll scatter. They'll be easy targets – the second you get a clear shot, shoot them dead.'

It was a good plan – if you were a psychopath.

'The Protrudes are not winning this war. We're going to take them out, one by one, if it's the last thing we do.' Nick stopped near Felan and a sinking feeling entered his bloodstream. 'Get to work.'

Chairs scraped across the wooden floor in a flurry of movement. Felan made to follow. Nick settled a hand on the boy's shoulder, and Felan's skin crawled.

'Not you, Felan – I'm not done with you yet.'

Nick yanked him to his feet when the door closed. Felan shielded his face with one hand and braced for impact. Conditioning, and fear, and pain.

But there was none.

'You poor boy.' Nick spoke like he was speaking to a young child. 'I'm not going to hurt you.'

Felan risked a peek. Nick was looking at him with something akin to pity. He grabbed Felan's chin with gentle fingers and turned his head further into the light. Panicked, Felan tried to turn, but Nick had already seen the marks on his face, marks Nick hadn't inflicted.

It was a small victory.

'I see Bruce got you again.'

How the hell did Nick know it was Bruce? 'Yes.'

The man tutted. 'It wouldn't happen if you just behaved.'

Felan squirmed. His touch burned. 'I know.'

'Do you? Because, from what I hear, you're not behaving.'

Nick let him go. Felan resisted the urge to rub away the ache – he wasn't going to give Nick any more satisfaction, thank you very much.

Wait. What did Nick mean by that?

'Tell you what, Felan. I'll make you a deal.'

'Deal?'

'If you do this for me, I won't come after you.'

'What?'

'I'm not as dense as you think,' Nick snarled. 'I know what you and Blaez are planning – and I'm going to come after you if you go through with it. But if you do this, I'll let you go.'

'We aren't planning to leave – we want to stay!' He put as much honesty into it as possible, but he thought it was obvious – even he could hear the lie. He might've been able to keep the secret alive if he hadn't opened his mouth to begin with.

The man glowered. 'Don't lie to me, Felan. You're smarter than that.' Nick turned his knife around.

Felan froze. He had scars from that knife. Scars he knew would never fade; a constant reminder, a constant battle, a constant *shame*.

'If you even think about trying to run, you won't like the consequences.'

'I know,' Felan whispered. He couldn't look away from the sharp piece of metal. He swore it was eyeing him up.

'That's my offer,' Nick said. He pointed the knife at Felan. 'Now what do you say?'

Felan said nothing.

'I saved your life,' Nick said. 'It's about time you saved ours.'

Chapter 41: Groundwork

There was no interference on the stream. It was crystal clear – unlike Felan's conscience.

It felt like he was drowning in warm air and bright monitors, and he could see everything, including the people they were trying to kill. No, not trying, *going*. He saw the people they were *going* to kill.

Had Felan eaten any food that morning, he'd have been sick.

'You don't owe anything, to anyone, no matter what you might think,' Blaez said. It wasn't as easy as she made it sound.

'Nick saved me.'

'He didn't. He made you suffer. He made me suffer. That's not what I call saving.'

'I should be grateful.'

She looked almost sad. 'Do you really believe he'll just let you go?'

Felan forced himself to watch the stream, taking notes, but why did he want to help kill all those people in the first place? Was it because of fear? Was it a need for safety? Or was it for something completely different? He'd said he wouldn't hurt anyone any more, so why was he breaking his promise to himself? Why was he letting Nick ruin his life? Why was he *allowing* it?

The Protrudes might deserve as good as they gave, but who was he to decide that?

Felan pushed himself away from the computer. Staring at the live stream made him feel ill. 'He's not going to let us go, is he?'

'He's guilting you into staying.'

That's exactly what Nick was doing. Why hadn't he seen it before? Felan checked his phone for the tenth time that day. Still nothing. Not a word.

'We're still running, Blaez,' he reassured. 'I just need more time.'

'I thought you were staying because you wanted to *help*?'

For the first time that day, Felan smiled. 'Not exactly – I'm waiting. Tristan *will* try and get in touch, I know it. I can't exactly go out and find him, can I? Not while Nick's breathing down my neck, not while we're doing what we're doing.' Felan bit his lip. 'I just need more time.'

She seemed to be deciding on something. 'So, no helping Nick?'

'I'm not pulling the trigger. Never again.'

***

His phone buzzed once. It fell silent.

You just have to ask.

Chapter 42: Perspective

Robotically, Felan changed his clothes: black trousers, black shoes, black jacket. Invisible in the dark, the way Felan always wanted to be.

He slid his belt around his waist, pistol holstered, knife sheathed, and pulled the jacket back down. It concealed his shame. It concealed his dirty secrets. There was little he could do about the rifle except stuff it into an empty satchel and pray. The rifle kept up their appearances: they were going to do as Nick said. They were going to obey.

He cast a long look around the bedrooms and the hallways, the brown walls, the empty space, the secret space. Secrets. He didn't want to be a part of them any more. He hated how unclean they made him feel.

Blaez paced back and forth. She bit her nails; she was never going to be rid of that habit. Felan wanted nothing more than for her to stay out of harm's way – another reason why they had to go, no matter the threats on their lives.

They had to try.

'Is there anything else you want to take with you?'

'Not one damn thing.' The clothes Harvey had given him remained at the Warehouse. The first gift he'd ever been given. Pity clothes. He had nothing, nothing worth taking anyway, except the purple brooch Blaez had gifted him months ago – it would sit on his shirt forever.

'Ready?' she asked.

'Ready.'

He thought it would be freeing, leaving.

It was anything but.

Felan was convinced someone was following them, but every time he looked over his shoulder, he couldn't see anyone, or anything, but black, and dark, and cold. And the silence. The silence followed him everywhere. It ate away at his voice, forced the words back down his dry throat, down into his stomach that perpetually churned. Fear choked him too, squeezing his throat hard enough to leave a bruise, choking him into submission. He rubbed his tattoo, something he would have forever. He supposed he could get a cover-up, but that wasn't the point. He knew it would still be there, underneath, hiding. Always hiding. Lingering where he didn't want it.

'Where is everyone?' Blaez asked.

They stood in the centre of a square, in a small village far outside the Fringe, very similar to the one the Protrudes had raided, but not quite the same. Empty. Everything broken, useless. There was no one. Nothing.

'Gone.' The last time he'd walked by, there had been people.

'Where?'

It wasn't the only abandoned village. Part of him thought the apocalypse had finally come, but he knew the Protrudes were probably to blame, and maybe he was too. The rest of him hated how messed up his life was, and how messed up society had become.

Blaez's question remained unanswered.

Their bags seemed to grow heavier, and mile after mile Felan himself grew heavier, so he blamed it on the baggage; an excuse. That's what society was; an excuse for the lack of change.

'He said he'd meet us here,' Felan said, glancing up the deserted street, the same street he'd discovered Randi on all that time ago. 'Let's find somewhere to hide until he shows up.'

'I wouldn't do that if I were you.'

All the air in the world couldn't fill his lungs any more – not with him so close. If snow had been falling, it would have frozen again, into stronger ice, before it started to sizzle and melt and die. *How did he find out this time?*

'Why do you make it so hard for me, Felan?' Nick asked. He stood beneath a broken street light. 'Why do you make me so angry?'

The man had no visible weapons. He was alone, though a Nick like this had a tongue as sharp as any knife. A Nick like this got what he wanted. It was some horrid form of charisma. Masochistic. *Sick.*

'What are you doing here?' Felan asked. He angled himself so he was in front of Blaez. He would not touch her; Felan would make sure of it, if it was the last thing he did.

Nick leered. 'Do you really think the people of this city are going to welcome you with open arms, especially when they find out what you are? After they find out what you've done?'

Felan bit his lip. Didn't he know that already? Hadn't he thought about that before he even considered texting the number back? Who *was* going to help them, even if they got out? Who would *care*? They'd rejected him the first time – what would stop them from rejecting him again?

'You'll be safe with me,' Nick promised. 'I'll protect you, like I did before. I'll save you – again. You have a home with me, Felan. With us. Don't throw that away now.'

'Don't listen to him,' Blaez said. 'He's trying to get into your head.'

His mother would be ashamed if she could see him now. She'd be so ashamed. She'd saved his life, and he'd tossed it down the drain like rubbish. He didn't even get to say goodbye. She sacrificed her life for him, and this was how he spent it.

It should have been him that day, and every day since, not his mother. It should never have been his mother.

Nick was right. No one was going to help them. No one was waiting for them to come home. No one cared, and no one ever would. What was the point in even trying?

Felan found himself nodding. All he saw was Nick, and a place to stay. All he saw was Nick, and *familiar*. At least with Nick, he knew what to expect. With Nick, he knew when to duck.

'There's a good boy.' Nick smiled. It looked odd and distorted upon his face. 'Now come with me – I need to keep you safe.'

'Okay,' he agreed. The punishment was okay. Nick cared enough to punish him. Nick cared enough to help him. Nick cared, and the city didn't.

'Snap out of it!'

Felan blinked. Snap out of what? Nick was giving him a home. Nick *gave* him a home. Nick cared about him. Nick cared about all of them. He cared about them even when they made him angry. Nick put time and effort into him. No one except his mother had done that.

Felan looked down. Blaez's small hand encircled the entirety of his arm. 'Let me go.'

'He's on his way, Felan,' Blaez said. 'We're getting out of here.'

'Didn't you hear him, Blaez?' Nick said. 'He wants to come with me.'

Blaez put herself between him and Nick. 'How can you sleep at night?'

What was she doing? Nick was helping them. Nick wanted what was best for them. No one else had done that before. Felan's words failed him. He couldn't breathe. Why couldn't he breathe?

'I'm helping you,' Nick said. 'I help kids like you. I give you homes, and all you do is hurt me.'

'Because you're making us do things we shouldn't be doing! You're hurting us!'

'No!' Nick roared. 'The city hurt you – not me! They gave up on you! I didn't!'

Felan remembered that first day without his mother. He hadn't slept at all; far too awake, far too afraid, far too scared that his dad would come in after him. He'd sounded so angry and Felan hadn't understood what he'd done wrong.

Then his dad had showed up in the dark, and with those angry steps of his, he'd yanked the door off the frame and grabbed Felan by his shirt. He'd yelled. A lot. He'd slapped him once or twice. He'd thrown him to the floor. The floorboards had shaken that night, and at the age of seven, he had stayed where he was, too afraid, too afraid of his own dad. And when the front door slammed shut, Felan had crawled into a corner and cried.

His dad had beat the hell out of him. Nick punished him when he disobeyed. Both situations left him bleeding, and hurting, and questioning everything.

Had there ever been a difference between the two?

'Stop getting in my head,' Felan cried out. 'Stop it!'

Nick's laughter made it worse. 'You were always so easy to manipulate. You were always so eager to please. You would do anything for recognition.'

'Shut up!'

'Now now, Felan – is that really how you speak to the man who saved your life?'

He could do it, couldn't he? He could say it. He wanted out, so he could say it. He thought it might make him feel better.

'I don't want anything to do with you any more.'

It made it so much worse. His chest tightened at the sight of Nick, standing so nonchalantly in the middle of the dimly lit street. His chest tightened at the thought of escape. It scared him how afraid he was. Nine years, and he was still afraid. Nine years, and he'd got nowhere.

'Hmm,' Nick said. He didn't move any closer. He watched them with that evil glint in his eyes. 'Edward's awfully young for drop-offs, don't you think?'

Felan pointed his pistol at Nick. He didn't remember doing it. It didn't scare him like it should have.

'Put it down, Felan,' Blaez hissed. 'Put it down!'

He shook her off. He held the pistol steady.

'You've given me no choice. I have no one to cover your drop-offs – he'll have to do it. You never know, maybe he'll do what you were too weak to do.'

'Anyone can see us!' Blaez tried again. She tried to force the pistol down.

Nothing could abate Felan's anger.

'He's a kid,' Felan choked. He wasn't sure if it was anger or fear he choked on. Maybe it was a bit of both. 'He's an innocent little kid. You won't do it.'

Nick eyed the pistol with the most twisted smile Felan had ever seen. 'Neither will you.'

He turned and vanished into the night.

Chapter 43: Choice

Blaez's arms wound around his waist and pulled him close. It was his fault. It was always his fault. He stroked her hair, played with the now not-so-choppy ends and smoothed them down.

Always his fault.

'He'll be okay,' Blaez whispered. 'Edward will be okay.'

Felan was stupid to think Accalia could fend Nick off. He'd rip her to shreds the second she stood up to protect the poor kid. And Tala – Nick would do what he wanted and no one would bat an eyelid.

'I have to get in position before the bombs go off,' he decided, pushing his friend away. This was the only way.

'What? No! Felan – he's on his way!'

'Exactly. You can still go.'

'Not without you. We made a deal,' Blaez reminded him.

He looked away. 'Edward's in danger.'

And Tristan appeared, dressed casually, like he'd said he would be. Bang on time, like he'd said he would be. Ready to help, like he'd said he would. 'Are you guys ready to go?'

He had to do this. Blaez could still get away, and that was good. If he stayed, he could protect Edward. He could help Accalia. If he stayed, Edward wouldn't have to do the things Nick wanted him to do.

'Felan? Blaez?'

'I'm not going with you,' Felan mumbled. The street light flickered.

'We agreed you'd both come with me.' Tristan came close, too close.

Felan backed away. 'I have to do what Nick says.' For Edward. For Accalia. For everyone else that was going to get hurt if he didn't do it. How could he live with that on his conscience?

'You don't.'

That was easy for him to say. 'He's going to hurt Edward. I have to go back.' He rifled through his satchel, his mind racing. First aid kit, spare jumper, out-of-date cereal bars, an old bottle of water, loose change, paper; he shoved it all at Blaez. 'Take it. I don't need it. Take it.'

She let it all drop to the floor. The first aid kit split open. Coins tumbled and rolled like they were in a circus ring.

'No! What are you doing? You need to take it all and go while you still can,' he said, tongue numb, lips uncooperative, stumbling over every syllable. He dropped to his knees and gathered up the pieces. His hands wouldn't stop shaking, and he couldn't keep a grip. 'Dammit.' Frustrated, he tried again. Coins slipped through his fingers. Bandages unravelled at his touch. The bottle spun away from him when he tried to grab it but missed. 'Dammit!'

He didn't realise he was crying until something warm landed on his hand.

'Felan – stop it!' Blaez was next to him. She scooped everything up in seconds and dumped it back in his satchel. 'You're not going anywhere but with us,' she said.

He lunged and grabbed the satchel from her. Why had she put everything back in? He didn't need it. 'No. No, I need to get in position. I need to help,' he said.

'No.'

Felan hurried in the direction of the Protrudes, crying, gasping, unable to control himself. What would Blaez think of him? What would Tristan think of him? What would happen when he went back? When he killed those people? Would Nick accept him with open arms? Would he punish him for trying to leave?

What if nothing changed?

'Felan!'

Tristan appeared in front of him, blocking the mouth of the alley he needed to go down.

'Take Blaez and go. Take her. Please take her.'

'I'm not leaving you. Not again.'

Next thing he knew, he was running. He was running towards Tristan, focused on his face, to punch it, to hit it, to make it go away.

Tristan dodged the punch and spun around, crushing Felan against his chest. 'Stop,' Tristan grunted.

'I can't. I can't. I need to go... I need to go... I need to go!' Felan twisted, and turned, and kicked at the man's shins; but he held fast, and Felan couldn't break free. He headbutted the man's chin – the man acted like nothing had happened. Felan couldn't breathe. He elbowed Tristan's side. Nothing. The man squeezed him tighter.

'Edward. I have to help Edward.'

Blaez ripped the satchel from his hands and tossed it over the wall.

'I need that!' he yelled.

Why was she helping Tristan now? She didn't know him. *He* didn't know him. He should never have trusted him in the first place. He should never have tried to contact him again. They should have left when they had the chance and now it was too late. Now he had no satchel, no rifle, and no way of helping Nick. No way of helping Edward.

No way of keeping Edward safe.

'Not any more,' Blaez said. She was crying again. She was so small, like a child, like Edward. The night made her even smaller, hidden by a shadow, like the moon behind a cloud.

'I have to.' He tried to break free of the arms that trapped him. He tried to make *any* progress. It was futile. His body grew limp. Drained. He couldn't even hold himself up any more.

Tristan loosened his hold. It felt like an uncaging, but he still couldn't breathe. He stumbled on weak knees. Tristan held him up. He was so *weak*.

'Felan – think! Do you really want to help kill a hundred people?'

'I already did,' Felan said. He'd watched them for weeks. He'd told everyone everything he knew. 'I don't have a choice.'

'You do! You have! You can choose to walk away!'

Felan wanted to curl up into a ball, and he would have, had his body obeyed him. 'I have to stay. For Edward. I can't leave.' He couldn't leave. He'd never be able to leave. He'd never get away. He'd never get away...

'Yes, you can. You're a child – you're both children. I'll get you out of this. I can get you help – but I need you to focus,' Tristan said. 'Can you do that?'

Felan nodded. His cheeks were wet. Everything was sore. He inhaled cold air. It burned.

'Harvey wasn't the only double agent, Felan. I'm one too. He wasn't loyal to Nick, or Maddison, and neither am I.'

He couldn't breathe again. Harvey? Why was Harvey in this conversation? Why was Harvey even relevant? He didn't get it; they knew each other? They must have if they were both Protrudes.

Thankfully, Blaez was there to ask the questions, because Felan thought he might pass out. Too much, too soon.

'Who are you loyal to?' Blaez asked.

'The cops. Social workers. Child protective services. The people that try to keep this city safe. The people that try to help children out of terrible situations. I'm a social worker. Harvey was a cop. I can help you,' Tristan said.

Felan took it like a punch to the face. 'Who would want to help kids like us?'

'You've been manipulated. You've been threatened. You've been beaten. That's child abuse.'

Felan *hated* that phrase. *Hated it*. Just like how he hated the nurses that said it like it meant nothing, like it was just words, just like saying 'hello' in the mornings. It made him feel completely and utterly worthless, like he meant nothing, not even to the nurses that tried to help – *tried* being the key word. No one looked for him when he ran. No one cared.

Nick was there in the back of his mind, stood shoulder to shoulder with Felan's father. They were both the same. Nothing had changed, just as Felan had thought.

The next flood of tears dripped down his cheeks.

'Felan, you've done nothing wrong,' Tristan said. 'Absolutely nothing wrong.'

'It doesn't matter,' he cried. 'It's too late. We've done things.'

'Maybe you have, but what you're about to do is a lot worse,' Tristan said. 'You need to make a choice.'

'What choice? *I don't have a choice!*' he roared. If it hadn't been for Blaez and Tristan, he knew he would have collapsed. Where had all his energy gone? Why couldn't he stop crying?

'I won't let you do something you'll regret for the rest of your life,' Tristan said firmly.

Felan didn't want to look at him. 'I regret everything already.'

'Exactly – and this won't make that guilt go away, Felan. It'll make it ten times worse... but right now, we can walk away, and this never happened.'

Could he? Could he really just walk away from all of this? What about Accalia? Would she feel betrayed? Would she hate them for leaving without her? Would she hate them for abandoning her there alone? And Edward – what would happen to him?

'Felan, I need an answer. Otherwise, I can't help you.'

Tristan had come when Felan asked him to, and that was the most an adult had ever done for him in nine years. 'Please just get me out of here,' he sobbed.

He hung his head low and his tears fell to the ground. He couldn't stop crying. He couldn't stop. He couldn't stop, couldn't stop, couldn't...

'Okay, okay. It's all going to be okay,' Tristan said. He patted Felan's shoulder once. 'Let's go.'

With Tristan on one side, Blaez on the other, they helped him walk. He was too scared to walk by himself. He was terrified. What would happen now that he'd defied Nick again?

'Where are we going?' Blaez asked.

'Far away – we can't be around when the bombs go off.'

'Let's hurry,' she agreed. 'It won't be long.'

In the dark, they probably looked like the weirdest trio ever, ambling down the street because Felan couldn't find it in himself to move his body. His mind was turning, always turning, but his body wouldn't move. When he asked Tristan what was happening, he nearly cried in relief that Tristan had an answer.

'It's the shock,' Tristan said. 'It happens. It'll wear off soon enough – I wouldn't worry about it too much. Here, Blaez,' he directed. Tristan fumbled in his pocket and held out a tiny key. He unlocked the door to the block of flats, and they stumbled inside – he made sure to lock it behind him. 'I'm upstairs,' he said.

Tristan used another key to let them in when they reached the next door. It was pretty basic for a flat. A cosy front room with two sofas led into a small kitchen, in which sat a table with two chairs. There was a tiny bedroom right at the back with an en-suite bathroom.

And a fine layer of dust coated the furniture.

Tristan disappeared into the kitchen and came back a few minutes later. 'You'll be safe here until I can get you to the station,' he said. 'And I hope you're okay with oat milk – the milk in the fridge went out of date two months ago.' He handed Felan a mug of hot chocolate.

Blaez took the second. 'It's fine,' she said. 'Thank you.'

Felan said nothing. He curled up under a blanket on the sofa, as far away from everyone as he could get. The mug in his hands was hot, almost too hot, but he didn't care. He needed a distraction.

To his dismay, Blaez sat down right next to him and curled up into his side. Tristan collapsed onto the other sofa and sipped on what smelled like coffee.

'How did you and Harvey get mixed up in all this?' Blaez asked.

Tristan set his coffee down on the wooden table in the middle of the room. He sank back into the chair – it looked like he was about to fall asleep. He started to talk.

'It was something I suggested, and Harvey backed me. See, we'd been friends a long time,' he said. 'Twelve years ago, I proposed that we had to understand before we could help. We couldn't properly understand if we didn't know first-hand what it was like, what was going on.' He frowned. 'They were wary at first – who knew what could happen to us in there? It took years, but eventually they agreed. After more meetings, and careful planning, Harvey and I were placed in the field, bang in the centre of the whole operation – each of us in one of the two most dangerous gangs in Guadalupe.'

Blaez gasped in all the right places. 'That's so dangerous!'

'Yeah – they thought so too,' Tristan said. 'It worked as we hoped it would. Every couple of days, we'd meet back at the station and report our findings. But we were away from the station for weeks at a time, and we had no way of contacting each other – and we needed to, otherwise it wouldn't work – hence why Harvey became a double agent for both Nick and Maddison.'

Felan nearly dropped his drink.

'We could work even when we were away from the station. We were working around the clock, but Nick grew tired of Harvey's games and his failure to bring back any useful information – Harvey grew obsessed with getting you guys out of there.'

And Felan had done nothing but condemn Harvey for betraying them.

'Then it was just me. I kept going, feeding information back to the cops. How many kids, how they got there, what they were being forced to do... what I was being forced to do. And then your friend showed up.'

'Randi!' Blaez said.

Tristan nodded his head. 'I tried to get him out – Nick got there first.'

Felan put his drink down and pulled the blanket over his shoulders. 'That's something I never understood. I know Nick sent him away to get information, but he never gave up the location of the base.'

'I told him about our plans, and he wanted to help. He wouldn't let me get him out, not without his boyfriend, or you guys. I tried to explain to him that we'd get to you all, but he wouldn't listen. He left without saying anything. By the time I realised what he'd done, it was too late.'

The guilt returned. Again. 'He came back for us?'

He'd condemned Harvey. He'd condemned Randi. He recalled Randi's last words: 'I tried.' That boy had tried to save his friends, and Felan hadn't seen it.

'Yeah. But Nick got there first. Again,' Tristan said bitterly.

Felan realised something. 'Randi never went to the cops. It was you and Harvey!' he exclaimed. 'Caleb, oh no...'

Blaez clocked on. 'I know, Felan,' she whispered. 'I know.'

'He died thinking Randi betrayed him...' He trailed off. God. It was all such a mess.

Tristan's hand froze as he reached for his coffee. 'Caleb's dead?'

Felan nodded. He'd cried himself out. 'He helped set up some bombs not too long ago – it went wrong.'

Tristan's face crumpled. 'I'm sorry.'

He shrugged. 'Don't be.' It happened, and they had to move on from it. No use crying over something they couldn't change.

It went quiet again, but it wasn't an awful silence. Felan couldn't stop staring at the window, and every time he blinked, he prayed he wouldn't see Nick leering through it.

Blaez poked his arm. 'He's not gonna find us here.'

Felan couldn't be bothered to get up, so he stole Blaez's hot chocolate and took a sip. She took it back without complaint, although she did poke him again, a little harder than before, with a cheeky smile.

'You weren't like the other kids I helped, Felan.' The redhead stood up and closed the curtains. Beneath the window sat an ottoman that Tristan rummaged around in. 'I wouldn't forget them, but I never stopped to wonder about them. With you, I always wondered what happened to you after I left.' The man retrieved a blanket and threw it to Blaez, who smiled and buried herself within it.

Felan glanced up and Tristan made eye contact. Felan couldn't look away. No, he didn't *want* to look away.

'I see now that I should never have left you there,' the man said, sitting back in his chair. 'I should have waited for your father, and I should have taken you to the station where they could have helped you. Instead, I put my job as an undercover agent above your life, and for that I'm eternally sorry.'

Felan could've shouted. He could've screamed. He could've cried. He could've punched Tristan in the face. He didn't. Of course he didn't.

It might have happened to him, all of it, but it had been his choice to let it control him. It had been his choice to dwell on it for so long. It had been his choice to deny it. The easy thing. Evolve or repeat – something he'd learned from Accalia while training: '*You can keep repeating by doing the same thing, the easy thing, or you can do what's hard and evolve.*'

Felan was done being bitter. 'You couldn't have known this would happen,' he said to the man.

'It was my job to protect you. I failed.'

Felan tapped his fingers on the arm of the sofa. 'You're here now, aren't you?'

Blaez nudged her way closer. Felan lifted his arm and let her cuddle into his side. She'd fall asleep if she wasn't careful.

'I'm resting my eyes,' she said.

'Yeah, yeah.'

He stayed awake long after the sirens stopped screaming.

Chapter 44: Testimony

'Someone's coming around to pick us up.'

Felan jumped to his feet, the television nothing more than white noise in the background. Blaez threw the blanket off and joined him. She pressed her shoulder against his.

'Where are they taking us?' Felan asked.

'To the station.'

'Then what?' Blaez joined in.

The man shook his head, a smile on his lips. 'Then we get you guys somewhere safe. Somewhere Nick can't find you.'

'What about the others? When will they be getting out?' Felan wondered if Accalia had stayed behind with Edward. He wondered if she'd picked up a rifle and used it. He wondered if she hated them for leaving.

'This is the part of the job that no one likes,' Tristan said. He slung a messenger bag onto the sofa and began to pile things inside. 'We can't just rush in. It has to be done carefully and methodically – if we rush in, they'll disperse and regroup and we'll have to start all over again,' he said slowly.

The way he phrased it jogged his memory. 'Mr Bailey said something similar – it was you!'

Tristan froze. 'You've met Mr Bailey?'

They told him about what they'd overheard the night the cops came to the Warehouse.

'Mr Bailey's a good man,' he said. 'He has a heart. He listens.'

'Is he the one coming to get us?' Blaez asked.

'Yes. He should be here soon.'

That was good. He already liked Mr Bailey – he sounded like a guy who'd give him a chance. But the others...

'He's right, Felan,' Blaez said. 'The best thing we can do for the others is wait and help Tristan as much as we can. We know things they don't. We can tell them everything.'

'I guess so.'

'Felan, look at me.' He did so without complaint. 'I know what you're thinking. You think I'm a coward for not going back to help. You think you're a coward for listening to me.'

'No.'

'Yes. Yes, you do.'

'Blaez...'

'We can't help them if we end up like Randi. We can't help them if Nick kills us first. I know, Felan – I'm scared of what'll happen to us now.'

They both simultaneously looked over at Tristan; he watched them with something akin to pity and Felan hated it.

'What *will* happen to us?' she asked.

Tristan looked exhausted. 'I'm doing my best, but most people in the city... they criminalise kids like you. They don't give you a chance. They see the knives in your hands, and they condemn you for it – they don't see the people forcing them on you, or forcing you to do their bidding. They don't see abuse; they see choice.'

'What do we do?' Felan asked.

Tristan sat the bag beside the front door, next to Blaez's bag, and Felan's weapons. 'I won't lie to you – it won't be easy, this transition. People will hate you for what you've done, whether you've done it or not,' he said.

'I hate myself for what I've done,' Felan whispered.

Tristan put a hand on Blaez's arm, and his other on Felan's. 'You have to know one thing,' he said, looking from Felan to Blaez. 'It was not your fault. None of this was your fault. There was nothing you could have done.'

'I killed a man,' Felan said. 'I've used my knife. I've sold drugs to people and ruined their lives; all because I was too scared to run.'

'Exactly. Manipulation – it comes in many forms,' Tristan explained. 'You've been manipulated. That's abuse, and that's what we're trying to get the city to see.'

'Edward...' He trailed off.

'Accalia will keep him safe. You said so yourself,' Blaez reminded him. 'We have to put ourselves first. It's the only way things can get better.'

'I'm scared.'

'I know,' she said. 'I'm scared too.'

***

'Won't Nick be watching us?' Blaez asked, peeking out of the window.

They were waiting inside for Tristan to hurry up, and for Mr Bailey to arrive.

'No,' Felan said.

'How do you know?'

He looked up and down the street. 'Because he would have stopped us by now. There's no way he's watching.'

A cop car turned the corner and Felan fought the urge to run. He couldn't remember the last time he'd even been in a car – maybe he never had been. They were dangerous. They'd killed his mother. They'd ruined his life.

He gave himself a quick once-over. Although the old clothes Tristan had given him were a bit too big, they were clean: a pair of jeans, a jumper he'd been given the night before, and a pair of shoes that didn't have holes in. Tristan helped him stuff newspaper in the toes so they wouldn't fall off his feet.

Blaez tugged at her shirt. It was the smallest thing Tristan could find in his wardrobe, but it was still huge. She opted to keep her black trousers on, as they weren't that bad.

'This is massive!'

'It's an extra small.'

'Shut up.'

They walked outside just as Mr Bailey stepped out of the car. He shook their hands and introduced himself. 'Are you guys all set?' he asked with a smile. Like Felan had guessed, the man was cool and easy-going, and just seemed to want to help. Tristan trusted him, and if Felan trusted Tristan, he guessed he could trust Mr Bailey too.

'Waiting for Tristan,' Blaez said.

'I'm always waiting for him,' Mr Bailey said with a laugh. 'He's rarely on time.'

Tristan had been on time last night, Felan remembered. He'd been on time when it mattered. 'I like him,' Felan said, swallowing a lump in his throat.

'Yeah – I like him too. He's one of the best,' Mr Bailey praised. 'You're in safe hands with him.'

Tristan showed up a minute or two later, bag in tow. 'Let's go,' he said, ushering them to the car. 'Let's not linger more than we have to.'

Felan climbed in after Blaez, her satchel sat between them. Tristan had given him a carrier bag to put his weapons in. Apparently, they needed to take them to the station.

He flinched when Mr Bailey closed the door, and he reached for his knife on instinct, forgetting it was in the bag at his feet. He couldn't help but think he was being trapped again.

'Felan?' He jumped and looked up. Mr Bailey stared at him through the mirror. 'Don't forget your seat belt,' he warned.

It wasn't a threat, he told himself. It was a simple reminder to stay safe. With that in mind, Felan strapped himself in. He hated how restrictive it felt, like something was holding him down.

'Have you ever been in a car before?' Blaez asked him.

'I don't remember,' he said. 'You?'

'No. This is a first for me.'

'What do you think of cars so far?'

'They're quicker than walking. And running,' she said.

He looked out of the window. In a moving vehicle, the world was faster, and blurry. It was going too fast and needed to slow down. They drove past the bakery where Felan had scrounged a bread roll and some water. They drove past the pharmacy they'd robbed that one time, where they'd stolen that elderly woman's pills. They drove past Jubilee Bank, then Vermillion Bank ten minutes later. Felan recognised particular street corners where he did his drop-offs.

He recognised the Slum.

Next to him, he could tell Blaez recognised it too, a faraway look in her eyes.

Mr Bailey continued to drive, and finally they pulled into the police station, a place Felan had never been to before.

Being escorted inside was a feeling Felan never wanted to experience again.

He saw the judgemental looks the other officers gave them, and he turned his head downwards in an attempt to hide the bruises on his face.

Officers muttered to each other, and he couldn't tell if it was about him or not. He didn't think he wanted to know. He wondered how many of those men he'd helped injure in the past, how many of those men had lost a friend because of his actions.

Then he heard the voice, and he grinned, despite the situation. He couldn't have been any more accurate in his mental description of the cop, though he was even bigger than he'd thought. Definitely an extra, extra large in uniform. Maybe even a triple XL. Some of his buttons were undone, and Felan saw a few stitches ready to burst around the arms. He wanted to laugh.

Instead, he ducked his head back down and let himself be led by Mr Bailey and Tristan.

Tristan opened a door and they walked inside. There was a small table with four chairs. On the table stood what looked like a microphone.

'The room is soundproof,' Mr Bailey reassured. 'Anything you say in here stays in here. It's in strictest confidence.'

'What about the microphone?' Felan asked.

'It's routine. We record everything you say in case we need it later.'

'To use against us?'

'No. Not at all. It's handy to have an audio record as well as a written one – we can listen to it later to check our notes are correct. I promise it's nothing to worry about. All we're going to do in here is ask a few questions,' Mr Bailey said. 'I'll be writing down key points of your answers, but it's vital you answer as truthfully as you can.'

'Are we going to prison?' Felan asked.

'Not a chance. You're not in any trouble regarding the law. I can assure you of that,' Tristan said. 'After we're done in here, we need to get you somewhere safe. Preferably out of the city. Somewhere new.'

Out of the city? That sounded like a dream, a dream Felan thought he'd never live out.

'Before we start... I know this is going to be hard for you, but I need you to hand in your weapons. I should have done this at the front desk, but I thought it'd be easier without an audience,' Mr Bailey said.

Blaez handed over her satchel without complaint. She slid her pistol and knife over the table. Mr Bailey put them safely in a box on the floor.

'Felan?' he encouraged.

Felan was glad Blaez had thrown his satchel over the wall, because all he had left was his new pistol, and his knife.

The pistol was easy enough – he'd never wanted it anyway. He'd shot Tristan with the old one, but they looked identical. He caught the man staring at it as Felan handed it over. He never wanted to touch that thing again.

He withdrew his knife from the bag and turned it over in his hands. He'd killed someone with it. He'd stabbed people with it. He'd used it. But he loved his knife, more than he cared to admit. More than he should. So much so that he was ashamed to feel that way. He'd had it the whole time, by his side, like a friend. He'd had it so long it felt like an extra limb. To give that up...

'I've had it for so long.'

'I know,' Blaez said. 'It's time to let it go.'

'I don't know if I can.'

She inched her hand over to his and touched the hilt. 'Let me,' she said.

He didn't remember how long he sat there for, debating. It must have been a while, but neither adult looked bored. Not frustrated. Not angry. They waited, for him.

'I'm sorry,' he said quietly. He passed his knife to Blaez and stuffed his hand into his pocket. There. But already his hand itched for the weapon – even more so when Blaez slid his knife to Mr Bailey, who placed it in the box.

'We'll do this at your own pace,' Tristan said. 'If there's something you don't want to answer, just say so, and we'll move on, okay?'

He was thankful for the huge pockets in the jumper – he could get his hands lost in the fabric, clenching and unclenching them, until the itch faded. If it faded. His gaze flickered up to Tristan, back down.

He felt naked without his knife in reach.

'Would you prefer it if you were asked individually, or together?'

'We've nothing to hide,' Blaez said, so softly he almost missed it. Her answer abated the itch – he didn't want to be alone. They'd do it together, like they always did.

'Okay. We'll ask you questions one at a time,' Tristan continued.

'Fire away,' Blaez said.

'How long have you been involved?'

'A few years?'

'You're new to all this… whereas I've had years to come to terms with it.'

Felan blanched. Here he was, practically destroyed after less than one year, and she was still standing after years of the same treatment, a time frame he'd never fully comprehended the meaning of until now. She'd told him before, back at the start, and he'd ignored it. He'd known her for so long, and he'd never brought it back up again. He'd never asked her.

Then again, there were lots of things he'd never asked her, lots of things he should know but didn't. They were friends, and he didn't even know her birthday.

'Less than a year,' he muttered. The questions reminded him of the Elders, the time they were interrogated after they watched the Protrudes invade a whole town. Randi had been with them. Randi had been alive.

'How were you treated?'

'At the start, it was everything I ever wanted. I know now that was the whole point,' Blaez said bitterly. 'They treated us like family to make us want to stay.'

Felan pulled up his sleeves. Many white lines stood stark on his skin, though a scary amount were still new, still raw. 'I have scars from where Nick punished me.'

'What did you do while you were there?'

He lost track of who asked what – he just wanted to get these questions over and done with.

'Robbed places, sold drugs. We hurt a few people along the way,' Felan listed off. He ignored the scribble of the pen.

'Did you get a choice of what to do?'

'It was selling drugs or killing. For me, that wasn't a choice,' Felan said. He kept his face neutral. The carpeted floor was really interesting for some reason.

'What drugs did you sell?'

'Mostly cocaine. A little bit of ecstasy. Maybe the odd bit of heroin?' Blaez stopped. 'Are we going to get in trouble for that? Supplying drugs to people?'

'No – the only person who'll be in trouble is the person who forced you to do it in the first place,' Tristan said. 'You've done nothing wrong.'

Blaez settled back down in her seat. Felan kept his hands scrunched up tight in his pockets. He hadn't even cared enough to know what he had been selling to people.

Mr Bailey turned a page. 'What weapons were you made to use?'

'For me, a sniper rifle. A pistol sometimes. Knives. That sort of thing.'

Felan wished he had his hands on the hilt. 'A pistol. My knife. My fists.'

They asked about the beginning, and when Felan couldn't find the words, Blaez was right there, ready. 'You had to win a fight. If we didn't win, we were chucked back out onto the streets – there was an incentive to win. No one wanted to get thrown back out again,' Blaez said. 'Even as young as we were, we had to fight.' Felan pulled his sleeve up higher. 'We got a tattoo after we won. It was something we rightfully earned. I remember being proud of that tattoo.'

Tristan's hand twitched on the table.

The questions started to get repetitive after a while, and so did the answers. Felan kept his to the bare minimum; Blaez was a trooper and gave as much detail as she could. They could have written novels with the information she provided. With Felan, they probably couldn't even scratch together a shoddy haiku.

'What's the headcount of the Wolves now? Just so we have a number to work with.'

'Seventeen. Eighteen including Edward; he's a child, Tristan. No more than twelve,' Felan said. And he'd left him there with Nick, knowing full well what Nick would do to him.

'Apart from Edward, is there anyone else you're worried about?'

'Accalia,' Blaez said. 'The others… we tolerated each other.'

'You weren't close to the others?'

'No.'

'Can I have the pen?' Felan asked.

Tristan handed it to him without speaking. While the numbers floated in his head, Felan scribbled down the coordinates of the base. He pushed the papers back.

'It's underground.'

'What is?'

'The new base.'

Mr Bailey took the numbers down on a separate piece of paper – Felan assumed he would be passing it to his colleagues; they could keep tabs on the area by the coordinates.

'If you need me to, I can hack into their cameras.' He'd do whatever he could, if it meant getting Accalia and Edward out of there.

'You can do that?' Mr Bailey asked.

'I did it all the time.' With Randi. Dead. With Harvey. Dead. Just him. Alone.

'I think that's enough for now,' Tristan said. He fiddled with the microphone; Felan thought he was turning it off. 'Thank you, both of you. I know that can't have been easy.'

Felan shrugged.

'We'll be staying here for the rest of the day,' Tristan said.

Felan took that to mean they (as in himself and Blaez) would be staying at the station. That was fine by him. As long as they could stay with Mr Bailey, he didn't care what happened. He knew one thing for sure – he had to tell Mr Bailey everything. He was the cop, not Tristan. He would know the proper procedure for murder.

Tristan said he needed to run some errands, and Blaez stood up to follow. Seeing his chance, Felan grabbed Mr Bailey's sleeve. 'Can I talk to you? Alone?'

The cop looked down in surprise. 'Sure – we'll catch you guys up!' He closed the door and waited.

Felan hated how much his head spun. 'As much as I trust Tristan, I just wanted to be sure,' he said. That was about all he could manage.

'Shall we sit down?' Mr Bailey invited.

Felan nodded, thankful for the distraction, no matter how small. 'I…'

He stopped. He couldn't say it. He couldn't say it because he was a coward. Always had been, and always would be. He bit down hard on his knuckle to stop his hand from shaking.

'Felan – look at me,' Mr Bailey said. 'Nothing you say will change our minds about you, or Blaez.'

How could he be sure? Mr Bailey didn't even know what he was about to say – no one would look at him the same way; he'd be criminalised for sure. But he had to say something. He couldn't keep this quiet – not something as serious as murder. He had to do *something*.

'There was a guy,' he began in a whisper. The memory came back all too easily, like muscle memory. 'He came up behind me and strangled me. He was bigger than I was. I couldn't move. I... I remembered I had a knife and, and I swear it was self-defence. I stabbed him once, or maybe twice. I can't really remember, and then he, he... I didn't want to hurt anyone.'

He ducked his head and prepared for the blow that followed. He squeezed his eyes shut, tense, heart spilling out of his mouth, running, from him, running. Seconds went by. Nothing. He expected the delay – Nick had done it before. So had his father. The anticipation boiled the air right out of his lungs.

'It was self-defence, like you said. If you hadn't retaliated, you wouldn't be in this room right now.'

'How am I not in any trouble?' Felan cried, looking at Mr Bailey in disbelief. 'I killed someone!'

'You can trust Tristan when he says you're not in any trouble – and you can trust me when I say it too; Felan, you've done nothing wrong.'

'I felt his blood on my hands – I still see it,' he said shakily. 'Every day I see it.'

'I'm sorry you went through that. I truly am.'

Someone apologised to *him*, because *he* killed someone? That made no sense. Had he accidentally taken hallucinogenic drugs at Tristan's instead of a paracetamol?

'So, I'm not going to prison?'

'No. Now let's go and find Tristan before he leaves.'

They found Tristan saying goodbye to Blaez by the front door. Before Felan could tell the man no, Tristan engulfed Felan in a bone-crushing hug. Somehow, he found himself hugging him back.

'Take care – I'll see you very soon, alright?'

'Are you going back?' he asked.

Back to what? Surely there'd be no one left. Nick would have killed them all. No survivors.

The man seemed to have come to the same conclusion. 'No. I've done what I came to do,' he said.

'What are you going to do now?' Blaez asked.

Tristan smiled over his shoulder as he pushed the door open.

'I need to keep you two safe!' he called.

Much to the dismay of the other officers, Felan threw up in the bin in the corner of the room the moment Tristan was out of sight.

'Now come with me – I need to keep you safe.'

Chapter 45: Acme

'I would have fared the same with Maddison, wouldn't I?'

Blaez was passed out on his lap again. He found it sweet, how she trusted him enough to be that close while she slept. The fact that she trusted him at all was a miracle in itself. She was still with him, after everything. She still wanted to be with him. He watched a strand of hair shiver every time she breathed.

'We're going to stop them,' Tristan said. 'I promise.'

Because he was a kid, alone on the streets, he'd been targeted by those who'd used it to their advantage. It just so happened that Nick had got there first. And although he knew it would have been the same regardless, he still thought of what his life would have been like had Nick never showed up that day.

'What was Maddison like?' he asked. No matter how many times he thought of her, he could never form a mental image in his head. All he could see was high heels and painted nails and a faceless shadow just out of sight.

'A monster.'

Even from across the room, Felan could see the lines Maddison carved into the man's forehead. 'Like you said, you're going to stop them.'

Tristan hummed and stared at the ceiling.

Felan sank lower into the sofa, glad of the extra pillows Tristan had offered – *someone* appeared to have stolen most of them. The culprit cuddled up to him even more in her sleep. It was crazy, how one minute she could be a complete danger to everyone around her, and next transformed into what he could only describe as a living teddy bear.

With a yawn, he pulled her closer and let the waves of tiredness wash over him. He wasn't sleepy, not by any means –

he just needed a little rest for the time being, until he felt brave enough to close his eyes.

'I've found somewhere for you to stay,' Tristan said. 'Somewhere they won't find you.'

Felan tried to act indifferent while tucking a shivering strand of hair behind Blaez's ear. 'Are we staying together?'

'I would never dream of splitting you up. It wouldn't be fair to do that.'

'Thank you,' Felan said. He hesitated. 'About the other night, I don't know what I was thinking.'

'You were thinking what Nick taught you to think, Felan. It's nothing to be ashamed of.'

'Will it ever go away?'

'It'll take time. You know that.'

Time. It always came back to time with Felan.

Tristan flicked the lights off when he left the room. Felan lay with his eyes on the doorway, Blaez snoring softly against his chest.

He didn't remember falling asleep.

***

'Weisworth?'

The name sounded strange on his tongue. He imagined it to be cold, maybe haunted; it wouldn't surprise him if it was a ghost town. He wasn't at all that educated on places outside the city of Guadalupe.

'It's up country,' Mr Bailey said. 'A lovely rural town. Very quiet.'

'Mrs Walters is excited to meet you,' Tristan added. 'It's been a while since she's had older kids under her care.'

Blaez held her train ticket under intense scrutiny. 'And how far away is Weisworth?'

'One hundred and sixty-seven miles,' Mr Bailey said.

'Goddamn,' Felan said. 'I knew you wanted to get rid of us, but this seems a little bit excessive.'

'I don't want to make the same mistake twice,' Tristan said.

Felan grinned at the man in question. 'You haven't.'

'It says here we leave tomorrow,' Blaez read, blinking. 'Is that right?'

'Yeah – train leaves at midday,' Mr Bailey said.

'So soon?' Felan asked quietly. As much as he wanted to get out, would they ever see Tristan again? Or Mr Bailey?

'The quicker we get you out, the harder it'll be for them to track you down.' Tristan reached into his pockets. 'I've got you guys a present.'

'Huh?'

'We'll need to stay in touch – legal reasons – so I thought I'd treat you.'

In his hands were two brand, spanking new phones. They weren't anything like the ones Nick bought – they were in an entire league of their own. Too much.

'I can't take it. It's too much. Even the train ticket was pushing it,' Felan said, laughing, but he meant what he said. He couldn't take any more of Tristan's money.

The man had been good enough to let them stay at his house for the last few days – it was getting ridiculous! He knew how much a phone cost. No way was he going to be able to pay the man back.

'I owe you your life, Felan,' Tristan said. 'I ruined your childhood.'

'And you've given it back,' he said. 'I don't need a phone.'

'I want you to have it. I want both of you to take them, and I want you to stay in touch.'

Felan took a phone. Blaez did the same.

'You have my number on there, and Tristan's,' Mr Bailey said. 'In case you ever need anything. We've spoken to Mrs Walters, and she's okayed for her number to be on there too. Everything's ready to go – we already packed the boxes they came in.'

'You've already packed our stuff?'

'Well, you didn't have much stuff to begin with,' Mr Bailey said. 'We've found you a few things to take with you; clothes-wise, other bits and pieces.'

Felan was speechless. They'd willingly spent money on him, even after what he'd done? Were they crazy? He thought they must be. No one in their right mind would spend money on a criminal.

'I'll know if you chuck the bag, Felan,' Tristan said seriously. 'You're keeping it, and that's final.'

'Fine.'

'Thank you,' Blaez said. 'Both of you. For everything.'

'Yeah – thank you,' Felan added sheepishly. He'd been so caught up in his thoughts that he hadn't even thanked the two overly generous men for everything they'd done over the last few days.

'It's been my pleasure,' Mr Bailey said. 'Don't be a stranger, you hear me?'

The cop left Tristan's flat soon after.

'Was that goodbye?' Blaez asked, worriedly.

Felan knew how she felt. He didn't even know where to *begin*.

'Unfortunately, yes – he's never been one for words. Likes to get out quick,' Tristan explained.

Something heavy landed on Felan's gut. 'What about you?'

'I'll be seeing you off,' he said.

'Really?'

'Of course. I'm not letting you guys go without saying goodbye,' Tristan said. His lips quirked upwards, but there was sorrow buried there too.

Felan swallowed. He stared at the train ticket in his hands.

Weisworth.

Somewhere else.

Somewhere new.

Chapter 46: Handwritten

Felan woke to a resounding crash.

He tore away the covers, peeked through the gap in the curtains and into the night.

The storm outside raged on. Rain splattered the windows. Wind howled through the tiny gaps in the frames. The whole building trembled.

He ran a hand through his hair in an attempt to tame it. He could've sworn he'd heard something that wasn't the storm. He searched every corner of his room, but he came away none the wiser. Every single thing woke him up now – every tiny, little noise he wasn't used to. He closed his eyes and listened. He could've sworn... Wait! Felan tiptoed to his bedroom door and peeped his head out. He looked up and down the hallway.

Maybe he'd imagined it. After all, it wouldn't be the first time he'd seen something that wasn't there.

Another thunderous crash sent chills down his spine.

He listened again – it was coming from downstairs. Felan debated. He could cower in his room until sunrise, but what if Nick was downstairs? What if Nick searched every room until he found him? Until he found Blaez?

He squared his shoulders and crept down the hallway towards the stairs, avoiding the creaky floorboards as he went. When he passed the shelves, he hefted a candlestick. It wasn't much in the way of a weapon, but he could knock someone out with it easily if he needed to.

The banging grew louder with every step. He kept peering over his shoulder, then forward, over his shoulder, and every time he looked, he thought he saw a scarred face looming out of the shadows, staring right at him. He blinked. The face vanished with the next flash of lightning. His grip on the candlestick loosened, and he cursed his sweaty palms.

He flinched at the next loud crash.

Maybe Nick was already inside. Maybe he'd already been in every room, done what he came to do, and now he wanted to play a game.

Felan held the candlestick so tight he didn't know what would break first: the stick, or his hand.

He was almost feverish by the time he checked the front room. The windows were bolted shut, and the curtains neatly drawn. He braved a peek outside, but there was only darkness. In all honesty, he didn't want to peek for longer than two seconds in case someone jumped out at him. He wouldn't put it past one of the kids to be playing a game with him.

He also wouldn't put it past Nick to follow them all the way up the country.

He crept further – the next crash made him duck, for some reason thinking the ceiling was about to collapse on top of him. A howling wind followed. He thought he could hear whispers. He checked every corner and crevice large enough for someone to hide, sure he was going to find someone from Guadalupe waiting for him.

He wished his heart wouldn't beat so loud.

The kitchen was clear, and the pantry – he checked them, top to bottom, and came away empty-handed.

A familiar burning sensation hit his sinuses. He rubbed his eyes furiously. He wouldn't cry. He could do this. He could defend himself against whatever, or whoever, was toying with him.

He pushed open the door to the playroom and saw the problem immediately.

The side window was hanging broken, and every time the wind caught it, it slammed against the frame. How the glass didn't break was beyond Felan.

The gap it left was big enough for someone to slip through, he realised. Shivers ran down his spine.

He searched the room, well aware of the billowing curtain and the water on the floor from the rain, well aware than anyone outside could be watching him...

The window crashed against the frame.

Setting the candlestick within reach, he forced himself to walk to the window, next to the impenetrable darkness, and solve the problem. He ran his fingers along the soaking latch and blinked the wind from his eyes. Okay, so it wasn't as bad as it looked – the window had slipped out of alignment and wouldn't shut. That was an easy fix.

Bracing himself on the windowsill, he yanked hard. It shifted with an almighty creak, but not enough to close it. It needed another tug, and fast. He was in full view of the darkness and the realisation that Nick could be *right outside...*

He yanked the window and it slammed shut with a bang. He pulled the curtains after he'd bolted the window down, and he choked on a sob he hadn't realised he was keeping at bay. He'd wake everyone up if he started crying. He sat on one of the chairs and tangled his hands in his hair, panting.

The tapping came next. A slow, deadly tap that he recognised all too well. He leaped to his feet and started to back away. The scraping of a fingernail along the glass, *right outside...*

The light flicked on. Without thinking, he lunged for the candlestick, ready to swing...

'Fee?'

He tossed the candlestick behind the sofa before she realised what was going on.

'What are you doing awake?' he asked gently. He didn't realise how hoarse his voice was.

'I couldn't sleep,' the four-year-old whined. 'I heard noises.'

'But why are you down here, hey?' He scooped her up and held her close. She cuddled into him instantly.

The scratching stopped. The tapping stopped. It all stopped bar the storm he'd locked outside. He'd clean up the mess in the morning. There was nothing to worry about. Nothing could get in.

But at least this time he wasn't the only one hearing noises.

'I came to find you.'

He sighed. If there was an intruder, and one as dangerous as Nick, and they'd found Gemma wandering around in the dark...

'Next time, if I'm not in my room, wait in there, okay? I don't want you getting hurt.'

'Uh-huh,' she mumbled.

He flicked the light off and carried her right back upstairs to her room. He shut the door behind him, firmly, and dragged her toy box over behind it. Just in case. She made grabby hands at her fairy lights, so he let her switch them on. He hoped they weren't bright enough to show his shock, and horror, and fear all at once.

'Come on,' he said, tickling her neck. 'Back to bed.'

She giggled, as he helped her crawl back under the covers.

'Can you read me a story?'

'Of course.' He picked a book from her shelf at random, sat beside her on the bed, and began to read.

She blinked up at him, awed, completely entranced by the story. Page by page, her eyes glazed over and before long she was gone. Still shaken, Felan tucked her in and pulled the blanket up high; she snuggled deeper into her covers.

He was wide awake now, so there was no point in going back to his own room, thanks to whoever or whatever was outside.

What if it was Nick, or someone from Guadalupe? Could they really have followed them all that way? What if *they* had broken the window on purpose? To see if he was actually there? If so, he'd played right into their hands. They knew he was there, and if they knew he was there, they'd know Blaez was there too.

'Dammit,' he cursed quietly. He settled himself on the floor, next to Gemma's bed, and stared intently at the door. He had to be awake if someone was lurking around in the dark.

He had to be awake if he wanted to protect everyone else.

***

Early the next morning, Mrs Walters offered Felan a hot chocolate and a biscuit.

'I apologise for the scare last night,' she said. 'You are safe here, Felan. They have no idea where you were moved to, but I understand that you're not going to adapt overnight.'

He nibbled on his biscuit. He couldn't believe he'd worked himself up so much over nothing. And he still wasn't used to the whole 'three meals a day' and 'snacks'. The fact that she let him have whatever he wanted was so foreign to him. She knew all about his background, of course – she'd spoken to Tristan and Mr Bailey at length about it. Felan didn't understand. Who would want violence around little kids? Especially ones who attracted trouble?

'Are you sure it's okay us staying here?' he asked for the sixth time. 'Because we can go somewhere else. It's fine.'

She looked at his arms and, when he looked down, he realised why. He'd forgotten to cover them with a jumper – his scars were on full display. He always kept them hidden, so even he forgot how ugly they looked; the gunshot wound was one nasty mess of bumps and tissue, and white lines criss-crossed up and down his arms. He dropped the biscuit and slid his arms under the table. He rubbed them uncomfortably.

It was bad enough when the little kids asked how he'd got them.

Mrs Walters busied herself at the sink. 'Enough of that. Go take a shower before the younger ones wake up, there's a good lad.'

He was in and out in five minutes. Years of quick, cold showers was a hard habit to break; he also didn't want to waste hot water when there were another seven kids yet to cycle through the bathroom. Better them than him. They deserved the hot water. They deserved the comforts Mrs Walters provided. Not someone like him.

He checked on Gemma. The kid was completely passed out – she wouldn't wake up till later after what had happened last night. With a smile, he closed the door and walked the short distance to Blaez's room, the door wide open. He knocked. She didn't reply.

She was sat on her bed, back to the door, in clothes that fit. They were old ones of Mrs Walters from when she was much younger.

'Hey there,' he said, knocking again.

'Oh, hey, come in,' she said, turning. She climbed to her feet. 'How'd you sleep?'

Felan left the door open a crack. One of the only rules: *'If there's more than one person in a room, keep the door open.'* He'd broken that rule last night, but they were extenuating circumstances. Yep. That sounded like a good enough excuse to hide what had happened.

'Not great. I got woken up by something, and then Gemma couldn't sleep.' He failed to mention his little adventure. Blaez would worry. She'd know he wasn't adapting well.

'She's a cutie,' Blaez yawned.

'What about you?' he asked.

'Better than you,' she joked half-heartedly. 'It will get better.' She hugged him tight. It stopped any more debris crashing to the floor. It stopped the waves from eroding more of the coastline. It stopped the hail from hammering down. She held him together, a small being in the direct path of a lightning strike, but that was okay. She was like those poppies outside in the flower bed; free, yet tainted.

'Thanks,' he mumbled.

'It's...'

'Fee?'

Felan peered over Blaez's shoulder and smiled at the little girl in the doorway. He let his friend go and walked over, crouching down so he was at eye level. 'Morning Gem – did you sleep okay?'

She stomped on the spot. 'You left my book on the floor!'

Blaez burst out into laughter. He hadn't heard that laughter in months. Crying happy tears, he bowed his head and swept Gemma into his arms.

***

A month later, they lay side by side on Felan's bed, staring at the ceiling. He'd taken the liberty of finding himself some glow-in-the-dark stars and planets; it had become a routine for them to stare up at them at night while they talked. Usually, Gemma joined them and fell asleep – this time she'd conked out midway through dinner and Felan had carried her up to bed.

'Did you get Tristan's message?' Blaez asked.

'Which one?'

There had been many since they'd got on the train – he hadn't replied to all of them. He didn't know how to. Blaez responding to every single one made him feel guilty. Tristan had saved his life, and he couldn't even drop him a text?

'About the interviews with the judge,' she said.

Ah yes. He knew all about that one. 'Yeah.'

Blaez turned onto her side to face him. 'What do you think? Are you going to do it?'

'I don't know. I don't know if I want to go back.'

'Me neither,' she said.

'We both know you're going back,' he said. 'I know you, Blaez.'

For the first time since they arrived at the orphanage, her eyes filled with tears. 'Are you angry with me?'

He buried his face in her shoulder. 'No. I'm proud to call you my friend.'

***

He turned the letter over in his hands. Blaez was already on her way back – she'd left two days after the interview summons arrived (a formality, apparently), after making sure everything was set.

He breathed the air that blew through his window. She was never afraid like he was. She always faced the problem head-on. But Felan? He'd be happier never going back there. Not because he was scared (okay, it was a little bit because he was scared). Blaez was scared too. It wasn't fear. It wasn't anger. It was the place. The memories. All those bad memories trapped in the confines of one city.

Felan pulled his sleeves up and ran his index finger along the bumpy, white lines. He traced the outline of the bullet wound – he still expected pain, no matter how long ago it had healed.

Memories of that city would never fade.

'You're not going, are you?'

He turned. Mrs Walters stood in the doorway with an armful of washing.

'I can't.'

'I spoke to Tristan and Mr Bailey yesterday – they're eager for the world to hear your story.'

He turned back to the window and looked outside at the unfamiliar ground. The garden expanded past the treeline, and visible just beyond it was a small play area. He saw Gemma playing with the other kids, excitable and innocent. He thought of how he read to her most nights.

'Evolve or repeat,' he muttered, thinking.

An idea sparked.

'Maybe I'll write my story instead.'

Author's Note

In 2019, almost 19,000 children were sexually groomed. There was an estimate of 27,000 children being involved in a gang, of which a majority stayed under the radar. An estimated 112,853 children are reported missing every year; many of these cases remain unsolved. And this is just in the UK alone.

In the US, nearly 800,000 children are reported missing every year. That's 2,000 children *every day*. While a number of reports are resolved, many involve situations where the case is permanent. And every five minutes, a child dies as a result of violence.

More needs to be done. It is as simple as that. We need to intervene earlier in a young person's life, and we need to make sure that they have safe places to go, trusted adults available, to talk to, to protect them. Without this support system in place, it leaves children vulnerable to exploitation. That should be the word we use. Exploitation. Because it is. It's exploitation. It's manipulation. It's *abuse*. These children should be recognised as victims, listened to, their stories heard – not criminalised for something they have no control over.

Children (and vulnerable people) are being systematically failed by those we trust to protect them. We need youth clubs. We need after-school activities. We need workshops. We need places that these children can go to... and not right into the hands of a criminal. More needs to be done to protect our children, and until this is deemed top priority, young people will continue to be exploited, manipulated, and abused. Children will continue to be involved in gangs and criminal activity that could have been prevented. But to some people, a child's safety is not top priority.

I hope the existence of Felan's story can be the start of change in our society for kids like him. They are out there, and they need our help.

So if you're reading this, and you do need help, then please talk to someone. Anyone. Help is out there. There are people out there who want to help you. You are not alone.

There is a way out.

Helplines – UK

Childline: 0800 1111 / www.childline.org.uk – free and confidential 24-hour helpline for children and young people.

The Mix: 0808 808 4994 / www.themix.org.uk – essential support for under 25s, from homelessness to break-ups.

Crime Stoppers: 0800 555 111 / www.crimestoppers-uk.org – give crime information anonymously… for anyone.

NSPCC (National Society for the Prevention of Cruelty to Children): 0808 800 5000 / www.nspcc.org.uk / help@nspcc.org.uk – free 24-hour helpline for children or adults, concerned about a child at risk.

Frank: 0300 1236600 / www.talktofrank.com - Honest information about drugs, for anyone.

Victim Support: 08 08 16 89 111 / www.victimsupport.org.uk – free and confidential support to help you move beyond the impact of crime.

Runaway Helpline: 116 000 / www.runawayhelpline.org.uk – for young people who feel like running away from home / have run from home.

Word 4 Weapons: www.word4weapons.co.uk – a leading weapons surrender charity in the UK for the last 10 years, supplying knife bins to a number of police forces, community groups, and faith organisations.

Gangsline: 01375 483 239 & 07753 351 256 / www.gangsline.com – a non-profit organisation established in 2007 to provide help and support to young men and women involved in gang culture.

Young Minds: 0808 802 5544 / https://youngminds.org.uk – the UK's leading charity fighting for children and young people's mental health.

Helplines – USA

Victim Support Services: Call 425 252 6081 / https://www.victimsupportservices.org – a non-profit agency providing peer support and advocacy for victims of crime

Childhelp National Child Abuse Hotline: Call or Text 1800 422 4453 / https://childhelphotline.org – the hotline is staffed 24 hours a day, 7 days a week, and offers crisis intervention, information, and referrals to thousands of emergency, social service, and support resources for child abuse victims, parents, and concerned individuals.

Darkness to Light: Call 866 367 5444 or Text 'LIGHT' to 741 741 / https://www.d2l.org – a free helpline for children and adults needing local information or resources about sexual abuse.

National Parent Helpline: Call 1855 427 2736 / https://www.nationalparenthelpline.org – available 10 a.m. - 7 p.m. Monday to Friday, this helpline provides emotional support and links to resources for parents and caregivers.

National Human Trafficking Hotline: Call 888 373 7888 / https://www.humantraffickinghotline.org – available 24 hours a day, 7 days a week, this hotline offers support for victims of human trafficking and those reporting potential trafficking situations.

Child Find of America: Call 800 426 5678 / https://www.childfindofamerica.org – a non-profit hotline for parents reporting lost or abducted children, including parental abductions.

National Centre for Missing and Exploited Children: Call 800 845 5678 / https://www.missingkids.org – a non-profit corporation who help find missing children, reduce child sexual exploitation, and prevent child victimisation. NCMEC works with families, victims, private industry, law enforcement, and the public to assist with preventing child abductions, recovering missing children, and providing services to deter and combat child sexual exploitation.

National Runaway Switchboard: Call 800 786 2929 / https://www.youth.gov – assists youth who have run away or are considering running away and their families, linking youth and families across the country to shelters, counselling, medical assistance, and other vital services. In addition, NRS works to prevent youth from running away.

Please visit **Child Welfare Information Gateway** for more information (https://www.childwelfare.gov)

Acknowledgements

I started writing *Opium* at 15 years old while sitting my GCSEs. I am now 21. Since then, it has undergone many drafts, many character names, and many endings.

Firstly, a huge thank you to my friends and family for your ongoing support. You have all been so encouraging and looked forward to anything I would share with you.

Secondly, a huge thank you to Dominic Wakeford and Sara Magness for editing the entirety of *Opium* and for giving me a shove in the right direction. Thank you to SpiffingCovers for designing me an incredible front cover, for helping me with the final steps to self-publishing, and for being there every step of the way. *Opium* would not be what it is without all of your help.

Thirdly, thank you to my Washingpool family. Thank you for watching out for me, for inspiring me, and for being so supportive and encouraging from the beginning. I love each and every one of you.

And finally, a big thank you to every one of you reading... it's only because of you that this message can be spread. Thank you for giving this book a chance.

I hope Felan's story inspires you as much as it inspires me.

So – let's aim to give children like Felan and Blaez a better life, because every child deserves a chance. Every child deserves to be fought for.

Let's make a change.

About the Author

Opium is Maisie's first novel. She wanted Felan's story to be a catalyst for change in society, and she wanted her first novel to start a conversation. But most importantly, she wrote it to inspire people.

She walked the Jurassic Coast Challenge 2021 in support of the NSPCC and raised money for the amazing charity – the only charity fighting to end child abuse in the UK and Channel Islands.

Training for the challenge rekindled her love of hiking, and in her free time she's exploring the Jurassic Coast, chasing sunsets, and taking photos of the beautiful scenery. The long hikes inspire story ideas and new characters.

She lives in Dorset with her mum and their two cats, and is, slowly, teaching herself to play the violin. She isn't quite sure how her neighbours are taking it though.

Follow Maisie on Instagram for writing snippets and updates:

@MKitton2206

Brief Explanations

Why Guadalupe?

I chose Guadalupe for one reason – it literally means *The Valley of the Wolves*. Later on, I discovered a few other meanings: *River of the Wolf*, *Wolf Valley*... it just somehow fit perfectly with how the Wolves in *Opium* are running around the city.

Why *Opium*?

Upon hearing the title, I had to tell many people, 'No, it is not a book about drugs.' A lot like choosing Guadalupe as the city name, choosing *Opium* just fit. It sounded right, and here's why.

A poppy is beautiful on the outside, but potentially dangerous on the inside – this is how the gang appears to Felan. The gang is everything he wants (a home, a family, and friends), and that is what he sees upon surface level. But, the inner workings of the gang are dangerous, which Felan begins to discover.

There are poppies growing in the flower bed at the orphanage in Weisworth, and there are also poppies on the front cover – they have connotations to remembrance, and also conflict. Felan remembers his mother throughout the book, and his father, and the damage the city of Guadalupe did to him.

And yes, I suppose you can argue the book is about drugs because Felan partakes in drug deals while he is a member of the Wolves – but the title isn't really about that.

It's about the idea of being addicted to something you really want. Felan wanted a home, and he was so focused on that aspect of the gang that it took a while to see what was truly happening.

So no, *Opium* is not a book about drugs, but seeing things beyond the surface level.

Milton Keynes UK
Ingram Content Group UK Ltd.
UKHW040730010823
426141UK00004B/300